Where the Oceans | Meet

A Novel

Bhargavi C.
Mandava

SEAL PRESS

Seattle

Seal Press
3131 Western Avenue, Suite 410, Seattle, Washington 98121
Email: sealprss@scn.org
www.sealpress.com

Front cover photograph by Susan Dumett
Author photo and interior art by Mark Sylbert
Cover design by Patrick Barber
Text design by Stacy M. Lewis

Printed in the United States of America
First Seal Press paperback edition, January 1998.
10 9 8 7 6 5 4 3 2 1

Library of Congress Cataloging-in-Publication Data
Mandava, Bhargavi C.
Where the oceans meet : a novel / Bhargavi C. Mandava.
I. Title.
PS3563.A4357W48   1996   813'.54—dc20   96-34887
ISBN 1-878067-86-9

Distributed to the trade by Publishers Group West
In *Canada*: Publishers Group West Canada, Toronto, Canada
In *Europe and the* U.K.: Airlift Book Company, London, England
In *Australia*: Banyan Tree Book Distributors, Kent Town, South Australia

Acknowledgments

I wish to acknowledge my mother, my India travel companion, teacher and best friend. My father, sister Chandra, and brother Amrutha, for their undying love. Nancy Nordhoff, founder of Cottages at Hedgebrook, where this book was written, all of the Hedgebrook staff, who strive to make it such a writers' paradise, and all of my Hedgebrook co-residents for their support; Holly Morris and everyone at Seal Press for their faith; Leslie Ferlinghetti-Price of *Poison Ivy Magazine*; Karen Williams for editing help and friendship; my dear friend, who is like a sister, Colleen McQuade for making me smile when I was crying; and, finally, my partner, Mark Sylbert, who encouraged me to write my first short story, and whose creativity, compassion and pure love charge my soul each and every day. God has truly blessed me.

FOR MY MOTHER,
whose love and spirit shed light in darkness

Where the
Oceans | Meet

The Lorry Driver

Ana removed the gold teardrop-bottu* from her forehead and pressed it on the mirror. Picking up a rag dipped in oil, she began wiping off the black Eye-Tex katika, which had smeared under her eyes. Her lips looked bruised from her new purple lipstick. The color matched many of her stage saris, and she had worn it every day for the past week. She rubbed the oily cloth over her mouth, but still she could not see the true pink color of her lips. She stood up, and the towel wrapped around her waist fell to the floor. Nothing she was looking at in the mirror felt or looked as it should. Was there something wrong with her sense of touch, or was her vision going? She stroked the lines under her lids and cheeks. As she stared into her reflected eyes, she swore she saw someone else moving behind the mirror. Like a dancing ghost trapped in ice, she glimpsed herself at seventeen. Picking up a soda bottle, she threw

---

* Refer to glossary at back of book for definitions of Telugu and Hindi words and terms.

it at the ghost, shattering the mirror. Later, in the bath, she wondered if she had wanted to set it free. A small part of her had, but mostly, she had wanted to destroy it. She just wanted to forget.

Ravi scraped a bit of splattered cow dung and mud from the mirror on his lorry. His life had been filled with dirt ever since he could remember. He didn't mind in the beginning, but at the age of thirty-eight, he was getting a little tired of it. As a child he had loved chasing the pigs down the street with his friends or walking on the dirt roads barefoot. And he had loved riding in his father's lorry. Both he and his father had the habit of referring to the lorries as being theirs, but in reality they belonged to the Tata Lorry Company. But Tata did not know what to do when the clutch stuck or know how much gas was in the tank despite what the gauge read. Ravi had been driving since he was nineteen, and this was *his* lorry.

After the last box of cotton sari fabric was loaded, he flicked his cigarette into the street. Lately, it took a lot out of him to pull the lorry's door shut. He yanked it down and decided that maybe all he needed to do was get on the road to Kanchipuram.

The pea-green of the rice paddy fields was so inviting. Ravi smiled as he thought about how deceiving appearances could be. He knew the field was not a field at all, but more of a giant puddle with thousands of grass blades shooting through the water's surface— thousands of arms reaching toward the sun. From the corner of his eye, he followed the women with wet, colored cloths wrapped around their heads and their skirts hiked up around their mahogany calves. As the women hunched over in the fields, the sun beat down on the shiny smalls of their backs. He knew the cool mud was a relief for their sore feet. Who did not welcome water and shade in India? He had gotten in the habit of wrapping his right arm in a wet rag to protect it from the sun's rays. Thinking about the sun made him notice how drenched the back of his shirt was. His tongue felt

4

thick and pasty.

Spotting a vendor with a cartful of seltzer bottles on the side of the deserted road, he pulled over. By now, it was amusing to Ravi how uncomfortable his presence made others. His burn scars made people stop breathing and choke on their words. Some pulled their children closer thinking, perhaps, that he had leprosy, but most understood the cause of his grotesqueness. He had gotten used to his hardened, bumpy skin, but there were occasions when the sight of his hand on the steering wheel startled him. As the vendor, pretending not to notice Ravi's scars, released the vacuum lever on the bottle, a loud *thup* escaped into the silence. Ravi took the bottle and steadily shot some of the fizzy liquid into his mouth. After he had quenched his thirst, he sprayed the remainder over his head.

By the time he arrived in Kanchipuram, Ravi was looking forward to a relaxing evening. He dropped off his load of fabric. The following morning, he would load up with the finest silks woven right there in Kanchi.

After eating some idli, Ravi checked into his usual brothel. A lot of drivers spent time behind the high plaster walls painted with lotuses. He turned the hot water on in the bathroom as he undressed. He hoped the steam would help relieve the pressure he had started feeling in his lungs. It was as if someone were pushing against his chest with their feet.

Towel wrapped around his waist, he stood looking out the barred windows. In the courtyard a woman was braiding another's hair in the looming shadow of a banana tree. The way the women smiled and stroked one another, he guessed they must have been sharing their dreams. The sadness in his heart gave way to more sadness, and Ravi knew this was the only way he could ever kiss a woman's lips and breathe in the scent of jasmine flowers in her hair. He had no choice.

He spun around when he heard a noise at the door. He saw the shadow of feet under the crack, but no one knocked or entered. A good five minutes must have passed before the doorknob turned. A young girl in her early twenties stood in the doorway. She was dressed in maroon cigarette pants and a matching blouse that shimmered with mirrors the size of his thumbnail.

Sitting on the bed, Ravi motioned with his hand for her to come in. The silver rings on her toes clinked on the stone floor as she walked toward him. She was new and scared. Many of the girls were frightened to death of him, but those who could not get out of having sex with him quickly learned that he was a gentle, sweet soul. He asked them about their dreams and spent hours kissing their necks. Those girls found themselves thanking him—even praying for him to come back more often.

As the girl bent down to kiss him, she placed her hands on his shoulders. Her lips first touched his forehead and then his right cheek. Then, she stood up straight and waited for direction. Ravi saw his face reflected in her myriad of mirrors and froze for a few seconds. Then, quickly, he slipped her arms out of the blouse and tossed it on the floor.

When the sunlight brushed his lids with its red palms, Ravi opened his eyes. Although it was summertime, he was covered in goosebumps. He saw all that was left of the girl was a slight depression in the pillow. He always hated the next morning. He never felt so ugly and alone. Flipping through the tattered spiral book in which he copied his favorite poems, he read a part of the *Gita Govinda*.

> For (*sang he on*) I am no foe of thine,
> There is no black snake, kama! in my hair;
> Blue lotus-bloom, and not the poisoned brine,
> Shadows my neck; what stains my bosom bare,
> Thou God unfair!

He closed the book and turned on his side. Seeing a long strand of black hair that clung to the sheets like a dead snake, he began to weep.

Ravi heaved himself up into the seat of the lorry and placed some samosas swaddled in newspaper beside him. The grease from the fried dough was already soaking through an ad for the latest movie featuring the popular actress Sridevi.

As he changed gears, the lorry jerked forward, spilling the black metal statue of the god Vishnu that perched on the dashboard to the floor. Ravi scowled and stepped on the brake. The glue that had held the idol in place must have dried out, he thought as he picked up the figurine and kissed it. Untying the string that bound the samosas in the newspaper, he wrapped it around the base of the idol and tied it to the visor. He then pushed it flush against the windshield. Ravi did not want the god to fall near his feet again.

By lunchtime, the goosebumps had turned into bone-shivers. Ravi was about six hours away from Pune, but did not have the energy to continue driving. He parked the lorry and wandered into a sweet shop, where the proprietor recommended a doctor whose office was nearby. Dodging scooters, rickshaws and school children, Ravi wandered through the busy streets with address in hand.

He pushed open the rose-painted wooden door. Walking past the delicious honeysuckle bushes that lined the walkway, Ravi stepped up on the veranda. After speaking with a nurse, he settled in a wicker chair and waited with four other patients. A small boy played hide and seek behind the pleats of his mother's sari. Ravi remembered how he too had loved to play with his mother's sari. The cloth had felt cool on his cheek and there was plenty of material in which to vanish when shyness overcame him. When he was cold, her sari became a blanket; when he was hot, it was his shade. His mother was always a tug away. When the boy noticed Ravi, he froze. Ravi smiled, but the boy did not smile back. Instead his mouth dropped open, and he began to howl. His mother did her best to quiet him, but he cried louder still, burying his contorted face in the folds of her sari. Ravi flicked open a newspaper to shield himself from the heat of their gazes.

✦

"Breathe," said the doctor as he held a stethoscope to Ravi's chest.

He then placed the cold disc on Ravi's back and took a deep breath, instructing Ravi to do the same. There was the scratching of pen on paper and then silence.

When Ravi turned around, he just caught the tail of the doctor's white lab coat swishing around the corner of the doorway. He turned back to the wall and stared at the poster of the human heart. Blue blood, red blood, ventricles and chambers. It looked so logical on paper, but what a mystery this human organ was! If it were merely functional, then why was it that the emptiness he felt shooting through his being seemed to originate from his upper left chest? Was he leaving his senses when he felt his heart deflate and slither down his pants' leg when a beautiful woman spurned his good attentions? And why was it that when he felt happy, his heart felt light and satiny like a rose petal being fondled by a spring breeze? There was more to the human heart than was explained on this poster.

Ravi looked toward the hall when he heard footsteps. The nurse walked by carrying urine and blood samples—the yellow and red sloshing as her hips swayed. Hopping up on the examination table, he sat swinging his legs. What a nice life he must have, this doctor, Ravi thought. He was handsome and earning a fine salary. His beautiful wife must tell him how much she missed his company all day long. And he must cover her with kisses to show her how much he missed her, her slender arms curling around his neck as he lifts her off her feet. On top of it, doctors had godlike stature in India. Never mind that rivulets of corruption trickled into almost every aspect of the Indian social system and that prospective medical students who had wealthy enough parents could buy themselves treasured seats in medical schools and assure their acceptance. Those crinkled, dirty pieces of paper clamped mouths shut, unlocked doors and bought brides. The wealth was not what Ravi craved. It was the fact that being a doctor automatically made a man a great catch.

The familiar smell of hospital disinfectant wafted into his nostrils, turning his stomach. He saw a barefoot boy in knickers on his hands and knees cleaning the hallway floor. The doctor, writing on his clipboard, stepped between the boy's hands.

"You have pneumonia," he announced flatly as he nervously clicked the pen in his hand.

"Pneumonia?" Ravi repeated.

"Yes. You are very, very sick. Tell me, are you married?"

"No. Why do you ask?" responded Ravi, his voice pinched with irritation.

"I was trying to ask you politely, that is all," said the doctor as he continued to write intently. "Have you slept with prostitutes?"

Ravi leapt up, teeth bared and gnashing like a babirusa. He could not believe the doctor was asking him this. Was it written on his face?

"It is not my intention to be rude or crass, sir, but I am asking because many lorry drivers are known to do this, which is really fine considering the loneliness you must feel in such a profession—a very demanding profession, that is."

With each of the doctor's words, Ravi's bruised expression intensified as if he were being kicked in the face. The doctor stammered, finding it impossible to cushion his questioning.

"What do you know about me to say such a thing?"

"Please. I am asking because of sexual diseases."

"I do not have any diseases."

"I am concerned that you might be HIV positive—that you might have AIDS."

"Well, if you think I do, just give me a shot and I will be on my way. You will not have to look at my ugly face anymore."

Ravi pulled up the sleeve of the examination gown and thrust out his arm toward the doctor. But the doctor just stood there shattered as if Ravi had just danced on his heart.

"Please try to understand that you could be very sick. I want you to check into the hospital so we can run some tests."

"I cannot do that. I must go back to work. If you just give me some medication for the pneumonia—"

"You need rest. A lot of rest and sleep. Driving is much too strenuous for proper recovery."

9

"I do not think you understand, Doctor. I must fulfill my duties. It may not seem that way to you since you are a doctor. You are thinking, I deliver life, he delivers saris. But my job is also very necessary and of significance."

The doctor looked at Ravi for what seemed to be the first time. His black eyes were glistening.

"Tell me, is your job more valuable than your life? Is this job your life?"

Ravi didn't answer.

"Is this job your life?"

The doctor sighed deeply. Ravi watched him write on his pad of paper again. He looked so important standing there. Whatever he did, he looked so damn important.

"I am sorry," said the doctor as he slid his gold pen into his shirt pocket. He handed him a prescription.

After walking back to his lorry, Ravi spent some time sitting on the fender, watching the traffic go by. He ate purple grapes and spit the pale green pits toward the gutter. As he watched mud-caked feet, bicycle wheels, cows' hooves, pigs' feet and autos scurry by, he felt so severed from his people. Since the fire, he was an object of pity and fear. Did they really think they were so indestructible? Did they think they were so different from him? With that, he threw a cluster of grapes into the middle of the road. They were so firm, however, that they did not burst. Instead, they rolled in various directions. He waited for them to be crushed. A full minute must have passed before a rickshaw puller's toe came into contact with one. Rather than being flattened, it was knocked into the safety of the gutter. He could not believe the luck of those grapes! Then, by the time it took him to fish a cigarette from a pack and light it, their luck had changed. Within moments, the heroic spheres were destroyed. First one, then another, and another, until all that remained of their existence were a few phlegmy blotches and some torn skin. Of course, he thought with a grin: That is how death comes—

unexpectedly and in multiples. Ravi felt as if he had died in the fire. And now, again, he felt his toes teetering on the brink of death.

"Let me borrow that lipstick, Ana," implored Jewel, one of the newer dancers at the Beach Club in Pune.

Ana shook her head as she rubbed gold eye powder into the curve of her brows.

"Why not—come on, we all share here," persisted Jewel.

"No, Jewel," Ana said firmly. "No offense, but I don't need your herpes to add to my list of problems."

Ana did not mean it as a joke, but Kalpana and Rumi, two of the other dancers who were on that night, burst into laughter.

"You are such a high and mighty terror, Ana," said Jewel as she brushed out her auburn waist-length hair. "You think you are better than the rest of us with your light skin? Just because you don't have sex with them, you think you are better?"

Ana stood up and smoothed her lavender-colored sari sprinkled with gold stars. She walked over to Kalpana and turned her back to her so the other dancer could fasten the clasp of her teardrop necklace of pink glass stones.

"There," said Kalpana.

"You know, it's not that I think I am better, Jewel," said Ana as she looked at herself in the mirror. "I think I'm luckier."

"If you're so lucky, why did your mother and father sell you to begin with?" shot back Jewel.

"Ana!" yelled the club manager.

Ana, her lips pursed, walked out silently to the stage.

As the disco ball bathed her in dozens of rainbows, Ana glided through the ocean of twirling lights like a mackerel, her silver chain slinking around the slight swell of her belly. When one of the lights hit her face, Ravi gulped the delicious flick of her kohl-lined eyes. He could not hear the jingling of the bells on her anklet, but he could imagine it. Ana had that kind of delicateness. It forced one to take notice of her subtleties like the heart-shaped beauty mark on her chin, her long, smooth fingers and the smallness of her waist. It did not matter that she was gyrating her half-moon hips to the Indian pop band cover of "That's the Way I Like It." Somehow the glaring of the red, blue and yellow lights and the filthiness of the city beyond the club's walls were forgotten as she lifted a finger to her garnet lips and spread a hush through his tired body. He came here to relax—to remember what it felt like to sleep in a white bed and wake up to the smell of dosai on the grill.

Ana was the prettiest of all the dancers he had ever seen, in Pune or otherwise. She was also the only one who would look Ravi right in the eye.

Looking into his glass, he remembered how as a child he'd nestle comfortably into heaps of brownish cotton that had warmed in the afternoon sun. It was the kind of plushness in which you wanted to bury your face—a grand bottomless cloud. He licked the beer foam from his upper lip.

As Ana unraveled her lavender sari, Ravi thought about his mother's most precious possession. It was a white shawl of the finest silk. Every day, after her morning meditation, she would unlock the bureau and take out the shawl. She would hold it to her face and breathe deeply into the cloth. She said it smelled like her dead husband, but he always thought it smelled more like musty sandalwood. He wished she could have seen how flawless the cloth was, but she was blind.

How he would like to give Ana that very shawl. Picturing the whiteness of the silk against her torso quickened his breath. He would run up to her and cover her bare shoulders. His nostrils flared when he remembered the fire. Everything had burned, including his mother, who could not find her way out of the house. She died in the room with the bureau.

He drank some beer to ease the ache in his throat. Ana was naked now, and his worries dissolved in the expanse of her wheat-colored flesh.

Ana was covering Kalpana's shift since her three-year-old daughter, Rani, was running a fever. Kalpana had brought Rani to work with her the day before to keep an eye on her. In between numbers, they all applied cold compresses to her overheated body to keep her temperature down.

"Promise me that you will take her to the clinic tomorrow," said Ana.

Kalpana nodded yes, but Ana knew she was worried about missing another day of work.

"I'll work for you tomorrow night, okay?" said Ana reassuringly.

Kalpana smiled and left, cradling Rani, who had begun to cry.

The club was practically empty the next night. Men crawled in and out like roaches, disappearing into the night after they had had their fill. The man with the scarred face, however, stayed for the bulk of the show. He sat at the same table as he had the night before. The other dancers hated him, saying it turned their stomach to look at his disfigurement. They nicknamed him Hanuman because, as Indian folklore went, Hanuman was said to have, in his greed, mistook the sun for a delicious orange. After he bit into it, his mouth was scorched and he took on the appearance of a monkey. As Ana moved to the music, she stared right into the man's eyes. His scars had never bothered her much—until tonight. Tonight, anger raced through her as Jewel's words echoed in her head.

"My parents didn't sell me off," she thought. "They married me off to Khalifa. There is a difference."

In the next second, that difference seemed as flimsy as that which differentiated her from any other prostitute. How was she superior to the whores who worked in Mehaboobki Mehandi, Hyderabad's red light district? And how was a high-priced call girl in Delhi or Madras any better than those whores in Hyderabad? She stared at the man and imagined how he must have screamed when his face was on fire. She tried to imagine how it would feel to scream with blazing lips and see through blazing eyes. She wondered if, on certain days, he began clawing open the wounds in a desperate search to find his true self? Did he want to tear open his face as she had wanted to tear off her skin? Did he remember how it felt to die while still living?

By two in the morning, Ana had danced ten hours straight. She sat on a stool in the dressing room and rubbed her aching feet. The buses stopped running at midnight, and to take a rickshaw home would cost her four rupees. What a nuisance, she thought, since her tips—fifty rupees in total—were nothing to shout about. Actually, it was only twenty-five rupees, since she planned on giving half to Kalpana to help pay for Rani's clinic bills. Although she was much too tired to even wash off her makeup, Ana slipped on her chappals and started to walk home.

She kept her pace quick and her eyes alert for troublemakers. She was always tense on the streets. Even in the daytime when she was vegetable shopping or buying sandalwood face powder or perfume at Akbar's Fancy Shop, she kept her eyes peeled for Khalifa's men. She took a pack of Goldflake cigarettes out of her purse and lit one. In front of a hut of palm fronds, a mother paced with her wailing baby, its cries piercing the stillness that had settled over Pune. A lantern hanging in a banyan tree cast a warm light that encircled mother and child, and Ana remembered what was once her sense of home. Startled by the sound of a breaking bottle, she glanced behind her and started walking faster. Maybe she was being paranoid and Khalifa had long forgotten about his young bride who had run away from him in Hyderabad over a year ago. Still, a part of her knew that he was vengeful and that he would trail her like a shadow.

When she reached her apartment complex, she had to step over a drooling man snoring in the entryway. As she pushed the door open, a voice startled her.

"Ana?"

She spun around, a scream caught in her throat. It was the man from the club.

"Do not be frightened, please," he said. "My name is Ravi."

Ana dashed inside and slammed the lockless door, pushing against it to hold it closed. Her heart was leaping inside of her.

"I don't know why I followed you home—like a stray puppy. I just needed to see you again. Please, Ana."

He did not try to push the door open.

"I don't want to hurt you, Ana, please," he pleaded.

The two of them stood there for a minute breathing in the humid air that stunk of urine, whiskey and burning wood. She was so sick and tired of being afraid.

"I am sorry to scare you," he said.

"I am not scared of you," she retorted, adrenaline charging through her.

With that, she threw open the door. Her hair was loosened, and she stood before him like a wild horse ready to trample on his chest and crush the life out of him.

"What do you want?" she demanded.

"I—I don't know," he stuttered.

"Yes, I think you do—you're spending all your days and nights wondering what it must feel like to hold this whore? Go ahead, touch me."

Ravi stepped back.

"You are angry with me . . . "

"I am not angry, Ravi. I am excited. You've come to me, and I am willing to destroy this monster for you. I'm ready to chop its head off and cut its tail to pieces. They've made you believe a beautiful woman is all you need to be happy."

She began to laugh. He tried to smile.

"You believed it, didn't you?" she continued.

She saw that she had hit a nerve. Ravi looked down at the ground, overcome with shame. His eyes welled up with tears.

"I'm sorry," she said.

"But I love you, Ana," he choked out.

"You don't. How can you love me when you hate yourself? God brings the clouds he wants us to taste within our reach—the others are unattainable. He has given us both storm clouds, and we have to live with them hovering over us, blocking the beautiful sun. These are our lives."

She walked up the stairs to her apartment, and he did not follow her. He sat down on the stairs, catching his breath. Her words were smoldering in his mind, burning truth into illusion.

Upstairs, Ana filled a basin with water and stripped off her sari. She began washing the city grime off her body. She scrubbed furiously until blood rushed to the surface of her skin, making the icy water feel warm and her pale skin rosy.

Ravi managed to fall asleep for a few hours in a cheap hotel, but awoke from a dream in which he was about to be swallowed by an immense wave of flames. He sat up and peeled off his sweat-soaked clothing. He walked over to the open window and filled his lungs with the muggy air. As he reached for a cigarette, he halted midway when he saw himself in the foggy, distorted mirror. In the morning light diffused by the translucent curtains, his perspiring body appeared to be covered in a light golden sheen. He did not recoil at the sight of his nakedness. He moved closer and placed a palm on his reflection's cheek. As he stared at his face, he noticed how smooth and babylike his skin was in certain places. As he looked deeper still, beyond the scars and bumps, there were crisp mountains and clear rivers. There was Africa on his chin and Sri Lanka on his neck. What divine mirror was this? If only Ana could see how the storm clouds had parted! Would she be able to see these continents floating on his cheeks and the honey-colored wings stirring on his back? It didn't matter; it only mattered that he saw this new world.

Ravi ran from the room, shot past the hotel desk clerk and headed for his lorry.

"The monsoon is expected, sir!" warned the clerk as Ravi ran out the door.

✦

Ravi had an incredible urge to drive, to move. Once on the road, he floored the gas pedal. The Vishnu statue rattled against the vibrating windshield. Panting, he drove until he had left Pune behind and all he could see in his filthy rear-view mirror was a glowing finger of sun breaking through the clouds. Suddenly, slamming his foot down on the brake, he stopped in the middle of the road. When he pulled on his door handle, a wicked wind slapped him and threw the door open. He did not notice that Vishnu was pirouetting only inches from the floor

Catching his breath, he used his newly found strength to open the back door of the lorry. He took out a razor from his pocket and began slicing open the boxes. Cutting sari-length strips from the spools of luscious silks, he threw them up in the air with all his might. Up they went, fluttering heavenward like drunken butterflies shrouded in gold filigree.

Exhausted, he fell to his knees and began to laugh. He couldn't remember when his shoulders had felt so light. Taking off his pants and shirt, he shrouded his nude body in a piece of orange silk, which he tied like a dhovti around his waist. He emptied a petrol can over the remaining boxes and then dropped a lit match on a gasoline-doused heap of unraveled cloth. Letting his feet lead him, he began walking down the road, his lorry blazing gloriously behind him.

The Tailor

"D o you understand?" asked the lady with crooked teeth. "I don't want you to nod yes-yes ma'am and then stitch whatever you fancy. Make sure you write it all down."

Leeladhar shook his head from side to side indicating that she need not worry. He stared at the gold dripping from her ears, neck and wrists and wondered why such a wealthy woman who had left India behind and moved to the United States had never gotten her horrid teeth fixed.

"Do you know how many tailors I've employed? I'll tell you—four. You're number five."

She looked at her daughter, who was starting to squirm.

"Mother," said the girl in hopes of silencing her.

"What? It's the truth isn't it? My poor daughter is being abused because of her creative tastes. Can you imagine that? Tailors wielding sewing needles like knives." The woman laughed heartily at her own wit.

"You need not worry, Mrs. Badari," replied Leeladhar softly.

"You wrote down her measurements? The last one didn't take into account that a woman's hips are much wider than her waist. I asked him how he could make such a foolish mistake. He picked up the skirt and wrapped it around himself, showing me that it fit him. I don't think he's ever seen a woman naked."

Her daughter snickered. And so did the two assistant tailors sewing in the back of the shop. Leeladhar smiled.

"He just stood there with the skirt still wrapped around him, blushing. What a waste, I tell you. A terrible waste. We bought the material in Delhi. A really lovely pattern. You can imagine how I felt when she tried that on. My heart shattered along with my dear Sukuntula's in a thousand pieces."

The daughter looked at her feet and spun the pink bakery box she was holding by the string. It was from Andhra's Sweet Shop, which was a few blocks away, on the other side of Besant Square.

"Now, you do understand that the armholes on this dress need to be large enough so she can move her arms about," said the woman, lifting her daughter's arm up like a mannequin's.

"I have the measurements, madam," said Leeladhar. He was getting tired of listening to her droning. He picked up his heavy scissors and began cutting a piece of white khadi cloth along the blue chalk outline.

"The first one made the armholes way up here. I told him that he's not going to wear the dress and that he shouldn't in his discomfort and embarrassment try to cover up Sukuntula. Remember the neck should be at fourteen inches on the blue dress."

"I have that right here," he said.

"The reason I'm trusting you is because you're young. I don't want you to do what you think is right. I want you to do what I tell you."

Leeladhar handed her a receipt for the three small bundles of material.

"When will you have them ready?" asked the girl.

"In a week."

"Very good," replied the woman. "We'll be back next Wednesday. Remember—don't think too much," she said jokingly with one foot over the doorstep.

"I stitch from my heart, madam," he said.

She hesitated for a few seconds and blinked at him. Leeladhar's breath caught in his throat. He wondered if it was not a reassuring thing to say. But it should not matter. It was the truth. At that moment, the woman's eyes darted to a lizard peeking out from behind the fluorescent light tube.

"Very good," she said and spun on her heel.

Leeladhar watched them get into a white Fiat. Their driver shut the door, shooing off a beggar girl.

"It is a good thing your grandfather was not here," joked Chetan, one of the assistants. "He would have tossed her out on her golden ass."

"It is difficult getting what you want," Leeladhar said, picking up his scissors again.

Leeladhar pulled the shop's gate down. The traffic around the square had quieted down, as it always did at nightfall in Vijayawada. He was getting on his bicycle when a dove-gray Ambassador car pulled up.

"You work at Yaxi Tailors?" called the driver.

He nodded and pushed up the kickstand with his foot.

"Please tell Mr. Bhaskaraiah that Mrs. Valuri would like him to pay her a visit tomorrow afternoon."

Leeladhar nodded again, adjusting the package of shirts he was bringing home to work on after dinner. He pedaled past the car and melted into the swirl of activity. The colors whizzed past him—a blur of yellow autos, red rickshaws, bright saris and brown skin. He wondered why the Valuri family had summoned his grandfather. It was inevitable that their only daughter, Navina, was getting married. But so soon? Too soon. He hoped the visit was for other purposes.

When he entered the house, his grandfather was taking out his teeth. Leeladhar hated it when he had to talk to him like that.

"Good evening, grandfather. Mrs. Valuri sent word with her driver for you to go to their house."

"Ahhh, it is the wedding."

"But he did not say anything about a wedding."

His grandfather dropped his dentures unceremoniously into an empty mango pickle jar.

"I will go after lunch."

"I will come with you," Leeladhar offered a little too eagerly.

"No. You must stay in the shop."

Leeladhar stared at the teeth as the disappointment spread from his ears. His grandfather's lips looked as if they were being vacuumed into his throat.

"It is such a pleasure having clients for whom money is not an issue," he warbled. "They are good people."

Leeladhar hated seeing him toothless because it reminded him that his grandfather was sixty-two years old.

"My water, son."

Removing the cup that fit into the mouth of the stainless steel water jug like a cork, he poured his grandfather some cool water. He stared at the Sai Baba of Shirdi silver etching plate as the old man drank deeply, making disgusting sucking noises. Leeladhar noticed one of the bulbs that encircled the image of the saint had burned out.

"Sleep well, grandfather."

Leeladhar stared at the back of his grandfather's bald head as the old man prepared for his visit to the Valuri house.

"We are finished with all the shirts," Leeladhar said.

"You are a good son, Leeladhar. You are more of a son than your drunken father. You know how important this shop is to me—to keep it in the family. When you take pride in your work the way you do, it makes me proud as well."

With that, he adjusted his gauzelike dhovti between his legs and walked out the door.

Ultimately, it was words like that that made Leeladhar's frustration dissipate heavenward like an autumn fog. When the air cleared, he saw his grandfather's love solid like an imperishable mountain before him. He had no choice but to keep climbing. It would be a long, painful fall.

The rest of the day was spent cutting cobalt-colored material for convent skirts. He remembered when his grandfather stood behind the counter, scissors in hand. He must have clothed half the village. Did they remember him at all? Mrs. Valuri did for one. She always raved on and on about the old man's talented hands and keen eyes.

"You have flair, Bhaskaraiahgaru. It is a gift from God. You cannot learn that—you are born with it."

Mrs. Valuri's mother considered Yaxi Tailors part of the family. And so, Mrs. Valuri did as well. Leeladhar longed to be truly part of that family. He was the perfect man to take care of Navina. He was hard-working, dependable, loving and gentle. If only he had a chance to show her, to touch her life somehow.

The next day, grandson and grandfather waited in front of the Sai Baba Sari Shop. They were meeting Mrs. Valuri and Navina there to help with the selection of the material for the wedding. Leeladhar had fallen asleep without eating dinner the night before after learning about the upcoming marriage. This morning, however, he woke to a feeling of acceptance. It was ludicrous for him to think that he could ever marry a girl like Navina. He was wasting his time with idle dreams.

"They are late," he said glancing at his watch.

"Rich people can afford to be late," said his grandfather with a smile.

The gray car pulled up, and the driver got out and opened the back door. Mrs. Valuri stepped out draped in an overstarched indigo sari laden with jheri. Navina exited on the other side and walked slowly around the back of the car. She was dipped in a sheer rose sari that clung to her slim form and brought out the apricot in her skin.

"Namaste, Bhaskaraiahgaru," Mrs. Valuri said putting her palms together.

"Namaste, madam," Basha said.

"Come, dear child," he said to Navina, who tipped her head down slightly.

"My, how your grandson has grown!" exclaimed Mrs. Valuri.

Leeladhar tucked his chin close to his chest.

"He has a good head for colors and fabrics," boasted Basha sweetly as he removed his sandals and pushed them toward the pile. "I am sorry they do not have seats here."

They sat down on the mattresses on the floor.

"The selection, you will see, will be well worth it. It is my grandson's favorite shop."

"The bigger fancy stores do not have as much variety," said Leeladhar.

They all sat cross-legged across from one another.

"Navina is very picky, so we will see."

Leeladhar's and Navina's eyes met for the first time. They quickly flew away as soon as they landed, however, like skittish sparrows.

"Show us some wedding saris," Basha said to the two salesmen, a fellow with a lazy eye and a gaunt teenager.

And so began an aggressive symphony of sensations as flattened spindles of sari fabrics were unfurled. The teen boy shook out the cloth, and down it fell, making a noise that sounded like four handclaps. Silks from Kanchipuram, Benares, Bangalore and Pochampalle, Mysore crepe and silk chiffons. Parrot-greens with elaborate jheri borders, scarlets sprinkled with golden mangoes, pearly damasks, peacocks grazing in fields of marigolds, and lotuses floating in oceans of blue. Within minutes, they were all waist-deep in saris—the space between Navina and Leeladhar bridged by the coolness of the fabrics.

"Show me that one," said Mrs. Valuri, pointing to a traditional pattern in olive.

Leeladhar saw Navina twitch her nose.

"That is lovely," said Basha, running his wrinkled hand over the cloth.

Mrs. Valuri slapped her thigh.

"The mosquitoes are eating me alive. Do you like it, dear?"

"It is not bad."

"Now, Navina, you are not going to wear the same boring colors." She turned to Basha as if Navina had suddenly vanished. "She has a terrible habit of wearing the same colors for days. Last week it was gray."

"How about this one?" asked Navina, pulling a peach-blossom pink from under the pile.

"You see? She is wearing pink, and now she wants to buy only pink."

"I think it is a beautiful choice," said Leeladhar, thinking his voice did not sound like his own.

"My sister already gave us a pink sari."

"But, madam, there are many colors in the word pink," explained Leeladhar. "This pink glows with warmth and excitement while the one she is wearing is cool and reclusive. I mean no disrespect, but the olive you have chosen is much too heavy for her slim figure. It is stiff and tiresome, while the pink one is fluid and spirited."

Mrs. Valuri and Basha stared at him with stone faces.

"He is right. I think it is lovely."

"Well, Bhaskaraiah, you spoke the truth. Your grandson has a way about him."

"He does, he does."

"Ahhh!" Mrs. Valuri squawked as she smacked the back of her neck. The crippled mosquito trembled, clinging to her perfumed handkerchief.

The sun was setting when Navina walked into Yaxi Tailors the next evening. Leeladhar was explaining to Chetan how to stitch the blue dress for the crooked-toothed lady's daughter. He was suddenly overwhelmed with work. Basha was home recovering from a cold. Leeladhar stopped talking when he saw that Chetan was staring dazedly straight ahead.

"Oh, madam, hello."

"Are you busy?"

"No, no. How are your plans going for the wedding?"

"I guess they are fine. I am not too involved with it. It is difficult with my mother. She is a bit of a tyrant. She ordered me to come here and give you my measurements."

"She called to tell me to expect you."

Leeladhar picked up his measuring tape. His hands began to tremble as he unrolled it.

"Arms," he mumbled. Navina offered him her left arm.

"Eight and a half."

He reached for the pencil behind his ear, but dropped it. When he bent down, he noticed her toes were painted to match her carnation pink sari. He moved behind her and stretched the tape across her shoulders.

"Thirty-nine."

Facing her, he slid down to her waist.

"Twenty-four."

He moved up to her ribcage.

"Twenty-seven."

His heart started beating faster as he loosened the tape and leaned still closer. He could smell the sandalwood talc she had powdered herself with after her bath. He reached around her back and encircled her breasts, barely grazing her right nipple.

"Thirty-six."

As he wrote down the figure, he desperately tried to think of other measurements he could take to keep her with him a little longer. He picked up the tape and wrapped it around her rounded hips.

"Thirty-five. That is it."

"Good. You will be done with the jackets next week?"

"Yes. Absolutely."

She smiled her thanks and left.

"Remember, you are stitching her jackets for her *wedding*," teased Chetan.

On Wednesday morning, Leeladhar rode his bicycle into the rising sun on his way to the shop. He had plenty of work to do. He wanted to finish cutting the material for Navina's petticoats and jackets. Jackets were very tricky to stitch since women's breasts were so different. There were so many shapes and contours. It was an essential piece of the Indian woman's wardrobe. Many women were on an eternal search for the tailor who would fit their breasts properly. He hated the way some tailors stitched the breast cups into unnatural, stiff points. It reminded him of how sugar syrup stretched and broke off into hard peaks as it cooled. When he stitched jackets, he made sure they fit the woman naturally and, most importantly, comfortably. She should not have to lift her breasts to fit into the cups or squash them to fasten the hooks or rearrange them to match the nipple darts. This is why female customers raved about his work. Once they stepped into Yaxi, they were lifetime customers. Leeladhar had his grandfather to thank for the genes that gave him the gift of imagination, because, except for the occasional pornographic film and the time he saw his father sucking on his mistress's breast, he had never really seen a woman's body.

"Are you finished?"

Leeladhar saw the woman with the crooked teeth smiling at him. He went in the back to find the dresses, face ablaze. He had forgotten all about them and had not had a chance to check the assistants' work.

"Are they done?"

"Yes, yes, Mrs.—"

"Badari," she finished for him.

He handed them over to her. She looked at them skeptically and held up the blue dress to her daughter's frame.

"Pull it over your dress."

The girl did as she was told.

"Oh, dear. You've done it, too, haven't you? You've made the neck too high. The hem is too low. It's much too big. There's too much material on the sides."

He listened, tapping a piece of chalk on the counter.

"Let's have a look at the others."

"The buttons suck," said the girl.

By the way she was twisting her face, he concluded that she did not like the buttons.

"These are also ruined. I cannot believe my eyes. I trusted you, and this is what you've done."

"I will fix them, madam," he said sweetly, although his hands were shaking.

"They're all that dreaded umbrella pattern."

"Tell him in Telugu the buttons suck—tell him that, Mom."

He bit the skin of his lower lip until he tasted the saltiness leak onto his tongue.

"How many times do I have to come back to your shop? Are you going to take the cost of petrol off your bill?"

"I can't wear these," the girl sputtered.

"I will have them ready tomorrow, Mrs. Badari."

"Good because we're leaving for a tour on Friday morning."

He reached impulsively for his scissors.

"Never again will I do this, Sukuntula. It's not good for my blood pressure. You will just have to buy your clothes back home."

With that, the woman and her daughter stomped out of the store.

Leeladhar was sorry he had agreed to stitch the dresses in the first place. He hated dealing with Indians who lived in the States. They always came in with their complicated ideas for some grand article of clothing. Did they think he could read their silly minds? Most Indian tailors were not designers. They sewed clothing, period. But this was something Indians from the States did not understand. They insisted on paying thirty-five to sixty-five rupees, the equivalent of one to two U.S. dollars, for a high-fashion work of art. Was all the aggravation worth it? He rarely ended up thinking so. But he welcomed a challenge, and most of the time he got it right. He slammed the scissors down on the counter. Chetan poked his head in and grinned.

"We really stepped in some extraordinary shit this time, eh?"

But Leeladhar refused to smile.

After fixing the girl's dresses, Leeladhar finished marking the fabric for Navina's petticoats and jackets, as his grandfather was coming in to check over his work before they started cutting the cloth. Leeladhar rubbed the sweat and grease from the sides of his nose. It was a scorching day, and the fan was merely blowing hot air his way. The heat was making his head throb. Picking up the wedding saris, he settled in the back room in front of his sewing machine.

When he finally looked up from his work, Leeladhar saw the darkness of the street through the shop window. His grandfather had come and gone, raving all the while about the jacket patterns his grandson had come up with. After Basha helped him cut the cloth, he left whistling down the street with some of the fabric so he could start stitching the jackets at home. It was agreed that Leeladhar would work on the saris and petticoats in the shop. That must have been two hours ago, Leeladhar thought. He had stitched the falls—borders of cloth stitched on the inside of saris to prevent them from getting dirty—for six out of the seven saris. He stood up and shook out the final sari—the one Mrs. Valuri was hesitant to buy. The pinkness pooled at his feet, inviting like a warm tongue. He felt the silkiness of the rich pallu that would be draped over Navina's strong shoulders and across her bosom. He breathed deeply into the fabric and swore he could already smell her scent there. At once, he dropped the sari. What was he doing? Why was he torturing himself like this? She was getting married not to him, but to another man! He wished the groom dead. And in the next second, he wished he hadn't wished that. His eyes started to tear from exhaustion.

He sat back down and began stitching the fall into place. His heart was racing, and his head filled with flashes of light. Why was it that he felt so many urges that he had to hold back? He remembered temple goddesses: curvaceous hips thrust forward, bellies exposed, plump breasts bared, nipples erect. Worship was torture. The human libido was not something to be ashamed of, yet he could feel the barbed manacles. Worse, he witnessed others who managed to break free. Most men's urges leaked out in the most perverse ways—pinching a tantalizing buttock, elbowing a breast in a festival crowd, touching a woman's knee or foot with their own while sitting on the bus, surreptitiously brushing a finger across a young girl's breast while handing her mother a box of sweets, ogling shamelessly. The balance of boldness and subtlety in the acts was always astounding. Mostly, they went unnoticed by passersby. But Leeladhar knew because he was always watching. He had many of the same thoughts as those men, except he never acted on them. As the rage shot through him, he stepped harder on the pedal. The fabric he was feeding into the machine bunched up as his fingers stumbled. The pain he felt as the needle pierced his fingertip brought him back to his senses. He gasped and pulled his hand away, clenching it to help stop the pain.

When he pulled out the bent needle from his sewing machine, he saw that his blood had fallen onto the sari. Panic and shame seized him, and his initial instinct was to scrub the spot clean—erase his foolish affections and forget the girl. But as he stared at the two beads of red, the bright rays of his love broke through and struck him. The plum shades of the border made the blood practically unnoticeable. He ran his finger lightly over the tops of the drops and watched as the thirsty silken threads drank him up.

The Pillow

As Sindhura bent over, pencils of sunlight raced down the length of her muscular calves. The armpits of her blouse were soaked. As she straightened, a rivulet of sweat ran down from her clavicle and vanished into her cleavage. She squeezed her breasts together to stop the tickling. The white sun was shooting through the foliage of the lithe silk-cotton tree before her. How different the sun was when she watched it dip into the cool blue glow as she walked home. Her father had been so in love with the tranquility of dusk that he had named his only daughter after the most scarlet of sunsets. Perhaps Sindhura liked the evening sun so much because she felt as if her father were walking her home.

Her eyes fell to the boat-shaped fruit she held in her hands. It was heavy with life, seams bursting apart with brownish puffs of kapok. She imagined her belly would feel like this when she became pregnant. Impulsively, she glanced behind her and lifted up her skirts.

Sunil's eyes opened as wide as his mouth, as he froze sand-wiched between two hibiscus bushes, following the sleek line of her calves to her thighs. Peripherally, he saw not the pale blur of pant-ies, but a magnificent thatch of blue-black. She tucked the pod into her waistband and walked toward the hibiscus bushes. Then she abruptly turned and searched the ground. When she found her shadow, she laughed at the sight of her bloated stomach. He let out a nervous chuckle. She heard the odd sound and ran back under the shade of the tree and looked about. She pulled the fruit out from beneath her skirts and squatted. She waited a good ten minutes before she was convinced that the noise was just a parrot flirting in the breeze.

Her father had taught her how to make pillows with kapok. He believed in being self-sufficient, so their backyard had been laced with all sorts of practical fruit-bearing trees. When her parents died in a bus crash, she and her brother had been taken in by their uncle, who lived in a modest house in Eluru. Since their death, Sindhura had started making more and more pillows to earn her keep. She sold each pillow for thirty rupees. In the chief marketplace on Eluru Road, many liked her pillows best because she stuffed them with extra cotton and took the time to embroider birds and flowers on the covers. Her father had shown her this hidden plot of land where silk-cotton trees grew. The trees were on government land, so she guessed she was stealing in a way. Whenever she walked to this secret place, she was very careful that no one saw her. If these trees were discovered, others would gather the cotton and she would soon run out of materials.

A look in her basket revealed that she was three pods shy of stuffing a pillow. She headed toward the nearby trees. Sunil started to get up, but she was upon him much too suddenly. He sat as still as he could. She crouched, parting some brush. He felt as if he were choking on a bird, the poor thing's wings flapping about below his tonsils. Just when he thought a scream would escape his lips, she stood up wielding a long bamboo stick. He nearly jumped out of his skin, concluding she had seen him spying on her all along and was now going to give him the beating of his life. At first, he thought it a horrible notion, but after a second's thought, he waited in heavenly anticipation. If this was the way she chose to touch him, so be it. He craved any type of contact with this beautiful creature.

Whack-whack! But he felt nothing. When he opened his eyes, she was gone. *Whack-whack!* He peered through the shrubs across the way at the silk-cotton trees. She was knocking the branches with all her might. On hearing a cracking noise, she would drop to the ground, covering her head with her slender arms. When he heard a twig snap, he, too, braced himself out of anxious concern for her. He peeked through his fingers and saw a plump pod crashing to the ground behind her, just grazing her mud-caked bare feet. After the fifth try, two more pods pirouetted and fell down. She picked up the fruit and marveled at the steadfastness of the two lovers who clung to each other by a single green branch. Tossing the pods into her basket, off she went. Sunil stared at her as she walked away savoring his last morsel of magenta. Slowly, he began to feel the coolness of the dirt around his knees. He slapped his back, just missing a mosquito sucking his blood.

When Sunil arrived home, his older brother, Nagu, was sitting outside, engrossed in a comic book.

"You are late," informed Nagu without looking up.

Sunil knew that meant Nagu had probably eaten his share of dahl and rice. He wondered how Nagu could read the same faded comic over and over again. He guessed the child Nagu had stolen it from had not bought another one just yet.

Inside, his mother was fast asleep. She worked hard, and for what? Her husband was an alcoholic and spent their meager funds on carousing, while her elder son was lazy as could be. Sunil had decided on his fourteenth birthday that his family was like quicksand. He was not going to let them pull him down. That was when he started selling samosas to save money. He sold ten samosas for nine rupees. Most of the others sold ten for ten rupees. Every day, directly after school, he would run to the restaurant by the train station and pick up the hot vegetable turnovers swaddled in newspaper. He would wave the bundles under passengers' open windows or if the train was stopping for more than five minutes, he would climb aboard to hawk the snacks. He had to board as soon as the train stopped because if he ended up behind one of the crippled beggars, he'd get stuck in a compartment. He always made sure he had plenty of coins, because customers were understandably wary if he said he had to return with their change. The village was crawling with crooks and indolent beggars. On sight, he was no different.

If his calculations were right, he would have enough money to leave Eluru and travel up to New Delhi by the time he graduated from school. In a big city like that, he could land a good job. He was studying business, and cities are always bustling with business. He would write to his mother often. Maybe he would even have enough money left over to purchase a camera. Then he could send her some pictures as well. Sunil reached deep into his knickers and gently— Nagu always had his ears pricked for the jingle of money—spread some rumpled bills and a handful of change on the bed. Opening a hair oil bottle he took from behind the armoire, he deposited his day's earnings.

Minutes later, on the roof, he bit into a soggy samosa. The black sky began to tumble like a kaleidoscope with images of the woman he had seen among the silk-cotton trees. Her thighs were emblazoned in the speckled night's constellations. As his eyes landed on the brightest star, he made his wish.

Two pillows tucked under each arm, Sindhura headed for the marketplace. On a side street, a block away from the sari and trinket vendors, she would stand with her perfect pillows. Tourists always fell in love with them. Usually, they bought a pair. Other girls sold kapok-stuffed pillows, but she did not mind the competition because it kept her alert. One squeeze, and buyers would hoot how Sindhura's pillows were wonderfully fluffy, much more so than the other girls'. She would swell and gleefully pocket the thirty rupees.

Sunil, too, was on his way to the marketplace this morning. His mother had sent him to buy dahl and cabbage, which he obediently did, although he was sick of eating the yellow mush. His mother was an excellent cook, and she tried her best to prepare enticing meals, but with rice or pulka, it was always dahl. He punted a piece of soda-bottle glass up the road. He wondered why his brother never went to the market for his mother. His brother was still snoring when he left. His mother had given up on Nagu a long, long time ago. Once, when Sunil had taken his mother to the temple, he heard her praying that Nagu would find a girl to marry and leave them be.

As Sunil ran to kick the glass, he tripped over a spinning puppy chasing its tail. The tolling in his head gave way to high-pitched laughter. Annoyed at such blatant ridicule from a girl, he collected himself proudly and stood anchored to the spot. His tangled brow unraveled at the sight before him. It was the delightful face that had been making him toss and turn at night. She hushed as he stared at her. Eventually, his smile budded mysteriously like a jasmine flower. She beamed back at him. He dusted the dirt from his legs and walked toward her.

He looked at the pillows. Panic seared through him as he envisioned her lifting her skirts. He was at a loss for words. Out of nervousness, Sindhura shook her petticoat this way and that. Seeing her naked ankle did not help matters much. Sunil stared at his feet. The weight of the silence was unbearable. She started digging her toe into the dirt.

"How much?" he bellowed in an attempt to compensate for his reticence.

The force of the question startled her, and she gasped, taking a step back. He looked into her eyes and saw a flash of fear. It was not his intention to frighten her. He noticed that her breath had quickened, her chest bobbing ever so slightly as a flower does when stirred by a bumblebee.

"How much?" he asked soothingly.

"Thirty rupees, babu," she replied sweetly.

Just then, a cackling group of wealthy tourists stepped out from some rickshaws and walked toward them. Sindhura handed them a pillow.

"Fifty rupees," she said.

"Wow! I'm gonna get two."

"The one with the peacock is terrific."

Sunil watched them carefully.

"I like the ones with the flowers."

The tourist handed over a hundred rupee note and clutched the two pillows to her chest.

"Thank you."

Sindhura gleamed as they crossed the street making their way to the bead and jewelry stands. She looked at the boy walking away. He moved so slowly that she deduced he must have injured himself during his spill, or, perhaps, someone had trampled on his heart. He seemed terribly sensitive for a boy.

Sunil could bear to turn around only when the bazaar racket had become faint and the colors of saris had bled together. Everyone said how the action of city life was invigorating, that it made even the most unproductive fellow productive. He questioned this as he slid down against a wall. No matter how busy life appeared around him, it was still somebody else's business. He felt as if he were running when others were walking on water; and when he was walking, they were swinging by him like spider monkeys. Would it matter if he went up north to a modern city? He rubbed a chip of plaster between his thumb and forefinger. In a fit of frustration, he threw it. If it were a bottle or marble even, perhaps he would have derived some satisfaction. Innocuously, the plaster plopped down in the middle of the road. In fact, a rickshaw driver stepped right on it with his bare foot as he ran by with a passenger perched like a king on his throne. No matter. The real trouble bubbled to the surface. She had called him "babu," a term of affection for young boys. She saw him as a child. She did not seem all that much older. There could only be two years between them. That wasn't too much. Actually, it was an insignificant issue. He knew what he had to do.

Over the next few weeks, Sunil skipped school several days and put in long hours selling samosas. He had saved thirty rupees, but Nagu had filched two rupees and some change. This bright day, Sunil decided he had better carry his savings with him to the market. He filled his mother's plastic vegetable bag with eggplants, bitter gourd, onions, rice, wheat flour and dahls. His father must have done well at cards last night. On his way to the marketplace, he tried to resist looking down the side street, but he could not. She stood behind the blanket on which she had laid out her pillows. His eyes ricocheted to her shapely form. He turned away.

"Babu," she called.

He picked up his pace.

"Babu!"

His feet started to kick ahead of his body. He felt a hand on his shoulder. He was confronted with bloodshot eyes and yellow teeth. The stranger pointed. Sunil looked over at the girl, who was waving a pillow at him. He walked toward her, every elephantine step cautiously planted. He stared at the pillow she held out to him. He reached for it. It had an emerald cover with a small golden peacock embroidered in the upper right corner.

"Thirty rupees for you only."

He held it close to his face, attempting to sleep in mid-air. He heard her chuckle, and this made him shake with laughter. There was something so intimate about laughing together. He wanted to make love to her right there in the middle of the bustling market. Would anyone notice? His hand moved down toward his pants. He pulled out some bills from his pocket and smoothed them out on the blanket. He continued fishing in all of his numerous pockets. He had to distribute the cash in case his brother got hold of him. They laughed. When he handed her the last paisa, she waited for him to tuck his pockets back into his pants.

"Have sweet dreams," she bade.

He smiled until a firebolt struck him, exposing his deepest thoughts. He felt pink rising to his ears, and he turned to run.

"How can I not?" he yelled ecstatically when he was halfway down the road. She smiled, shaking out her blanket. It was an early day for her, and she felt completely rejuvenated. This boy filled her with warmness. What a handsome man he would grow up to be, she thought.

Hugging the pillow, Sunil ran through a field to a secluded spot. He admired how it melted into the grass, the peacock shimmering like a lost jewel among the blades. He sighed and rested his head on the cushion, staring at the clouds dancing above him. He pictured her delicate hands coaxing the silk cotton from its lair. There she was, stepping from cloud to cloud, cupping hunks of fluff and stuffing them into her velvet sack. And as she bent down, he was drawn to the darkness between her breasts. He knelt in front of the pillow and felt every inch of its plushness. It was as inviting and irresistible as a woman's bare breast—her bare breasts dangling before him. He tenderly kneaded the softness, his hands trembling. His skin prickled. He never felt so alive. How he wished she would fall right through the clouds and into his arms. He heard a scream. He sat up, his arms wide open to catch her. He blinked at the emptiness. A goat herder carrying a stick with a bell hiked through the green behind him.

That evening, when Sunil arrived at home, he noticed extra chappals on the veranda. Peeking into the front room, he saw his brother in an overstarched shirt slumping next to his father. There was a man who was about his father's age lighting a cigarette. He knew his parents were trying again to arrange Nagu's marriage.

Sunil went to his room and slipped his pillow into a white case. Picking up a towel, he headed into the courtyard. He dunked his hands into the brass cistern and splashed his face. As he shook the tin of tooth powder into his palm, the pink dust sprinkled down his leg. Looking in a piece of broken mirror hanging from the guava tree, he mixed the powder into a paste and scrubbed his teeth and gums with his finger. He could barely hear them talking. He turned and looked at the doorway, but just caught the tail end of a sari pallu. He applied some hair oil to his short hair and combed it neatly.

On the way back to his room, he heard a familiar chuckle. Then, he saw the woman of his dreams sitting next to his mother. She smiled at him.

"He purchased a pillow from me just today."

"Is that so?" said his mother. "Bring it here, Sunil."

Sunil went to his room and brought out the pillow. The women, caressing the peacock, raved about Sindhura's sewing talents. Finally, it floated back to his trembling fingers.

He made his escape as quickly as he could to the safety of his room. He could not believe that she was going to marry his brother of all people. What miserable destiny was this? He could hear them laughing as he sat on his bed hugging his pillow. When his mother entered his room to call him for dinner, he pretended to be asleep. She stroked his hair before she left. As he tossed in and out of a light sleep, Sunil could still hear them talking. They must have reached an agreement regarding the marriage.

The guests had barely stepped out of the house before Nagu burst into Sunil's room.

"Where did you get thirty rupees from? Are we in love, little monkey?"

He lay facing the wall, as his brother taunted him.

"Do not worry. She is going to be my wife, and you can have a look now and then. But looking is all. She can only be yours in your pathetic dreams."

Nagu snatched the pillow from under his head and waved it above him.

"Jump, monkey, jump."

Sunil jumped, but Nagu kept raising it a bit higher out of his reach. Then, all of a sudden, electricity shot through Sunil and he tackled his brother. They fell on the bed, Nagu still digging his fingers into the soft pillow. Sunil started punching.

"Are we angry, monkey?"

Sunil beat his fists into his brother's stomach again and again.

"Owww! Easy!"

Sunil pulled the pillow down. As they struggled, his hands and arms began pressing the softness into his brother's smug face. He pressed down with all his weight, muffling his words. He could not listen to another horrible word. Nagu was unusually weak. Perhaps it was because he stuffed himself fat eating Sunil's share of dinner. He felt an incredible strength surging through him. He felt for the first time in his life that he could crush his brother like a roach. He pushed as if he were trying to close an iron door. He wanted to shut it so he would not have to listen anymore. He wanted to sleep. He pushed and pushed into the golden peacock until his brother was quiet.

The Bath

*I*t *must have been moonglow way up in the blue, it must have been moonglow
that led me straight to you. I still hear you saying, dear one hold me fast,
and I started prayin', oh lord please let this last.*

Mrs. Vidya Chitra turned up the volume of the tape recorder on
the bathroom shelf. She always played the same cassette during her
bath. It was a bootleg compilation she had purchased at a book fair
in Madras two years ago.

"Are you coming?" she hollered through the crack of the wooden
door.

"I am coming, Ammagaru," came the respectful reply.

Within a few moments her servant, Munjee, entered cradling a
silver canister.

"What were you doing? You know that I am getting cold."

"The milkboy had come, Ammagaru."

"You did not forget to lock the door, did you?"

Munjee gave her an assuring nod and knelt down on the cool

granite floor to test the warmth of the water in the bucket. Mrs. Chitra breathed deeply and began to relax as she looked at her servant. Munjee's lavish tresses, when set free, cascaded down her back like a waterfall. She was wearing the cabbage-green cotton sari Mrs. Chitra had given her for Dasara. Mr. Chitra's malevolent sister, Hema, had given it to her as a gift, and Mrs. Chitra had in turn given it to Munjee. She remembered wearing it only once. She had had a horrible fight with Hema at dinner, and that was that. It was a bad luck sari. But it looked nice on her servant.

Mrs. Chitra took off her jacket and tossed it on top of her discarded sari in the corner. She then stepped out of her cotton petticoat and added it to the crumpled pile. She turned around so Munjee could take off the gold chain around her neck. It was a wedding gift from her husband's family. It was a traditional gift—a thick gold chain from which dangled two golden breasts with diamonds sparkling on the nipple peaks. The breasts symbolized the virginity and purity of Parvati, the goddess of courage and war. She laughed at the thought of how her life had changed since her wedding day. She was forty-six years old, and her husband, Tilak, was not interested in her anymore. They slept in separate rooms. She supposed she had lost interest as well.

Mrs. Chitra stared into the mirror and checked her breasts for any lumps as Munjee loosened her straggly braid. Her thumb scraped across some stiff black hairs around her areola. She had stopped plucking them years ago.

"I am so cold," whispered the old woman.

Munjee reached through the bars and pulled the window closed. She turned on the hot water tap. After unwrapping her cotton sari so it would not get wet, Munjee opened the door and dropped it outside. Munjee always left her petticoats on. She was a modest one.

The room was already filling up with steam. Mrs. Chitra sat down on the wooden stool and stared at the white wall with hand-painted lotuses. When she had commissioned them, the artist was surprised at the generous price she offered. He was a lovely young man who wore a hat made of straw. Everyone was so curious—typically, no one wore hats in Vijayawada (aside from the few young men who managed to procure baseball caps from relatives in the States). But, then again, there was nothing typical about Jan. He did not have a moustache. He had catlike hazel eyes and a smooth, shaved head. He was African and had traveled to Egypt, Italy, Madagascar, Australia. She had met him at the vegetable market on Besant Road, haggling over a three-foot snake gourd. He was adventurous and so charming to talk to over a cup of tea.

The condensation dripped down the walls in streams, running through the pink lotus petals. They looked so real when they were wet. Jan, at first, had been resistant to take the job.

"Lotuses?" he had repeated quizzically.

"Yes, lotuses."

"Fine. I'll do it."

"But you are hesitant."

"Well, it's just that I won't have much freedom . . ."

" . . . in a lotus?" she finished for him with the kind of amused smile a grownup sheds on a child.

So, she bought one of his "original" paintings. It was a self-portrait—a nude of Jan eating a mango. His legs were wide open. How her husband had despised it!

"This is art!" she had trumpeted.

"It is vulgar," Mr. Chitra denounced.

His lips had barely moved, but still he managed to extinguish some of her zeal. Then, there was the deafening sound of papers being shuffled about on his desk.

"It has passion," she said more softly, more doubtfully.

"I will not have it in the house, Vidya."

The words landed like slaps across her already hot face. Impulsively, she began tearing at her sari. She stripped off her jacket and petticoat and stood staring at the back of his head.

"Look at me."

He turned around slowly, taking his time. His eyes widened at the sight of her nakedness.

"Tell me, Tilak, am I vulgar?"

He stood up as if she were holding a butcher knife.

"Have you gone mad?"

She looked down at her hands for a weapon. After all, it was not as if she had never fantasized about it. But she was holding only Jan's painting.

"Why are you so afraid?"

"I am not afraid. Have you no shame?"

He rummaged through some drawers and picked up a stack of papers from his desk.

"I have some business to take care of."

He walked out at exactly seven minutes to ten. She stood in the middle of the room naked and tearless. It was seven minutes to ten on a chilly night, and she was alone. The next day, the painting mysteriously disappeared, and she never asked him about it.

Wiping the moisture drops settling on her eyelids, she wondered where Jan was right now. He had said he would write to her and let her know of his whereabouts. She was hoping to see the world through his travels. But she never heard from him again.

"The walls need to be cleaned—I can smell the mildew," she said, punctuating it with a sputtering sigh.

"I will wash them tomorrow morning."

Munjee ran a comb gently through her hair.

"How many?" Mrs. Chitra asked routinely.

"Still seven, Ammagaru," Munjee replied. She was referring to the silver strands in Mrs. Chitra's hair. They were well dispersed and unnoticeable from a distance. Munjee poured some amla hair oil into her cupped hand and began massaging Mrs. Chitra's scalp.

"I believe the oil really helps keep it black. You are only twenty now, Munjee, but it is never too soon to start, I tell you. One day, you will suddenly notice your thick hair is thin and weak and wonder what happened. You must be alert." She could just see the swell of Munjee's pregnant belly. She was due in two months.

"I don't have as many worries as you do, Ammagaru."

"Once your first child is born, you will see. You will start feeling like you are trying to catch a train. Always late, just missing it."

But she knew she was lying, because her daughter, Gayatri, who was attending school in London, never gave her much to worry about. Her disconcertednesss ran deeper than that.

She felt as if there was a knot the size of a cricket ball at the base of her skull. Munjee's ministrations relieved the tension. She had strong fingers. Every Friday morning, her servant girl bathed her and tended to her beauty rituals. Mrs. Chitra looked forward to it each week.

Munjee pinned up Mrs. Chitra's hair to let the oil soak in and condition the withered roots. She washed her hands and opened a bottle of body oil. Mrs. Chitra closed her eyes, and her nostrils soon filled with the aroma of sandalwood as warm hands began rubbing her tired body with oil.

"Your skin is very dry, Ammagaru. It is drinking up the oil immediately."

Mrs. Chitra did not respond. Her servant's sweet voice was being drowned by a louder one in her head. It was the voice that reminded her that Munjee, after all, was a servant and that all servants were never to be completely trusted. Some thieves had robbed the house next door last week in the middle of the afternoon. The wife had been in her own dreamland, entertaining some guests on the veranda. The thieves took jewelry, five thousand rupees and four sovereigns. Although she would have liked it otherwise, robberies like that kept Mrs. Chitra miserably alert. She could not let Munjee get the best of her like that. That was when they slipped into the house in the dark of night.

"Do not be so rough," snapped Mrs. Chitra. "You are not skinning a chicken."

Munjee conveyed her apology through her hands. She unscrewed the canister and scooped up some root powder. It contained scented khus-khus, turmeric root and chickpea flour. Adding a little water, she made a paste and rubbed it over the expanse of her back. A moan escaped Mrs. Chitra's lips as Munjee's fingers dug into her buttocks and moved down to her calves. She felt a slight breeze as Munjee stepped in front of her and began spreading the cool yellow salve on her neck, breasts and stomach. The steam was thick now, and all she could see were betel-nut-colored hands reaching for her.

After the paste had dried, Munjee began rubbing it off using the heel of her palm. Mrs. Chitra sucked in some air through her clenched teeth. It felt as if the first layer of her skin were being torn off. She could feel bits of the paste mixed with body hair and the dirt from deep inside her pores dropping on her feet.

"Do you remember the story of Ganesh?" Mrs. Chitra said, continuing without waiting for a reply. "The goddess Parvati had collected the grimy paste after her bath and used it to fashion a young man. One day, she told this son not to let anyone enter as she bathed. He carried out her orders—even when Parvati's husband, Siva, came home from fighting a battle with an evil demon. Siva, angered by the son, whom he saw as an indolent brat of a servant, chopped off his head. Parvati, upon finding her son slain, demanded her rash, impulsive husband breathe new life into him. So, Siva went back to the battlefield and returned with the elephant head of the demon he had slayed. He placed it on Parvati's dead son's neck, and he was reborn as Ganesh, the god of obstacles."

She heard Munjee turning off the hot water. Then Mrs. Chitra felt hands pushing her legs slightly apart. Munjee began kneading the inside of her thighs. As her hands moved down to her calves, Munjee rested her head on her leg. Mrs. Chitra did not ask her to move it. It felt good having the weight of someone on her. The steam was dissipating, and she could see the rosy glow of her servant's skin. Munjee had never given her any reason not to trust her. Mrs. Chitra had stopped taking a daily inventory of the butter laddoos, kaza and Mysore pakum in the store room long ago. Munjee never took more than what she gave her for meals. Once in a while, she would ask for permission to pick some kamala oranges from their tree. Mrs. Chitra usually watched her from the corner of her eye as she picked the fruit. She always plucked two—not greedy at all. But there were those ten or so occasions when Munjee had claimed to have *forgotten* to wash down the veranda in the afternoon before she went home. Perhaps she had truly forgotten. She must have. Munjee was a good girl. Letting her shoulders slump, Mrs. Chitra stroked her servant's hair. She was a good girl. As Munjee looked up at her and ran her fingers back and forth on her thigh, Mrs. Chitra slid into another world.

Suddenly, there was the sound of a steel vessel bouncing on the slate veranda. Mrs. Chitra's back tightened, and she gasped.

"Thieves!"

Then the impatient, thorny voice of her husband.

"Munjee! Where are you?"

"Your master is home!" shouted Mrs. Chitra. She stood up, shaking Munjee off her like crumbs from her lap. "Get up, get up! Go down and see what he wants. Do not be so lazy, Munjee!"

"Yes, Ammagaru."

Munjee jumped to her feet. She wiped her hands on her petticoat, opened the door and wound her sari about herself as quickly as she could. Then, Mrs. Chitra heard her delicate footsteps falling like mustard seeds down the stairs.

The tape player clicked, switching to the other side. In the next second, the sound of a pining saxophone filled the misty room.

The Sugar-Cane Field

Bujji rose before the sun and walked along the paved road into town. His father had arranged for him to operate a sugar-cane juice cart a while back. Bujji hated fussing with the gummy contraption, which seemed with his slightest laxity to take the opportunity to harm him. He always had to be on guard as he fed the strips of cane into its metal jaws that chomped down and extracted the milky juice. Often, he would burn himself on the machine's motor. Bujji took special care when it came to his right hand—his drawing hand. He could not help but imagine the machine's teeth sinking into his finger and then sucking him in up to his arm socket. He would cry out, but who would help him? The street was always bustling with activity. Would anyone even notice? And then he would just be another crippled child on the streets of Amaravathi.

Coins jiggled in Bujji's pockets as he wove down the winding road. He patted a cow on her forehead as she passed, the bell around her neck swinging with the landing of her heavy hooves. Cows had such forgiving eyes, and he decided as he walked that they were probably the most gentle creatures on earth. He wondered how to convey this emotion in his paintings. That was what the master artists did. How could he paint this infectious serenity radiating from such an ordinary animal? It would, he imagined, come to him in time. He would eventually learn how to paint the rain—the way the silver swam in the base of each drop and streaked like tinsel in the moonlight. This was the secret all artists had to discover for themselves.

Bujji picked up the motor and hooked up the machine. As soon as he flicked the switch, he had an urge to abandon the growling beast and run off to the bookshop. Since having been scolded by the proprietor for touching one of the enormous European art books, he looked only at the religious digests. He would spend hours thumbing through the magazines of gods and goddesses slaying demons. He was captivated by the fierceness of the colors the artists used to show the rivaling forces of good and evil.

"How can I see such a sight on this cramped street?" he thought out loud. "Divinity needs space. Gods and goddesses would never appear by this silly sugar-cane cart. They walk through temple walls. They battle in open fields. How can I hope to paint this power if I cannot witness the way immortality moves? Do the arrows of a god move faster than those of a demon?"

As questions bounced noisily like marbles in his head, his shoulders drooped with despair. When he reached home, he was thankful that his father was out. Bujji did not have the energy to face his father's usual prodding about his supposed selfishness. Selfish? Bujji was the one working to help with the bills since his mother had died. Was that not enough? In fact, everything Bujji did was preceded by the adjective "small." Even his nickname, Bujji, meant "little one." He wished people would call him by the name his mother gave him—Upendra. It demanded importance. But it is human nature to call small things by sweet-sounding names. Unfortunately, it is terrible when one grows out of the name. For example, the girl whose father owned the cool-drink stand on the corner had named her new puppy, Chinna, another endearing word for little-ness. However, the wee puppy grew into a mammoth beast. How silly it was for her to continue calling the dog Chinna, but that is exactly what she did. In fact, the dog's fanglike incisors, its panting, slobbering mouth and darting eyes, made Chinna a frightful sight. Bujji shivered at the thought as he emptied his day's wages into a metal drinking cup.

The next day passed very quickly. It was as if Bujji had somehow left his body. He was in a perpetual daydream, thinking about all sorts of things· How perfect his life would be if he did not have to stand beside this awful cart. How easy it would be if he could deliver soda to the rich. Why did people like to drink sugar-cane juice when gnawing on a piece of stalk was so much more satisfying? And how splendid it would be if he could rise early every morning and paint. He stuck a long cane stalk into the machine's mouth and looked at his hands. They were black and sticky from the sap. He remembered the time he had fallen asleep without cleaning them and had awak-ened to the stings of red ants crawling on his palms. It was so hard to get his hands clean. His paintbrush would stick between his fin-gers and make his stroke jerk across the page. At times, he liked the mistake, but mostly, he despised the loss of control. Bujji became so obsessed with thinking about putting paint to paper that he de-cided to turn the motor in earlier than usual. By late afternoon, he was running down a side street.

The tip of his brush had barely touched the paper when the red chased its fingers across the greenish sky. Bujji watched the libera-tion soundlessly. When the flowing ceased, he smiled with pleasure at the rays that fanned themselves from the sphere pressed be-tween the mountains. Actually, this was a sunset. He stared at the sun in his painting and remembered what an old beggar man on the riverbank had told him once.

"See how when the sun opens his hand at dawn, the beams run over the land mindlessly like young children—and how they return!" he had squawked agog, exposing his tobacco-speckled gums.

The rays were drawn back into their father's smoldering palm at dusk. Slowly and simultaneously, they were tucked into their beds. Bujji was enthralled by the beggar's sheer joy. Ever since their meeting, he had paid the sun more attention. He looked at his painting and decided that the father was certainly closing his hand.

When Bujji awoke, it was well into the night. He heard a rumpling sound as he sat up. He smoothed the curling ends of his painting and tucked it in his pad with the others. By the time he arrived at home, his father had already returned from an evening of drinking and playing cards. He must have lost quickly, Bujji thought, because he was home so early. He also must have spilled some whiskey on himself because the small room was filled with the sour smell. Bujji's shoulders jerked when he heard his father's booming voice.

"Where were you?" he half-growled, half-yawned.

"I fell asleep near the river, Nannagaru. I was painting."

His father moved toward him, his face held high in the shadows, his body outlined by the flickering flames of the fire behind him.

"You did not do your chores. Instead, you have been playing. How will you ever grow into a man?"

"But I like painting better than running around the village, Nannagaru," answered Bujji.

"Do you not care that the other boys make merciless fun? Have you mistaken your brush for a sword?"

Bujji started stepping backwards until he felt the wall behind him. His father moved closer until he stood before him like a flaming tree.

"I do not like to run with the others, Nannagaru. I prefer to sit and think—and paint."

"Do you think you are so much better? What insect burrowed

into your small head and told you that you are a prince? Or do you think God appointed you as his painter? Do not think for a moment that you are better than the ordinary fellow. If I am nothing in this life, you are beneath even that because you are my son. That is your duty."

Bujji's face sagged, and he looked at his feet. His mind raced as the heat of the echoing words began to sear into his soul. He wanted to look into his father's pock-marked face and shoot some spears right back. But he felt as if lead thumbs were pressing down his eyelids. He held out the pad he was clutching. He hoped his father did not notice how his hand was twitching. If he did, perhaps there was a chance he would think it was just the way the flames were dancing on the walls. His father snatched the pad from him and opened it. One of the paintings fell and slid under a chair.

Bujji waited, not blinking or breathing. Laughing, his father walked over to the fire and tossed in the pad. Roaring, he slapped him with an open hand and scooped him up under a long arm. Bujji's head swung limply from side to side with his father's every stride. He tried to see where he was being taken, but he found it difficult to focus his eyes. He was seeing spots from staring into the brightest part of the fire. When his father stopped walking, he knew where he had brought him. He smelled moss and water. They were at the well.

In one swift motion, Bujji found himself flipped upside-down. His head started to fill up with blood as his father hung him over the well. When he barked, his speech was slurred.

"You will learn to do as I say!" his father commanded. "Who do you think you—"

Before his father had finished, he lost his grip on Bujji's ankles. As Bujji plunged into the deep well, he heard the "are" fade as if he were traveling on a speeding train. Maybe this was a train, and they were going through a tunnel. The dank air patted his tears, cooling his swollen cheek. Then his ears were filled with the sound of wood on wood. When his father heard the splash, he looked into the blackness of the well.

"Upendra! Upendra!"

As terror bit, he collapsed onto his knees and groped for a branch with which to rescue his only son. He clawed frantically, his body stretching longer and longer until he was prostrate. Eventually, his gasping sobs gave way to snores.

When Bujji opened his eyes, he was looking up at a sea of crushed sapphires. As he blinked, his hands jumped to his face to keep the water from splashing him. After a moment, he peeked through his fingers. The liquid blueness still hung above him, swirling slowly. He sat up and realized that it was the sky rather than the ocean he was gazing upon. He looked at an enormous green field before him. He turned around and saw he was leaning against a skinny tree.

Where was he that the sky looked like this and a field spanned so far and away? Had he actually run so long that he had wound up in another town—another country, perhaps? He concentrated, and what he did remember was falling, brushing up against the most wonderful colors—many more than what his watercolor box offered. He remembered seeing sage, ruby, peacock, turquoise, flame, saffron, slate and pearl. And there was a lavender that was neither too purple nor too pink—the color of the most delicate flower or a young girl's lips. As he mused, the color filled him. Bujji scratched his hand and threw himself backward against the tree. His skin was lavender! He could not believe his eyes. Where was he that the power of thought was so potent? Did he crash through a rainbow and accidentally gulp a piece of the spectrum?

As he asked himself question after question, he did not notice that his skin was once again ruddy-brown. He noticed the transformation when a drop of dew landed on his nose. An almond fruit was rotating from a stem above him. After it spun in one direction, it would unwind itself. Then, noiselessly, it broke free and landed in his hands. He smelled it and began peeling off the skin with his teeth, spitting out the bitter flesh. Patiently, he continued until he was greeted with the sight of one perfectly shaped almond of the whitest white. It was much too beautiful to eat, so he dropped it into his shirt pocket and walked into the field.

He had taken but a few steps when he saw an immense bald eagle swooping down at him. The bird's beak was open, and its piercing eyes seemed transfixed on Bujji's. As it flew past him, Bujji covered his head and ducked. He knew immediately it was not an ordinary bird because it did not have a shadow. When he looked up, his mouth flew open. He saw the chubby back of—could it be?—the god, Krishna. He inched closer, his eyes growing wider and wider at the greatness before him. He gawked for several minutes at Krishna, who sat upon the eagle, playing with his toes. His indigo body sparkled, bedecked with gold and pearls, and his plump lips glistened from eating sweet butterballs. Bujji stood drinking in the brilliant stream of colors—the turmeric-colored silk against his blue skin and the azure of the peacock feather sprouting from his black tresses.

"Climb aboard," bade a voice.

Bujji was confused as he did not see anyone speak. Trembling from head to toe as he was, he still vaulted aboard the bird. He held on tightly to the mess of white feathers as the majestic bird spread its wings. Bujji did not feel the wind blow stronger nor did he feel the sun get warmer upon their ascension. He looked down and was immediately struck by the immensity of the field below. The greenness went on and on, and he thought it most appropriate because it was a green that should not be contained.

They must have covered some distance, but it was difficult for Bujji to tell because it did not feel as if they were moving at all. He could not even find the almond tree he had sat under earlier. As the eagle landed, Bujji suddenly remembered whose chariot he was riding. He was in the presence of a god! When he worked up enough courage to turn around and look at Krishna once again, he saw that he was gone. Brow furrowed with thought, Bujji stepped down from the bird. When he turned around, it was gone too! In its place was a bag of arrows. He ran in circles looking for a hole in the earth and sky and even in the air. He could not understand how the eagle had vanished. He picked up the bag of arrows. They did not seem at all like the arrows of a god. They were very light and sharp, but seemed quite ordinary. Should they not have golden tips or garnets or, at the very least, a magic feather bound to each end? So absorbed was he that he did not see a black form growing larger in the west of the field.

By the time he looked up, Krishna was once again before him. What a treat it would be to have a live god to paint! As he was thinking about the proper way to ask Krishna to pose for a painting, something flew by his head and nipped his ear. He looked up in the sky for the eagle. When he wiped his ear and looked at his fingers, he did not see the remnants of the bird's dropping. He saw blood. It was only then that Bujji realized he was in the middle of a battle.

Krishna was shooting arrow after arrow at the ferocious beast, Narakasura. Bujji was awestruck at how the demon looked like the simplest of men. There was nothing special about him at all. Should Narakasura not have rivulets of blood racing from the corners of his mouth? Should he not have many, many hands wielding villainous weapons and in his teeth, arms and legs torn from poor street urchins? Narakasura looked Krishna up and down and started laughing. The earth rumbled from his peculiar elation. Krishna aimed his bow at the quaking demon and whispered a mantra. Arrows sailed right into Narakasura's mouth. His tongue shot forward like a snake as he spit out the daggers like a mouthful of splinters. Krishna continued his attack ceaselessly, but Bujji noticed that he was running out of arrows. What was he going to do? Just then, he remembered the bag slung across his shoulder. Hiding behind Krishna's leg, Bujji fed him with an endless supply of arrows. It must have been a special bag because it always remained full of ammunition.

The battle continued for several days, and with each impaling blow and incantation, Narakasura grew weaker. The demon finally fell after Krishna hurled his wheel of blades and cut his throat. Bujji anticipated Narakasura's toppling to sound like a mountain crumbling, but it was actually more like a leaf falling from a tree. When Bujji turned to pay his respects to Lord Krishna, he saw his eagle chariot already a kilometer away. He hurried after him across the field, staring into the sky. He kept running faster and faster until he found himself fighting for air. What he thought for certain was his last breath ballooned into a thunderous scream as he felt the field beneath him drop.

As he fell, Bujji forced himself to open his clenched eyes. Instinctively, his arms jutted forward to brace himself for the shock of landing, but he found he could not move them. When he stopped struggling and took a really good look, he saw that his hands were entwined between sugar cane stalks. He caught his breath and realized he was sprawled in a huge field of sugar cane. Lying so close to the ground, he felt his heart beat. It was pumping so hard and so loudly that he could feel his chest lifting from the earth. He tried to understand what had happened. He found it hard to believe that it was a dream. It was all too real. But he decided it all had to have been woven by his active imagination.

Bujji stared at the families of stalks before him. They were beautiful the way they grew so closely together—the way family members should, protecting one another. He liked everything he saw in this small world—the strength, the sweetness. He loved this field. This was surely a place the gods would visit. He reached for his watercolors. But when he lifted the lid, the colors were gone. It was as if someone had washed them away with water. Maybe it had rained. Did he have a bath and forget to put them aside? Perhaps he swam in the river. He frantically racked his head for a clue to the truth. Creeping on the ground, he hunted for an arrow or an eagle feather. As he did so, out from his pocket slipped the pearlescent almond. He stared into it and saw his father, tears slipping off his wrinkled cheeks as he carried Bujji's limp body in his arms. And he saw him dumping his body on a roadside for fear of being jailed for his own son's murder. Bujji's mind suddenly filled with whiteness, and he remembered. He remembered falling and hitting his head; taking his last and first breath, in succession. Bujji smiled because it was in a well—in the smallest, darkest of places—that he had seen God. He took out a pencil and began to draw the families of sugar cane.

The Wedding

N avina stepped out of the bathroom naked. There was no one home. Hanging the thin cotton towel on the drying rack, she walked over to the vanity and looked at herself in the mirror. Would her groom mind that her right breast was slightly smaller than the left? Well, if he did not like it, then that was too bad. She was willing to accept him for who he was, whatever that meant, so he should do the same in return. Her breasts were round and firm. Even after two children, and at the age of fifty-eight, her mother still had nearly perfect breasts. It was hereditary. She examined her buttocks and then bent over to look at herself upside down. The towel wrapped around her head unwound and fell to the floor. Her long wet hair spilled out, the heavy drops at the tips brushing the marble. In that position, she whipped her head up and down to knock the water from her hair. As she shook it out, a wet lock wrapped around her wrist. She picked up the towel and rubbed it into her scalp to help dry the roots. Her mother always said she would get a head cold if she did not dry the roots immediately since her hair was so thick.

Opening her closet door, Navina scanned the neatly stacked saris and decided she wanted to wear one of her mother's saris. She put on a pink blouse and petticoat and went downstairs, where she wrapped herself in a violet print. The silk chiffon was cool against her skin. Sitting down at the vanity, she combed the knots from her hair. For a moment, she froze, her eyes locked on those of her mirror image. It struck her suddenly that she would be leaving home. The day after the wedding, she would be leaving with her new husband for Madras. They would stay there one night and then leave early the next morning for New York. She looked down at her mother's things, the black bun-pins, jeweled haircombs and silver tins of kumkum. Her mother had resisted the modern wave of fashionable stick-on bottus. Opening a small bottle of perfumed oil, she breathed in the smell of jasmine deeply. She smoothed some sandalwood talcum powder over her face, neck and shoulders. Navina would miss her mother and the house, but was excited about seeing the States. She was excited to become a wife.

When she went to get the flower basket from the front room, she was taken aback to see someone sitting on the veranda in one of the bamboo chairs. She peeked through the curtains. It was the tailor from Yaxi. She flushed with embarrassment as she recalled having walked through the house half-dressed. Then, she thought she was being unreasonable and paranoid. He could not possibly have seen her. He had opened the gate and let himself in. Even the servant, Lalitha, was at the market. She thought for a second and opened the door.

"I did not hear you ring the bell," she said.

"That is okay, madam," he said smiling. "I was not waiting too long." He stood up, holding two stuffed bags at his sides. "Won't you try them on?"

"My mother is not home."

But then Navina thought her mother might get angry with her for not trying on the blouses and sending him away.

"Well, I suppose I can try them on."

He walked closer and handed her the bags. She walked into the house, and he followed. Actually, she would have preferred he waited on the veranda.

"I thought it would be best to bring them by as soon as they were finished," he said apologetically.

"Yes, thank you. Please sit down. I will try one blouse on. All of them should be similar, no?"

"Yes, but also please try on the pink sari."

She looked at him questioningly.

"It is just that I take great pride in my work. I am always deprived of seeing it on the model. It would be a favor to me."

What harm could it do? She smiled graciously.

"I will be just a moment."

She went into her mother's bedroom and shut the door. She dropped the bags on the bed and turned to bolt the door. Walking over to the mirror, she unhooked her blouse. What an odd request, she thought. But this tailor shop had been in the family since her great-grandmother. Her uneasiness was put to rest as her hands excitedly reached for the saris. They were beautifully stitched and pressed. She pulled out the sari and petticoat.

As she tried on the pink blouse, she turned to face the mirror. She imagined her husband-to-be swooning at the sight of her. She took out a photo of him that his parents had given her father. Ajay was a thirty-two-year-old doctor and quite handsome. He was tall and broad-shouldered. She was lucky. All of her college girlfriends were so envious. Her mother looked for the usual characteristics— a good income and fair skin color. He was light, but Navina was lighter. That was always more appealing—the woman being fairer than the man. She had a B.A. and was considering furthering her studies. His decent income would allow her the chance to do that. Then she would happily bear children. Navina was so aglow, admiring herself in the mirror, that she forgot about the tailor.

When she finally walked into the living room, he stood up. His eyes roved over her from head to toe.

"Breathtaking," he said. "How does the blouse fit?"

"Perfectly."

"Are you certain?"

He moved toward her.

"Let me see."

He walked behind her and carefully moved her damp hair aside.

"Here—it seems a bit tight," he said pushing between her shoulder blades.

"I think it is fine, really. Your work is flawless."

He circled around her.

"What about the breast cups?"

"I think they are also fine."

"Take a deep breath and see if you feel any tightness."

She followed his directions and shook her head.

"Good, good. One more thing to check."

He moved beside her and slid his index finger around the border of the blouse against the side of her ribs. She was shocked at his boldness, but did not object.

"That is also good. The arms are not too loose?"

"Everything is fine," she said with a hint of nervousness mixed with impatience.

He adjusted her pallu over her shoulder, taking time to display the rich border. Then he took several steps back and looked at her, cradling his chin in his hand pensively. She was used to being stared at and having her appearance commented on, but this was strange. It was the first time that a man other than her father was giving her his opinion. She trusted that he really wanted to make her look her best for the wedding.

"You really have a head for design as mother said, no?" she said in an attempt to fill the awkward silence.

"I am more of a painter than a tailor sometimes. Good tailors have to be."

"Maybe you should go to Bombay and be a tailor for the cinema stars?"

"This sari is mesmerizing," he breathed, not acknowledging what she thought to be a splendid suggestion.

"I am glad mother finally agreed to buy it."

"What kind of chappals will you wear?"

"I bought two pairs with mother yesterday."

"Let us have a look."

His enthusiasm had rubbed off on her. She practically skipped off to her mother's bedroom to retrieve the sandals. As she was rummaging through the shopping bags for them, his voice startled her.

"This is a beautiful house."

She whirled around, jolted that he had followed her.

"I am terribly sorry," he said. "I did not mean to frighten you."

"That is okay. People always say I'm as jumpy as a rabbit."

Opening the box, she showed him two pairs of golden-trimmed leather chappals.

"Good choices. They will work well with all the other saris."

He walked over to look out the window. He picked up the photo on the bureau and looked at it in the sunlight.

"Is this the lucky man?"

"Yes," she said smiling broadly.

"What is his profession?"

"He is a cardiologist—a heart doctor."

"Yes, I know. Tell me, why do all the beautiful women marry only doctors?"

Navina began putting the chappal boxes back in the closet.

"Do you know this fellow?" he asked with concern.

"I met him a few weeks back. My family knows his family."

He put the photo down and turned to face her.

"If you knew that as a tailor, I could give you everything you could ever want, would you marry me?"

She could not believe what she had just heard. Her mouth hung slightly open.

"I must ask you, Navina. Would you marry me?"

She looked at him and decided he must be joking.

"You are a great flatterer and very funny, too!" she said with a hearty laugh.

Opening a drawer, she took out an envelope.

"Did you bring the bill?"

He reached into his pocket and gave it to her. She handed him the money.

"Here is an extra twenty rupees for being so punctual. Mother will be thrilled."

The tailor walked out of the bedroom and out of the house without uttering another word. Perhaps he was disappointed with his tip, she thought as she locked the door. He seemed a bit moody, but he was a creative type. She remembered reading a letter in an advice column from a reader who complained about the terrible temper of her artist husband. The response was to take the oddities of one's husband along with the beauties.

Outside on the second floor veranda, Navina sat with a basket of flowers in her lap. She wound the string around the base of each jasmine bud and made a small knot. The buds were tightly clenched now, but they would open at sunset. She was amazed at how some flowers closed at night and some opened. Not unlike humans, she thought. She heard the gate.

"Ammagaru," yelled Lalitha.

"I am coming," Navina called down.

She opened the door for the servant, who was carrying two bags brimming with vegetables.

"When Mother comes, tell her I am upstairs."

Navina headed back up the stairs, feeling her scalp with her fingers. Her hair was almost dry. As she wove it into a single plait, she thought about the tailor touching her hair. Next time, she decided, she would not let him into the house. Picking up a pin, she secured the garland of jasmine blossoms where her braid began. She peeled off a black-colored felt bottu from the paper and pressed it firmly between her eyebrows. Then she sat down with a current copy of *Women's Monthly*.

"Warding Off the Mistress," she said aloud, half shocked. "Although your husband may seem attached to the other woman, you can lure him back to the nest." She hoped she would not be put in that position.

Lalitha walked outside and presented her with a tray of tea and butter biscuits.

"Did Mother say when she will be home exactly?" queried Navina, sipping her tea.

"No. She did say she had many errands."

Just then, they heard the driver opening the squeaky driveway gate. Navina looked down from the veranda at the car and then followed Lalitha downstairs.

"Here you are," her mother said as she handed a box to her.

They were sweets from Andhra's, the best confectionery in Vijayawada.

"What did you get?"

Her mother just smiled as Navina slipped the string off the box.

"M*mmm*. Kaza. My favorite."

She bit into one of the coconut-sprinkled rolls. She offered her mother one, but she declined.

"What else did you buy?" she asked eagerly.

The driver, Eswar, walked in cradling bags and boxes of goods.

She licked the sticky honey from her fingers and went to relieve him of the packages.

"Wash your hands, Navina."

She walked to the sink in the hallway.

"Eswar, be here tomorrow at nine o'clock," she heard her mother tell the driver. "I have some errands, and then we have more wedding arrangements to make."

"Yes, madam."

"What shall I open first?" asked Navina, walking past Lalitha who stood in the doorway anxiously waiting.

"Lalitha, bring me my tea," ordered her mother.

With a frown, the servant headed into the kitchen.

Navina tore into the boxes and bags, spreading out the glittering saris.

They would be gifts for some of her aunts and her future in-laws. She clapped her hands at another pair of chappals, these in oyster-pink. Seeing them reminded her of the tailor.

"I nearly forgot. The tailor came by with the saris and blouses."

"He finished a day earlier than he had said. Good. Go try them on and show me."

She got up as Lalitha walked in with a cup of steaming tea.

Navina stared at the beggar boy tapping on the tinted car window. Eswar swatted his hand at him as if the boy were a fly. The poor could smell money a kilometer away. If she had been on foot, the boy would have followed her from store to store all along Besant Road. They were trained to know by the way a woman was dressed if she was rich and, therefore, more likely to spare a few coins. The boy walked away reluctantly. She stared at Eswar sucking on a cigarette and at the dust billowing around him from the passing cars. A sickly old man spit a red stream of killi juice mixed with saliva in the street. After the sun dried the moisture, it would remain, an ugly stain on the road. Those were the stains her mother warned her not to step over. People suffering from bad luck spit on the ground like that hoping that someone else will take on their ill fortune, she had told her. Navina wondered how on the traffic-thick streets of India one could manage to avoid stepping over these stains. They seemed to blanket the ground in certain spots. When she was little, it was a game to hop over the phlegm and dung. At twenty, she found herself looking ahead rather than down at the ground. She looked over at her mother, who was dropping off some material for her blouses at Yaxi. The tailor stood in the window, writing on a pad of paper. As her mother crossed the street, Navina saw him looking at the car. She turned away.

"Eswar, take us to The Palace," said her mother as she sat down. "We are starving."

The waiter set two steel plates with various curries down on the table. Another waiter came and dished out some piping hot white rice. As she mixed the rice with a potato curry, Navina noticed she and her mother were the only two women in the hotel restaurant. Most men ate out to get away from their wives and relax with their male friends. Her father was different. Ever since she could remember, he had taken them out to eat and to the cinema. They also went on short vacations to visit temples and other places of interest. She knew that it was different in the States. Families ate out more often and went on summer vacations for a whole month at times. It was a good way to give a housewife a break, she thought.

They ate quietly. Her head was reeling from all the places they had been to thus far—the goldsmith, the caterer, the florist and the bangle shop. She admired the organizational skills her mother possessed. Nothing ever seemed to intimidate her. She bustled about town like a bee sampling flowers, singing cheerily, but not once forgetting that she was on a mission. Until it was accomplished, she would not sit still. It was a way to entertain herself, Navina supposed.

Three days before the wedding, Navina sat flipping through a book of mehndi hand designs at Chandra's Beauty Salon.

"What do you think about the black stain, Amma?" she asked turning to her mother who was reclining beside her getting a facial massage.

"I prefer the red, Navina," she said in a distorted voice because her cheeks were being vigorously rubbed.

"What do you think about this one?" she asked holding up the traditional mango and lotus pattern.

"Anything would be lovely on your slender hands, dear."

"I think this is it," she said resting the book in her lap.

"Have you selected?" asked the beautician walking toward her.

Navina pointed to the design.

"Good choice."

With that, the woman walked off and returned with a piece of plastic with the appropriate pattern cut out of it. She placed it on Navina's hand and began filling in the design with the henna paste.

"I want it to be the brightest red, all right?"

"We cannot guarantee the exact shade. The henna will continue to ripen for a few days and will become darker. I *can* say a bride who has visited Chandra's Beauty Salon has never been disappointed on her wedding day."

"Well, what do you think it will be like to be married?" asked Navina's friend Anju.

"I imagine it would be nice, like a clear, breezy morning or dipping in a cool lake," replied Saraswati, who was sitting on Anju's bed.

"What?" said Anju incredulously. "I think more on the lines of rolling in hot sand and then diving into a fiery volcano."

They laughed. They looked at Navina for an answer.

"I think it will be a bit of both—volcanic and oceanic," said Navina.

"Are you going to do it here or wait until you get to the States?" asked Anju, guzzling a Thums Up cola.

"Leave it to Anju for being tactful," mumbled Saraswati, biting into a laddoo.

"We will be alone in Madras the night before we leave . . . so."

"You must be so excited, Navina," said Saraswati. "You are so lucky to get such a good match. I hope I am as lucky as you."

"Imagine, in two days you will be married, and in three days you will be on your way to the States!" sang Anju, admiring the henna pattern on Navina's hand.

"So, tell me your big tips on kissing," Navina said.

"Do not overuse your tongue—flick it like a butterfly's wings," said Anju.

Navina stuck out her tongue and batted it lightly between her lips.

"Like this," said Anju moving toward her. "Imagine I am Anil Kapoor."

"He is beautiful," mumbled Saraswati dreamily.

With that, Anju kissed her on the lips, mouth slightly open. When Navina opened her eyes, they stared at one other for a moment and then burst into nervous laughter.

Later that evening, when Navina was walking around the corner back to her house, she was dreaming about kissing Ajay's lips. She pictured herself laying on his chest listening to his heartbeat. How would his hands move across her breasts? Had she already fallen in love?

"Navina. Navina."

She turned to Saraswati.

"Sorry, I am just daydreaming. Good night."

"I will see you tomorrow," said Saraswati as she headed for the first house on the street.

Navina looked up at the clouds moving across the yellowish sky as she walked on. A storm was coming. As her eyes fell back down to the road, she just had enough time to sidestep a glob of sputum. As she stopped to open the gate, she heard a whirring noise. She turned and saw the silhouette of a bicycle. In the next instant, she felt a splash across her face.

"Let us see who you will marry now!" the man hissed.

Suddenly, her eyelids, lips, cheeks and neck seemed to be on fire. Eyes clenched, she clawed at herself in an attempt to tear off her skin.

"Amma, Amma!" she screamed, impaling the peaceful twilight.

Lying in the hospital bed, the words rung in her ears.

"Let us see who you will marry now!"

Navina wanted to cry, but the tears would not come. She tried to open her eyes, but could not. She felt as if her head was going to explode. Her face and neck felt as if they were still on fire. If she was in a hospital, why were the doctors not helping her? Why weren't they making the pain stop? She strained to make sense of the voices she heard.

"Who would do this?"

"Acid causes irreparable damage in certain cases."

She thought it was her mother. She tried to call to her, but found her lips would not move. They felt heavy as if someone were pressing down on them. Was someone kissing her?

"These attacks are on the rise."

"Where is the groom?"

"Why, dear God, why?"

Navina pursed her lips and tried again.

"Amma," she managed to whisper. It did not sound as if the voice was her own.

"I am here, Nanna." said her mother.

"Navina," her father cried.

Why were they so sad? Why were they not telling her everything was fine? Panic filled her, and she began to writhe and kick on the bed. She just wanted to touch her face. It felt as if someone was holding her down. She tried to open her eyes. Was she blind? As she tossed and ground her head into the pillow, she crushed the jasmine blossoms in her hair. When the scent reached her nostrils, she became still. She could hear someone weeping softly as she drifted into sleep. Her hands lay limp and open, palms stained blood-orange.

Amaravathi Road

Veena was glad they were finally moving. The wind felt good on her face. Brad kept trying to get the auto taxi driver to go a little cheaper, and it was driving her crazy.

"Just because it's thirty rupees to a buck does not mean we have to throw our money away. We can get a car for just eighty-five more rupees."

She knew he had a point, but she really didn't care. She was tired of standing in the sun haggling over what was the equivalent of about a buck-fifty. It wasn't that Brad was cheap, but he just didn't like people taking advantage of him. Living in New York City had a way of doing that to people. Deciding what kind of transportation to use had even been a topic of debate. The buses were out of the question—they were too crowded. Veena objected to bicycle rickshaws because she felt terribly guilty sitting back as if she were a queen while a man as old as her father and dripping with sweat pedaled them to their destination for a few rupees. Brad felt that taking a car would be safer, but she pushed for the auto, a three-wheeled taxi—a modernized rickshaw that ran on gas and accommodated two people. She liked that they didn't have any doors and were open.

The driver said something and pulled into a gas station.

"What did he say?" asked Brad turning to her.

Veena shrugged. He knew she recognized only a few phrases and a handful of words in Telugu, but he kept asking her to translate anyway. She couldn't help but feel a little incompetent. She found it much easier trying to communicate in English. She wasn't comfortable being Indian, being an Andhra. Funny thing was, she wasn't comfortable being American either. Luckily, many Indians understood English.

"What are you doing?" Brad asked the driver.

"Petrol," said the driver, his teeth gleaming.

He stopped the auto beside the pump. Brad got out "to stretch," which really meant he wanted to keep an eye on what was going on. As one of the men pumped the gas and the other measured some black liquid, probably oil, in a measuring cup, they tried to look in the backseat as much as they could while doing their work. Veena's lips turned up in a small smile. She was not gracious all the time. It depended more on if the stare was a curious one or a negative one. Sometimes as she and Brad walked down the streets, they heard women giggling and caught men making faces. Passersby definitely stared more in the smaller towns because they were less used to seeing an Indian woman with an American. It might have been the first time some of them had ever seen a white man, much less an NRI (nonresident Indian) with a white man. Sometimes the way the eyes followed her, Veena felt as if she were in a movie.

She thought of her cousin, Ajay, who decided on an arranged marriage although he had lived in the United States since he was a teenager. His decision had come completely out of the blue and much to her dismay. She felt as if he had betrayed her. They always used to sit together at family functions and talk about school and the opposite sex. She wondered if he thought any less of her, knowing all the boys she had liked in high school and college. Was he disappointed

69

that she hadn't married an Indian man? Sometimes, disappoint-ment crept into her own heart, but she knew it was a mirage. Was it her fault she had never met an Indian man she could relate to—one who she was attracted to immediately and not one she would grow to love? This was ridiculous. She was debating the virtues of men based on their skin color, their ethnicity. She knew better than that.

"I married Brad because I love him, period," she confirmed to herself.

"What?" Brad asked defensively, looking at the driver's outthrust hand. "What does he want?"

"Ten rupees," the driver replied.

"No, no," said Brad firmly. "You didn't say anything about pay-ing for the gas, too."

The men looked at Brad and then back at the driver.

"Ten rupees," the driver said again, still smiling, but now his fin-gers fluttered.

"Honey," she coaxed.

"Christ," Brad said, throwing up his hands and slapping them down on his thighs.

He dug into his fanny pack and gave one of the gas station at-tendants the money. As Brad climbed back in, the driver yanked on a stick near his feet to start the engine.

"It's like a lawn mower on wheels," Brad remarked, trying to keep a sense of humor about it all.

She smiled. The driver repeatedly squeezed the big rubber bulb of the horn hanging near the side mirror to clear a path down the crowded street. There were no lanes. People crossed wherever they wished. There was, however, an odd order in all the chaos. She looked out as they turned off the main road.

"What is this road called?" she yelled over the noise of the auto.

"Amaravathi Road," said the driver.

"Amaravathi Road to Amaravathi—that makes sense," said Brad sarcastically.

She went back to looking at the spanning fields. Fields of rice, millet, turmeric, squash and what looked like cotton.

"What is growing there?" she asked the driver.

He answered her in Telugu, and she could not understand his reply. The fields were sprinkled with colorfully clothed workers.

"How can they work in the sun like that?" said Brad, taking off his safari hat.

"It must be over a hundred degrees."

"I guess they must be used to the heat," he concluded.

A man was walking on the side of the road with a giant basket of flowers on his turbaned head. He had doubled up the ankle-length cotton cloth wrapped around his waist so it was above his knee. He was shirtless and barefoot. The mid-afternoon sun lit up the muscles on his back and legs, giving them the sheen of black satin.

Veena looked over at her husband. He sat gripping the leather strap and metal bars to brace himself for the bumps. She remembered when she had told him where she wanted to go on their vacation. They had just taken a walk in Central Park and were having brunch at Tuli's.

"Why?" he had asked, sipping his soda.

"I wanted to go two years ago, but remember you seduced me with your description of Greece."

"What about Australia?" he asked, trying to appear casual.

"I know it's supposed to be pretty there and all, but I really want to go to India—south India."

"Are you sure about this?"

"I've been putting off a trip there for a while now," she said, busily cutting into her stack of apple-walnut pancakes. "I'm ready to see it with my own eyes." She waited a moment and asked, "You don't want to go?"

"It's not that I don't want to go. I guess I'm just anticipating not speaking the language and all that. Have you ruled out the north already—you know places like New Delhi?"

"I just said the south because I think it might be a little more down-to-earth. You know, less modernized. Besides, I was born there, and I know a little Telugu."

"Oh," he said picking up his knife.

She poured some more syrup on her cakes.

"Did you think about going with your parents?" he said, slicing into a fat sausage link. "I mean, doesn't your mother want to show you the homeland?"

"My mother says she's too old to go. Besides, I think it's important that we make this trip together," she said. "I want you to see where I'm from."

"You grew up here though."

"I know, but that's where I'm from."

His knife slipped, and a chunk of the sausage landed on the floor in the middle of the busy diner. They looked over at it and laughed, as did some other patrons.

"See, look at that," he said, smiling. "It's some kind of omen. We're going to India."

So here they were, going forty-five kilometers an hour on their way to the Amaraswara temple. It was not listed in their guidebook, but the hotel clerk had told them about it. He said it had one of the most auspicious Siva lingams in all of India. Supposedly, it was more of an attraction for Indian tourists.

Brad reached for her hand, and she held onto it tightly. She kissed him on the cheek.

"Thank you," she said.

"What for?" he asked.

"For saying yes to this."

"I'll just get you back next year by picking a really cold place."

She laughed. They became silent again, and the clamor of the auto filled their ears. She leaned forward and retied her hiking boot. It was too hot to hold hands.

Up ahead, the rows of acacia and tamarind trees lining both sides of the road reached toward one another. Their tangled branches and leaves made a spectacular tunnel that glowed. The air was cooler as in a real tunnel. But instead of being dark and claustrophobic, this tunnel was inviting and magical. As they moved through the dappled light, she took off her sunglasses.

"Look," Veena said.

Brad nodded and smiled.

When they came out at the end of the tunnel, the sun seemed brighter than before. She put her glasses back on. What amazed her was that Indians here lived so close to the earth. They walked with bare feet on dirt roads or wore sandals they could easily slip on and off. Their clothes were washed not by machines, but in the rivers on stones. They ground grain in stone mortars outdoors. They took their tea on their roofs or on their front verandas, watching the parrots flirt in the clouds at dusk. They heard the crane's hollow coos, telling them it was a new day and, at sunset, that it was time to. close the windows and doors because the mosquitoes were coming. It had been a long time since she had read a book under a tree. The buildings blocked out most of the sun from their New York apartment. There was light, but not beams in which she could see the steam of her coffee rise in the morning. She realized in the next moment that she was longing. Was it that she was just infatuated with her strange motherland? They seemed to have everything in New York City. Her husband was a wonderful man, and she loved her job as a magazine editor. Their apartment was spacious and close to the Metropolitan Museum of Art and Central Park. They had rooms with spectacular views—even a rooftop garden—and cultural stimulation galore. But in all her self-convincing, something as delicate as an eyelash in her mouth was making her stir, making her retaste her tongue and her life.

They had been driving for about a half-hour. They were only twenty miles away from their destination, but that didn't mean it took twenty minutes to get there. The driver had to keep slowing down to let lorries and cars pass. Honking his horn, he had to dodge potholes, oxen, stray dogs and bicycles in addition to the pedestrians. Just then, he swerved around a cock crossing the road.

"Christ!" blurted Brad as they were thrown forward.

"You okay?" Veena asked.

"Yeah," he said, settling back into the seat.

He took out his camera and loaded some film. Fiddling with it, he looked through the lens and then put it away again.

They saw a man walking with a plastic container. He made his way into a patch of trees and brush.

"I can't believe they're just plopping down and shitting on the side of the road," marveled Brad.

"I guess it's strange to us, but it's not unusual to them," she said as she pulled her long hair into a ponytail.

"Veena, they're actually taking a dump in public. It's weird."

"How do you mean?"

"I mean aside from being unsanitary, it's just weird seeing a truck pass by while you're doing your thing, that's all."

"I think it would be kind of nice, actually, to look up at the sky and be around all those trees," she said looking right at him.

"I don't know if I could do it," he said, shaking his head.

"You've never whipped it out and peed in public in New York?" she asked.

"Yes. But that's different."

"Why is that different?" she asked, annoyed that he was dragging her into this at all.

"Because that's pissing, and this is shitting, that's why," he replied, his voice cracking. "You can't tell me that you'd join them?"

"If I had to, maybe I would."

"Besides, I only pee in public because of dire necessity. There just aren't a lot of public bathrooms in New York. You know that."

"Oh," she said, stretching the two-letter word out smoothly like a piece of taffy.

"What is that supposed to mean?" he asked, cocking his head to the side.

"Oh, it means *oh*. What else could *oh* mean, but *oh*."

They both stared out of their own sides of the auto. Veena noticed her breasts were hurting from being knocked up and down driving over the bumpy road. She crossed her arms and held her breasts up to cushion the jolts.

"Are you mad at me or something?" he asked, none too apologetically.

"No," she said.

"Well, what is it then?"

"Nothing. I was just thinking how you hate losing control."

Even her own words amazed her. They had barely been born in her mind before they slid onto her tongue and were unleashed on her unsuspecting husband artlessly like spitballs.

"What?"

"You can't shit on the road because it means giving up control, and you won't do that. It's the same thing that makes you go nuts when someone is asking you for a bit more money than they should because they know you're a tourist."

"You're pissy because I haggled with this guy? Is that it?"

"No, Brad. I'm not pissy. It was just an observation. Look, I don't want to fight about this. I want you to know that it's okay to feel uncomfortable. We're the foreigners here. I feel it, too. I'm just not fighting it."

What was going on here? They usually had wonderful times on their trips. He was acting so immature, it seemed. He was always impatient, but this was more like arrogance. Why was he ruining everything? She felt as if he wanted to erase her culture. It's true that she was raised in the United States, but she had been born in Eluru and raised by Indian parents. If he hadn't wanted to come, he should have said so. It seemed he didn't want to take the time to understand what he was seeing. He wanted it fed to him. He wanted to be entertained. Was he always like this? Well, she was going to try to have a nice time. She didn't want to fill up the silence with words. She didn't have anything else to say. She certainly didn't want to apologize. Why should *she* be sorry? She wasn't. She readjusted her arms. Holding them up was helping.

As she took a deep breath, her nostrils filled with an awful smell. Looking out, she saw they were passing a pen overflowing with chickens. It was much too small for them, and the chickens were walking on each other's heads. The cocks were running freely, pecking along the roads for food, while the chickens were imprisoned in filthy pens. She made a slight snorting sound. In the next second, she was glad he did not hear her over the noise of the auto's engine.

"Ugh," Brad said, in an attempt to reconnect. "What is that?"

"Chickens."

Her eyes fell to the ground passing beneath them. A part of her felt ashamed: She didn't want him to smell the bad smells or see the unsanitary conditions—the backwardness of her people. She thought of their other trips. God, they had seen some beautiful places. They had backpacked through Europe, both east and west. Her mind raced with the images: artists selling their etchings in Budapest; the glass blowers of Venice; the Klimts in Vienna; the eeriness of Mont-Saint Michel in France. They had gone to Hawaii when they were married four years ago. That was fine for a honeymoon, but they both preferred vacations that had elements of surprise and made them earn their dinner. They had even toyed with the idea of doing a bike tour of Ireland and Scotland, but when it came down to it, they were never in good enough shape for it. They really weren't into the resort scene much—sipping on mai-tais and playing tennis and shuffleboard with couples from Montauk. She had an occasional glass of wine with pasta or fish. He liked his beer. She was thirty-one, and he was thirty-six. Maybe he was just getting too old for trips like this. No. She knew that wasn't it. Maybe he was just going through some changes right now.

As her eyes refocused on the passing road, she saw a boy in knickers lying face-up in the dirt. He was frothing at the mouth.

"Oh my God," she cried.

"What's the matter?" asked Brad.

"There was a boy lying in the road. It looked like he got hit by a car or something. Stop. Driver, stop!"

The driver stopped the auto.

"The boy, go back to the boy."

"Wait a minute, did you see anyone else around?"

"I don't know. Brad, I think he might be dying."

"I don't think we should get involved," said Brad shaking his head. "I mean, what if they say we did it or something?"

The driver looked back and forth at them, trying to understand what they were saying.

"I think we should take him to a hospital or doctor," she insisted.

"Veena, I understand that you're upset, but I want you to really think about this. We don't speak the language, and it's really none of our business."

"How could you say that?" she practically howled. "Turn the auto around."

"No, wait. They have their own way of handling things here. You can't just come to India and run to everyone's aid like Mother Teresa."

"To feel compassion for another human being is—"

"Look, Veena. I'm not saying it's bad or that you're crazy. It's just unreasonable, that's all."

"I'm an emotional woman who is overreacting—is that it?"

One of them was being completely irrational, and as they continued shooting arrows back and forth, it was becoming less and less clear to her who that was exactly.

"No. I am just asking you to think about it. Please. Remember, you're the one who said we're the foreigners here."

She sat there for a moment looking at her hands. There were flecks of red, blue and green splattered on the boy's neck and chin. She thought she saw what looked like a paint box near his body.

"I'm sorry you saw it," he said as he put his arm around her.

She rested her head on his shoulder, and he kissed her on the forehead.

"Let's go," he said.

"Okay?" asked the driver.

"Yes, okay," said Brad.

♦

"Where will you wait?" Brad interrogated the driver when he stopped in front of the temple.

"I will wait," the driver replied.

He didn't ask for his payment ahead of time, which was good, because Brad probably would have started arguing with him, Veena thought. She got out and looked up at the temple rising above the surrounding wall. It was not as elaborate as some of the others she had seen in the guidebook, but it was nice. Brad put on his knapsack and stood next to her. Everyone was staring at them. The driver parked under a tree across the street.

"Guide, guide, guide," twittered a balding man walking quickly toward them.

Brad looked at her, and she shrugged.

"How much?" she asked.

"You give what you like," he replied.

Brad seemed to like that, so they proceeded. They deposited their hiking boots at a stand and took two claim tickets. Their guide was barefoot.

"You let me say," the man said as they walked toward the entrance. "Camera?"

"Yes," answered Brad.

"Don't say," the man advised.

They stopped and admired the colorful paintings of gods, goddesses and saints that covered the walls surrounding the temple. There were swans, peacocks, snakes, pots of gold, blue skin, tridents, elephants, lotuses, monkey heads, potbellies, golden crowns, sitars.

"These are fantastic—what is all the writing under each painting?" she asked the guide.

"Advertisements for sari and handloom shops," he replied.

They walked inside the wall.

"You take offering?"

He walked toward a woman sitting on a piece of burlap with

baskets of flowers around her. When she saw them coming, she jumped into action. She held up pink and yellow flowers she had strung together in one hand and, in the other, a bunch of leaves with some loose flowers on top.

Brad had already answered negatively for them, but Veena wanted to buy some flowers.

"Yes," she answered quickly.

Brad just looked at her. She took a garland and paid the woman.

"Coconut," another vendor called as they walked to the door.

There was a guard at the entrance. He stopped them.

"Hindu?" he asked Brad.

The guide answered for them in Telugu. The guard seemed angry at first, but then softened up. He said something authoritatively and pointed at Brad's crotch.

"You must leave your belt—no leather in the temple," their guide translated. "Give it to me, and I will go check it at the shoe stand."

Brad obediently took it off and watched as the man rushed off with his belt into the crowds. They waited on the side of the steps and watched worshipers stream into the temple.

"Come," said their guide as he rejoined them.

"What is your name?" asked Brad.

"Srider."

"Srider," repeated Brad.

They stopped in front of what looked like a ticket booth.

"You need ticket," explained Srider.

"How much?"

"Forty rupees for both."

"Twenty rupees each, *huh*?" said Brad in a tone to indicate he was displeased.

"Come, we will wash our feet," Srider said and waved at them to follow as he walked down a set of stairs.

The steps went right up to a body of murky water.

"This is the Krishna River," said Srider proudly. "It is sacred."

The guide washed his feet, and they followed his example. Hardly anyone was there except for some men with an orange fishing boat. When they turned to walk back up, she saw that a small group of people had congregated at the top of the stairs to watch them.

Srider did his best to answer their questions. He told them what some of the stone carvings represented and that the lingam and yoni were symbols of Siva and Parvati. He told her what to do with the flowers and to turn three times clockwise.

She and Brad waited in line. Eventually, the line split up, and some people walked on one side of the railing, while the others walked to the opposite side. The sacred lingam was up front on the altar, and they had to lean forward over the railing to see it. The white phallus was adorned with red kumkum and lots of flowers and coconuts. The lingam rose from the yoni, which encircled it like two hands at the base. She could feel the weight of stares upon her, but she didn't care. The priest walked down the center aisle. When he approached, she held out the flowers.

"Ticket," he said impatiently.

Brad frantically patted his pockets on his shirt and shorts.

"Here," he said with relief after finally locating them.

The priest took the flowers and put them on a tray. He collected everyone's offerings and placed them around the lingam. Then, he proceeded with the prayer. Veena didn't understand what was being said, but she felt good anyway. Although her mother did pujas in the house, she had never forced her to participate. Now, a small part of her wished she had grown up with a stronger sense of religion or at least had a better understanding of Hinduism.

In college, she had studied all the religions, and, in fact, there wasn't a religious scripture she had come across that she didn't like. It was what people did to the texts that was unappealing. Brad, on the other hand, never really gave religion much thought. He had been raised in an Irish Catholic family, but had stopped going to church after he turned eighteen. He hated all the restrictions. He didn't even have a Bible in the apartment. They never really talked about what they were going to do when they had children. She wanted them to have a sense of both Hinduism and Catholicism and let them decide for themselves. But would that just confuse them? All they could do as parents would be to teach them to respect creation and be good, honest people. That was pretty much what all religions taught anyway. Deep down, she felt disappointment. She wished she had listened to her mother more patiently when she told her stories. Soon, those stories were going die with her mother, some untold, most forgotten.

As the priest continued mumbling the strange words, Veena thought about the boy in the road. His lifeless face and body consumed her. She hoped he was okay. She prayed that he was okay.

"Turn," she reminded Brad when she saw the others turning.

The priest walked down the aisle again. He had white marks on his forehead. He was shirtless and, although he was gaunt, he had a potbelly. She noticed a string that was tied diagonally about him like a sash. He poured some liquid into their right hands. She had been watching the others, so she knew to wave her hand before her lowered head before drinking it. Brad slurped it right up.

"Names?" asked the priest.

"Veena and Brad Shanley," she answered, smiling.

He chanted a prayer looking down. His lips barely moved.

Then she heard him mutter their name "Chaney" twice. Brad let out a little chuckle. They were offered a tray with a bowl filled with kumkum. Some people had dropped coins onto the tray. Veena took some of the crimson powder for both of them. She dipped her finger in the powder and pressed on her forehead and then on Brad's.

On the way out, they passed another priest breaking coconuts on a wooden bar. There was a long line of worshipers waiting to get a bit of the blessed water drizzled in their cupped hands. Brad grimaced as his bare feet touched the wet stone-ground.

"Be careful—it's slippery," he warned as they walked through the puddles of coconut water.

They met Srider at the back of the temple, and he pointed out a sculpture of a bull.

"This is Nandi," he said. "Look through the horns at Siva. This lingam is different because it is white. Normally, lingams are black."

They leaned over the bull and did as he had demonstrated.

"How much do we owe you, Srider?" asked Brad when they were outside.

"Here," Veena said handing over a twenty-rupee bill.

"Oh, madam, thank you," he accepted. Then he quickly added, somewhat apologetically, "But I must pay the guard."

"Really?" asked Brad.

Veena gave him another twenty. He bowed his head in thanks and walked them to their auto. Brad took out his camera and took some shots of the temple from a distance.

"So, what did you think?" asked Brad, once they were heading back in the auto.

"It was nice," she said. "Peaceful. What about you?"

"It was strange. I wish I understood more about the rituals." After a moment, he asked, "Do you think they sell the flowers again?"

Veena looked at him blankly.

"You know, the flowers you bought," he said, peeling a banana. "He didn't give them back to you. I was wondering if they took them back out front and sold them again."

"I don't think they do that because there were lots of flowers all around the lingam," she said, surprised at what he had asked.

What a silly question, she thought. Maybe she was just not in the mood to talk because she was preoccupied with the boy. They were coming up to the spot where she had seen him, and she wanted to make sure he wasn't still there. It was across from a sugar-cane field. There was the field. She didn't see the body. She was almost sure this was the spot. She waited until they drove a little further. Her eyes hunted under the trees alongside the road for the paint box, maybe a brush. But there was no sign of the boy.

"He's gone," she said right before they entered the tunnel of trees.

"What?" asked Brad as he flipped through the guidebook.

"The boy lying in the road. Someone must have taken him."

"See," he replied omnisciently.

She was glad that she had prayed for the boy in the temple. She asked for him to be taken care of because she was unable to help. Her mind flashed to the image of him—legs spread, the whiteness at his mouth, the paint drops on his chin and neck. His eyes were closed. They had been moving much too fast for her to see if he was breathing.

It suddenly hit her that the lingam was a representation of Siva and that Siva was the god of destruction.

"Isn't Siva the god of destruction?" she asked out loud, already knowing the answer.

"I think so," answered Brad.

She felt as if she had been punched in the stomach. Had she asked The Destroyer to save the boy? She sat in shock for a moment and tried to catch her breath. Did Siva dance on the boy's chest, expelling the last breath from his lungs? Did she ask him to do *that*?

"What's the matter?" asked Brad. "You're sweating."

"I feel sick."

"What is it? Want some water?" he asked reaching into his knapsack.

She tipped her head back as she put the bottle to her mouth. Some of it dribbled down her shirt. It brought her back.

"Feel better?"

She nodded. She thought back to her classes and remembered the balance that the Hindu Holy Trinity is said to maintain with creation, preservation and destruction. She was in India. Death had a different meaning here. She felt somewhat relieved. He put the back of his hand on her forehead.

"You feel a little hot," he said. "I hope you didn't catch anything, you know, a flu or something. I'm sure walking around barefoot on the wet ground at the temple didn't help."

"What did you ask for in the temple?" she asked.

"What do you mean?"

"Did you pray for someone or something?"

"No. I think I was too nervous about them catching me with my camera in my bag," he said.

Catlike eyes shimmered in the twilight as the headlights of passing cars reflected off people defecating by the side of the road. A woman, who had perhaps straggled behind in her chores, was carrying water back home beneath the purplish sky. The brass jug was hoisted on her left shoulder, and her right hand curled around her head and held onto the lip to hold the vessel in place. Her left hand was poised elegantly on her hip for balance. Her legs were muscular, and their length was only hinted at as her long skirt swayed about her ankles. Veena turned around to look at her face as they passed. Her braided hair was smoothed back with oil, revealing a pretty face and pierced nose. She wondered if this girl had any inkling of her beauty and if it mattered at all out here.

Brad was dozing off, and every time the auto hit a bump, he would jerk his head up and then fall back asleep. She thought about putting his head on her shoulder, but a part of her did not want him to sleep. A part of her wanted to jump out of the auto and delve into the shadows flickering all around her. It was a strange feeling she could liken only to the time when they had gone to Disney World's Space Mountain—the part of the ride when they were moving fast, cutting through the pitch-black. She had wanted to dive into that darkness then. Now, she had the same urge. The same unreasonable urge. Why was she feeling this uneasiness? The hairs on her arms were standing up. Her heart was beating fast. She took deep breaths to slow herself down. Is this what falling out of love felt like? Strange, it felt as if she were falling in love all over again. Smoke was billowing up from heaps of sugar-cane roots being burnt to make way for the new shoots. She moved closer to Brad, and his head naturally dropped onto her shoulder.

The Lizard

She sat on the edge of the cot, eyes lazily following the trans-parent story in a Telugu newsstand soap opera weekly. The ball of her foot brushed the burgundy floor as she swung her dangling leg. Her eyes darted from the page to a flicker of movement on the ceiling. A lizard about half the length of her hand was watching her from the corner of the room. His sage-spotted skin was so smooth, she wanted to run her finger across his spine. She had tried to catch one when she was a little girl, but the tail had broken off in her hand. She thought she had killed the poor thing. Later, she learned from a servant that a new tail would grow in its place. She wondered if it hurt. Suddenly, the lizard shot out of the room through the bars of the open window. She waited for him to come back, and after a moment, she shifted her position and sat on her left leg.

As she found her place in the story, she started tapping her foot, the silver ring on her middle toe clinking on the floor. As her eyes skimmed over the words, her face felt warm as if an invisible hand were inches from her cheek. She looked up and saw that he was watching her again. He was rust-colored now, but she knew it was him. She put the book down and stood up. The cot moaned as her sari slipped off her shoulder. She stepped closer and reached for him, her fingers fluttering with anticipation. He moved toward her hand, head tipped upward in a sleek line of elegance. She almost stopped breathing. He trusted her.

"Divya!"

Her mother's squawk ended it all. With a twitch of his tail, he vanished.

"Divya!"

Divya jerked her head, her face twisted with the anguish of treading on the shards of a broken spell. As she wandered onto the front veranda, her sari tail crept behind her. The golden threads woven into the cloth shimmered in the frisky sunlight. Noticing Divya's dragging pallu and her exposed torso, her mother shot her a disapproving look. She adjusted herself, throwing the trail over her shoulder and tucking it at the back of her waist.

"I am going to the market," announced her mother. "I cannot trust that Priya with the vegetables. Every two eggplants she buys for me, she takes one home. Do you need anything?"

Divya shook her head and settled into a bamboo chair. She watched her mother's enormous oval hair bun disappear around the blossoming mango tree. She pulled her long plait in front of her and stroked her fingers through the soft tuft. She remembered when her mother wore her hair in a braid, too. It was not proper for her to do so anymore because of her age. The town's people might gossip that she was still trying to attract suitors and maybe even that she was having an affair. So, Divya's mother spent sunrise winding those thick raven locks into a tight, netted bun. By afternoon tea, she would start picking at the pins and grumble about how her head throbbed.

It wasn't that Divya hated having long hair exactly. She hated not having a choice and that women had to grow their hair long because it was what men found desirable. Why were they all wasting time with physical attributes? She imagined Parvati in a battle, her long braid swinging behind her as she hacked away at evil. Surely all that hair got in the way! Of course, it did. Maybe she used it as a weapon? Nonetheless, Parvati was a goddess and a married one at that. She, too, had to be desirable for her husband, Siva. There was not a doubt in Divya's mind that the first painter to depict the goddesses was a man. Women were imprisoned by their hair. Holding her braid in a nooselike loop, she laughed out loud. She knew she would have to find a different hairstyle for herself by the time she was her mother's age.

"Would you like some tea, Ammagaru?" asked Priya, the servant girl.

"Send for a drink from the shop," said Divya.

Priya displayed a grin with three teeth missing as if to say, "Oh, how wicked you are," and skipped into the courtyard. Divya knew that if her mother were home, she would have to settle for tea. It was not an easy task to bargain with her mother. Divya pictured her rooted to a spot in front of a cart piled high with eggplants and squash, mercilessly haggling with the vendor, whose spine would suddenly turn to custard. With a wiggle of his neck, he would hand over a sack of vegetables, and the corners of her mother's maroon lips would curve the slightest bit. She would bless him with that sprinkle of gratitude as if she were showing him mercy. Should the poor man have needed to wave away a fly at that particular moment, he could have easily missed that smile altogether.

It was obvious to everyone that although her father was the head of the household, he was merely a puppet in his wife's busy hand. Or maybe his floppiness was sheer disinterest in family matters? Divya used to be able to talk to him, but now he seemed to be more of a ghost. How she missed sitting in his lap while he played cards and smoked British cigarettes! He would give her a thimble full of betel nut, which she would wedge between her cheek and gums, sucking on it until it was time to go to bed. Now, she had to sneak the betel nut from a silver canister tucked behind the bottles of scented oils in her mother's armoire. If she was caught chewing it, she was scolded for her nasty habit and lectured on how terribly unfeminine it was.

"Ammagaru," a voice called from the yard.

Divya got up and walked toward the back of the house. She saw a man standing at the gate.

"What is it?" she called.

"I have an invitation," he replied.

She walked down the stone path lined by her father's prized garden of orchids, gardenias, banana trees and flourishing tulsi bushes. Every night, he would drop five sacred tulsi leaves into a glass of water. In the morning, he removed the leaves and drank the water, which he said gave him incredible strength and vitality. The tulsi was not easy to grow because it required more than just knowledge of gardening. One also had to have a good spirit. Her father loved telling the story of when his mother had placed a few leaves over a cancer-stricken woman's body in hopes of making her well. Instead, the woman had died and so had the three tulsi shrubs lining the walls of their yard.

"The power of the tulsi is more than we can comprehend," her father had said.

Divya opened the gate and took the invitation from the man.

"It is from Mrs. Hema Supanni of Eluru for Mrs. Radha Khanna of Guntur, Ammagaru," he said.

Divya nodded and pulled the gate closed. The invitation was for a baby birthday party. Mrs. Hema Supanni was one of her mother's friends, whom Divya found to be unbearably pretentious, and the party was for her grandson, Ganesh. She thought about ripping up the invitation, but thought better of it. That was the reason it had been hand-delivered—Hema wanted to make certain it was received. (The postal service was terribly unreliable.) Divya sat back down in the bamboo chair on the veranda. Hopefully, her mother would not insist on dragging her to this tiresome affair. Babies were decent and all, but that hinged on the fact that they were not her own. She did not have any desire to become pregnant. Under the guise of *oohing* and *aahing* over the bundle of chubbiness and drool, the women at the party would undoubtedly take the opportunity to flaunt their gems and latest fashions.

If she had to go, maybe she could take her friend Tara along. Her mother would probably protest, reminding her that Tara was not a proper girl and that she had her own image to look after. Tara had been a proper girl until she fell in love with Aamir, a Muslim boy. She was prohibited from seeing him and he from seeing her, but they somehow managed to do so anyway. Tara was so busy going to school to get her engineering degree that Divya hadn't seen her for almost two weeks. She picked up the phone and dialed her number. If she were free, they could go fabric shopping on Besant Road. Divya had a few saris for which she needed to find matching jacket material. Maybe Tara could just come over, and they could catch up. But there was no answer at Tara's, which Divya thought odd.

"Miss Divya," whispered Priya.

Priya was standing so close that when Divya came out of her daydream, it took her a full five seconds to realize the blurry auburn she was staring into was Priya's bony arm. The bottle of Gold Spot was sweating with moisture from the heat of her hand. Taking the soda from her, Divya guzzled it quickly. Priya rubbed her big toe on the peacock's face on the floor tiles as she waited in the doorway. Divya hated making people wait. She took another sip and poured the rest into the steel cup sitting on top of the clay water jug. With another toothy grin, Priya walked off with the empty bottle. Divya had just finished the orange pop in the cup when her mother entered, swinging her pink plastic market basket.

"An invitation came for you," said Divya.

"Oh, good. I was expecting it."

She followed her mother into the kitchen and sat down near the stone mortar to help her with dinner. Her mother handed her a tray of woven straw, and after pouring some black gram into it, Divya began picking out the stones. Her mother cracked a coconut on the ground and caught the water in a glass. She gave her the pale gray liquid, but Divya declined.

"You used to love it when you were little," her mother said accusingly.

"I am not thirsty, Amma. You have it."

Mrs. Khanna shrugged and downed the glass in one shot.

"It was not that sweet anyway," she assured her in case Divya was feeling as if she had missed out.

Picking up a blunt knife, she began prying the white meat from the shell.

"I got a letter from your Aunt Sita in the States today," began her mother. "Her daughter is still very sick. Your silly father wants to send her some tulsi, but I told him it is illegal. Besides, the girl is mentally ill. What could tulsi do for her now?"

Divya tossed the grain up in the air and caught it in the tray.

"How did Usha get sick?" asked Divya.

"Like the body, the mind also needs protection. My sister was not very strict with her, and the strangeness of the land and its ways confused her. I also have my own suspicions about drugs and such. I do not think any of this would have happened if she had been married."

"Maybe the illness is hereditary, Amma?"

"We don't have lunacy on my side of the family. It most likely stemmed from that puny husband of Sita's. It breaks my heart. Usha was a beautiful girl. Such a shame."

When Divya felt the silence thickest over the house, she grabbed a rolled straw mat and carefully climbed the stairs to the roof. This was where she used to sleep when her cousins lived in the house. She remembered drawing with chalk on the cement floor with Usha, who had left India when she was ten years old. Divya had been only six and always surrounded by children, so she didn't feel the pinch of loss. She could not help but think, however, what her cousin's life might have been like if she had never left.

Since maturity, Divya had slept in a barred room on a bed that made her legs itch. Her mother insisted it was not safe for a young woman to sleep alone on the roof and that there were scores of incidents in which rowdies climbed to rooftops to rob and harass people. Regardless, Divya could not breathe in that stuffy house at times. That night, she unrolled the mat and stretched a sheet over her body. Her eyes flickered over the sky and settled on the softness of the moon, which hung like an eyelash on twilight's cheek. Where would she be sleeping in a year's time, and who would be her husband?

The modern age made her mother skittish, and Tara and Usha made her anxious about the disintegration of tradition. Under that tanklike demeanor, she was eager to get her time-bomb of a daughter married off or "settled," as she preferred to call it. Divya never really disobeyed her mother more than the usual pilfering of betel nut powder or sneaking to the cinema. She was not in love with anyone, and she did not write secret letters. But there was that time when she was fourteen and had fallen from the roof onto the third-floor veranda. Her head had split open, and she had had to get twenty-one sutures. She told her parents that she had fallen from the ladder, but she knew her mother had decided that it was a failed suicide attempt. Since then, the very fact that she never gave her mother anything to worry about made her mother worry all the more.

But Divya did not shudder at the thought of an arranged marriage. Rather, she welcomed the changes it would bring to her narrow life. Excitement caught her heart, and her ears warmed from the thought of leaving India behind and venturing into the universe.

As she became drowsy, she thought about the lizard. Was it a male or a female? Was there such a thing in the lizard world? She wondered what it would be like if she could lose her tail, too. If when they had a hold of her leg or her arm, she could keep running. Or change color so they would walk past her as if she were just one of the beggar children washing at the water pump. What would it be like if she could run and run, unraveling herself until all they had in their clutches was the mound of her wrinkled sari?

✦

When the last corner of night's cloak was vacuumed into the pin-prick of a star and shaken over another part of the world, Divya opened her eyes to a sky smeared with the powdery orange of dawn. She quickly rolled up the mat and scurried down the steps. She heard her father gargling in the garden and smelled the smoky wood heating the cauldron of bath water. Her mother was nowhere to be seen, and Divya thought how odd that was. By this time, she was usually cooking up a tiffin of idli and sambar. As she put away the mat, her father came up the path, wiping his chin with a towel.

"The parents of a suitor are coming for breakfast, Divya. Your mother told me to tell you—"

Her father cut himself off when he saw his wife marching in.

"Never mind. She will tell you herself."

With that, her father handed the reins back to her mother, who rushed her numb daughter into a bedroom, reciting a detailed list of instructions.

Within an hour, Divya was dressed in an orange and gold tissue sari. It was a sudden meeting because the suitor and his family were from the States and in a hurry to get back. What her mother did not tell her was that the groom's first choice had fallen through. She did not tell her that she was the understudy.

"He is a doctor," her mother crowed. "He has a job at a good hospital in New York and is making a good income. You will be very comfortable. His parents described him as being forward."

Her mother had just finished fastening a jasmine garland into Divya's long braid when Priya entered.

"The guests are here, Ammagaru," she said, more excited than both mother and daughter.

Licking the tip of her finger, her mother wiped away a smudge of katika under Divya's eye.

They went out onto the shady veranda and greeted the guests. Divya knew from the looks on their faces that they were extremely pleased at the lightness of her skin. It made up for the larger amounts of money and property that darker, and consequently, ug-lier girls had to offer. As she sat down in a chair next to her father,

Divya noticed the suitor's mother had short hair. When she looked at the groom himself, she saw he had a pleasant face and a thick moustache. He was sharply dressed in a suit that was obviously not from India. As she stared at her hands in her lap, she could feel his eyes upon her. She looked up and met them, unwaveringly. Their bond was interrupted by Priya, who pranced about with a tray of sweets and tea.

"Divya graduated at the top of her accounting class," her mother boasted.

"Ajay is a cardiologist," his mother said, beaming.

Through the ribbon of Priya's looped braid, the prospective bride and groom glanced at one another and smiled with embarrassment.

After consulting an astrologer, the wedding date was set. Her mother bustled about taking care of last-minute details, and her father was working on getting her passport and visa in order. Divya sat on the slate ledge under the guava tree, dotting her left palm with henna paste in a plastic tube. None of it seemed real. She was going to be married and join her husband in New York City—a place she had only seen pictures of at the library.

"Amma," she called.

Mrs. Khanna sat down on the floor. She placed Divya's right hand in her lap and began tattooing her palm with the paste.

"You did such a wonderful job on your other hand," her mother said.

It was her mother's way of apologizing for the little argument they had had earlier in the day. Divya wanted to have their tailor stitch some backless jackets for her. It was the latest fashion. Her mother had said that it was inappropriate.

"Only desperate girls do that," she had said.

She stared at her mother, whose hair was loose and hanging about her shoulders. There were dozens of white hairs mixed beautifully into the black.

"Your hair looks pretty, Amma," she said.

"Yes, but what a nuisance it is," complained Mrs. Khanna.

"Why don't you cut it like Ajay's mother?"

"Your father adores it, that is why," she said, prickly with resentment.

Just then, they heard a rustling in the branches above. As they watched a parrot tear into a perfectly ripe guava, Divya saw her mother's anger dissipate.

That evening, Divya retired earlier than usual. She sat on a cot and looked at the moonlight that slipped in between the bars on the window. The room was so illuminated that she thought there must be a full moon. Just when she was going to have a look, she saw a shadow on the floor. Her eyes moved to the window and rested on the lizard hanging upside-down. How interesting to have the power to turn the world on its side, she thought. She cautiously approached him. He moved back. She held out her elaborately decorated palm, and into this palace he stepped like a prince. His underside was cool, and she could feel him breathing. She could not resist stroking him with her finger. And as she did so, his eyes darted and he jumped through the window in one swift movement as if riding the wing of a breeze. Divya gasped and pressed her face against the cold metal bars. He was gone. She should not have been so eager. How could she blame him for not trusting her? Her mother's marriage advice rattled in her like pebbles in a can.

"Behave yourself, Divya. As anything else, too much freedom can choke you."

As she drifted off into sleep, she thought about Usha. Tomorrow, she would secretly ask her father if he would pack some tulsi when it was time for her to leave so she could take it to her sick cousin in the States.

Ten Acres

Mrs. Auni Badari tore off a piece of paper from an envelope in her purse. Rolling it into a sharp point, she picked in between her teeth.

"Mom, that is really gross," said her daughter, Sukuntula.

Sukuntula was seventeen and always complaining about something or other. Mrs. Badari tossed her makeshift toothpick out onto the passing road.

"This thing feels like it's going to fall apart," her daughter said, referring to the intense vibration of the auto taxi.

"It won't. The road is just rough. The damn politicians make election promises of cheap rice and better roads, but this is what you get in the end."

"What if it did break down? We're in the middle of nowhere going to a stupid field."

"A field can never be stupid. And when you are nowhere in India, you are everywhere."

"Ahh-yuh."

Mrs. Badari hated it when Sukuntula said that. *Ahh-yuh.* It was as if she were slamming a heavy door in her face. She hoped, eventually, the door would open and she and her daughter could really share their thoughts. She had a feeling it would be a long wait. But then again, realization came unexpectedly like a cool breeze—remembered for a second and then forgotten, a part of your skin and then suddenly invisible.

Opening her purse, she fished out the paper with the directions for getting to the Eluru land that her father and mother had left her. She had never seen it before. And if she was going to fight for it, she needed to see it. Her greedy brother, Tilak, was occupying all ten acres and refused to give her any money for the crops he had harvested on it for the past five years. He was also preventing her from selling the land to interested buyers by telling everyone that she had already sold the land to him. Even her two sisters, Hema and Varija, refused to help. They threw up their hands and shook their heads, but that was it. False sympathy. He was probably paying them off, too.

On top of that, everyone was acting as if she were the intruder. They asked her why she had waited so long to take action. What people didn't understand was that she didn't live in India. Three summers had passed after her mother's death before she could come back for a visit. No one helped her with the paperwork and red tape. In India, you were on a perpetual line. There were always people ahead of you and a six-month wait. That is, unless you happened to drop a wad of rupees on the registrar's desk. Getting to that desk was another adventure in itself. India was crawling with corruption.

"You know, I want to tell you that I'm thinking of changing my name," said Sukuntula, flipping her poodle-permed hair back away from her face. "I hate it."

"It's a beautiful name. It means—"

"Yeah, I know. Raised by the birds. That's great. I mean, what were you and Dad thinking when you came up with that one? Do you have any idea what I've gone through on Long Island? The class gets hysterical when the teacher asks if I have a nickname."

"Nickname? Can't they say the whole name?"

"Mom, that's not the point. I want a nickname. But what do I have to choose from? Suck, sucky, sukun, kunt."

"Sukuntula, your name was not meant to be butchered. Besides, we did not know how to say Christine or Michael when your father and I arrived in the States. We learned. They can learn to say your name correctly."

"I am so glad Tiffany came up with Ula. I really like it. Ula."

"Why can't they call you Suku for short?"

"Ula. It sounds like Uma."

The auto hit a bump, and they were thrown forward.

"Easy!" Mrs. Badari warned the driver. "Uma? Uma is an Indian name."

"You know, like Uma Thurman, Mom," said Sukuntula, excitedly. "She's awesome."

Mrs. Badari hadn't the faintest idea who her daughter was babbling about. Sometimes she just had to let her run at the mouth like an old faucet. Sukuntula was really a good girl. Hopefully, this was just a negative period in her life. As she stared at the paddy fields they were passing, she became lost in her own worries.

"Aww, forget it," her daughter muttered.

If Mrs. Badari died before selling the land, Sukuntula would never see the money. She was seventeen, unmarried and needed the security of the funds. There would be no one for her to rely on after she and her husband died. Besides, her father and mother had left the land to her. Tilak had threatened their mother with a knife and forced her to sign a counterfeit will. She knew because her mother had written her a tear-stained letter. The subregistrar was bribed, original documents were destroyed and official-looking documents were fabricated. Her parents had actually left her more land, but the ten acres were what the fraudulent will said they had left her, and so it was. Her siblings thought that since Mrs. Badari lived in the States and was married to an engineer, she had no need for the land or rupees. Tilak thought that since he was a male, he should get more. He thought since Auni had a daughter and not a son, she didn't need all that land.

"You have a very big house," they had said over and over again.

It was ridiculous. If she were a millionaire, would she be running around in the scorching sun, hunting down selfish kin and bribing arrogant officials suffering from inferiority complexes? No. She had better things to do. They didn't care that the measly ten acres was rightfully hers—even if she *were* a millionaire. She just couldn't believe that the brother she had cradled in her arms was torturing her like this.

"Stop here on the right," she said to the driver.

"Here?" asked Sukuntula.

Mrs. Badari stepped out of the auto and stood in the dirt road. Three women were sauntering by, balancing trusses of grass on their heads.

"Are you coming, or do you want to wait here?" she asked her daughter impatiently.

When the driver turned around and stared at her, Sukuntula quickly got out of the taxi. The field women snickered as they passed. No doubt they were laughing at her daughter's knee-length, flowery dress, which was pretty, but inappropriate for south Indian travel if one were Indian.

"We'll be back in ten minutes," said Mrs. Badari to the driver.

A boy rode by on a bicycle with a basketful of fresh eggs. He turned around and looked at Sukuntula with fascination.

"You cannot sell cracked eggs at the market," quipped Mrs. Badari in Telugu to the boy, and he sped away.

Stepping over the trench separating the dirt road from the land, she and her daughter began walking on a weed-covered path about a foot in width. Mrs. Badari wrapped her sari pallu around her head as a shield from the harsh sun.

"What is this stuff?" asked Sukuntula referring to the tall stalks flanking the sides of the path.

"Sugar cane. Brown sugar comes from the red cane; white from the lighter ones."

The sun was breathing fire. She reached into her bag and took out two yellow-colored umbrellas.

"Here, take this," she said handing her daughter one.

"No thanks, Mom."

"There's no one to impress here, Sukuntula. You'll get sunstroke."

Sukuntula begrudgingly took it, making a face at the clown carved on the wooden handle.

"Where'd you get these? They're so loud."

Between the grassy weeds and cracked earth sprouted purple and pink flowers. Without irrigation from the well, which was conveniently located on her brother's forty acres, the fertile land would have dried up. She knew her father did not think any of his children would charge the others a fee to use the water supply, but that was exactly what was happening. She looked at a headless palm tree in the distance. Most likely, the top was torn off during monsoon winds. The rains were so unpredictable in India. Then again, was there a place on earth where life was otherwise?

"So, how'd we get the land anyway?" Sukuntula asked.

"We come from a long line of agriculturalists—"

"You mean, farmers," her daughter corrected as if she had caught her mother in a lie.

"Yes, farmers. In reality, our ancestors were Rajasthani warriors, and back in the 1500s they helped to keep invaders out of northern India. The king Krishna Deva rewarded them with estates in Andhra Pradesh. That is how we moved down to the south. Later, we were forced to stay in A.P. because the Aryans invaded and overran the country with their inferior civilization. They are the ones who introduced the terrible caste system."

"What caste do we belong to?"

"The same caste as the famed Untouchables, the Sudras."

"Are you serious?" Sukuntula asked fearfully.

"It's not as bad as it sounds," Mrs. Badari replied with a chuckle. "In the final book of the *Rig Veda*, it states that Brahmins, or priests, came from the head of God, from the shoulders came the kings and warriors, from the thighs came the Vaisyas and, finally, from the feet came the Sudras. Our subcaste is Kamma, which means we are not as bad off as the Untouchables. We probably came from the knee or calf."

She lifted up her sari.

"Be careful here—there's a hole."

"But how could the foot of God be any less important than the head, shoulders or thighs?" asked Sukuntula innocently.

"It can't. I personally think the class system was added to the Rig Veda to give the priests more power. We're Untouchables, but our milk, rice and vegetables that we grow aren't untouchable to them. I think the Vedas were also altered to say that women were unworthy of priesthood. Once, there were priestesses, but suddenly they weren't permitted to wear the sacred thread anymore. It's all sexist, classist, materialistic bullshit."

"Mom!" Sukuntula ejaculated and then exploded into giggles.

In the astonishing crudeness and wrath of her words, she managed to link arms with her rebellious daughter for a fleeting moment. The connection felt good.

"It's true—all of that bias is so a part of the Indian culture now," she continued.

When they reached the telephone pole, Mrs. Badari stopped walking.

"This is it," she said as she twirled the yellow umbrella on her shoulder.

Her daughter was respectfully silent. All around them, green. They stood firmly like two giant dandelions in the center of the field. Mrs. Badari felt like one, too. A weed that the remaining members of her family were trying to yank out by the roots.

"What is this?" asked Sukuntula, kneeling to take a closer look at the crop.

"Brinjal—Indian eggplant. I think there's a marker over there. I think our land goes up to that hut."

"Look, a bird," said Sukuntula, pointing to the telephone wire.

"A crane."

Sukuntula took a photo of it as Mrs. Badari looked back to the expanse of green before her. If the solid jade hills did not surround this land, would it have gone on forever? This rich motherland, once cultivated, fed millions of Indians over the centuries. It belonged to her and was her sole responsibility to nurture. It was not about money. It was about respect.

"What are you going to do with the money, Mom?"

"I don't know. Set it aside for your marriage."

"But I'm not getting married," she protested.

"You will someday."

"See? Why are you so cool one second and then say something so backwards the next? You're always contradicting yourself."

Mrs. Badari considered her daughter's words for a moment and knew the answer. Fear. The fear of her own parents' and Indian society's disapproval of her unorthodox life frightened Mrs. Badari. As her upbringing sprinkled light over her life, it also cast a shadow. And light and shadow were inseparable, weren't they?

"If it's not for your marriage, then you can use it for something else. Things should be easier for you."

Sukuntula plucked a pink flower and stared into it for a second and then handed it over to her mother.

"I'm going to walk around," Sukuntula said and turned away.

When did the world change so much? When did her brother become greedy and malicious? Mrs. Badari closed her burning eyes and remembered her mother's letter.

I remember your small footsteps on the garden path. They were indistinguishable from your brother's and sisters'. Sixty-three years later, my children have shown their true faces. Now, dear Auni, you are an angel amongst these devils.

Mrs. Badari had planned to use the letter against her siblings in court, but while she was visiting her sister Hema, it had miraculously vanished from her bag. It was stupid to think she could trust anyone. After her father had died, they had all turned on her mother. What was her mother thinking when she closed her eyes for the last time? Was she cursing the womb that nursed such demons, or was she muttering blessings for being able to move on? What would her own life have been like if she and her husband had never left India? She turned and looked to her only child. She hoped Sukuntula knew how much she loved her, but she could not help feeling they were speaking different languages. Should she let go of Sukuntula before her daughter moved on and left her behind? Would that be less painful? Sukuntula was walking toward her.

"Look, I found a brush and a painting," Sukuntula said as they rejoined each other.

The colors on the curling page were faded and washed out.

"It's a sugar-cane field," said Mrs. Badari. "We've got to start back. I told the driver we'd only be ten minutes."

"Wait," said Sukuntula as she focused her camera on her mother with the green spilling all around her. "Smile."

As they headed back down the narrow mounded path, Mrs. Badari thought about the vicious battle that lay ahead with her siblings. She had seen and touched the land. And if there was a shred of justice left in this country, she would truly own it.

"Mom, I'm not sorry you guys decided to move," said Sukuntula as they walked toward the road. "There's no way I could deal with living here. The women are treated like servants. They're so pushed around."

She nodded, staring into the spinning yellow of her daughter's umbrella. What could she say? It was true.

"I don't think I could live here either—not anymore," said Mrs. Badari, acknowledging that the family she once felt a part of was gone forever.

"Do they have a good name in Telugu for women who don't take crap, Mom? You know, stand up for what they believe in?"

"My father used to joke around and say 'kanchu vattalu' when describing daring women to my mother," said Mrs. Badari with a snort. "It's not a good thing—more of a vulgarity used to describe aggressive women. It literally means bronze-balled."

"In school, the guys just say 'bitch' or 'dyke,'" chattered Sukuntula. "This jerk, John Mangino, called me and Tiffany dykes on the last day of school. I couldn't believe that. Just because we're close and tough doesn't mean we're dykes."

Mrs. Badari laughed out loud, knowing that in the center of that emerald earth, something very different from sugar cane or eggplant had taken root.

The Artist

Jan took off his straw hat and put it beside him on the berth. He was sitting in a train headed for Cape Comorin, or Kanniyakumari, the southernmost tip of India. "Kanniya" meant virgin, and "Kumari" was the name of a young girl. A bony hand reached in between the bars and waved a small bag of popcorn.

"One rupee, one rupee."

He shook his head, and the boy waited, drinking in what was probably his first sight of an African man. It was hard to say, though, because Indians tended to stare at anyone who wasn't, well, Indian. Even Indians who were living abroad in England and the United States were treated differently from the natives. He looked at a woman in a lavender sari bordered with gold stars. She was standing away from the waiting areas, as distant as she could get from the crowds. Her pallu was wrapped around her face out of shyness or perhaps from disgust at the unsanitary conditions of the station. Regardless of her desire to remain inconspicuous, people were staring at her. What was it? She did have a beautiful face. But it was the sari. Amidst all the grayness of the station, the color was vibrating the way fallen jacaranda blossoms do on lawns. And it was her skin. It struck him then that this violet hue was what he needed to enliven Indian flesh on his canvases. He looked at her honey-colored hands and saw lavender, green and even brick red. Impulsively, he took out his watercolor box, and in the next breath, thought better of it.

Another brown hand jutted through the window bars, this one trembling and offering nothing in return. Looking into the girl's wilting eyes, Jan dropped a fifty-paise coin into her hand. Her tawny-colored hair was dull and matted. When she broke into a grin, he saw that two of her front teeth were missing. She put her hands together in prayer while bending her head down in thanks. As she walked down the platform to beg at the next sleeping compartment, he saw she was dragging her right leg. He closed the window.

A garbled announcement was made, and the woman in lavender began to walk. Actually, the others walked; she glided gracefully like a swan. Yes, there was certainly something different about her. She reminded him of Padma. Suddenly, he wished he hadn't met Padma at all. As soon as the thought materialized, he knew how useless it was. He had met her, and there was no going back. Initially, he had planned on going back home to London. But he knew it would be dangerous to run with such an experience on the tip of his tongue. So, Kanniyakumari it was. After that, he'd go to Madras and then head back to England.

He reached into his pocket for his ticket and faltered when he felt metal. He took out the gold nugget, and as he rolled it between his fingers, his thoughts turned back to Padma: It was a late June afternoon, and the air was drier than usual in Nilambur, a small town in the state of Kerala. It was a hundred degrees—remarkably high for a tropical rainy region. The teak plantations lining the road crackled in sanguine expectation of the coming monsoon rains, which were late. He was carrying his portable easel under his arm. A water canteen jostled at his hip. He stopped to wet his handkerchief and tie it back around his neck. It was then that he heard her laugh—a delightfully childish cackle. His eyes searched amongst the grayish-yellow trunks, but saw no one. Then rustling and a young woman spilled out onto the road with a chubby black puppy nipping at her heels. She clapped her hands as it barked and tried to jump up and catch her sari pallu, which she wagged before him. That was until she saw Jan standing on the roadside. She stepped back and adjusted her sari, covering her breasts and the bareness of her stomach. She had stopped laughing. Even the puppy had become still; the only thing moving was its tongue as it panted.

"Hello," he had said, showing her his upright palm.

He immediately felt silly for doing so. He hoped she didn't think he was ignorant enough to confuse the Native American greeting for an Indian one. Would she even know that? Thinking back now, he guessed he had raised his hand because he wanted to convey that he was coming in peace.

She stared back at him. When he walked toward her, she bent down and picked up the puppy. It, in turn, took the opportunity to scramble toward her shoulders and lick her face. She struggled with it for a moment and finally put it down. The puppy, serving as a messenger of sorts, ran back and forth between two, leaping at their knees and barking. Jan laughed heartily, and she joined in.

"What is his name?" he asked.

"Share."

He laughed because "Share" meant tiger.

She went her way, and he went back to the room he was renting from a widow in Nilambur. She overcharged him, but he didn't mind because she needed the money. She cooked two different vegetable curries for him and respected that he sometimes worked well into the night. It was good that she offered him meals because it allowed him to keep his contact with people in the village down to a minimum. It's not that he didn't like the people. What he disliked and was tired of was the attention he got by way of looks and whispers. The children still chased him about asking for change whenever they spotted him, but even that slowed down as his stay lengthened. He spent much of his time painting in the remote quiet on the outskirts of the village or in the privacy of his room. The arrangement with the widow made him feel as if he belonged—not just a tourist passing through town. He remembered when she had even volunteered to sew a button on his shirt for him.

The next time he saw the young woman was by the Chaliyar River. Her name was Padma. It meant lotus, the pink fragrant flower that sprung pure and clean from the murkiest waters. To Hindus and Buddhists, it signified remaining untouched by the sin and vices of the material world. The lotus in its purity symbolized enlightenment.

"In the *Odyssey*, Homer wrote about the lotus-eaters," he told her. "They were a tribe in North Africa who ate the fruit of the lotus. It made them indolent—dull and lazy."

He didn't know if she understood, but she smiled. They spoke in a mix of Hindi, English, Telugu and Malayalam. He learned that she was nineteen years old and had spent the last six years panning for gold. She had never finished school.

"Family business," she said.

She was the youngest and had three brothers and one sister. Both of her parents had died of natural causes. She was going to be married when her brothers had saved enough money for her dowry.

"How much?"

"Three thousand rupees."

"Isn't it strange to have to be paid to marry a woman?" he exclaimed. "And a beautiful one on top of that!"

She smiled and twisted her head out of shyness.

Their friendship developed slowly like a streamlet trickling down a mountainside as the sun's heat melted the ice. They never planned to meet. He always tried to bump into her when she was fetching water or washing the laundry by the river. The closest he ever stood to her was when she showed him how she panned for gold.

"White with brown good," she said handing him a rock. "You take only brown part."

Her brothers went up into the mountains and hunted for the white rock with the brown stains. They broke off choice pieces with a mallet and ground those into a powder. The powder was then panned with sand and water until gold with small amounts of mercury was left behind. This mercury-gold amalgam was collected on a cloth and burned with a kerosene lamp. The result was almost a hundred percent pure gold.

"The white rock with brown is good because those are quartz veins and they have gold dust," he clarified. "Quartz is good."

"Quartz, quartz," she mimicked.

"How much do you sell the gold for?"

"This much, forty rupees."

He was stunned when he saw the large size of the nugget she was showing him.

He later understood why—much of the village was involved in some way in panning for gold, and it was an illegal profession. The buyers knew they had the upper hand because it was a highly competitive underground business.

"How come your family doesn't fish? Wouldn't that bring in more income?"

"Not allowed to fish in monsoon season," she explained. "Too little fish, too many men."

She was right. It was spawning season. He remembered a guide in Cochin had talked about the problems with fishing. The coast of Kerala was lucrative for fishing because in the married waters of the Arabian Sea, the Bay of Bengal and the Indian Ocean were shoals that included several varieties of fish. Unfortunately, there were too many fishermen and poachers.

When he asked her to pose for a painting, she had declined. While beating clothes, she kept an eye on him as he stood in the distance in front of his easel. She would sneak up on him and peek at the canvas.

"What is that?" she had asked once.

"The Chaliyar," he replied, pointing with his brush.

"When did you see an orange fishing boat like *that*?"

"I didn't."

She smiled and went back to her work.

The next day, he painted her and Share sitting under a tree. She was nervous at first, but when she began playing with the puppy, she forgot all about being a subject. He concentrated on blending the right colors to match the brown of her skin.

"It is nice," she said simply when she saw the portrait. "You make me look nice."

Walking along the banks of the Chaliyar, he collected stones that were softened and shaped by the river's strong hands. He gave the prettiest of these to Padma because he wanted to give her something. He knew a painting was out of the question. Such a gesture would raise too many eyebrows.

"They are beautiful," she said.

For a moment, she stared intently at the riverstones in her hand.

"But the life drains from them when you put them in your pocket."

Having said that, she tossed them back into the muddy water.

"I guess you don't feel that way about gold?" he said, partly amused and partly hurt by her honesty.

"Gold is always happy!" she gushed.

Later that week, she took him deep into the forest. She explained to him that the hunters in search of white and brown rocks were often chased away by farmers and forest guards. Jan knew that gold panning contributed to deforestation and increased the threat of landslides. So, the hunters had to go into unmapped areas of the forests and mountains. This proved to be invigorating as well as dangerous.

When they had walked for about fifteen minutes, she stopped

and told him to close his eyes. Taking his hand, she led him closer to their destination. It was the first time they had touched.

"Okay," she whispered.

When he opened his eyes he saw a swing hanging from a giant banyan tree. She sat down on the worn seat. Her father had built it for her when she was a child. The mother-trunk of the tree was practically indistinguishable from the other trunks that had sprung up all around it.

Rocking gently, she tipped her head back

"Look up," she said.

He stared into the mess of leaves and branches scraping the roof of the sky's mouth.

"See how small we are," she said laughing

He looked at her sloping neck. She floated like an angel amidst the lush leaves. The whiteness of her sheer sari pallu, wrapped around her head like a scarf, stood out against her black plaited hair. He sucked on the brush to smooth the bristles and began to paint.

He was leaving in two days and woke up anticipating having to say goodbye. She had told him she would be at the swing that afternoon. He went, but she did not come. He set up his easel and painted the swing, empty and motionless. As he walked back, he dug his heels into the cracked earth that waited so patiently for relief. For days, the villagers had been jabbering about a storm that was on its way. They believed the monsoon would bring good luck—the riverbanks would be bathed, and the rain's fingers would lay bare morsels of gold. But the air was so dry, Jan could taste the dust on his tongue.

When he returned to his room, he uncovered the painting of Padma on the swing. Her innocence radiated as the lining of a cloud that had closed its enormous fist on the sun's rays. He put the one of the swing on his easel and began painting her into it. Except this time, he painted her without her sari. He imagined the color of her nipples and the curve of her hips.

As he was completing the portrait, he heard a crash behind him. It was the widow. She had dropped a steel plate of rice and curry on the floor.

Her mouth hung open. She bent down and quickly began scooping up the food from the floor with her hands.

"Don't worry—I will get something at the food stand," he said.

She looked back at him with small eyes.

When he returned from dinner and opened the door to his room, he found it had been ransacked and all of his paintings were gone. He asked the old woman, but she pretended not to understand what he was asking. She looked grief-stricken.

He heard a commotion outside. To his horror, he saw Padma, bound, being paraded naked through the village streets. She was crying silently, her head hung in shame and bobbing gently like that of a bird with a broken neck. He ran outside to stop them, but the crowd raised wooden sticks at him. He was struck on the shoulder and head.

"Leave Nilambur!" they cried.

His eyes locked on the leader of the pack. It was Padma's eldest brother, but Jan did not know that because they had never met. The way his eyes burned into him, Jan knew if the sea of bodies weren't between them, this man would have lunged at him.

Jan screamed, but their voices were louder.

"Let her go!" he yelled. "Stop it!"

Two policemen in khaki knickers stepped in between him and the crowd. But he kept screaming.

"You don't understand! Nothing happened. We were friends. I painted her. Nothing happened. Listen to me! She is innocent. Let her go!"

A strong wind began to blow down on them. The clouds were white and puffy and raced all around Padma, making the painful scene inch by in slow motion before his eyes.

It occurred to him at that moment that her nipples were dark brown. They were not pink as he had painted. The crowd's chants became fainter as they marched down the dirt road toward the river.

"Please listen to me! I didn't touch her!" he yelled.

But he knew that he had.

When he was packing his things that evening, the widow told him that Padma had been found floating in the river. She had drowned herself. The old woman said the people were mad because Padma had killed herself and that they could not understand how she could be more ashamed to be naked in front of her own people than to be naked in front of a black. They just did not understand that. She said that he had better leave before he caused any more trouble. She didn't want any more trouble. She didn't want them coming to her house.

"They are very angry," she said.

Jan didn't know what to believe. Was Padma really dead, or was the old lady lying so he would never come back to Nilambur? Was it Padma's choice? How could it be? They had murdered her. He had murdered her.

As he walked to the riverbank, he did not notice the funny way the sky, drained of the last drop of blue, was breaking open like a watermelon. The monsoon had finally arrived. He was concentrating on his moving feet, which felt like bricks. He needed to see Padma again, just one more time on the swing.

By the time his eyes met the bank of the Chaliyar, thunder pealed and the heavens began spitting out torrents of rain like black seeds. His backpack was getting wet, but he didn't care. He needed to hear her carefree laughter ring through the treetops, making monkeys stop and listen. He needed the monsoon rain falling in sheets to whip him. He needed it to wash him clean again. His mouth filled with the sweet, warm water as he fell down on his knees in the mud and cried. As lightning struck, he thought he glimpsed the shores filling with glistening bodies dancing in celebration.

When he rose, he was soaked to the bone. He wiped the water from his eyes. As his vision cleared, he saw lying in front of him, in the mud, a nugget of gold.

Paradise

"They look like penises," she said, looking skyward at a palm tree. Sitting at the Paradise Bar on the beach on the Malabar Coast, Veena and Brad were eyeing a family of palmyras swaying a few feet away. This palm variety was split into visible sexes. The female bore palmyra fruit, while the male had clusters of black snakes at the core of the fanlike leaves.

"Guess that one is a male," he said.

The bars dotting the shores of the state of Goa consisted of long stakes driven into the sand, topped with roofs of palm fronds. They were lopsided patches of shade where tourists could quench thirsts and gain relief from the sweltering sun.

"I hope he doesn't fall," said Veena, referring to the man, dressed in a loincloth and silver belt, inching up one of the palm trees by using the footholds carved into the bark.

The man cut a gash in the top part of the trunk with a machete and then secured a pot under the dripping sap. Before sunrise, the colorless extract was called neera and was consumed by young children as well as adults to improve strength and vitality. After sunrise, however, the neera fermented and became toddy, the foamy white liquor sitting before them in dainty rose teacups. It had a pungent smell. The waiter, Subbaiah, called it "coconut beer."

"One, two, three," Veena said, and they upended their cups. She scrunched her face.

"If the neera is for strength, the toddy is for inspiration. I will have one more, Subbaiah," Brad called to the waiter.

"Me, too, please," Veena said giddily, as her head began to feel light. "I like it better than the other stuff—feni."

Feni, a spirit distilled from cashews, was big with the locals. The young man in knickers nodded, beaming bright teeth.

"Two more coconut beer," he said as he walked off.

"It is a fucking amazing thing, Veena. They give this stuff to babies like vitamins—then *whammo*—it's bum juice."

"Yeah," she agreed.

"I am so glad we came to India," he said.

She burst into infectious laughter, and he eventually joined in.

"You know what this is like?" he said.

"What?"

"It's like *Gilligan's Island*."

She laughed.

"Stranded in paradise," he said.

"Except *they* were too pissed off to realize it."

On the soft forest floor were sprinkles of light falling like fine sand sifted through the fingers of leaves and branches.

"It's magical," Veena said. "I feel like I'm floating."

She held her arms out and skipped in a circle.

"God, look at the size of this tree," he said. "It must be twenty feet around."

"What kind do you think it is?"

"I think it's a banyan," he replied.

113

She threw her hands around the trunk and hugged it.

"It's amazing," Brad said as he bent down to look at the roots.

"Take a picture," she said, arms still wrapped about the tree.

"You're drunk."

"Come on, take a picture," she cajoled, pressing her cheek against the cool bark dreamily.

"Okay," he said and took the cover off the camera lens. "Say *toddy*."

"Toddy."

As soon as he clicked, they heard a branch creaking in the tree-tops. Veena stepped back and looked up. A rhesus monkey vaulted from branch to branch and then sat looking down on them.

"Oh, there's a baby hanging on her," said Veena with delight.

"I see it," said Brad as he snapped the shot.

Some of the branches were naked and looked as if they were gnarled limbs scraping the pale sky. It amazed him how well the monkey was camouflaged in the foliage, her curling tail another twisted branch. In the next moment, she flung herself into the thick of green and vanished.

Brad looked at Veena, who was still searching for the monkey. A strand of her chestnut hair clung to her open lips. She turned and looked at him. He could just see a glint of her perfect teeth. Brushing her hair aside, he closed his eyes and kissed her softly. She moaned and slid her hand down onto his neck. As they fell to the soft forest floor, he held the small of her back.

"God, I love you," he whispered.

"I love you, too," she said.

He opened his eyes and pulled away when he saw someone was watching them.

A bearded, barefoot man was towering above them.

"Is it a snake?" Veena shrilled, sitting up on her knees next to Brad.

They were at the feet of a swami. He appeared to be the survivor of a fire: His face, neck and chest were horribly scarred. He was striking in a orange dhovti and a hot pink cloth that was draped loosely over his head, his well-oiled hair falling past his shoulders. The man started laughing. Both Veena and Brad stood up slowly and took a few steps backwards.

"If only you feared men as well as you fear snakes," the man said. "If only you liked snakes as much as you like men."

He laughed some more and then became quiet. Red and intense, his eyes focused on the ground.

"Ants," he said pointing to the grass.

Their eyes fell to the lush blades and spotted the shiny creatures busily marching along.

"Yes," whispered Veena.

"When they take off their black coats," he said in English and then completed the sentence in Hindi.

He turned around and began walking away, tapping his bamboo walking stick on the ground. They watched the last bit of his pink crown vanish into the forest.

"What did he mean by that?" Brad asked.

"I don't know, but it definitely wasn't Telugu," said Veena with conviction. "He looked kind of crazy, don't you think?"

"Let's go," said Brad, disturbed that the moment was broken on such an enigmatic note.

After eating a lunch of curried fish, they walked along Calangute Beach. They passed three men, one of whom was smoking a pipe. The other two were kneeling stupefied.

"Guten Tag," one of them called drowsily.

Brad and Veena nodded.

"What are they smoking?" she asked after they had walked on.

"I'm not sure. Maybe opium—something strong."

"I can't believe they're doing that out in the open," she said.

"Well, there's no one around to tell them they can't," he replied.

Veena scooped up some sand in her hand.

"It's white, but up close it's got these beautiful bronze bits."

He picked up a shell, looked at it and then threw it back into the ocean. There were some children playing up ahead, making cones out of the sand.

"Those kids are making lingams out of sand."

"And yonis," she said. "Cool."

"They're phallic symbols of the god of destruction. That's cool?"

"He is also the god of reproduction and fertility, remember," she countered. "And the yoni is Shakti or Siva personified as Parvati. I think it's beautiful."

"Okay, so we're talking penis worship here?" he said, smiling.

She gave him a look indicating that he should know better.

"Look, swings," she said, pulling him by the arm as she started veering to the left.

She sat down on the wooden seat and pushed off with her feet. He sat beside her and squeezed the sand between his toes.

"Wow! Brad, start swinging, close your eyes and then open them after a moment."

He did as she said and opened his eyes.

"Isn't it amazing? You feel like you're in some shitty park in New York and then when you open your eyes, you're sitting on the beach looking at the Arabian Sea."

"Yeah," he said, and she fell silent, continuing with her game.

The sun was striking the waves brilliantly, dusting them with what looked like crushed pewter. He could stare into it forever. Looking over at Veena, he saw that she had her eyes closed. Lately, he felt as if they were pulling and pushing into each other as the tide and shore. He watched some fishermen draw in a massive net. He could just hear their haunting chants. Two bare-breasted tribal girls, glass-beaded necklaces glinting in the sun, sauntered down the beach holding hands. He looked over at Veena who still had her eyes closed.

He remembered the fiasco with the Van Gogh umbrella. Early in their relationship, maybe about a few months into it, they had been browsing in the Metropolitan Museum of Art Store for Christmas and New Year's gifts. He had picked up a display umbrella with Van Gogh's *Starry Night* printed on it. He was just kidding around, but she responded enthusiastically to it.

"Oh, how pretty," she said.

"Yeah," he said and put the umbrella down.

Well, a year had passed before that misunderstanding was cleared up. That Christmas, she got him the *Starry Night* umbrella and he got her a *Starry Night* tote bag with a box of Impressionist notecards. Finally, when they were fighting over something trivial, it had all came out: She had hated that *Starry Night* umbrella from the start, and so had he.

"Well, why did you say it was pretty, then?" he had asked.

"I thought you liked it. Why do you think I pretended to like it? I didn't want to hurt your feelings."

"Do you see what happened? You pretended to like it, and you pretended to like the tote bag and the address book, too. Lies all lead to shit in the end."

"I didn't lie."

"Look, Veena. Just trust that you're not going to crush my little heart if you breathe the wrong way. Our relationship should be able to hold up even if you hated the umbrella and I loved it. Trust that we're stronger than that."

She appeared to be happy, but what was she really feeling inside? Was she just pretending again? In the sea breeze, her hair was fanning out behind her head like a peacock's plumes. He loved her so much. He wanted her to be happy. She opened her eyes. He smiled at her.

"What do you think he meant?" she asked.

"Who?"

"The man in the forest."

"I don't know. Maybe that fear of snakes and other creation points to fear of ourselves."

"Hmmm."

A stray dog paused by the water to bite at a flea.

"What do you want to do the rest of the day?" she asked, picking up momentum on the swing.

"I'd like to see St. Cajetan. It's modeled after St. Peter's Basilica in Rome."

117

"Okay," she agreed.

As she swung higher, one of her chappals flew off her foot and scared the dog, who limped off down the beach. Brad watched the ocean's tongues slowly lick at the sand lingams as a child savors an ice cream cone.

He breathed in deeply. There wasn't a smell of incense here as in the temples. It was different, cool and musty. It was familiar. He could smell the history, and the memories rushed back to him. He wondered if the handful of kneeling women and men were there to enjoy a respite from the heat. As he walked down the aisle, one of the women looked up at him. In her eyes, he saw something flicker. She was smiling although her lips did not move. She went back to praying.

Veena walked down the sides of the church, looking at the sculptures and stained glass. Brad thought how she always gravitated toward the artistic aspects of things. She was walking around as if this were a museum rather than a place of worship. She did not spend much time looking at the crucifix. He never liked looking at it either. He hated blood as a child. Standing in the center of the church, he looked up at the ceiling and found himself asking for things. He asked for peace and health. He asked for the success of their marriage. He prayed for Veena's happiness—that she would find what she was searching for. He prayed that he would be forgiven for not stepping foot in a church for over ten years.

"Did you know that generations of Portuguese rulers are buried in the crypt downstairs?" she asked as they pushed open the doors and walked into the sun.

"No," he said, squinting as he put on his sunglasses.

"I read it on a plaque over there. It said that thirty-two years after Affonso de Albuquerque set up Portuguese colonies on Goan shores, Saint Francis Xavier came as a Christian missionary and started converting the Hindus into Christians. That stuff really pisses me off."

Brad was not in the mood for this discussion. It had become

gusty and the wind was blowing up dust from the road.

"I think it's ludicrous to walk around thinking there is only one path to God," she continued. "It's such a self-righteous attitude."

"You don't think it's ludicrous to pray to an elephant?" he asked.

"And you don't think it's weird praying to a guy with bloody thorns around his head? It's such a violent image. That's not what I'm saying."

"What are you saying, Veena?"

"I just don't think it's right to go and force a strange religion on people. I mean how would you like it if the Indians came over to the coast of Maine and forced you to practice Hinduism. How would you feel praying to an elephant every day?"

"Weird. I already told you that," he snapped.

"What's the matter?"

"I just don't feel like dissecting the whole history of Christianity, that's all. Look at the crusades and the KKK—every scripture can be misused in regards to practice. It can be used to persecute instead of liberate. I know it; you know it."

He realized that though they were walking, he had no idea where to. He felt as if he was trying to get away from her and she was chasing him.

"Where are we going, anyway?" he asked, stopping short.

She turned him around by the shoulders and looked him in the eye.

"I'm sorry, Brad. I just realized you were in a church. I was being insensitive. Okay?"

She always demanded his forgiveness. She almost bullied him into it, at times. She couldn't stand the fact that he could be mad at her.

"Okay," he said and started walking again.

"Are you serving dinner?" he asked the hotel clerk.

"Yes, go ahead to the back, please," the clerk replied, looking up from his writing. "You know, the monsoon is expected tonight. You should probably stay inside."

"A monsoon?" Veena parroted.

"Yes, tonight. It is mostly wind, but the rain will come in the middle of the night—we hope."

"Thank you for letting us know," said Brad, and they walked into the back.

The restaurant was practically empty, probably because it was only five-thirty. They sat near a window overlooking the street. A waiter came over with a pitcher of water.

"No, thank you. Bring us a bottle of mineral water, please," Brad said, gesturing with his hands.

But the waiter finished pouring the water anyway.

"I want it all—I'm starving," Veena said, looking through the menu.

"Well, you can. It'll probably only come to thirty bucks tops if you did order one of everything."

"It's so incredibly cheap," she said, closing the menu.

They looked out on the street. A cow had decided to sit down in the middle of the road. The traffic stopped briefly and then continued, splitting around her.

"They call them brake inspectors," joked a different waiter as he opened the bottle of mineral water.

They laughed. The waiter had a large birthmark on his cheek.

"I will have this, number seven," Veena said, pointing to the item on the menu.

"I'll have number twelve, and some cutlery," he said.

"So, there is a monsoon coming," Veena said, probing for more information.

"Yes, we are expecting it tonight, but sometimes the monsoon turns back over the ocean," answered the waiter. "Sometimes the rain starts and stops. Sometimes there is too much and there are floods. Sometimes there is drought. It is unpredictable."

She nodded, and the waiter walked off, smiling broadly. Brad glanced at his wife and then looked out the window. He wanted to talk to her. He wanted to ask her why she was drifting away from him. The pretending was wearing him down. Maybe he hadn't wanted to come to India because he felt this would happen. He had a sickening feeling that their lives as they knew them were going to come to an end. He felt so different from her, and she felt so alien to him. But nothing was happening—that was the strange part. They weren't really fighting. There were no affairs. They were talking, discussing.

"It's so surreal here, isn't it?" she asked.

"How do you mean?"

"When you look around, you don't see what you normally expect. A cow in the middle of the road. I feel like I'm in a Dali painting."

He smiled. She was so enthusiastic. The waiter brought two bowls of spicy tomato soup and two sets of cutlery.

"Is that your fantasy?" he asked.

"What?"

"To be in a Dali painting?"

"Oh, I don't know. I like to be shook up. I feel so dead lately."

He blew on a spoonful of soup. He knew it. This was it. Had she fallen out of love with him?

"Spiritually, I feel dead," she clarified.

"So do you want to go live in an ashram?" he blurted because he couldn't wait for her to say it. "Because if you do, I just don't know if I could wait for you."

She dropped the spoon in her bowl.

"What? I don't want to live in an ashram. Not right now anyway."

Her brow furrowed. The waiter approached them with a serving tray on his shoulder. He put down plates of biryani, lamb, vegetable and lentil curries on the table. Veena dished some of the biryani onto her plate and began eating with her hand.

"Can we have another mineral water, please?" asked Brad, and the waiter nodded.

"Why couldn't you wait for me if I did?" she said as she pushed a small ball of rice and lentils into her mouth.

He looked out the window as if he hadn't heard her.

"Why is sex so important to you?" she said, her voice crackling.

"It's not that important to me," he said. "Mutual happiness is."

While he mixed the lamb curry and rice with his fork, she kicked her leg under the table.

"Look, I don't want you to think I'm unhappy with the marriage or with you," she said calmly. "I just think we can share so much more. We can make love on a spiritual level."

"Did you know there is a sect of Hindu swamis who eat human flesh?" he asked, a part of him not believing what was coming out of his mouth.

"What?" she asked, taken aback.

"I read about it on the plane. First, they eat their own feces and drink their own urine. Then they graduate to eating human flesh that they steal from funeral pyres—"

"God, Brad, we're eating here," she interrupted.

"When they get really good, they can eat raw human flesh, which means they steal bodies before they get burned or get lucky by finding a dead body in the middle of a field or something. Some of them even have sex with the dead bodies. Okay? Is that enlightenment?"

"I can't believe you believe that shit. It sounds like the Indian *National Enquirer* to me. Then again, maybe there are people who do that. What does that have to do with us?"

She pushed her plate away from her and sighed.

"It seems like you're so desperate to get enlightened," he said. "You want to catch up on all the culture you've missed growing up in New York. I feel like you're blaming me for missing out."

"Yeah, a part of me feels I've missed out. But I know that if I grew up here, I'd be a different person. And I *like* who I am."

"Do you like who I am?" he asked softly.

"Of course I do. Please, don't blow this all out of proportion. It's just that I really think we can grow. Don't you want to take it to the next level?"

"We're not talking about a video game here, Veena. I understand what you're saying, but how do we do that? Seeing you miserable doesn't make me feel good."

"I'm not miserable. I'm just questioning the way I live my life—

not with whom I live it."

"It just seems like you're questioning everything—including us."

"Sometimes, I am. But that's not necessarily a bad thing. That's how we change for the better. It's not like something is broken and we can just fix it."

A great sadness fell over him as he stared into her eyes.

"Look, I don't want you to do things you don't want to, but I want you to be more open-minded. That's all. I guess what I want is for us to admit that we don't have all the answers."

"You mean you want me to admit that," he said defensively.

She didn't answer right away. Instead, she picked up a shaker and studied the rice mixed in with the coarse salt granules. She shook some out on the table and felt their texture with her index finger.

"I just want us to look—*together,*" she said.

Brad wanted to retort, but his mind was suddenly blank. Together. They were husband and wife, and they were going to look together. Was that all she wanted? What was he panicking about anyway? There were no choices here. He loved Veena. He couldn't imagine his life without her. His eyes fell on her collarbone. The sun was hitting the silver necklace she had bought from a street vendor.

"Your neck—it's green from the necklace," he said.

"What?" she asked as her hand went to her neck. "He said it was pure silver."

"It's green."

She contorted her face, struggling to look at herself, but soon realized it was impossible. Brad laughed, and she soon joined in.

"I'm sorry, Veena," he said.

"Me, too," she said, reaching for his hand.

The waiter was walking over with another bottle of water, so they separated.

"I don't have all the answers," he said.

She smiled. They watched out the window as they ate. Outside, the merchants were filing by with baskets of dried fish, colorful flowers and several varieties of bananas. In the swirl of activity, they saw the mysterious man clothed in orange and pink making a beeline through the crowd as if on a mission. They looked at one another knowing that they had both seen him.

"Do you want to follow him?" she asked.

"Don't you?" he volleyed.

At that moment, the waiter brought over the check.

"Tell me, is there a saying that goes like this: When the ants take off their black coats," Brad asked him.

"When the ant takes off its black coat," the waiter repeated, not finishing the thought. "H*mmm*. When the ant takes off its black coat—I do not know. Sorry."

He refilled their glasses with the mineral water and walked to another table. Brad and Veena looked at each other for a moment and burst into laughter.

The Lovers

Tara sat with her suitcase between her knees. She looked at the station clock. It was seven o'clock. Would Aamir come? Of course he would, she assured herself. They were in love. She looked at the passengers boarding the train waiting on the track. It would be leaving for Tirupati in ten minutes. She looked at the tickets she was holding in her clammy hand. Destination: Hyderabad. Time: 20:10.

Tara tucked her sandaled feet closer to the suitcase as a woman swept the floor. The dirt billowed up and surrounded the woman, but she did not seem to notice. She continued to sweep, hunched over with her left hand behind her back. Tara breathed into her embroidered handkerchief. Some would say this woman was one of the lucky ones—one who nabbed a government job. Some would say she was one of the lazy people who sucked the government dry like leeches. She watched the woman sweep the pile of papers, peanut shells and other garbage over the edge of the platform and onto the tracks. When she turned around, Tara smiled at her, but she did not smile back.

Tara fanned herself with the tickets. It was exceptionally hot. The noisy fans did not help in the least. She was glad they had gotten an AC/Sleeper. By the dawn, she and Aamir would begin their new lives.

"Train 0789 on track three leaving for Bangalore in five minutes," the man announced.

His voice was barely audible with the static of the microphone and the train engine growling in front of her. She looked at the clock again. This was the first time she would be traveling without her father or mother. They had gone to Madras occasionally to visit her mother's sister. And there was that one time when a friend of her father's was visiting from the States.

Her father's friend had expressed interest in going to the Ellora Caves. So, they made a special trip there by car. She was about fifteen years old at the time. It was the rainy season, so not too many other people were there. The Hindu, Jainist and Buddhist temples and caves were elaborately carved right into the mountainsides, with long sets of crooked steps leading up to the separate enclaves. She liked it because, as her parents and the visitor walked beneath umbrellas through the mist, she got to wander around through a wonderland of goddesses, gods, saints, Buddhas and bodhisattvas. Almost all of the friezes and statues had arms, legs, trunks and other pieces missing. There were headless gods and earless, trunkless elephants. She walked ahead, passing a giant sculpture of the lovers, Siva and Parvati. Their noses were broken off, their faces marred.

"Look at this, such a terrible shame," she heard her mother remark. "It breaks my heart."

"How could they be so vicious?" asked the visitor.

"They" were the Muslims. They had desecrated the Hindu temples.

"They are cruel, angry people," answered her mother matter-of-factly. "Look. The poor elephant."

Tara rolled her eyes and lost them in the curve of the grassy mountain. She climbed the stone steps. Her pulse quickened as she ventured into the darkness of the caves. She did not have a flashlight, and it was hard to see. A "tour guide" tendered to walk with her and illuminate the statues, carvings and ceiling paintings. He held a piece of a broken mirror in his hands. She told him that she could manage. He did not stand and watch her, but instead walked off. He probably hoped she would become frightened and decide to give him the fifteen rupees. But she went on ahead alone.

She sighed, breathing in the mustiness. It was odd that although there were no doors to speak of and each of the temples and caves had several openings, the crisp mountain air did not blow through here. The camera knocked against her stomach as she walked. She paused to look at a wall carving of a devi holding her lover from behind. Her breasts were pressing into his back as they embraced. The stone was weatherworn and felt smooth under her fingers. It looked as if they were dancing, or as if they were making love. Tara took a photo. The flash lit up the entrance to another cave.

Gossamer kissed her face as she entered the smaller cave. Was it the spiders she was smelling? She accidentally touched the walls with her hand. They felt strange. She could barely see at all. It was such a deep cave. She picked up her camera and pressed. The shutter clicked, and the flash illuminated an enormous carving of Parvati. There were bats hanging against the walls and from the ceiling. She held the camera away from her face this time and lit up the cave again. Parvati was beautiful.

"Tara!"

Her mother's voice startled her, and she became disoriented. Red spots from the flash danced before her eyes.

"Tara!"

As she walked out, bats flew out of the cave and toward the silhouette of her mother, who was standing with her hands on her hips in the arched entrance. Her mother screamed when she saw the bats and swatted her hands at them. They glided into darkness.

"Do not be so scared, Amma. They are just bats."

Her mother grabbed her by the arm.

"Why are you always running off and worrying me so? I was scared to death!" Then more calmly, "Come on now."

As they made their way down, a sunbeam burst through a rain cloud.

"It is raining again," her mother grumbled.

"To complain of such a refreshing shower in the monsoon season is foolish," her father warned, and her mother scowled in silence.

When Tara looked back, she saw two goats, one black and one white, munching grass high on the mountainside. The light shower sprinkled down on them, too. But they, like Tara, did not seem to mind.

She had always wanted to go back to the caves. And when she told Aamir about them, he, too, had seemed excited.

A man waddled by, carrying a bag. He paused for a moment to hike his dhovti between his legs.

"Hurry up, move, move," he barked, looking behind him.

His wife was trying to keep up. Could he not see that? She did not want to miss the train either. Tara hated it when men talked to their wives as if they owned them. She glared at the man as he stood on the steps of the train waiting impatiently for his wife. He did not give her a hand up. In fact, as soon as he saw that she would make it, he headed for the compartment. As Tara watched him through the open windows, he pushed the suitcase under the seat and sat down. His wife eventually joined him as the train began to move. He must have felt eyes upon him, because he looked right at Tara. As the train picked up speed, they stared at each other through the metal bars. She hoped he felt her disgust.

Looking into the blur of the train, she thought about her own life. She had never wanted to feel imprisoned by her culture, but she always had. These identities and roles that were already nicely sketched out for women and men were ridiculous. She remembered when she had asked her father for money to start a women's shelter last year.

"What? That is none of your business," he said. "Never get in between a husband and his wife or his children. Understand?"

No, she did not. She hated that she could not go out to the movies alone, could not take a moonlight walk alone, could not do anything alone except daydream and read in her room. If she were married, then that would be different. But, then again, who said her husband would have the same interests? Looking back at the clock, she watched the second hand revolve and realized this was the first time she had been alone in public at sunset in a long while. She was usually helping her mother in the kitchen or reading in her room. Sometimes, she watched the sun set from the roof veranda. She felt so lonely up there lately.

As a teaboy ran by and stirred the languid air, she welcomed the breeze. She felt as if she were breathing in everyone's exhalations. Turning her head slowly, she glanced at the man leaning against a column. He had been staring at her for some time now. What was he looking at her for? Had her mother found out she was not studying with Divya? She remembered a newspaper story she had read last month.

> The daughter of a Congress functionary was kidnapped after her court marriage to a Hindu youth of her choice and smuggled into Kashmir, where she was forcibly married to a Muslim. Indian authorities inquired, but were consistently told the woman was dead.

She turned and looked the man in the eye. After about ten seconds, he looked away and walked over to the cool-drink stand.

A small boy in knickers and suspenders walked up to her.

"Hello, there," she said.

His mother pulled him back onto her lap as she sat down next to her. Then she handed him a biscuit, which he nibbled on, resting his small shoe on Tara's suitcase. She thought back to when she and Aamir were little. The roofs on top of their three-story houses had been their playpens. Once, he had tossed her a plastic gun across the low wall, and she had tossed him a stuffed puppy toy.

Then one day, Aamir told her to close her eyes. They were about six years old, she calculated. She waited and felt something hit her on the arm. She looked down. An orange and pink rose lay at her feet. As she reached for it, she saw his feet in front of her. She slowly looked up at him. He had joined their two roofs with a wooden plank. She broke into a big smile as she sniffed the rose. That day, they played marbles. She beat him, but he was not upset. The next day, they decided to play dress up. She took a sari from the clothesline and wrapped him up in it. Then she combed his hair and stuck a waxy gardenia behind his ear. He looked as if he were a little king with that mound of purple cloth shrouding him. She was just about to put a bottu on his forehead when her mother walked onto the roof.

"Tara!"

The shout made her arm jerk, causing the kumkum to smear. She handed Aamir the mirror.

"Tara! Get inside right now!"

She stood up as he looked at himself.

"Go! You, too. Go back home now."

When Aamir stood, the sari slid down and fell at his feet. He carefully stepped out of it and walked across the plank. Her mother took the wood down and held it up at her side, vertically like a door. Aamir looked at Tara from the wall and smiled. He still had the gardenia behind his ear.

Tara smiled to herself at the memory. Just then, the boy beside her put a half-eaten biscuit on her lap.

"Why, thank you," she said.

His mother tapped his hand, and he took the biscuit back. As Tara looked up from his wet, glossy eyes, she noticed the strange man was back. He was looking at her again. What was his problem? Where was Aamir? Her mind flashed.

Riots broke out in Srinagar in Kashmir when a Pandit girl married a Muslim after converting to Islam.

The little boy kicked her leg.

"Bharat!" his mother scolded.

After her mother had caught her on the roof with Aamir, she would not let Tara play there unattended. The servant watched her, or her mother sat there sifting through rice or lentils for stones.

"You are Hindu, Tara," her mother said, pointedly. "That boy is not Hindu. You cannot play with him."

"Why?"

"Cats do not play with dogs, do they?"

Tara shook her head and drew on the roof with chalk. She drew a picture of her and Aamir in a garden of flowers. Her mother did not tell her it was a nice drawing.

"Look, Amma," Tara said, pointing.

She looked at it, sliding her glasses off her nose, but still she did not speak.

When Tara was about eight, she walked home with Aamir after school each day. Her mother had paid a rickshaw driver to drop her off and pick her up at school. Tara went to school in the rickshaw, but she always walked home. One day, she and Aamir wandered into the tar pits and she got some of the black goo on her frock and knees. Her mother tugged her around the house by her ear, while her father gave the rickshaw driver a slap for not bringing his daughter safely home. She found out later that Aamir's father had given him a terrible beating.

Now, the man was pretending to read a newspaper. She looked at him, but he would not meet her eyes. Her mind raced: What if Aamir's parents had discovered their plans? What if her mother had gone to Divya's house and discovered Tara wasn't there after all? What if Aamir's parents sent him away and she never heard from him again? Could she go on? She could not see her life without him. She closed her eyes, and a picture filled her mind: It was Aamir being beaten by his father. As the pain seized her, she stood up abruptly. When her head cleared, she sat back down. Her thoughts drifted back again.

She had taught Aamir how to climb a coconut tree. He was making the mistake of trying to use his thighs rather than gripping his feet on the trunk. They would race up the tree and she would always catch him. But by the time Tara had turned thirteen, they had stopped climbing trees; in fact, they had stopped playing together completely. He never had time to see her, and since she had started menstruating, she was suddenly considered a woman. Her playtime consisted of sitting with neighborhood girls, making stupid faces at a baby. What was wrong with them? Why did they want babies so badly? What was wrong with her?

She and Aamir met in their secret ways, but it was rarely in person. It had become impossible for them to meet in public. Over the past couple of weeks, she even had to restrain herself from meeting with her best friend, Divya. Divya's mother was always suspicious, and Divya herself was not such a smooth liar when her mother cornered her with questions. It seemed their parents had spies all over Guntur. They never felt safe.

"You cannot lock me up forever," she had told her mother. "You are going to have to trust me sometime."

After her mother was sure she and Aamir had grown apart, she again let Tara sleep on the roof on especially hot nights. Tara smiled when the memory of one of those special nights came to her: She had been lying on a straw mat, staring at the constellations, when she felt rain on her face. She sat up and began rolling her mat up, but then she saw the night jasmine flowers sprinkled on the roof.

"Aamir?" she whispered.

"Yes. I am here."

She tossed a flower back to him.

"Good night," he said.

"Good night."

On her neck, she felt the coolness of the jasmine buds slipping from her hair. The man watched as she took out the pin and refastened them to her braid. She closed her eyes.

After a low-caste college lecturer from Bihar married a Brahmin girl, he was made to disappear and his wife was forced to commit suicide.

Suicide? Could Aamir's parents do that? Could hers? She opened her eyes, and train 8976 to Hyderabad was pulling into the station. She looked for the man, but he was gone. She looked at the clock. Seven-forty-five. Where was Aamir? What was she going to do if he did not come in time? Did they catch him? What could have gone wrong? Frantic, she started fanning herself with the tickets again. Her parents were in the midst of interviewing prospective matches for her marriage. Did he change his mind? If he did not show, then she would go ahead without him. There was no turning back now.

Clusters of passengers stood waiting to board the train. She stood up to stretch her legs. One of the tickets dropped out of her hand and fell on the ground. A hijra scampered by and stepped on it. She lunged forward to get it before it was kicked farther away from her. As her fingers reached for it, she saw someone was standing in front of her. Black shoes and pinstripe pants.

"Aamir!" she said, trying hard not to throw her arms about him.

Looking into his brown eyes, she had never wanted to kiss him more than right then, but she had to resist because it wasn't a proper thing to do in public. They certainly didn't need any more attention drawn to them.

She could feel his warm breath against her cheek as he bent down and reached for her bag. He took a deep breath, and she knew he smelled the flowers in her hair. The buds had opened, and their sweet fragrance swirled around them.

"I can manage," she said picking up her suitcase.

Delivery

Kishore watched the sacrifice. He did not make a move to stop them. He remembered when he was seven, he had done it, too. It was only fair. Slapping a foot up against the wall, he took out a crumpled cigarette from the front pocket of his tattered khaki shirt. The younger boys were piling over each other to toss their ingredient into the giant mortar. There was a huge crack in the stone, and it was the latest addition to the plot of government land that was serving as a garbage pit and their playground. Pink worms, white spiders, fire ants, water bugs and a lizard's tail. Kishore stared at the glistening creatures crawling maniacally to escape. All were alive except for the flies and mosquitoes. They were hard to catch alive. Brown hands jutted in and out of the mortar, knocking the creatures down into the pit. Someone tossed in pieces of bottle glass. The lizard's tail was still wiggling.

"Do you see it? It's still moving!" yelped Bindu, the most skittish of the gang.

Kishore remembered his mother had told him why the tail kept moving after detachment from the body. The lizard sits motionless nearby, waiting. The tail squirms, distracting the predator. At just the right moment, the lizard runs like a streak of lightning and is gone.

"Come on," said one boy.

"Do it!" yelled another.

The biggest boy of them all, Rama, lifted the pestle high in the air and brought it down, crushing, grinding, pounding. Someone threw in a rotting, fleshy guava fruit. The boys cheered, unified by the mass execution. Kishore walked off, flicking his cigarette butt. He knew they would stop soon. He knew they would see how much they themselves as orphans were like those insects. Then they would stop.

At sixteen, Kishore stood out from the weedy lot he ran with. His skin was a rich coffee color and his teeth were like milk. He was always putting oil in his hair and combing it to keep it clean and shiny. He cursed only now and then, and he was the best at shooting marbles. He also spoke the best English. Sometimes he would read to the others from the book he had found on the top sleeping berth on a train headed for Calcutta. It was a medieval romance novel called *The Wolf and the Swan*.

Victoria knew that the moment her eyes met his, her life would change. She tossed and turned with those green embers seared in her mind, his name on the tip of her tongue. What was his name? Did he see the world as she did? She knew by the way he looked at her that he did. She couldn't explain what she was feeling. This man was known throughout the land for his ruthless slayings. She couldn't find an explanation to quiet her stirring. She longed for another look, another chance.

Kishore would skip over the big words, but he got the gist of the plot. The others would ask questions, and he would try to explain in Telugu. What he did not know, he made up. After all, it was just a story.

◆

The sun was starting to dip into the river. The laundry women plucked the saris from the warm rocks, folded them and bundled them up in lunghees. Heaving the blooming baskets onto their heads, they made their way back to town. Kishore weaved through the traffic of pedestrians, rickshaws and autos. Everyone was yelling and honking horns. Over the clamor of engines and vendors' squawks, Kishore heard the rumbling of his stomach. All he had eaten since daybreak was a handful of finger bananas and a mango. The deep-fried aroma of samosas turned his tongue to honey. A boy in a convent uniform waited for his after-school treat. His blue and white uniform, starched and bright, made him look like a doll. They stared at each other, and in the boy's eyes, Kishore saw a flash of fear, then contempt. Did this scrap think Kishore was going to knock him down and steal his samosas? Did he look that ravenous? They both watched the vendor fill a newspaper funnel with the vegetable turnovers. Before the grease had started to soak through the paper, the boy snatched the package and hopped aboard a cycle rickshaw that was waiting for him. He sat with his feet dangling from the open back of the rickshaw as it pulled away. When he thought he was at a safe distance, the boy opened the steaming newspaper and bit into a samosa. He smiled victoriously and waved at Kishore through the crowd. For a second, Kishore thought of chasing after the rickshaw, which was not going very fast, and teaching the brat a lesson. But he was too tired.

"If you are not going to buy anything, get moving, boy," ordered the vendor.

As Kishore started walking away, the vendor scratched under his turban and filled another paper funnel for a customer.

The sun was going down unusually fast today. The packed dirt road was even a little cool on Kishore's bare feet. He decided to run home the rest of the way.

Hissing, a train snaked toward the moon. Fashioned from pieces of plastic, paper and other refuse, the track-side tents shimmered in the nightglow. It was a wonder how he remembered which tent was theirs, since they all looked alike in the dark. He stepped in something wet and wondered if it was cow shit. The smell of fermenting fruit and vegetables and polluted sewage was everywhere, so it was hard to tell without light. He hoped it was not human shit because the smell was harder to get rid of. When he walked in a puddle, he stopped and rinsed off his feet. Sometimes, the stench embedded in the soil was not washed away even by the rain.

Walking past a man urinating on the tracks, he continued to the tent. Rama, who was tending the fire outside, greeted him by proudly pointing out the yams he had stolen.

"Good," said Kishore. "I have started chewing on my own tongue."

He could already hear the boys were in a raucous mood inside. Parting the flap of blue vinyl, he ducked in. Just then Bindu, the youngest at nine, came crashing into the tent, his arms embracing a large pink box.

"Look what I got!" he roared.

The boys' irritation quickly evaporated at the sight of the box, on which was written Andhra Sweet Shop.

"How did you manage it?" asked Kishore.

"It fell into my lap from the heavens," joked Bindu, and they laughed.

Bindu placed the box down and lifted the cover carefully to reveal luscious sweets—giant butter and dahl laddoos, orange pretzel-shaped jilabee and halva. Everyone snatched their favorites.

"Save me something!" squealed Rama, who walked in with some charred yams on a piece of cardboard. "The next batch is still cooking."

"God, sweet and sweet—now I am craving a hot pepper bhaji!" said Gandeev, licking his lips.

Sitting in a circle, the boys ate and exchanged stories about their day's adventures of playing pranks and thieving. Two of the boys had snuck into the cinema, and they proceeded to act out a love scene from the film.

"Oh, Prasad."

"Oh, Lakshmi."

They bellowed with laughter. One of them kissed the air as the other narrated. There was silence. When the breeze blew the flap of the tent open, Kishore could see the fire reflected in their eyes.

"Then their lips came together, wet and warm, eyes closed."

Gandeev, the instigator of the bunch, stood up.

"It is not like that at all. It is not lips coming together, but mouths."

He picked up a laddoo and locked his lips around it, gently sucking the sweetness.

"You've had plenty of practice on the neighborhood pigs, *eh*?" quipped Rama.

The tent filled with snorting noises as the boys laughed and slapped Gandeev on the back. Kishore got up to check on the fire, which was now a small heap of red and copper. Bending down, he brushed the ants off a yam chunk and popped it in his mouth. In a nearby tent, a woman sang a soothing song to quiet a crying baby. He wondered about his own mother. Did she sing like that to him? Would the sight of her son eating off the ground fill her heart with anger or sadness?

Climbing over tangled limbs, Kishore crawled from the tent, which was melting from the hot sun. Bindu was already up and entertaining himself by drawing a goddess in the dirt with a stick.

"Where are you going?" asked Bindu.

Kishore shrugged, and he tagged along. It was a silly question because there was nowhere and everywhere to go. There was no one to tell them to go to school or send them on an errand or check that they had washed the backs of their necks and behind their ears. Sometimes it felt like freedom, and sometimes it felt like prison.

As they walked into the village, they passed open tiffin halls filled with men eating idli, dosai, puri and vada on banana leaves. Kishore remembered his mother sending his older brother, Nikhil, to the government banana grove to steal leaves for meals. He would go along and enjoy the silent walk. Nikhil had never talked very much. Kishore's questions were usually answered just by watching him. A man dumped some water from his glass onto the banana leaf and wiped it clean with his hand. The droplets that clung to the green made Kishore think of home.

"You see, we eat the bananas, and the leaves we use for plates—the Creator does not waste anything," his mother's voice echoed in his mind.

Kishore felt his throat tighten as he thought how senselessly his mother's life came to an end. What was the purpose of her death? And what was the purpose of his life?

They washed up at a public water pump. Nearby, a sow nursed her young.

"Kish?" began Bindu. "How come you did not kill the bugs in the mortar the other day?"

"I didn't want to."

"Did you ever want to?"

"Yes, a long time ago."

"When did you stop?"

"I got sick and almost died when I was nine. My mother took me to the clinic, and I got an injection. After that, I decided that I didn't want to do that anymore."

As they walked down the road, Kishore picked up a half-smoked cigarette off the ground. He lit it, took a drag and handed it to Bindu.

On a deserted stretch of Bandar Road, they came across a lorry smashed into a tree. Kishore wondered if it had anything to do with the upcoming elections. It was not unlikely for lorry drivers who were so committed to their candidates to crash their speeding trucks into each other in a mindless dare. Was it loyalty or childishness? Did they cast their votes before they died? Fortunately, the driver here was fine. Bricks were strewn all over the road. There was a traffic jam, and people were agitated.

"We'll help you," said Kishore to the distraught driver, who was

139

cursing those honking their horns.

Within five minutes, the bricks were collected and stacked back onto the lorry. The driver thanked Kishore and Bindu and gave them a ten-rupee bill.

As they walked away, Bindu could hardly contain himself.

"I cannot believe he gave us ten rupees!" he screeched. "Do you think he made a mistake and thought it was a one-rupee bill? Kish, when are we going to split it?"

"Do not worry so much, Bindu," assured Kishore. "Let us break it here."

They walked up to a drink shop. The dust on the road had coated Kishore's throat, and he wanted to blow his whole share on ice-cold drinks—maybe a soda and a glass of almond milk.

"Could you give us two fives, sir?" asked Kishore.

The man looked at the bill in the sunlight as if it were fake. Then he handed him two ragged five-rupee notes. One of them was torn, which was probably why the man agreed to do it in the first place. For some reason, it was always difficult getting people to take a torn bill. Kishore handed Bindu the better of the two fives.

"What are you going to get, Kish? Should we tell the others?"

"It is your money, Bindu. Do what you will with it."

"Maybe I will get some idli," he said.

Just then, the proprietor put a help wanted sign in the window. Kishore could not believe his luck!

"Sir?" he asked excitedly. "I would like the job."

"I do not hire beggars," he replied, looking them up and down.

"I am not a beggar," said Kishore.

The man opened a Thums Up and tipped his head back. Kishore could see his tongue through the opening of the clear bottle.

"I will need a five-rupee deposit for security," said the man.

When Kishore handed him back the torn bill, the man's brow twitched with annoyance, but he did not say anything. He handed him a wire rack with six glasses of hot tea.

"What are you waiting for?" his new boss snapped. "Go, go. Sell them while they're still hot."

◆

For every glass of tea, Kishore would collect one rupee, twenty paise of which were his to keep. He walked out slowly toward the incoming train so as not to spill the tea or break the glasses. A broken glass would cost him one rupee. Working steadily for five days, he collected an average of three rupees a day. He gave five rupees of the fifteen to the boys for food. As long as the tea was piping hot, his customers were happy. On the sixth day, his boss said he wanted to promote him. He was to deliver cold drinks and soda to the houses in the village. He would get to keep any tips. Kishore was glad not to have to push through the crowded trains and worry about breaking any glasses. Bottles of soda and cold drinks were much easier to carry.

He left to deliver his first order—two Gold Spots, one Thums Up and two Limcas to a fancy house around the corner. He waited in the yard as the family guzzled the drinks. Peering into a bedroom, he was riveted by the shelves of books and photographs. It must be a very big family. At his next delivery stop, he saw a letter on the floor. He cocked his head to the side to read the return address. It was from the States! Just then, the servant returned with the empty bottle and sent him on his way. Kishore caught a glimpse of a woman, maybe four years or so older than he, gliding toward the veranda. She was dressed in a royal purple sari bordered with parrots. She had the most graceful hands he had ever seen. He was so swept up in watching her that he nearly fell over backwards. Ears hot, he burst through the back-gate door. Standing against the plaster wall, he took deep breaths until his heart slowed.

Over the next week, try as he could, Kishore could not shake the vision of beauty he had witnessed. He became friendly with the servant, Priya, and learned the woman's name was Divya, meaning divine. What a fitting name, Kishore thought. Priya also told him that Divya was promised to a doctor. Every day, as he inched closer to handing the Gold Spot to Divya himself, the sharp claws of hopelessness sank deeper into his heart.

Later that week, after making a delivery, Kishore learned from Priya that Divya was leaving for America the next day. What could he do now? She was going to leave Guntur for the States. Forever. A meeting between the two of them was impossible. Kishore looked down at his filthy knickers. What would a goddess want with a pauper? Nothing. Nothing at all. The answer echoed in his head until he was tempted to vanish. He ran and ran until he collapsed under a tree.

The next day, he awoke to a sweet bouquet mixed with pain. A woman had pushed a cart piled high with jasmine garlands over his foot. He stood up and patted the dust from his clothing. His cool skin drank in the rays drizzling from the apricot sphere in the cloudless sky. The goats by the roadside, the drunks behind the tobacco shop, the school girls with ribboned pigtails crammed into rickshaws, the men in silk lalchees and the swami on the riverbank were all bathed in a tranquil tenderness. It was a day just as any other day, laced with rude and blissful awakenings. With this realization budding, Kishore started walking.

At the drink shop, the boss paced. When Kishore opened the door, the bell on the door jingled.

"Where were you?" growled his boss.

"Forgive me, sir, but I—" Kishore began.

"It is no excuse! You will go back to selling tea."

Kishore did not speak up because he thought it was probably all for the better. Seeing the richness of some people made him feverish and turned his stomach. It just made his own life all the more difficult. He picked up his rack of glasses and was heading out the door, when a car horn honked outside the shop. His boss signaled for him to see what the commotion was about.

As he approached the driver, he noticed the luggage tied to the roof. The driver asked for a Thums Up and a Gold Spot. Kishore tried to see who was in the back seat, but the windows were dark. He re-trieved the drinks and walked back to the car. The driver was light-ing a cigarette. Kishore opened the Thums Up and handed it to the driver. As the driver walked around to the other side of the car, Kish-ore opened the Gold Spot. He watched breathlessly as the window lowered. As light splashed in, Kishore saw Divya's delicate hand break through, reaching toward him. He handed her the bottle, standing with his legs apart and his arms stiff, anchored by the sight of her. He could just see her lips, the color of coral one would find in the most secret of reefs. He stood there and wished she would drink more slowly or maybe want another one. In seconds, the or-ange fizzy pop was gone. She leaned forward and held the empty bottle out the window. And Kishore saw her face for the very first time. She was even more beautiful than he had imagined. As his hand moved toward hers ever so slowly, their fingers touched. How soft she was! As their eyes met, her lips curved upward like a cres-cent moon. She was actually smiling at him. The driver started the engine and began to drive away. Kishore stood motionless as he saw her brightness eclipsed by the rising window.

"Damn lazy fellow!" muttered his boss.

Kishore stared vacantly at the car.

As Kishore shuffled toward the train tracks, the rack jostled and tea splattered his legs. Numbly, he waded through the crowds. Some-one pulled on his arm. It was Bindu.

"Hello, Kish."

Kishore nodded, and Bindu tagged along beside him.

"Where have you been?" Bindu said.

"Can't you tell I am busy? Do you think I want to spend the rest of my life in that stinking tent?"

Bindu stopped short. As Kishore continued on, he felt the strength drain from his body. His legs felt like jelly, and he remem-bered when his brother Nikhil had walked away from him. Turning around he walked back to Bindu.

"Come on, let us ride the trains for fun," said Kishore, and Bindu's face lightened.

They entered a vacant sleeping car and sat down. As the train started to move, the rainbow of activity on the platform smeared into the blue of sky and the green of the rice fields. They could hear the voice of the ticket collector coming closer.

"Could you read to us from the book later?" asked Bindu.

Kishore nodded and handed Bindu a glass of tea. It was still hot. Kishore touched the glass to his lips and let the warmness fill him.

Hijra

Seshu walked up the stairs to the cheap hotel, a few blocks from Andhra's Sweet Shop on Besant Road. He tossed the bags on the bed and turned on the fan. The sun was white and hot. He poured some water from the dirty plastic pitcher into his mouth. Wetting his handkerchief, he wiped his face and neck. The balcony door was open, but the room was still stuffy. He looked at the sheer cotton sari that hung lifelessly in the portal to block out the blinding light.

Stretching out on the bed, he thought about what he had to do. He probably would be home by about eleven o'clock that night. Reaching in the bag, he took out the detonating device. It would set off the bomb five minutes after it was activated. What time would ensure that B. T. Sankarani got the scare of his life? What time would be the perfect time? According to his official itinerary, Sankarani would be leaving Vijayawada and going back to Hyderabad this evening on train 8976, leaving at 20:10. A friend at the railway station had secured the ticket for Seshu, and he would be sitting in the compartment beside the corpulent politician and his guards.

Seshu wasn't sure if the bomb would actually kill someone, but he knew it would certainly cause some damage. He wanted the old bastard to realize he had made a mistake when he spouted all that nonsense about the dwindling power of the Dravidian Youth Force. He wanted Sankarani's heart to leap into his throat and choke him. He reset the detonator clock to three minutes. That would give him enough time to get off the train. Justice in India would be delivered by their hands. Tonight, they were going to show all of Andhra Pradesh and Tamil Nadu just how powerful the DYF could be and make sure they knew that their demand for Dravidistan was to be taken seriously. They spoke for millions of aboriginal peoples of peninsular India who wanted their independence because of past and present oppression by northern Aryans, who were still forcing their pathetic concept of "civilization" on them. The Dravidians had been enslaved many centuries ago because of their darker skin. The prejudice was still in full effect, and it was up to the DYF to abolish it once and for all. Tonight, they were going to take back the power that was lying in the hands of old fools who loved strutting from state to state in silks and khadi. They wanted to pulverize the pompous film stars who thought they could run a nation because they could lip synch to songs on the screen. How could they be so blind to the infiltration of western ethics that were driving a stake through India's heart?

He dumped the rest of the contents of the bag onto the bed. Out fell an olive and yellow sari with peacocks. It was a nice pattern. He smiled as he held up the green jacket and remembered his conversation with Trinadh.

"I am telling you, the jacket will fit you only," Trinadh had cooed. "My chest is much too broad and, you know, my mother is not that fat."

So, it was decided that Seshu was the one who would dress up as a woman and plant the bomb on the train. It was the perfect disguise. The hijras were an accepted part of society and were seen milling about smoking in groups on the streets. He remembered looking at the hijras with fascination when he was little. It was rumored that some of them were prostitutes and that was looked down upon. But the fact that they wore women's saris was not astonishing or considered terribly abnormal. Seshu had agreed to do it if the others held their tongues, and they all promised they would not rib him.

It was five o'clock. He stood up and began unbuttoning his shirt. Suddenly, explosions hammered the silence, and Seshu fell back on the bed, covering his head with his arms. In the next second, he realized it was just firecrackers. He walked onto the narrow balcony and looked down. A funeral procession was passing. An old man's body adorned with flowers was being carried in the traditional style on seven steps made of raw wood. Seshu took out a pack of Charminars from his pocket and lit one. At the head of the cavalcade, carrying the pot of fire, was a young woman. That's odd, he thought—it was the duty of the eldest son if the father had died, and of the youngest son if the mother had died. Under no circumstances should a woman lead the procession. He laughed out loud. The woman had short hair and a loose gait. He knew she did not live in India. Suddenly, his laughter gave way to anger. She was bringing her ridiculous western ideas to the homeland, and these fools were letting her turn their world upside-down.

The men set down the body at the intersection of the two streets and showered the corpse with popcorn kernels to ward off ghost-souls that might inhabit the shell. They stopped at every crossroad, waiting for a moment to make sure the old man was really dead and would not suddenly spring back to life. Why did they hold onto silly superstitions and discard solid traditions? Did this woman have any idea how ridiculous she looked? Everyone was laughing at her. Again, some children set off fireworks to alert the village that someone of importance had died. Seshu flicked his cigarette down on the roof of a passing car and watched it smolder.

He wondered what would flash in Sankarani's mind when he felt the heat of the fire on his face. He had behaved so poorly in the past year that he probably would not have a clear idea which of his enemies had got to him. Would any of his precious guards throw themselves over his body to shield him from the explosion? Probably not. By the time they were checking the old man's charred wrists for a pulse, Seshu would be in a car on his way back to Vijayawada. He was excited by their plan. The DYF needed this to set the record straight. They would not be ignored any longer.

The procession was drawing people out from their houses. Children climbed walls to have a look at death, and adults solemnly peered into the creeping cars at mourners. The dead man was bathed and dressed in new silk clothing. It was necessary for the body to be purified before it was sacrificed to Agni, the god of fire. After they reached the open fields of the cremation grounds, the woman holding the fire would walk around the body three times, break a water pot at the body's head and then ignite the head. Sometimes, if the family was wealthy, pieces of sandalwood were burned with the body. After the corpse had completely burned to ash, they would walk away without ever looking back again. Then, the few immediate relatives that had actually witnessed the cremation would bathe and indulge in a delicious feast the women had been preparing all day at home. Death of the body was briefly mourned, and then the eternal life of the soul was celebrated. Seshu wondered, if the bomb killed Sankarani, what kind of funeral he would have and if there would be a large turnout. If he was killed, would people want to find the culprits and hang them? Or would they shake their heads for a day, forget all about the movie has-been and secretly hail the DYF as heroes? Soon, they would find out.

Walking back inside, Seshu tossed his shirt on the bed and stepped out of his pants. He looked at his naked body in the mirror. Tucking his penis and testicles in between his legs, he stroked the triangle of pubic hair. The mirror was warped and made him look wavy and more feminine. Trinadh's girlfriend, Pankaja, had given him some chunnis—the long scarves with which college women hid the curve of their breasts when they wore salwar-kameez outfits. The brightly colored silks would trail in the breeze seductively as beauties sped by on scooters. He draped a canary-colored chunni over his shoulders and wrapped a deep orange one about his waist. The chiffon was cool against his overheated skin. Through the sheer fabric, it looked as if he really were female. Someone knocked on the door, and Seshu pulled the scarves off of himself as if they were snakes. He glanced at the door. It was bolted.

"What?" he snapped.

"Chai?" someone called back.

"No."

Seshu waited for the voice to fade. He pulled the petticoat about himself and tied the strings at his waist. It was a bit short, but that would be fine since it was just an undergarment. He tried on the jacket and hooked it in the front. After stuffing the chunnis into the breast cups, he unceremoniously grabbed at the softness and admired his work in the mirror. As he shook the sari, the bulk of the material fell around his feet. He began slowly winding it around him. Pankaja had taught him how to wrap one properly, and he had practiced several times with her. After he tucked the pleats in the front at his waist, he flipped the pallu over his left shoulder. Sitting down on a stool, he fastened the fake hair attachment to his shaggy hair and pinned up the long ponytail into a bun. That was the style in which most hijras wore their hair. After shaving the stubble off his face, he applied katika, powder and a red bottu. He clipped on silver teardrop earrings and a cheap necklace. The final touch was a pair of glittery, but worn-out chappals. He tested them out. They were easy enough to walk in. Standing up on the bed, he surveyed himself from head to toe. He looked convincing as a woman, but not too convincing. Although he was small, the lean muscles of his arms and back were straining against the jacket cloth.

Carrying a small bag with his clothes and shoes, Seshu snuck out the back of the hotel unnoticed by the clerk. Andhra's Sweet Shop was within walking distance. Trinadh's family owned the shop, and he was arranging for the bomb to be planted in a cake. His family had no idea what was happening. He did not want them to be involved. Trinadh's father was a retired brake inspector, and he would not approve in the least. It would make him look bad. Taking bribes and buying lorry-loads of teak and rosewood for next-to-nothing for his personal use was fine when he was working, but now, he was angelic. A few passersby looked at Seshu and then looked away.

As he pulled open the shop's door, a bell tied to a string tinkled. A man walked past him stuffing a sample piece of laddoo into his mouth. Seshu walked up to the counter and waited for the young boy to finish transferring sizzling jilabee to the display tray in the window.

"Yes?" the boy said, a bit taken aback to see a hijra in front of him.

"I ordered a cake," said Seshu, attempting to sound like a woman. "The name is Rao."

"Let me check," the boy said in a frazzled voice and went in the back.

There was a box sitting on the table behind the counter. That was probably it. The door opened, and a glittery woman walked in. She glanced at Seshu and rang the bell impatiently.

"Hello?" she called.

He noticed she already had a five-hundred-rupee note in her hand.

"Hello?" she called again.

"Yes," said the boy, as he hurried back to the front.

"I ordered a birthday cake," she said. "I am in a rush."

The brass bell on the door jingled as another customer entered.

"Okay," the boy said as he dashed into the back room.

He brought out another cake box and put it on the table behind the counter. Just then the woman dropped her money on the floor. Seshu instinctively bent down and picked it up for her. She nodded her thanks.

"That will be a hundred rupees even," said the boy to Seshu.

He pushed the cake box at him and took the money Seshu had laid on the counter. Seshu got a fleeting glance of Trinadh, who was smiling in the back room. He probably did not want to see his best friend dressed as a woman lest he burst out laughing and blow his cover.

"I special-ordered pineapple cream instead of the elachi—I hope you have it for your sake, because I came here all the way from Eluru," he heard the woman say as he walked out.

"How much to the railway station?" asked Seshu.

"Ten rupees," said the rickshaw driver.

"The station is not that far. I will give you seven."

The driver nodded, and Seshu climbed aboard the red carriage with vinyl lotus appliqués. The smell of sugar wafting up from the cake box was making his stomach turn. Maybe he was just nervous. The warm wind blew against his cheeks and stroked his sari as the driver pedaled faster. There was not much that could go wrong. His confidence surged again as he looked at the dark street lined with twinkling lights from killi and cigarette stands. He looked up at the statue of Karl Marx as they drove through Marx Square. A cow lackadaisically plopped down in the middle of the road as a crowd waited to gain admittance to the latest film. Tonight, Seshu thought, this banality would be decimated and they would make history.

"Six-thirty," he heard a teenager mutter as he walked up the stairs to the station track.

That was one of the names people called the hijras, because at six-thirty, the hands on the clock came together—indistinguishably. The hijras were called kojjas in Telugu, which meant neither this nor that.

He stopped on track three and checked the ticket for the number of the train. This was it. Walking along the platform, he searched for the correct car and boarded. There were already two people sitting in his compartment. Ideally, he would have had the compartment all to himself. But that, unfortunately, was not possible. At

151

least only one other passenger would be boarding now. The other two would board at a later stop. He went to Sankarani's compartment and reached for the handle. A guard threw the door open and glared at him. He showed him his ticket.

"Next door, Miss," the guard said, his scowl breaking into a smirk.

Seshu walked back to his compartment. As he slid the door fully open, a man and woman who were clinging to one another, stiffened and separated as if they had just touched a hot flame. He felt like an intruder. A man entered hurriedly behind him and stowed his briefcase. They all watched as Seshu pushed the cake box under the berth across from him so he could keep an eye on it. He was just about to sit down when the man stopped him.

"I am very tired," he announced. "I am going to raise the seat so I can sleep."

If he slept, then Seshu had to sleep as well. The man was already hooking up the chains to secure the bed. Then, balling up his sweater for a pillow, he climbed up to the second berth. Seshu sighed and laid down on the first berth with his bag of clothes under his head. At least it was air-conditioned. He wished the couple would go to sleep, too. Then he could slip away in the darkness.

He pretended to be asleep for an hour. The man above him was snoring, but the lovers still had not hooked up their berths. They were sitting close together, whispering in each other's ears. When Seshu cleared his throat, they faltered for a moment like disturbed bees and then resumed. He could tell by the man's features that he was not Hindu. She was, but he definitely was not. It was pitch-black outside. He checked his watch. It was fifteen minutes past nine. He looked up and saw the nuzzling couple was staring at him, frozen as if a snapshot. He could see their life stories written on their fearful faces. They were in love and running away to get married. Thousands of others as these idiot lovers were the future of India—reckless, arrogant youths who were burying traditions, diluting Dravidian blood and forfeiting history. These weren't true Indians. Seshu sat up abruptly and bumped his head.

"Toilet," Seshu informed them as he opened the door as quietly as he could. A guard was walking down the aisle away from him. The train was slowing down. Without giving it another thought, he took out the detonator and pushed the button. It clicked. In three minutes, the bomb would explode. He casually walked toward the exit and looked down at the ground that was rushing by although the train was slowing down. Unfortunately, it would be stopping at the next station. That meant that Sankarani would have access to police and medical attention more quickly. Seshu dove from the train and rolled into the mounds of overgrown grass on the side of the track. When he landed, he ducked until the train passed. Then, like a deer, he skipped lightly over the tracks toward the road. It was not until his feet hit the tar that he realized he had lost one of the chappals. Panting, he turned around and saw it sitting on the roadside. As he bent down to pick it up, he saw headlights. It was Trinadh.

"Let's go," he said jumping into the car.

"Did you do it, darling?" asked Trinadh, laughing.

"Of course," said Seshu as he reached into his cleavage and pulled out a pack of cigarettes.

He lit one and rolled down the window.

"Where is the detonator?"

"Right here. It felt so good pushing that button."

Seshu took off the hair piece and put it in the bag. He then began pulling out the chunnis from inside the jacket.

"You look like you are doing a magic trick," said Trinadh, who was watching him transform back into a man.

Seshu stripped off the sari and bunched up the cloth. After doffing the petticoat, he sat for a minute in his underwear letting the sweat evaporate on his body.

"You must not forget to put the sari back in your mother's closet, Trinadh."

"Yes, it will be described in the papers tomorrow, and we don't want them to get suspicious."

Seshu wiggled, pulling on his pants.

"That bastard will fry in one minute," he said as he checked the detonator timer.

"You know, you do not look half bad as a woman," said Trinadh.

Seshu smiled as he continued wiping the liner from his eyelids with a kerchief. He remembered the lovers in the train compartment and wondered how they could love each other more than they loved themselves? How could they live happily knowing that they must each kill their Moslem and Hindu identities? How could they tear up their roots without feeling the recurring pinches of sacrifice?

"Ten, nine, eight, seven, six, five, four, three, two, one, long live the Land of the Dravidians," said Trinadh, as he punched the fuzzy squeaking dog hanging from the rear-view mirror for punctuation.

But they did not hear an explosion. Instead, night rustled slightly as a crisp breeze blew through its dark covers. The two friends looked at each other as crickets and frogs ticked in their ears, a hundred voices echoing their failure.

The Sun Is Setting
in the Acacia

Nikhil stopped at the sweet stand to get some jilabee. He
looked at the batter spattered on the man's face as he spoke.
"Give me a small bag. Fresh."

The man nodded and skimmed the boiling oil with a spoon. After pouring some batter into a piece of white cloth, he squeezed
pretzel-shapes through the hole into the cauldron. Nikhil liked the
sizzling sound the cool dough made as it began to fry in the hot oil.
It reminded him of his little brother, Kishore. Nikhil used to watch
him burn spiders and roaches alive in fires made of camphor. The
fat roaches would run like mad and then pop like firecrackers. The
explosion made his brother laugh and laugh.

"When it is time for you to die, you will die like that," Nikhil had
told him. "You will try to outrun death, but you will not. The fire will
lick at your heels and the backs of your kicking legs. Your dark buttocks will become darker—if that is possible!"

Nikhil had been only half kidding back then. Now, he felt differently. After his mother was slain for speaking up for the rights of poor field workers, his attitude about killing had changed. She was found in a field of sugar cane, naked with her throat slit. He never told Kishore what had happened.

He glanced at his watch. Five to six.

"How much longer? Hurry up."

The man transferred the jilabee into a bowl of sugar syrup. Again, they sizzled. The fried dough was airy and readily soaked up the syrup. The man put the sweets in a bag.

As Nikhil walked down the Vijayawada street, he pulled out a sticky jilabee. It was still warm as he bit into it. A river of liquid sugar flushed against his cheeks and spurted down his throat. Even though he knew what to expect, it was a surprise.

Nikhil took off his sunglasses and looked at the timings for the films. He put down a twenty-rupee bill.

"The film has already begun," the ticket clerk informed him, tapping his fingers on the bill.

"It doesn't matter," responded Nikhil.

The clerk pushed the ticket and change toward him. Flicking his cigarette into the street, Nikhil pushed open the door and walked in. There were about fifty people dispersed in the three-hundred-seat theater. He sat behind two college-aged women. It was a Hindi picture.

The hero was chasing his love through a mango grove. "Give me a kiss-kiss, darling, kiss-kiss." She was dressed in a golden blouse with straps, her breasts pushed up so they jiggled when she ran. "Darling, I see your smile in the garden; I hear your voice in my dreams; are you for real?" she cooed. He looped around a tree and caught her in his arms. Out of breath, they paused, locked in an embrace. His lips moved toward her—an innocent kiss on the forehead. She leaned her head on his chest. The two women in front of Nikhil whispered and laughed.

In the next scene, the couple got jumped by some thugs. They tumbled, the hero landed some karate chops and kicks, but they got the best of him. In the end, his love was kidnapped. The plots were thin and silly much of the time, but most people went to the movies to escape reality. Why did so many people believe in fairy tales? The giggling women in front of him were behaving vacuously seductive, and he started to feel as if he were a character in one of the films. As he fished out a piece of jilabee, the bag made a crinkling noise. One of the women turned around and looked at him. When he reached into the bag again, they mumbled something and moved. Did they want him to follow them or leave them alone? He checked his watch. Twenty to seven. The women watched him leave.

By seven o'clock, Nikhil was walking to the house. He looked at the policeman standing on the concrete island in the middle of the intersection. He was standing amidst the chaos of traffic, twisting his moustache and gripping a wooden stick. When he blew his whistle, the line of scooters, cars, bicycles and auto taxis revved their engines and were off. As Nikhil passed him, he thought how his khaki uniform blended into the dust puffs vehicles were kicking up as they sped by. He looked like a ghost.

As he turned onto a side street, he passed a bar. On the metal doors was a painting of a bottle of Knock Out XXX Rum. On the bottle label, a boxer had just succeeded in knocking out his opponent. Nikhil laughed at the thought of triple X rum giving one the strength and stamina to box. Indian people were starting to believe their country was in such a mess because it lacked bars, blue jeans, fried chicken and colorful sneakers.

He pushed open the door and walked in.

"MBL Lager."

The bartender stopped combing his hair and handed him a bottle.

Nikhil sat down at a table and took out a pack of cigarettes. His last one. Good. As he lit it, he looked at the young men crowded around a table playing cards. They were drinking shots of Knock Out

XXX Rum. He thought about wandering over and asking to be dealt in. He could wipe them out. One of them kept pounding his fist down on the table every time he had a bad ha᎒ ᎒. Nikhil looked out the sooty window. Schoolboys in convent uniforms lingered outside the bar, trying to peek in. Their focus of interest changed when a car crashed into a rickshaw. The rickshaw driver was not carrying passengers, but crates of eggs. As the drivers argued, the boys began sliding in the mess of broken eggs and stomping on the ones that were still whole with glee. When the rickshaw driver tried to stop them, the boys threw eggs at him and ran off. Nikhil laughed and wondered if Kishore was running in the streets causing havoc like that. Car horns honked as traffic came to a standstill. When the rickshaw driver turned around, the other driver was getting back in his car.

Nikhil finished his beer and walked out. The rickshaw driver was standing in the middle of the street, helpless. Eggshells crunched under Nikhil's sandals.

"I saw everything from across the street," said Nikhil in a booming voice. "The driver of the car was responsible."

The crowd's eyes were upon him. People began to stir.

"No one was hurt; mind your own business," snapped the driver, jumping out of the car.

"The eggs are clearly hurt, and the rickshaw is clearly hurt," said Nikhil.

People in the crowd chuckled.

"Ashok!" a voice bellowed from the backseat, its owner hidden behind tinted glass.

The driver ran over and returned with a fifty-rupee note.

"Now you can celebrate," he said, waving it in the air.

"That is not enough. Because he is a poor man, you think he does not have any rights to share this street with you?" Nikhil asked.

The crowd became agitated and moved closer to the car.

"Who do you think you are?" someone yelled.

"Pay for the eggs!" hollered an old woman.

Some youths banged on the roof of the car. More money was

passed through the window to the driver.

"Five hundred rupees," he muttered, as he walked back.

The rickshaw driver took it, smiled and nodded. The crowd began to dissipate, and as the car drove off, hands smacked down on the trunk and roof to punctuate justice.

"You came like an angel," the rickshaw driver said to Nikhil.

Nikhil smiled and walked into the crowd.

"What is this? Clear the road! Move along!" yelled a policeman who had just happened on the scene.

The twilight sky was a swirl of pink and orange as the sun's embers smoldered in the coolness of clouds. As Nikhil walked past Ring Road to the house, he saw a black sow lying on her side in garbage, nursing eight white speckled piglets. She was oblivious to the darkness that was closing in on the town—the darkness that made people put bars on their windows and bolts on their doors.

"The sun is setting in the acacia," his mother would say as they watched the red sun disappear and blackness descend, with all its night-noises.

He looked at the pig. Anyone could have easily straddled her and split her open. But she had trust in the people. They stepped out of her way and the cars came to a screeching halt when she crossed the road. The people loved pigs. Hindus, generally, did not eat pork, and they respected all animals. A pig was not just a pig, but perhaps a god or goddess in disguise. How ridiculous, he thought. They had more concern for the sow than for each other. It occurred to him as he passed the sow and her babies that the rotting cabbage and fruits must have made a comfortable bed.

"Goldflake," he said, stopping at a smoke stand.

He unwrapped the pack and lit the cigarette, using the tip of the burning rope hanging on the side. An old woman crossed Bandar Road and bought a cigar. Her graying hair was cropped short, and her sari covered her naked breasts. Her skin was so leathery and wrinkled that he reassuringly glanced at his own. He watched her light the cigar, smoke puffing from her mouth like an exhaust. Women did not smoke on the streets in Vijayawada. It was unfeminine, people said. He wondered if the woman thought she was still exercising her freedom of choice, or was she just addicted as he was? People loved to think they were in control of themselves. When the stench of the cigar reached him, she turned it around, putting the glowing red tip inside her mouth—the nicotine was more potent smoked this way. She sucked on it hungrily as the piglets on their mother's nipples. Those who chose to smoke like that usually ended up getting cancer of the mouth and throat. He wondered if she knew and decided most smokers did not want to hear about cancer. When one is swimming in an ocean, one cannot perceive its size. He looked across the street at the dark faces lit up by cooking fires around the huts. As if for the first time, he saw where he had been living these past years.

Ducking into an alley, Nikhil used a car fender for a boost and climbed up to the roof. Once safely on top, he crossed over to the next building. Looking down from the wall of the roof, he saw a driver asleep in his rickshaw on the street. He lit a cigarette and looked up at the sky. Bats were flying through the indigo night in search of ripe fruit. An insatiable hunger seemed to be strangling the country like a clinging vine. It was not the type of hunger that was sated with what the land offered, like a deliciously perfect mango or the serenity of a sunset. It was a hunger that made a mother sell her child into prostitution and another maim hers so she could be a more believable beggar. It was what made the landowners greedy enough to treat the farmers as slaves. It was what made the government officials puppets in the hands of rowdies and the corrupt rich citizens. It was this very hunger that made Nikhil who he was. He had gotten used to the aching in the pit of his stomach.

He flicked his cigarette into the street. Sometimes when he was standing in a high place, he had an overwhelming urge to jump. Was this a natural thing to feel because of the pull of gravity toward the earth, or did he just want to die? He knew the instinct to die was as strong in humans as was the instinct to live. He saw his body lying on the dirt road below. His head was cracked open, and a stray dog barked at his feet. He pictured himself dead so he would know what it felt like. He wondered if he would have the time to really confront death, to understand it. Would it chew on him slowly like a cancer or shoot through him like a bullet? People said death and birth were similar. In that case, at death, he would once again become a newborn.

He thought about his mother. What was his mother thinking when death lunged at her throat? When she clawed at their faces and bit their hands, was she thinking about living or dying? Did she have a chance to count the number of men and knives it took to make her silent?

He took off his chappals and pulled on the roof door. As expected, it was open. He walked down the stairs, not making a sound. Opposite the Siva calendar was a framed black and white photograph of grandparents, which was adorned with a garland of curled sandalwood shavings. He liked it when they were not home. He could take his time. He looked into the glass showcase. It was filled with things such as tarnished cricket and badminton trophies, dusty books, ugly glasses with painted cartoon characters he had never seen before, New Year's cards, some photos of the old folks in front of the Statue of Liberty, fancy key chains, a box of hairbands and some ceramic birds. So much garbage, he thought, as he turned the corner.

Entering the kitchen, the only room with a light on, he saw a plate of butter laddoos on the table. How thoughtful. He ate one and guzzled some water.

Refreshed, he strolled into the bedroom to get down to business. As he took light steps toward the steel wardrobe, he brushed against the mosquito netting hanging over the bed. The bloodsuckers were buzzing in the air. Waving them off, he took out an awl and hammer.

That was when he saw the empty crib in the corner of the room. Several precise knocks and he broke the lock on the wardrobe door. They were much too old to have a baby. Why did they have a crib? Soon, he would be a father himself. He could hardly wait. Running his fingers over a stack of glittering saris, he pulled out a deep red one with a turmeric-gold border that crept up into the red about a half meter. His own wife would delight at twirling herself into such a rich color. But where would she wear it? They did not go to dinner parties or officers' functions. They did not invite friends and relatives to their hut and have dance recitals. In fact, if his wife was seen in public wearing this sari, she most likely would be accused of stealing it from her employer. They would heckle her and yell how her black skin and the bluish-green tattoos on her forearms gave her away—how they would laugh at a servant in red and gold!

Nikhil positioned the awl on the lock of the safe where the valuables were kept and brought the hammer down hard. It was a difficult lock to break. The awl kept slipping. He saw that his hands were shaking. He wiped off the sweat rolling down from his sideburns and under his jaw. He looked at the crib. She should have told him.

He went and quenched his thirst with some cold water from the refrigerator. Maybe it was for their grandchildren. He walked back into the bedroom. After several more hits, the lock broke in slow motion—in the most anticlimactic way. As his eager fingers reached to open the door, a piece of the jagged metal cut his hand. He pulled back and sucked on the blood. It was then that he felt another presence in the room. Was someone looking in the window? His heart lurched. He turned slowly and sighed when he saw it was just a statue. He was too jittery. He knew fear fed on itself. The moonlight was streaming in through the window, illuminating the black stone statue of Lord Venkateswara. There were red roses at The Preserver's feet and a strand of gold beads and pearls around his neck.

Nikhil's hands reached into the safe for the three stacks of hundred-rupee notes, the velvet sack of gold coins, two gold necklaces, a set of gold bangles and a box of precious stones the old lady was going to take to the jeweler to have set in a bracelet. Just as he was putting the box of stones in his pocket, he heard a noise. The front door creaked open. He quickly shut the door of the safe, but failed to shut the wardrobe door completely. He crouched behind the bed. Why were they home so soon? In just one more minute, he would have been gone. They would never have had to meet. Everything had changed now.

The light was switched on. The old man walked in and stopped short when he noticed the open doors of the wardrobe. As he moved to open the safe door, Nikhil stepped nimbly behind him and covered the man's mouth with his cut hand. He reached inside his jacket for the knife. As he put it to the old man's throat, he felt the man's body stiffen, rigid with fear. Together, the blood rushing through the old man's jugular and that pulsing in his own wrists drummed fiercely.

"What are you thinking?" Nikhil whispered.

In a fit, the old man began to struggle, kicking Nikhil's legs with the soles of his feet.

"Tell me, what god lets this happen?" Nikhil murmured as he dug the knife across the old man's throat. The body slumped at his feet. He turned to the statue of Lord Venkateswara and snatched the pearls. He went back to the old man and tore the gold chain from his neck. He accidentally stepped in the warm blood with his right foot. Grabbing a towel and pillow from the bed, he ran up the stairs to the roof. There, he wiped the blood splattered on his arms and hands with the towel. He shook out the pillow and put the loot in the case. Donning his chappals, he jumped to the neighboring rooftop and blended into the night. Below, a trail of singular red footprints led to the abandoned towel and pillow, suddenly so mysterious in the moonlight.

Nikhil let the cold water run, hoping it might get a bit warmer. He had asked for hot water, but it was an hour past the cut-off time for bucket service. As he poured the water over his head, he gasped for air. Was this how the old man had felt? No. He had not had time for

163

the fear to build. The water shocked Nikhil every time because he was waiting in expectation. The bathroom was so filthy that he did not feel clean when he was done.

He reached for his pants and took out the jilabee bag. He had such a sweet tooth. He sat down on the bed and popped the last piece in his mouth. He remembered when he was six and had gotten up before his mother on her birthday. He had wanted to make sure the first thing she tasted that morning was something sweet. She always did it for both of her sons on their birthdays.

"Eat something sweet, the whole year will be sweet," she would tell them.

So, taking a bamboo stick, he had struck a beehive hanging in a drumstick tree. He had seen some boys doing it once. He swung again and again, but nothing fell. The next time he hit it, the hive broke in half and fell down from the tree. He ran to it excitedly. Then, he pulled his hand back and screamed. The hive was not full of honey, but crawling with worms. He turned around and looked to make sure no one was watching him. He wanted to be certain it was not a cruel prank those boys had played on him. As he ran back home, tears streamed down his face.

"What happened, Niki?" his mother asked.

She smiled when she heard.

"That is because it is right before the full moon. The bees ate up all the honey. The worms you saw were babies. Anyway, you should not be bothering the bees. Did you not think they might love to nibble on someone as sweet as you?"

She tickled him, and they laughed.

Nikhil reached into the pillowcase. He counted the stacks of money, ten thousand each for a total of thirty thousand rupees. Out of town, he could get about a lakh for the necklaces. Last but not least, the velvet sack. Out dropped the gold coins. Twelve sovereigns shimmered on the tea-stained hotel sheets. He brought one to his lips and kissed it. There was a knock at the door. As he got up, he tripped on one of his sandals. Looking down, he saw the blood had darkened the beige-colored leather to maroon.

"Who is it?"

"Nikhil?"

When he opened the door, his wife, Munjee, stood blinking at him. She had a large bag at her side. She entered and collapsed in his arms.

"You are safe."

"Of course, darling. I told you not to worry."

He kissed her forehead.

"How could I not worry?"

"You left the door open as we planned. I walked in; I walked out. It is behind us now. Come."

He led her to the bed.

"All this?"

She sat down and flipped through a stack of money. She brought it up to her nostrils.

"Khus-khus," she whispered, the perfume too familiar to forget.

He scooped up the gold coins and dropped them into her cupped hands.

"Sweet music," he said.

She dropped them back into his hands.

"Golden rain," she said.

"Did you get the reservations?"

She nodded and took them out from inside her faded blouse. As he read the tickets, she looked at the gold chains. She noticed one had a broken clasp.

"A/C Sleeper. Good job, Munjee."

"Mr. Chitra," she whispered, her eyes wide.

She was holding the chain in her quivering hand. He saw the dark imprint it had left on the bed sheet. He wrapped his arms around her, and she cried into his chest. Stroking her hair, he stared at the design that lay like a crimson snake beside them.

Four Uncles

I told Bhupal to bring the video down," said Sekhar. "Those two are getting so irresponsible, I tell you."

Sindhura squeezed the liquid soap onto the sponge and began washing the dishes. She had been in the States for less than a week, and she had already learned that Sekhar was the sternest of her four uncles. Perhaps it was because his wife, Madhavi, had just given birth to a baby boy and he was a new father. Madhavi had taken the baby and gone to Georgia to visit with her sister for a few months. Sekhar and two of his brothers—Vyshna and Poorna—drove New York City cabs.

Vyshna, a bald, sweet-faced man, lived next door with his wife, Pushpa. They did not say why exactly, but they could not have any children. They were a playful couple. Pushpa said the word "bastard" a lot and whatever else was on her mind. Vyshna listened patiently. It did not mean that he agreed with her all the time, but at least he listened. They reminded Sindhura of her own parents.

Vyshna was addicted to playing the lottery.

"This is it," he would boast, waving the precious cards under their noses. "We're going to wake up millionaires."

"Are you going to share it?" Poorna or Bhupal, the youngest brother, would ask.

Vyshna would always say yes, and Sindhura believed him.

Pushpa had told her once that Vyshna's secret to picking the numbers involved the license plate numbers of the cars that cut off his cab.

"It's a silly obsession, but I'd rather have him doing math than chasing down the bastard who cut him off," Pushpa had said with a grin.

Poorna and Bhupal shared the apartment upstairs. They were in their early twenties, unmarried and always in search of fun. Bhupal was studying business at a city college and dreamt of importing crafts and textiles from India. Sometimes he drove a cab on the days the other three were not working. He did not have a license, but one of his brothers would sign out the cab and Bhupal would take over from there. He often returned it late at night, and the dispatcher never noticed or was asleep. Bhupal also worked part-time at an expensive French restaurant on the Hudson River. He talked about eventually moving out of Astoria and into Manhattan. Sometimes, he made fun of Astoria, but Sindhura couldn't understand his humor.

It seemed to her that Poorna was the only one of her four uncles who seemed to enjoy what he did. He loved meeting Americans, and as a cabbie, he often met a lot of rich women who told him he was exotic. In his spare time, he was taking writing classes at a community college and was working on a book about his experiences as a cab driver in the city.

"I hope he did not forget to bring the video home again," grumbled Sekhar.

"I will go upstairs and check," Sindhura offered as she finished rinsing the last plate.

As she walked up the stairs to Poorna and Bhupal's apartment to get the video, the smell of cardamom and cloves was swirling through the air. Someone was cooking chicken. She paused and looked at the numbered doors lining the hall. They were so mysterious. Whenever she tossed the garbage in the incinerator or went down to check the mail, she hoped she would run into one of their neighbors. Some of them smiled at her, and others just walked by pretending not to see her. Sometimes, she glimpsed the inside of someone's apartment and was struck by how different each one was decorated. There was a Polish man on the first floor in apartment nine who was in the habit of collecting stray cats. Bhupal said that he had at least ten and that it was against the rental policy. She always stared at his door when she walked past in hopes of seeing him or the cats, but it never opened. No one ever seemed to visit him, and she wondered if he were to get sick or die, if anyone would know until the landlord came knocking for the next month's rent.

She opened the door to her uncles' apartment with the spare key and spotted the video on the table. As she walked toward it, she heard a woman's laugh coming from one of the bedrooms. Sindhura froze. She felt like a thief. The door was slightly open, and it was pulling her toward it like a magnet. She wanted to look so badly, but she was terrified of what she would see. Before she could make up her mind, she found her feet walking closer to the door. Leaning forward, she saw Bhupal kissing a woman with red hair. Her eyebrows were penciled black, and the purple paint smeared around her mouth made her look as if she was bleeding. Her blouse was open, and Bhupal's head lowered to kiss her small breasts. The woman's arms and face were sprinkled with brown flecks. She helped Bhupal take off his T-shirt. Her milky hands ran over the expanse of his coppery, muscular back—he was the only one of her uncles who lifted weights. The fan hummed in the window. She could just see the wetness glistening above the woman's lip.

"I love your skin," she whispered.

"I love your skin," he said.

Then he became lost in sucking on her pink nipple. She moaned. Sindhura looked down at what she was holding in her sweaty hands—the videotape. She turned around and slowly walked out. Her aunt and uncle were probably starting to worry.

As she walked back down the stairs, she wondered if Bhupal had met this woman at the college. She wondered why he had lied to his brother Sekhar about having to study tonight. She wished she could have watched just a little longer. She opened the door.

"What took you so long?" asked Pushpa with concern.

"He had a hard time locating it," muttered Sindhura.

She sat down on the carpet. Her aunt put in the cassette and placed a tray of laddoos on the table. It was just the three of them since Poorna and Vyshna were working the late shift and Bhupal was supposedly studying.

"Have a pillow," her uncle suggested.

It was one of the pillows she had made back in India. They looked strangely small and delicate in her new home. They did not match the orange-and-green plaid couch or the blue carpet.

"Madhavi told me Sridevi is wonderful in this," said Pushpa as the film began.

Sindhura hugged the pillow, her fingers caressing the golden lotus she had sewn on the cover. She smelled the fabric and was reminded of her life that had come abruptly to an end in Eluru. She remembered the sweet face of the young boy who had murdered his brother—the man she was going to marry. Would she have been pregnant by now, sitting on a slate floor shelling peas instead of watching a movie? The ceiling creaked slightly, and she looked up.

Poorna had a way of drawing out the final word of each sentence and wrapping it in silk. Then he would hit people on the head with the swaddled word. It was a trap that made her other uncles feel stupid. He rarely talked to her that way, however. He just told her what do. To him, she was a blank canvas and he was the painter. He was dramatically honest and quite amusing. He wore mostly jackets with jeans and had a wide collection of hats and scarves. The others joked about how he dressed up to sit eight to twelve hours a day in a filthy New York City cab.

"People remember a marvelous scarf or hat," Poorna said smoothly.

It was thrilling to him, she supposed, because it was like putting on a show. He ran a hand through his thick unoiled hair, fluffing it up. It seemed that he was always looking at himself in the mirror. She never saw men doing that in Eluru, but she imagined the accessories for men here were much more exciting.

"You are not going to wear that, are you?" Poorna said when he saw her in the corner of the mirror.

"You don't like this sari?" asked Sindhura.

"We are going on a tour of New York, and that means we will be walking a lot. It would be best to wear some jeans and some comfortable shoes. No chappals."

"But chappals are comfortable, Uncle," she said.

"We are not staying in Queens, we are going to the city. You need something sturdy and closed, or else your feet will get filthy. Besides, you cannot walk quickly in chappals. Everyone walks very fast in New York."

"But India also has dusty roads strewn with garbage," she countered.

"The dirt is different here. It sticks to the soles of your feet. Somehow, the dirt in India is cleaner."

So, by the time they were walking out the door, Sindhura was wearing jeans, a plain white jersey and sneakers. Her underwear was riding up between her buttocks because of the stiff denim, and she wondered how women dealt with this. She never thought much about all the freedom wearing a sari gave her—the generous fabric swinging loosely about her hips and legs; the delight of the sun's breath on her bare midriff and the small of her back, and the vivacious colors and patterns she had to choose from. She never wore underwear under her sari either. It was unnecessary. Pushpa wore mostly jogging suits of an odd plastic material and donned saris only on special family celebrations. She had brought some jogging suits home from the store she worked in for Sindhura to wear, but

Sindhura found that the jogging pants made a funny sound when she walked.

"That is the World Trade Center," said Poorna as he pointed from his cab. "That is where that sick terrorist planted a bomb a few years ago. Did you hear about that in India?"

"No," she said. "What did he want?"

"Attention," he said flatly. "I think I'll take you to the Empire State Building, okay?"

"Okay," she said.

He began humming to the radio. She stared at all the people waiting on street corners to cross. There were so many people, and they all looked so different.

"There are jobs for all these people?" she asked with amazement.

"Yes, if you have a degree, the jobs are usually better."

"Even the women?"

"Yes."

She saw a dark-skinned woman with a leather jacket and a crew-cut standing on the corner as they turned.

"I think she is Indian," she said with disbelief.

"M*mmmm*," he said, expressing his delight. "Look, Sindhu, I want you to know that you don't have to do this crazy mail-order bride crap. I'll support you if you choose to go to school or get a job, whatever. It's important for you to experience life here first."

She nodded. He was referring to the newspaper ads that Sekhar, Vyshna and Pushpa were scanning for her marriage prospects. It was true that she had been upset when her wedding match was killed. She wanted to start a new life then. But now, everything had changed. She had a green card.

"What do you think you want to study in school?" he asked, speeding up through a yellow light.

No one had ever asked her what she wanted to do with her life. She stared at all the people's faces streaming down the well-paved streets.

"I am a good seamstress," she said. "Maybe a fashion school."

"Fantastic, Sindhu," he beamed. "That will blow Sekhar's mind.

He's probably thinking along the lines of computers."

Seeing Poorna's cab approaching, a man jumped off the curb and waved his arms wildly.

"Lesson number one—New Yorkers do not understand the meaning of 'off-duty.'"

She laughed, ducking close to the dashboard to see where the tops of the tall buildings ended.

"Push the button when you want to kill them," said Bhupal.

Sindhura picked up the joystick and held the button down. The goal was to kill off as many men with guns as possible. Wherever the joystick moved, the video screen view swiveled as well, and it was making her slightly dizzy.

"I tell you, you are going to spoil our niece's pure mind with that garbage, Bhupal," said Sekhar. "Why not read a good book instead?"

"It's good to get out your aggressions," said Bhupal.

"Are you making the rice upstairs?" asked Sekhar walking out of the kitchen.

"Don't worry, be happy," said Bhupal. "I'm going to spring for dinner."

"The others will be home in a half hour."

"Brothers," he said, rolling his eyes as he stood up. "Keep playing, Sindhu. I'll be right back."

"Be careful—you know what I mean," warned Sekhar as Bhupal put on his jacket and walked out.

"What do you mean, uncle?" asked Sindhura.

"Just because we aren't in India any longer doesn't mean the night doesn't hold dangers, dear. We used to say back home, 'the sun is setting in the acacia' to describe that eerie darkness of cricket-chirps and strange shadows that envelops a town in minutes. It applies here, too, although, there isn't an acacia in sight."

He sat down on the couch behind her. She played the game for a few minutes and handed him the controls. He tried, but the men with guns converged on him and riddled him with bullets. With each successive hit, his video face at the bottom of the screen under the word "Vitality" became bloodied and droopy.

"You have to play like a zombie like Bhupal if you want to get good at this," he said as he put the joystick on the carpet.

She laughed. This uncle had a way of always complaining with a smile.

"Are you happy here in the States, Uncle?" she asked.

He interlocked his fingers and stared at them.

"Happiness is elusive, Sindhu. Most people stare up at the sky waiting to see a shooting star. When they see it, an honest joy overcomes them. When the sky is once again black, they wish for the things they think would make their lives perfect and capture that joy they just experienced in a bottle. What they fail to see is that the night sky is not black—it is not sad. It is smiling with a billion shining teeth. Sometimes this smile is hidden behind a veil of clouds, but only temporarily. That is the nature of happiness. It sometimes hides and you must seek it out. The funny part is that it is everywhere. To answer your question, I miss India, but I am happy."

Bhupal, holding two giant flat boxes, threw the door open.

"Look who I found," he said.

Vyshna and Pushpa entered.

"Pizza—now I am happier," said Sekhar, and Sindhura smiled.

"I hope you got half of one with olives," said Pushpa to Bhupal.

"Where is Poorna?" asked Vyshna.

"He said he was coming, but he will probably be late as usual," said Sekhar.

Vyshna brought some paper cups from the kitchen.

"Now, Sindhu, here is your first sampling of what New York is all about," said Bhupal as he lifted the cardboard top.

He lifted a triangular piece, and the cheese stretched all the way from box to plate. Some of the pieces had discs of reddish meat.

Sindhura could not believe this was an Indian family. The men did not mind taking care of dinner or serving the women. It seemed so strange. She did not know what to do with herself.

"It smells good," she said.

Bhupal took out a giant bottle of Coca-Cola and twisted off the top. The cola spewed out and squirted Sindhura in the face.

"Just imagine it is champagne," said Vyshna, and they all laughed.

"Pizza is nothing without Coke," said Bhupal as he handed her the paper cup.

As Sindhura bit into the pizza slice, and then pulled it back from her mouth, the cheese stretched as if a piece of elastic. She let out an embarrassed giggle.

"What do you think?" asked Bhupal.

"It is good," she replied in between chews.

Just then they heard a strange noise at the door. It sounded like a grunt or bark. Bhupal got up and looked through the peephole.

"No one's there," he said.

As he started to walk away, there was a groan. He opened the door, and they saw Poorna lying in the hallway. He was bleeding profusely from a head wound.

"God!" said Bhupal as everyone jumped to their feet and ran to Poorna's aid.

"Quickly, to the hospital!" said Vyshna as they lifted Poorna and started down the stairs.

Sekhar, keys in hand, followed behind them. Pushpa grabbed clean towels and locked the apartment door.

"The bastards got him," her aunt said as she headed for the stairs.

Sindhura seemed to be the only one who was immobilized. She had never seen blood run like that. She imagined her parents must have looked similar to this after the bus they were on had crashed. Had Poorna gotten into a car accident? Who could have done such a terrible thing? Why were the others so calm? It seemed as if they had been expecting it to happen. Poorna's scarf, stained with blood, lay near the stairwell. She picked it up and ran down to the car.

While Poorna was getting his head sutured, Sindhu sat with Vyshna. Pushpa and Bhupal had gone in search of food, and Sekhar was calling the police. She could not believe that the "bastards" were neighborhood kids.

"Why did they do this?" Sindhura asked again because no one had answered her the first time.

"Because they are afraid," said her uncle.

"Of what?"

"That we are all more alike than we are different. They have a need to assert that they're right in their looks and whom they worship."

"They are afraid of being wrong?" she asked, still baffled.

"Do you know the story of the Sri Kalahasti?" he asked.

"I know that there is an original Siva lingam there, but that is all."

"In the forest, there was a spider who worshiped Siva, and to show its devotion, it spun a web on the lingam and yoni. This intricate and spectacular web served as a shield from the sun and an umbrella from the rain. Another Siva devotee, this one a snake, was very distressed to see this ugly web covering the lingam. After destroying the web, the snake surrounded the lingam with precious gems to show its devotion to Siva. Then, an elephant arrived and was upset that stones were burying the lingam. It spouted water from its trunk and washed away the stones, replacing them with fragrant gardenias, lotuses, mangoes and bananas. When the spider returned the next day, it was furious. Again, the three repeated their cycle. Finally, it came to a point when they all wondered who was destroying their puja. Who was the culprit? They each decided to find out. When the snake spied the elephant washing away his gems, he slithered up his trunk. It maddened the elephant, and he beat his head against a tree and eventually died. The snake died in the elephant's trunk, and the spider was crushed in the chaos. 'Sri' means spider; 'kala' means snake; and 'hasti' means elephant."

Sindhura nodded because she understood. Pushpa and Bhupal were walking toward them, their arms full of small bags of chips and other junk food. A nurse with blonde hair led a male patient down the hall. In the whiteness of the hospital, Pushpa and Bhupal stood out as if they were crows against a cloud.

"Have a snack," said Pushpa.

They were each sitting with a hand in their own bag of chips, crunching meditatively, when the nurse approached them.

"We are going to keep him for observation overnight," she said, glancing at Sindhura's sari and chappals. "You may see him for a few minutes."

As they walked to the room, Sindhura's heart was beating fast. She had hated hospitals ever since the bus crash. Her father had been dead on arrival, but her mother lived for a day. The sharp smells of the government hospital had overwhelmed her. She had seen a bat in the open hallway, and the paint was peeling off every wall. She remembered side-stepping past sputum on the steps and vomiting under a powderpuff tree that was beginning to close its leaves as dusk fell.

She held her breath now, as they approached the door. It was wide open. Poorna's arm was bandaged and his head stitched up. The area near his right brow was swollen, which made it hard for him to keep his eye open. There was a drop of spit dangling from his puffy, bruised lips.

"How are you?" asked Sekhar.

"Alive," he whispered as they surrounded the bed.

"How many stitches?" asked Bhupal.

"Fifteen."

"Racist bastards," spat Pushpa.

"The police are coming," said Sekhar.

"Do you remember what they look like?" asked Vyshna.

"Is anything broken?" asked Bhupal.

But Poorna did not answer them. He looked drowsy.

"Where is Sindhura?" he asked softly.

Trembling, she stepped forward toward the bed. He looked up at her and smiled. He reached for her hand, and she held it tightly.

"I do not want you to think this is what America is about," he said.

The Funeral

"What about mangoes?" Mrs. Chitra asked as they walked through the vegetable market.

"They look delicious, but they don't let you take fruit into England," said Gayatri in a slight British accent as she put the mango back in the basket.

"Only five rupee each," said the vendor in English.

"Five rupees?" repeated Mrs. Chitra sharply. "My daughter may live in England, but do not forget that I live around the corner."

The vendor smiled sheepishly and shrugged his shoulders.

"Now why can't you take one back? Are they afraid it has a bomb in it?" her mother asked, her voice pinched with sarcasm.

What a silly question. Her mother seemed a little obtuse since her father had been murdered. She was not her usual clear-minded self.

"No, Mum. It's because they're afraid of it carrying agricultural diseases."

Her mother nodded, and they moved on to the bananas. There

were six kinds overflowing from the baskets and hanging from jute strung up along the roof. Amrutha bale, a very sweet and cottony variety; chandra bale which was red and bland; green bale, a long, pale and sugary variety; kadu bale, a wild, small banana with an abundance of seeds; the native bontha, which was a green cooking plantain, and Gayatri's favorite, chakrakeli, the scented bananas she used to devour as a child. Her mother picked up a bunch of chakrakeli, which were larger than a finger-banana and smaller than the typical ones sold in markets in Britain.

"Can you believe there are so many kinds?" said Gayatri with excitement. "Many people think of a certain taste when you say 'banana,' but I think of the chakrakeli. It is so much more delicious than the London market bananas. Trying to find this subtle taste abroad is maddening, I tell you, Mum."

"There never is an absolute," said her mother.

"How do you mean?"

"When two people taste a piece of the same banana, they do not taste the same thing. We think we know the absolute, but how can we? Yet we insist on holding on so proudly to our notions and deductions."

Since her father, Tilak, had died, her mother was much more religious, or rather profoundly philosophical. She was having a hard time and found solace in Hindu and Buddhist scriptures. Gayatri wished she could spend more time with her mother. Just then, an agile langur suspended itself upside down from the roof of the stand and snatched a bunch of chakrakeli.

"Hey!" yelled the vendor, but the monkey was already gone.

Gayatri and Mrs. Chitra laughed, as did many other patrons.

"You see," said Gayatri, "all these to choose from, and a connoisseur of bananas went for the chakrakeli."

Her mother smiled.

"Did you know a wild rhesus monkey stole you when you were a baby?" she asked as they walked to the other side of the market.

"What?!" Gayatri cried, aghast.

"You were about six months old. I left you for a minute on the veranda, and when I came back, you were gone."

"How could you leave me on a veranda, Mum?"

"She was a mother. She grabbed you and climbed up to the roof of the house. The sweetest thing was she cradled you as one of her own. But I was terrified she was going to throw you from the roof."

"Fantastic," said Gayatri wryly. "Did she nurse me, too?"

"I put out a plate of guava and bananas, and she eventually put you down and went for the fruit. The thing that amazed me was that she was so gentle."

"Why do you think she did it?"

"Perhaps her own baby had been stolen or killed. Do you want some wood apples?"

Gayatri shrugged, and her mother handed the vendor some yams and wood apples with a ten-rupee bill. She took the change, and Gayatri put the items in her bag.

"Do you remember when you tried cooking a wood apple over the fire and it exploded because you didn't crack it on the ground first? It was so loud!"

Gayatri laughed and started helping her mother pick through a basket of eggplants.

"So, how come there are so few monkeys around," she asked. "What happened to them all?"

"They have been shipping them off for experiments or shooting them as they do to the stray dogs," her mother said without looking up.

Gayatri remembered an article she had read about the monkeys of Tirupati. They used to yank flowers from women's hair and jump on worshipers and slap them. People said that they behaved so because such vanity was not permitted at the temple of Venkateswara and the monkeys were the guards. In the article, it stated that the temple grounds were "cleansed" of the "troublesome and aggressive" monkeys. She smiled because she felt that description fit most men.

"They've shot all the monkeys in Tirupati, Mum," she said aloud.

"How much for the snake gourd?" her mother asked a vendor, not responding to Gayatri's statement.

"Twelve rupees, Ammagaru," said the shriveled lady sitting behind huge baskets of the giant squash.

The sun was shining in the old woman's eyes, where flecks of bronze and gold were flickering with a quality similar to iridescent fish skin. With age, Indian irises, which were big and jet-black, often softened and became the color of sandalwood. The woman stared at her, and Gayatri knew she was wondering what this short-haired girl in jeans and wooden fish earrings was doing in Vijayawada. They stared at her in India, and they stared at her in London. Where was she supposed to go? Her mother paid the woman, who took the selected squash and placed it over her knee.

"No!" said Gayatri, but it was too late.

She had snapped it in half.

"It was much too big to carry, Gayatri," said her mother.

The woman handed her the broken sword. The center of each celadon half glistened with diamond dewdrops.

As they walked to the car, Gayatri saw a group of lorries stopped in front of the temple of Hanuman. They were asking for blessings from the monkey god so they could avoid accidents on the road. Balls of white and yellow chrysanthemums festooned the sparkling chrome grills of the trucks. The contradictions of the culture ricocheted in her mind.

"Mum, the killing of monkeys and stray dogs is permissible, yet Hindus worship Hanuman and also the bull, Nandi, who protects all four-legged animals. I don't get it."

"Who has money for animal shelters when people are starving and children are being sold into prostitution?" her mother snapped.

"Where to, Ammagaru?" asked a spindly bicycle-rickshaw driver wearing an oversized red turban.

The old man looked like a top-heavy matchstick. Mrs. Chitra laughed at his offer.

"If we climbed aboard your chariot, you would surely have heart failure."

"But I am strong," said the old man, smiling as they walked past him to the white Maruti. Their driver relieved Gayatri of the bags of fruits and vegetables. She got in the car and continued their conversation.

"But permitting this type of killing will only lay down the tracks for other horrors. Remember the mass sterilization that happened in the seventies? They persecuted the Harijans and forced so many of them to have vasectomies. Isn't that ironic—men had to fight for their right to reproduce, and women are still fighting for the right to choose how, when and if they will reproduce at all."

"Your stunt at the funeral has put a terrible rift between me and your father's side of the family," her mother said, playfully chiding her. "His sisters think I am crazy and that you are an unmanageable brat. They are all bombarding me with marriage prospects for you. They all want you settled before you desecrate any more body parts with your tattoos."

Gayatri rolled her eyes, and then, with a smile, stroked the peacock tattoo on her forearm.

"How is this so different from decorating, excuse me, desecrating, your palms with henna?" quipped Gayatri.

"I hope you do not think you are going to start a revolution, because nobody is interested. Why stick your finger in shit and smell it? Shit is shit."

They passed groups of young women waiting for the bus outside a women's college. Gayatri met one of the student's eyes and smiled. She had on a cobalt blue sari and her skin was sable. The woman's lips curved up in a half-smile. Uncomfortable, she shifted the books she clutched against her bosom. Women in India did not usually smile at strangers. It invited trouble.

Gayatri walked into the bedroom and looked at the spot where her father had been murdered. There was not even a bit of stain left from which to imagine the blood that had been spilt on the white marble. With the servant, Munjee, gone, her mother had scrubbed the floor herself. Gayatri had asked her for details about the servant's whereabouts, but her mother refused to believe that Munjee had anything to do with the theft and murder. Gayatri understood. It would have been too much betrayal for her to bear at one time. It was a terrible murder, and the violence of it was enough for her mother to forgive her father for all of his misbehavior. Gayatri suspected that her father had had at least one mistress, although all of the property and other deeds went directly to her mother. He must have paid his mistresses well because none of them reared their ugly heads. To wash her hands of his greediness, her mother had made peace with her father's eldest sister, Auni. Auntie Auni lived in the States, and Gayatri's father had been unduly torturing the poor woman by occupying her land. Hema and Varija, her father's other sisters, were all for ganging up on Auni. It did not please her father's side of the family that her mother had given Auni the land that was rightfully hers. Gayatri's dear aunties and uncles were an insidious and wicked lot. That became crystal-clear during the days leading up to the funeral.

Gayatri turned on the ceiling fan. The mosquitoes were unbearable. Her old cradle was in the corner of the room. Apparently, her mother had been going to give it to the servant girl. She walked over to the bureau and looked at a photograph of herself when she was about three. She was sitting in her father's lap with a garland of lotus buds around her neck. It was taken at their old house in Tunuku. Her father was reading the newspaper, resting his chin on her head. She wondered when her relationship with him had changed. She had been closer to him than to her mother as she was growing up. She would accompany him when he played cricket and, on lazy afternoons, they were chess partners. She remembered the day she first beat him and he began to laugh.

"Did you let me win, Nanna?" she had asked.

"Of course not," he had replied with a smile.

He had never treated her like a girl. Maybe it was because he had wanted a boy so badly that he decided to just pretend she was one. When she was seventeen, her father began insisting that she get married, and it was her mother who supported her wish to study abroad. She wanted to go to the States, but her father said that it was much too far away. So, she ended up going to medical school in London. That was seven years ago, and she had grown further apart from him with each passing year.

She looked in the puja cabinet at the colorful paintings of the gods and goddesses. The white smoke from the incense streamed up to the ceiling. Would her father have approved of her behavior at his funeral? Traditionally, the eldest son was supposed to carry the pot of fire, but Gayatri was an only child. She was not supposed to ignite the body because, as a woman, she was not pure enough— as a woman, she would faint or fall grief-stricken with the pain of seeing her father's body burn. When Gayatri stated that she wanted to be the one to set her father's body aflame, all eyes were upon her. The nauseating scene quickly built in momentum and was over in a few minutes.

"What a ridiculous notion your daughter has put forth!" Hema, the unofficial spokesperson, had squawked.

Her colored hair was oiled and slicked back, its true length hidden under a massive artificial bun that was three-quarters the size of her head. Gayatri stared at it rising from behind her like a strange planet.

"He is my father, and if my mother is not going to do it, then it shall be my duty, Auntie," Gayatri had responded simply.

"Before he was your father, Tilak was my brother, dear," spat Hema.

"If the corpse were here, I do think you women would tear it limb from limb!" said Dileep, the eldest son of Varija, who sat plucking imaginary dirt from under his short finger nails.

Dileep was constantly eating and had such an aversion to exercise, she knew he'd be riding in one of the cars rather than leading the procession on foot to the cremation site.

"We are not at the sari shop quibbling over who saw which pattern first, Aunties," said another cousin, Jayadev, with an ear-splitting grin.

Jayadev was Hema's son. His face always shimmered with smugness. He lit a cigarette and stood in the doorway overlooking the courtyard. When he spoke, he did so with an authority only fitting a king with obsequious subjects.

"I, Dileep, Suresh, Chandram, Kiran and Nannagaru's good friend, Balajigaru, will handle it."

"Balajigaru? Who is your father's friend to *my* father?" blurted Gayatri.

The anger was rising to her ears and she started forgetting about the small words such as "Andi" that were customary to tag on to ends of sentences to show respect. She glanced over at her mother, who sat with her lips pursed.

"You watch your tongue, Gayatri!" Hema shot back. "Lord only knows what you do in London, but we live respectable lives here. Well, some of us do anyway," she added icily, glancing at Mrs. Chitra.

Mrs. Chitra met her sister-in-law's eyes. It only took Gayatri a moment to pick up on the vicious woman's insinuation that her mother was some sort of trollop.

"How dare you insult my mother," said Gayatri.

"Oh, how precious," Hema said caustically. "A warrior defending the woman who permitted a murderous thief into the house! A convenient arrangement, I imagine."

With those irretractable words whipping the silence, Mrs. Chitra stood up.

"I have heard enough. Although my husband was not an angel, he fulfilled his duties, and I will fulfill mine with dignity. My daughter, our only child, will lead the funeral, and she will ignite Tilak's body. I must say, in light of the unpleasantness of it all, your poison-tipped barbs have been most enlightening."

Hema looked to her husband, but he blinked back at her as if he were being forced to walk on broken glass with a sprained ankle. She waited. Nothing. Then, her face bristling with defeat, she charged out like a rhinoceros.

"Such a distressful death as this can make one less reasonable than one would like," wheedled Jayadev. "Think about how it would look. It is not worth splitting the family over such a matter."

He purposefully ignored Gayatri as he followed the others out.

It might have turned out differently if Varija's husband had still been alive, but he had been shot in a political fracas perpetuated by mob tensions.

"Your father was pigheaded, and you are pigheaded as well," Mrs. Chitra had said simply when they were finally alone.

The incense ash that was burning intact along the length of the stick fell silently on the richly engraved silver tray. Gayatri tilted her head and read the inscription. It said, "Good Luck." She looked at the goddess of courage, Parvati, a weapon in each of her four beautiful hands and a tiger at her feet. She thought back to the funeral, and wondered if her father had been angry or pleased. Either way, she was glad she had done it. She struck a match and lit another incense stick.

With firecrackers alerting the villagers, the funeral procession had wound slowly through the dirt roads of Vijayawada. Her cousins carried her father on seven steps of raw green wood. Her mother had remained at home as was the tradition. People looked out of their windows and over walls to see who had died. She felt the heat of their eyes upon her as she held the earthenware pot of fire high above her head, her own eyes focused straight ahead. When they arrived at the holy burial grounds, the field grass was cool as it brushed against her toes and ankles. The body was set down, and she walked around it clockwise three times. She took the fire pot and ignited her father's head. She looked up at the ghost shell before her and thanked him for taking part in her birth. She excused how he mistreated her mother and thanked him for raising her with love. Through tears and flames, she looked up and said that she would miss him and wished him well in his next life. Breaking the water pot, her clay jug of daughter-tears, she promised not to cry anymore and bid him goodbye. The black smoke was billowing up toward the clouds behind her as she began to walk away. She was not supposed to turn around, and she resisted the urge. The men were waiting for her under the shade of a tree, and she could not help but think they had been laughing at her.

"Did you not hear me, Gayatri?" asked her mother.

She was standing in the doorway.

"The rice is getting cold. Let us eat."

Gayatri followed her mother into the dining room, although she was not in the least bit hungry.

She tipped her head back and knocked the bottom of the glass so the last grape would roll into her mouth. They were the only customers sitting in the Dollop ice cream parlor until an Indian-American woman and her white husband walked in. They both looked miserably exhausted. The proprietor looked at them disapprovingly as they considered the ice cream flavors. The man was painfully sunburnt, his skin glowing like an ember.

"I've been craving this grape drink forever," said Gayatri as she put the glass down on the table.

She looked at her mother and realized she looked sad.

"Are you all right, Mum?" she asked.

"I am just thinking of all of my lives," she said as she stared into her mango ice cream.

"Do you mean your past lives?"

"No, in this life, I have died so many times. When I married your father, my life as I knew it died, and when I had you, my life as I knew it with your father died. All these deaths, and still I was not prepared. We are surrounded by death at every turn, yet we refuse to see it. We fool ourselves into thinking we can surpass it."

Her mother got up and walked out. Watching her move, as if in slow motion, Gayatri noticed her mother's age for the first time.

Massive clouds were blocking the sun like moving buildings. One minute it was blindingly bright and in the next, gloomy. A red-winged crow coasted through the eerily illuminated sky, which was swirling with the strangest pinks, yellows, oranges and blues. It felt as if the end of the world had finally arrived, and the flow of frenzied traffic only added to the fantasy. As they walked over the bridge that led to the road to Guntur, the sacred Krishna River split on either side of them. Gayatri stared at the spot where her mother had just strewn her father's ashes in the river. They had to go on a bit of a trek to do so because the water was so very low. She looked at the buffalo that spotted the shores like small rocks meandering toward the receding river line. Further down, washer women had walked for what seemed to be miles of beach to beat clothes in clean waters. She remembered how she watched the washer woman at their house when she was a child. Each time she would whack a sari on the washing stone, she would expel a gust of air from her lungs in the way of a song for stamina. There was a slight breeze when her mother set the ashes free, and the grayish powder blew toward the makeshift laundry lines strung out on the riverbank. Saris of vibrant colors were on one side and lily-white dhovtis and bed sheets, on the other. Unlike in washing machines, the women could wash all the laundry together here. Disparities of color and conscience were harmoniously diffused in the vastness of river waters.

"A part of me is glad you have a life for yourself in London, Gayatri," her mother said as they left the bridge and walked down a quieter street. "Lately, the crime has become terrible here. They are even snatching chains from the necks of schoolgirls. Navina, the Valuris' daughter, was doused with acid by an irate suitor, and the Sutrachilis' son hung himself from a ceiling fan over an exam. I think he was in love with a girl. It is frightful."

"Do you want to move to London, Mum?" asked Gayatri enthusiastically.

Mrs. Chitra did not answer immediately.

"I am much too old to move now," she said, finally.

"Oh, come on, it would be just brilliant. You've always wanted to be a painter, and there are loads of galleries where I live."

"Do you know what would make me happy? If you got married, Gayatri."

"You would love it there. I've got an enormous flat on a charming street with a cobblestone walk. We can set you up in a fantastic place in my building. There are dozens of cafes and galleries right downstairs and sari and Indian sweet shops in the Little India quarter not too far away. It's a really artsy neighborhood. And we can take trips to Paris and Florence. You know how you've always wanted to see Europe."

"I just want you to be happy, Gayatri."

"But I am happy, and I want you to be happy. Just promise to think about moving. You don't have to right off—in a year or so."

Her mother smiled and looked up at the dusk sky, which was now a purplish gray. The sun had suddenly disappeared, forever it seemed. Above a church was a bluish-white glow thrown from a cross made of two fluorescent light tubes. They stopped at a paan-wallah stand, and her mother asked for two beeda. They watched as the vendor laid out some betel leaves and filled them them with scented calcium, a red sugary paste, betel nuts, fennel seeds and a thin sheet of silver foil. He then rolled the leaves into two elegant funnel-shaped works of art and handed one to each of the them. Her mother paid him and casually popped the entire thing into her mouth, her left cheek bulging as if she were sucking on a ping-pong ball. Gayatri was surprised because her mother had never encouraged her to eat betel nut, much less killi or beeda. Although it was a good aid for digestion, she said it was unfeminine, especially for unmarried women, because it stained tongues and lips and mouths an unattractive blood-red. As Gayatri bit into the plump bundled leaf, the red juice trickled down her chin.

The Doctor

J unk," Ajay muttered as he tossed the mail on the table with two
bouquets of pink and white roses he had bought downstairs at
the Korean market. Picking up the remote, he turned on the stereo.
He had left in an Ella Fitzgerald compact disc in that morning, and
it began playing automatically. He had at least five hundred CDs and
cassettes to choose from, but he didn't have time to select one right
now. Ella's voice swung through the room:

"Say it's only a paper moon, sailing over a cardboard sea, but it wouldn't be
make-believe, if you believed in me; yes, it's only a canvas sky hanging over
a muslin tree, but it wouldn't be make-believe, if you believed in me."

He glanced at the answering machine. He was thankful it wasn't
blinking maniacally. Stripping off his clothes, he turned on the
shower. He looked around the bedroom, which was relatively in order. Then his eyes fell on the two down pillows, both of which
seemed to have indentations. He sprinted over to the bed and

fluffed them up. As he surveyed the bed again, a few feathers floated past his face. He blew at them so they would stay up just a little longer. In the next second, he walked through the bathroom mist and disappeared behind the tropical-sea shower curtain. As he washed his hair, he could hear his watch beeping in the bedroom. He had forty minutes. It was funny how, at times, an hour shot past as if a submarine missile, while, at other times, a minute sank slowly to the bottom of the ocean, ensnared by seaweed and interrupted by fish. He could be in the operating room for hours and have it feel like minutes or vice versa. As he reached for the soap, he froze in midair. It was the Crabtree & Evelyn sandalwood soap that Joanna had given him for his birthday. Pushing the curtain aside, he grabbed the rose decorator soap from the dish on the sink and began lathering up. That day, she had taken him to a restaurant in SoHo. It was a trendy place called Fa Caldo, Italian for "it's hot." He had to wake himself up. Turning the shower nozzle to cold, he gasped at the temperature change. As he stepped out of the tub, he took the sandalwood soap and pitched it into the garbage.

After pulling on some briefs and socks, he flicked on the switch in the spacious walk-in closet. Pushing some hangers aside, he gave some thought to wearing a suit. Instead, he pulled on a pair of Levi's and put on a button-down shirt. As he tied his shoes, he looked at the other side of the closet. It was empty except for the new pastel plastic hangers neatly pushed to one side. In the living room, he clipped the ends of the roses and arranged them in two vases. He put the pink ones in the foyer on the table and the white ones in the bedroom on the nightstand. Finally, he collected the garbage and picked up the two bags of soda and beer bottles from the kitchen and left. In a second, he was back to click off the stereo.

He walked to the corner to hail a cab. It was seven o'clock. Most of the rush-hour traffic would be thinned out. Stopping at the intersection of Tenth Street and Broadway, he looked up the avenue for a cab. The art exhibit in the windows of a New York University dorm building featured building blocks with jarring images of victims of recent wars juxtaposed with photos depicting gang violence and happy diapered babies. As he saw the cars coming, he held up his hand and looked back at the window. He imagined himself having to operate under the pressures of war. He had been working at St. Vincent's for only a year and a half, and it was, so far, a relatively calm experience. He had never lost a patient. Would he be able to handle an influx of war victims? Would he be able to become a human body mechanic—to detach himself as the veteran doctors and move from shrapnel-riddled stomach to crushed lung? A cab screeched to a halt. He leaned into the open window.

"Will you take me to JFK?" he asked.

"Sure thing," said the driver.

He got in and shut the door. The driver stepped on the gas, throwing him back into the seat. He rolled down the window a bit.

"Indian?" asked the cabbie.

He hated it when people asked him that. It was different, of course, when it came from people who were just curious about his skin color. But more often than not, they made bets on if he was from Sri Lanka, Pakistan, West Indies, Guyana or India. There was always this goddamn guessing game, and he hated it. What was the big deal?

"Pakistan?" continued the cabbie, turning his head a little.

"No. Indian."

He glanced at his taxi license. He was Indian, too. His name was Prabhadaokar, Vyshna.

"I am also Indian," the driver said with a big smile.

"I know," he said.

"How?"

"Your license. I know by your name."

"And your name is . . . ?"

"Ajay," he said. It sounded weird because he was so used to saying Jay.

The driver reached to turn up the volume on the tape deck. Ajay hoped it wasn't some high-pitched Indian movie singer. He waited.

No, it wasn't Indian. The driver began to sing along. Ajay closed his eyes.

"Since you came into my life you found a way to touch my soul, and I'm never, ever, ever gonna let it go. Happiness lies in your own hand. It took me much too long to understand how it could be until you shared your secret with me."

"You like Madonna?" asked the driver.

"What?"

"You like Madonna?" the driver repeated, turning down the volume.

"She's okay."

"Ohhh, come on. She is terrific. You listen to her? She's spiritual."

"No, I like mostly jazz," he said, and the cabbie shrugged.

As the music filled the cab again, Ajay looked out the window. He didn't want to talk to the driver and wished he would stop asking questions. He closed his eyes. The next time he asked him something stupid, he was just going to ignore him. He would think he was sleeping.

"It took me by surprise that you understood," sang the driver softly. "You knew all along what I never wanted to say, until I learned to love myself I was never ever lovin' anybody else."

Ajay drifted off with thoughts of Joanna. She was beautiful naked. Her breasts were perfect, heavy and pink. He wished he wasn't thinking about her right now. What was wrong with him? The last time they had sex was over a year ago. It was right before he left for India. Then he broke it off. He had to. He was not in love with her. He saw her at work, and she always looked into his eyes too deeply. She didn't understand. When he had come home that night from the airport, she was waiting for him in his apartment. She had lit what looked to be twenty or so candles and arranged them around the living room. She was sitting on the rug with some pillows when he opened the door. When she stood up, he saw she was wearing a transparent black shirt that reached her mid-thigh. The candles flickered when he took off his jacket and tossed it on the couch. She held her arms out. They looked like wings and the sheer black draping over them was pulling him closer to the luminescence of her milky skin. Gorgeous. She was so hard to resist.

"Surprise!" she had cried.

"How'd you get in?" he had asked before he could stop himself.

"The manager—did I surprise you?"

"Yes, you did."

"I couldn't wait until the hospital to see you. I didn't think I could contain myself."

"Look, Joanna, I'm tired," he began.

"Want a drink?"

"No, I just want to go to sleep."

"Bad timing?"

"Yes," he said.

He sat down on the couch, and she came over to him.

"What is it?"

"Joanna, I told you that it was over. I told you I didn't want to see you anymore. Didn't you hear me?"

"Why are you so angry?"

"I'm not angry. Well, I am. Yes, I am because I didn't expect to see you. You're just making this harder than it should be."

"What does that mean, Jay?" she raised her voice. "I'm just supposed to vanish? What was I—just so you could say you screwed a white woman?"

She stood up. He looked straight ahead, but he still could see her naked white body glowing amidst the circle of flames as she pulled on her jeans and sweater.

"Joanna, you know that's not true. I care about you, but I just can't keep lying to myself. I was attracted to you and you to me, but it just didn't work out."

"What am I supposed to think?" Her voice started to get jittery. "You break up with me, but don't give me one good reason why. What am I supposed to believe?"

"I'm sorry if I hurt you, Joanna."

He stood up.

"What is it, Jay? Tell me. You owe me an explanation. That's the least you can do."

"I can't explain it. I enjoy being with you, but it doesn't feel right. It just doesn't feel like it could last," he muttered, realizing how horribly cryptic he sounded.

"Nothing lasts," she said.

"That's what I mean. I don't think this infatuation will last."

"You think I'm just infatuated? I'm not. I love you."

"You're a beautiful woman, Joanna. This has nothing to do with you. It has to do with me. I'm sorry. I don't know what else to say."

"Why did you go to India?"

He walked away from her and looked out the window. He wished he had never gotten involved with her. It was a mistake. No, it was not a mistake. She was the best thing that had ever happened to him in a way.

"I'm not leaving until you tell me," she said firmly.

He turned around and looked her in the eye.

"I got married," he said.

Her lips started to quiver.

"To whom?"

"It was an arranged marriage."

"What? You married someone you don't even know? I can't believe this shit. You couldn't stand up to your parents? Or did you want a virgin? Was that it? What the hell is wrong with you, Jay?"

He really knew she was asking him what was wrong with *her*. He felt sick to his stomach.

"I never wanted to hurt you, Joanna," he said walking toward her.

She was furious as she fastened her shoes. Her face was wet and flushed.

"It's too fucking late for that, Doctor," she said and slammed the door.

Ajay looked down at the candles. He was standing in the circle of fires. He bent down and blew them out. The wisps of smoke spiraling toward the ceiling set off the fire alarm.

The driver honked the horn and swerved the cab, catapulting

Ajay back to the present.

"Watch it, clown!" yelled the driver at a car that had cut him off.

Ajay saw him reach for a pen and jot down the license number. He wondered if he was going to report the driver. They were going through the Midtown Tunnel.

"What airline do you want to go to?" the cabbie asked.

"Air India."

"Who are you meeting?"

"My wife—she is coming to live with me."

"Oh," he said with a big smile.

"Are you married?" asked Ajay.

"Yes. I live with my three brothers. Sekhar and I are married, and the two younger ones are still single."

"Where do you live?"

"In Queens—Astoria. Do you know it?"

"Yes. A lot of sari shops are located in Flushing. We went there when my mother and father visited from Chicago."

"So, what is she like?"

"Who?"

They emerged from the tunnel. The sun was just beginning to set.

"Your wife."

"We didn't have much time to get to know one another. She is pretty and bright."

"What do you do?"

"I am a physician—a cardiologist."

"Really? We went to the hospital last week."

"What happened?"

"Hey!" he yelled and honked the horn. "My brother, Poorna, got beaten up by some men."

Again, he jotted down the license number.

"That's awful," declared Ajay. "What happened?"

"Well, they jumped on him when he was coming home at about seven o'clock on Friday night. He was bringing home some Hindi videos. We were all planning to watch them that night. They beat

Poorna with their fists only, thank God. They screamed 'sand nig-gers' and 'Paki.'" They don't think we should be there because it was an Italian and Greek neighborhood before we came along. They want us to go back to our country."

"Is your brother okay?"

"He got fifteen stitches on his head. Wounds will heal, but he is scared to walk down the street again."

"Did they ever harass you before?" Ajay asked with increasing concern.

"A few times. They told us to leave and that when we cooked, our spices stunk up the building and street."

"They said that?" Ajay said with amazement. "Didn't you alert the police about that? That's harassment."

"We did, but the police said there was nothing they could do."

"They have to wait until a person is hurt again before they can do anything? It's ridiculous. Well, you're pressing charges now, aren't you?"

"We are still discussing that. It will be such a mess really. It might be best to just forget it happened."

"But you can't let them intimidate you."

"Ajay, this is not India. Our voices will not be heard as loudly here."

"Well then, you can't stay there. They know where you live."

"We are thinking of moving, but the rents are too expensive in Manhattan. Now my niece, Sindhura, has come to stay as well, and we must spend extra money on her. Her wedding match was suffo-cated by his younger brother, who was apparently in love with Sin-dhura all along. Another terrible shock—they say bad things happen in threes. She is the daughter of my brother-in-law's sister. When she and her husband were killed in a bus accident, Sindhu went to live with her uncle, my sister's husband. You know, the number of love-related suicides and murders in India is climbing?"

"Really? I was not aware of that," Ajay said.

"The cinema industry is responsible, I think. The young ones copy what they see."

"Like TV here. I still cannot believe they beat your brother. I mean, 'sand niggers,' it's obvious we're not—"

"Racists do not care if we are Indian, Arab, Pakistani, Hindu, Muslim, pacifists, terrorists. We all look the same—different from them."

Ajay's eyes followed an airplane in the night sky. They were getting closer to the airport. He wondered how many racists' lives he had saved. If they were able to choose between a white doctor and himself, who would they choose? Should he have the right to choose who should live and who should die? For the first time in his life, he felt completely useless as a doctor. How do you make someone like you? How do you make them understand? He thought back to the soap that Joanna had given him. Did she realize that it was made by a British company capitalizing on India? Did it even occur to her? He could feel his pulse beating faster in his neck. Why was he so angry all of a sudden?

"It seems odd that you would have an arranged marriage, Doctor," said Vyshna, looking into his eyes in the rear-view mirror.

"Why is that?" asked Ajay.

"You look like you were born here. I see more and more young Indian men and women with non-Indians. I pick them up at the Palladium and the expensive bars in SoHo. Poorna and Bhupal are the single ones, so they date occasionally—you know with the AIDS problem, they must be careful. I tell them all the time."

"True. Well, I've dated a fair share of women, and I didn't feel that they understood me. I felt they were too conscious of the fact I was Indian—that my skin was darker than theirs, that I was exotic, their ticket to spirituality. I want to be with someone who doesn't need an explanation about why I eat with my hands sometimes and who can converse with me in my mother tongue."

"Could you not meet an Indian woman living in the U.S.?" asked Vyshna as he turned into the airport.

"I've dated a few, but it just didn't work out. They had the attitude that I was going to take away their rights. We had a difference of opinion regarding the definition of the word 'independence,' I guess."

"You are traditional. There is nothing wrong with that."

"This country may be the land of opportunity and choices, but that does not mean I have to shun my cultural identity."

"This is what I tell Poorna and Bhupal. They should have arranged marriages and settle down. But I have faith that they will come around. Did you fall in love with your wife when you saw her?"

"No. But I think I can fall in love with her."

"Instead of meeting her at a bar, you met her at a wedding, right?" Vyshna said, beaming, as he stopped the cab in front of the Air India terminal.

"Yeah, ours."

Ajay gave him a ten-dollar tip, and Vyshna accepted it graciously.

As Ajay walked over to the customs inspection exit, he was amazed he had ended up talking Indian politics with a cab driver. There were all shades of Indians pressed up against the railings, their eyes focused on the automatic doors that opened and closed. He remembered what it felt like on the other side of those doors. Eighteen years ago, he had waited anxiously in a long line for the inspection officers to stamp his passport, hoping they wouldn't find the snake gourd, amla and other seeds his mother had asked him to bring. He was sweating as he stepped up and heaved his suitcases onto the counter. The officer looked at his passport, stamped it and let him through. There was no trouble at all. He didn't even ask him what was in the plastic containers that had started to ooze messy orange oil. Maybe he let him through so quickly because Ajay was only fourteen and wearing blue jeans. Maybe it was because the smell of mango and lemon pickle that filled the air was making him sick. Whatever it was, he was relieved. He hoped his wife would have the same luck.

He remembered their wedding night—her white and green sari, the large mole on her lower back, her fine-boned wrists, her unusually small waist and her disproportionately large buttocks. She was beautiful. They had only spent time together during the whirlwind of nuptials, beginning with a huge feast at her family's house and ending with the consummation. They actually hadn't had sex that night—the night that was foretold by astrologers as an auspicious time for baby-making. Instead, they had talked about wacky relatives and movie stars, politics and ice cream flavors, the Immigration and Naturalization Service and their dreams. When the doors swung open, people—some waving name-cards—leaned forward in anticipation. He hoped he would readily recognize her. After all, almost a year had passed by the time the glitch with her visa was ironed out. Still, how odd to hold up a card for one's own wife, he thought. A young woman pushing a luggage cart walked out. Was it her? No. Someone waved at the woman and she smiled, being swallowed by the crowd. She had made it to the United States. He wondered what dreams were fluttering in her heart. A steady stream of passengers was passing through now, and Ajay scanned their faces. What would she think of his outfit? Maybe he should have worn a suit. He looked at a couple embracing. Should he hug her when he saw her or just take her luggage? He felt so unsure of himself. He felt a tap on his shoulder.

"Ajay?"

He turned around and saw Divya dressed in a sparkling white and gold sari. She was radiant. Before he could speak, she wrapped her arms around him in an embrace.

"You made it," he said.

"Yes, it was a long journey."

"Well, let's go home, then," he said, taking the luggage.

The spicy aroma of pickle wafted up from a tote bag, and he smiled.

"Tomato pickle?" he asked, his mouth watering.

"Tomato, lemon and mango," replied Divya. "Is it too heavy? Give it to me."

"No, not at all."

Once outside, he started walking over to the taxi dispatcher.

"Ajay!" someone called.

When he turned around, he saw Vyshna across the street. He

waved a pink rose at him. Ajay was glad to see his familiar face. He felt as if their conversation had been much too short, and he regretted not getting his phone number. He picked up the luggage, and they walked over to the cab.

"You forgot something," said the driver as he handed him the rose and put the bags in the trunk.

"Thank you for waiting," said Ajay.

"My pleasure."

"Divya, this is Vyshna."

"Namaste," said the cabbie.

Divya just smiled. After they had settled in the back, Ajay handed her the rose.

When they got home, Ajay filled the tub and sprinkled rose petals in the water. Her mouth slackened, and he knew she was impressed.

"If it's too hot, turn this knob for cold water," he said and pulled the door closed.

When Divya emerged, he was busy dishing out the curries he had ordered from a local Indian eatery.

"There are no south Indian restaurants nearby," he began. "But I hope you will like this."

She was dressed in a transparent salmon-colored sari specked with white stars. Her shoulders were strong and her posture perfect. His wife was breathtaking.

"I am not so hungry," said Divya.

As she walked closer, he saw that her eyes were thrown open like a window in springtime and what he saw there was as magnetic as it was repelling. What on earth was he afraid of? Was she already in love with him? This was not love. Her thick lashes were clinging to one another like wet grass blades. She led him to the couch. After he sat down, she sat very close to him. She touched his face, and he held her hand. It was as soft as the petals he had plucked and tossed in the bathtub. When she leaned in and her lips met his, he could hardly breathe. It was as if he were kissing a woman for the first time in his life. Maybe it was because it was the only time it had really mattered. The brown of his hand on the brown of her neck was too much too fast. His heart was hammering from fear, from the joy of discovery. Before he knew what he was doing, he pulled away and stood up.

"You've traveled so far, Divya," he whispered. "You really must eat."

Her eyelids fell a little as she watched Ajay disappear into the kitchen. She thought back to when, in India, a curious lizard had crawled into her open palm. When she moved to stroke its back, the lizard had panicked and vaulted out of her bedroom window. Divya wondered if she had, once again, been too eager.

When Ajay awoke the next morning, the smell of dosai and coconut chutney filled the air. He had been craving them for a long time. He hadn't made love to Divya the night before. He wanted to get to know her and give her some time to adjust to her new home. He had taken off a few days from work so they could spend some time together and he could show her New York City. He wanted to take her to Central Park and the Metropolitan Museum of Art.

"Good morning," he said as he walked into the kitchen.

"Good morning."

"Did you find everything okay?"

"Yes," she said as she put a plate of sizzling dosai in front of him. "We need more flour and sugar."

Just then, his beeper went off.

"Damn," he said as he stuffed some dosai into his mouth.

He walked into the bedroom to check the number. It was his supervisor. He made the call with dread and walked back into the kitchen glumly.

"I have to go to the hospital," he told her.

"Maybe you can point out the market and post office," she suggested brightly. "I need to post a package to my Aunt Sita. I brought her tulsi for her sick daughter."

"I thought she was mentally ill."

"She is. The tulsi will help her."

He laughed at Divya's naiveté.

"Schizophrenia? I don't think so. If there was any chance of that, there would be whole farms growing it."

He noticed she looked a little hurt.

"It was a sweet thought to carry it all the way from India, Divya," he added. "But we have it here. It's called sacred basil."

As Ajay stepped off the elevator that evening, he smelled biryani and chicken. It was coming from their apartment. His mouth began to water.

"Divya," he called as he closed the door.

A jazz tape was playing. He walked into the kitchen and ate a piece of chicken from the steaming pot. She was probably in the bedroom.

"Divya?"

As he walked into the bedroom, the bathroom door opened and out stepped Divya into the hall in front of him. His mouth fell open. She was dressed in a skirt and blouse. Her hair was different. She was wearing it loose, and it was much shorter than he remembered.

"Do you like it?" she asked. "I went to the beauty parlor downstairs. Do you like it?"

"If you do, so do I," he said, trying his best to hide his disappointment.

She smiled and took his hand, leading him into the kitchen to eat.

The Servant

Indian buses made for neck-breaking journeys, so they were taking the train for the sake of the baby. Munjee was glad they had the compartment all to themselves. She hoped no one would join them, but she knew that would be impossible. Everything in India was crowded and overbooked. The baby kicked twice. She put a hand on her swollen stomach and looked over at her husband, Nikhil. He was sleeping, his tea glass precariously perched on the edge of the berth. But she did not want to save it from disaster. She wanted it to fall and break into a dozen pieces. Part of her wanted to walk on those shards of glass and feel each one pierce the hardness of her soles. Maybe if she felt the pain and saw the drops of blood bloom like roses on her feet, she would feel better.

She remembered the day she had told Mrs. Chitra that she would be quitting her job.

"Munjee, no," Mrs. Chitra had said, clutching her heart.

"Nikhil's mother is very ill, and we must take care of her. His brother sent word."

"When will you be leaving?"

"Next Wednesday. It is a good day to travel."

"Well, I knew this day would come, I suppose. I will miss you, Munjee," she said and walked into her bedroom.

But now, Munjee was going over her exact words because she wanted to be sure that they wouldn't accuse her. Nikhil robbed the house on Friday night, two days after they had supposedly left for Madras. Mrs. Chitra would not suspect her, but the police would. It occurred to her that she might have previously mentioned to Mrs. Chitra that Nikhil's mother was dead. If so, would she remember one day?

Nikhil's body was twitching. His outstretched arm was reaching toward her, his hand open and limp as a beggar's. What was he asking for in his dreams? Forgiveness or more riches? He was using the bag of jewelry and money for a pillow. Still, she could not bear to look at the gold chains.

"Wear it, and make it yours. It belongs to you now," he had said as he tried putting one of the stolen gold chains on her.

"No!" she screamed and backed away. "I cannot forget."

"You will."

Would she? She was glad she had convinced Nikhil to take a detour and stop at Tirupati before they started their new lives. She wanted to ask Lord Venkateswara for forgiveness. That was the god from whom Nikhil had stolen the pearl and gold necklace. He had tried covering it up by saying that he found the necklace in the safe, but she knew where it had come from. Had he forgotten that she was the Chitras' servant for two years? Did he think she was that stupid? It infuriated her that he thought he could use her like this. Was he planning to kill all along, or did he just get nervous? She looked out the window through the eucalyptus trees. She could see granite stones piled in pyramids, the tops of which were outlined with chalk so the workers could easily tell if thieves were stealing the stones. If the pile was disturbed, then a guard would be assigned to watch the rock piles at night. Everyone stole from the railway company. It seemed as if everyone was stealing from everyone in India. Probably that was why Nikhil was so calm. It had become a way of life. Maybe she would have felt differently if she was not pregnant. Life had been growing inside her for eight months now. She felt it growing every day.

Nikhil woke with a start. The glass fell, but did not break. It began to roll, so he held it between his feet. The creases in his neck and forehead glistened with sweat.

"What is it?" she asked.

He moved closer to the window so he could feel the breeze on his face. It must have been an upsetting dream because he did not answer her. She played with the orange glass bangles on her wrist. Neither of them had known that the old couple would be coming home. They should have been at the officer's function that Mr. Chitra had chirped about incessantly for a month before she had left. Munjee sighed, wishing she had never found out about the death. Murder. It was murder. How did her husband kill him? She suddenly had a thirst to know all the details. The question kept popping into her head. Had Nikhil killed anyone else before this? That was what she was itching to know, but dreaded learning. The sick feeling in her stomach was growing as the baby began to dance.

"Where is the water bottle?" he asked.

"In the big bag," she said, pointing under the berth.

He fished it out of the bag and twisted off the cap. He handed her the bottle, and she drank a little. The temperature was a hundred and four, and the water was already warm. The monsoon was predicted for any day now, but it had been fooling them for weeks. Once in sight, it kept turning around and heading back over the ocean. He tipped his head back and poured a steady stream into his open mouth.

"Are you hungry?" he asked.

"No, but you go ahead and eat. The pakodis are in a plastic bag."

He found them and sat down next to her. She looked out the window while he ate, but she could not stop thinking about that night. Finally, she turned to him.

205

"Nikhil, I want to know what it was like in the house that night," she said flatly.

"Where?"

"That night when you slit the old man's throat. What happened exactly?"

"Munjee, it is over," he said firmly. "Let's not dwell on it."

"No, I need to know. To put it behind us, I need to hear you tell me."

He stared at her for a moment and then looked down at his hand shining with pakodi grease.

"I was about to leave, when I heard the front door. He walked in, I jumped behind him and held the knife to his throat. He began to struggle."

"How did he struggle?"

"He began to kick my shins with his feet. I had no choice. It was over in a few seconds."

"Did you feel the life drain from him?"

"Munjee," he said, getting upset.

"Please tell me," she persisted.

"I did not hold him long enough. I grabbed the money and jewelry and ran to the roof."

"Was he still alive when you pulled the chain from his neck?"

"No, his eyes were open, but I think he was dead. Darling, I am sorry that I had to involve you at all. It was a bad idea."

She looked out the window at the blurry landscape.

"Did you ever kill anyone before, Nikhil? Tell me the truth."

She braced herself for the answer. She hoped he would say that he never had, but could she believe him? She had to.

"No," he said softly.

The word fell like a stone in a still pond, the rippling echo sending shivers down her spine.

By the time they reached Nellore, two other passengers had joined them in the compartment. One was a widow dressed in a white sari, and the other a man with bloodshot eyes. At first she thought that he had been drinking, but she did not smell liquor. When Nikhil stepped into the corridor to have a cigarette, he stared at her. She looked at the widow, who was asleep. She was Mrs. Chitra's age. A few wrinkles cut through her tea-colored skin beautifully as rills race across seastrands to rejoin the oneness of the ocean. Her hands were folded neatly in her lap. She wondered if Mrs. Chitra was also wearing white. The man continued to stare at her. When Munjee looked at him, he turned away. She noticed pieces of multicolored threads stuck to his pants. There was a lovesick sadness in his eyes, and it occurred to her then that he might have been crying.

She stared out the window wondering how she could love a murderer. How stupid she was for not knowing what Nikhil did when he robbed houses. He never talked about it, and she never asked. As they approached another stop, the train slowed down. On the side of the tracks, Munjee saw a pond with white and pink water lilies. The water level was very low because of the drought. Snouts up in the air, two pigs surfaced from under the sheet of lily pads. They were in heaven, diving down, digging up the roots and munching on rhizomes. They had already chewed up the lily fruits. She remembered when Nikhil had dived into a pond and retrieved a lily fruit the size of an apple for her to taste. The seeds looked like fish eggs and delightfully squirted in her mouth. It was a buttery-tasting delicacy, and here were the pigs devouring them by the kilo! It brought a smile to her face. Nikhil slid open the compartment door and sat down beside her. She wanted to tell him about the pigs, but she did not have the energy. Resting her head on his shoulder, she closed her eyes.

When they arrived at Tirupati, they had to take a bus to Tirumala, the mountaintop where the temple was located. They ate a quick, cheap breakfast and walked over to the ticket line. It was long, and Munjee waited on the side while Nikhil stood in line. She watched a pair of young girls slyly push their way closer to the front. They were purchasing tickets for those who did not want to wait in line and taking a service fee of ten to twenty rupees. The faster they got through the line, the more customers they could round up.

"Where do you think you are going?" asked an old woman.

The girls giggled. Then after a minute, they continued to inch their way closer to the front of the line. Munjee wondered what horrible sickness had sunk its teeth into the heart of India? Had people always been so greedy and selfish and this was simply the first time she had noticed?

Nikhil joined her with the tickets, and they headed over to the buses. There was not a queue to be seen. People were stampeding toward the arriving buses in a panic, as young and old alike shoved to get a seat. After three buses had come and gone, Nikhil became impatient. It was especially difficult for them because they had luggage. As an empty bus pulled up, he held people back with his arms wide.

"My wife is pregnant," he said at the top of his voice.

They managed to climb aboard and sit down in the front so it would be easier to disembark. She looked at the people scrambling up the steps and wondered if it was a game to them or if they were fighting others because they felt their reason to see Lord Venkateswara was most important. In less than a minute the bus was full and the driver was pulling away. As they wound their way up to Tirumala, Munjee's mind was stilled by the curvaceous hillsides and swaying cassia trees spangled with sunny petals and ruby pods.

Statues with wings, which symbolized Vishnu's bald eagle in human form, welcomed them. After storing their luggage, except for the bag with the money and jewelry, they found their way to a long zigzagging line where they could buy the special darshan tickets. They cost thirty rupees each. When she had come five years ago with her mother, they had waited in the "free" line. It had taken them six hours to see God.

"How are you feeling, darling?" asked Nikhil.

"I am excited," she said. "I want to offer my hair, Nikhil."

They were passing by an orchestra of barbers who sang to them, waving their shiny instruments. He gave her a questioning look. Munjee walked up to a few of the barbers and compared prices. When she settled on one, she asked to see the knife. She knew people who had gotten ringworm from dirty blades.

"Do you want to give your hair, too?" she asked her husband.

He shrugged.

"I guess I will look foolish with a bald wife if I were not bald as well," he said jokingly.

So, they made their way to the pushkarani, the tank of sacred water in which worshipers bathed before they got their heads shaved. Checking their chappals, they glided into the cool water with their clothes on. After that, they dried off and headed back to the barber. Munjee loosened her plait and sat down. Nikhil watched wide-eyed as the barber began first by hacking at her long hair with scissors. She could see the raven locks falling, tips heavy with holy water. Then she felt the cold blade pressing against her scalp.

The sun had been devoured by a hungry cloud. A man yelled that the smell of rain was in the air, and the crowd cheered. Munjee and Nikhil had waited for four hours and were inching closer to their destination. Whenever she could, she sat down on the seats on the side of the line while Nikhil saved their place. On one of the benches, someone had stuck a sticker that read, "Pirated cassettes are bad karma." Some young men in front of them laughed, but she felt sick to her stomach. The warning struck her like lightning. What if Mr. Chitra would be reincarnated as the baby growing inside her? She could not believe it had not crossed her mind until now. It was a sign from God telling her that sacrificing her hair was not enough. Her skin became clammy.

They entered through the temple doors, and she could feel the urgency of the crowd pulsing behind them. She felt lightheaded, partially from the heat and partially from the absence of her heavy braid. They each held their own cut hair in turmeric-stained cloths. The bundle was soft in her hands. Nikhil smiled at her, and she smiled back, letting him know that she was all right. She was glad he was not as resistant as he had been before about coming to see Lord Venkateswara.

"Why do you want to take me to a god who watched my mother be murdered?" he had asked.

"Because it is the same god who is giving us a child," she had said. "We will ask for forgiveness and start our new lives."

Guards stood at opposite corners directing the flow of traffic. Bodies pushed against one another as blood rushed through them as if through a singular vein. It was only in a place of worship that men freely pressed up against women and women ignored it. She glimpsed the black stone of Lord Venkateswara. They detoured into a quieter area, where a priest took their oblations of money and hair, while muttering prayers. Then, they rejoined the line, and when it was their turn, the guard tapped Nikhil on the shoulder to tell him to move along. They rushed to the front, and in a fleeting moment, she saw the sparkling diamonds set in the deity's tall crown. She did not even have enough time to think. On the way out, she stopped Nikhil and briefly looked back at the statue. Standing still, defying the angry guards, she finished praying.

As they followed the line out, they passed the fervid crowd straining their necks to see what lay ahead. A priest dished some prasadam into Munjee's and Nikhil's hands, and they waved the sacred sweet before their eyes before eating it. The floor was sticky and wet. As they turned the corner and walked outside, they passed glass chambers where temple workers were counting the money that was bestowed upon Lord Venkateswara. Much of it would be given to the universities of Andhra Pradesh. Since worshipers often gave money and jewels generously, Tirumala was one of the richest Hindu temples.

When Munjee had come here last, her brother had been sick and her mother had given all the jewelry on her body at the spur of the moment in hopes that Venkateswara Swami would cure her son. By the time they had reached home, her brother's fever had broken and the rash on his body had vanished. She remembered her mother taking off her bangles and gold-dipped earrings and dropping them in the large container covered with cloth. It was over six feet tall and very difficult to reach to discourage robbers. Her mother had told her that in the old days, people walked through the forest and up the mountain to Tirumala. The treasures were said to be protected by tigers and snakes who would kill off any thieves.

As they turned the corner, Munjee came face-to-face with the vat of jewels. Every step she took, it became clearer to her what she would have to do to ensure her first-born child's welfare, to have peace of mind. She snatched the bag from Nikhil and stood on her toes to reach the top of the container. In that split-second, she heard something fall in. She thought she had even glimpsed the Chitras' gems and gold cascade into the opening. But Nikhil caught her by the arm before she could let go of the bag. He thrust his hand into the bag and pulled out a stack of hundred-rupee notes. That was all he could salvage of the gold chains, twelve sovereigns, bangles, gems and thirty thousand rupees. As her husband looked up and his eyes locked on hers, she knew he had killed more than once.

The Beggar

Maya set down the plastic container of water and squatted to shit. The folds of the long skirt bunched between her legs and covered her somewhat. She fingered the mirrors stitched onto the pale blue cotton langa, off which sunbeams bounced, sprinkling stars in the shady, grassy spot behind her. She looked up as a lorry driver honked his horn at a passing herd of goats on Miryala Road, one of the main roads in Kondapalli. It was only eight in the morning, and she was already ravenous. She hated it when she woke up so hungry. Picking up the container, she washed herself with her left hand. She smiled when she remembered her mother's words: The right hand is for eating and the left hand is for shitting. A frog hopped toward a swampy area near the rice paddy field. Today, she decided, she would take a bath. ·

When she arrived at Godavari Canal, she hiked up her langa to her knees and walked down the steps to the water. Removing the pouch she carried on the inside of her waistband, she hid it under a rock. There were others washing further down the canal. Maya placed the small packet of newspaper on a stone and unwrapped it. One of the storeowners had gotten into the habit of giving her a scoopful of green gram flour once a week. It was cheap, and it probably made him feel he was doing his share of good deeds. Sometimes, she delivered groceries to houses for him, and he gave her a little money. She smoothed the olive powder over her arms and legs. She wished she could strip off her clothes and wash herself properly, but she could not as the only time the water was still was at night and she needed the sun to dry her clothes. Lifting up her jacket, she rubbed the flour onto her stomach and between her breasts, and it fell into the stream, blackened by the dirt from her skin. After she washed her face, she walked further into the stream until she was submerged up to her neck. Her langa floated up around her shoulders as her hands disappeared under the water. When she stepped out, she could feel how clean she was by the way her wet skin drank up the warm sun. She was grateful to the storeowner. Many of the others just washed with water.

Taking out a small comb from her pouch, she began combing the knots from her long brown hair. It was rough and dull because she rarely washed it. That was fine because she could not afford to look too clean. It would ruin her chances of begging some money for food. She had to look convincing. She worked alone, unlike many of the beggars, who were usually part of an organization in which the brokers took most of the money and gave them a little to survive. They were not fed too much because then they would not look like beggars. It was not easy to fake looking thin and sickly. It was hard enough getting people to reach into their pockets and flip a coin her way. She was fifteen, and at that age, they said she should go find work. But none of them would hire her to clean their houses. What was she supposed to do? It was true she was not missing an arm or dragging her leg, but she needed to eat, too. Her mother, who had spent many of her days as a child begging on the streets of Hyderabad, had taught Maya everything she knew. She told her how to avoid the pimps and how to look pathetic. It was an art, and it took a lot out of Maya in the beginning. She remembered when she was clinging to her mother's sari one day on a busy street. A little boy sitting in a car started playing peek-a-boo with her, and she played along. When her mother saw what she was doing, she pulled her by the hair.

"You must not smile like that, Maya," her mother had scolded, as the tears rushed down Maya's dirty cheeks. "You must not do that. It is bad."

So, Maya learned to smile when a piece of sweet was handed to her. She learned to smile when someone tucked a rupee in her small hand. Mostly, she learned to smile in private. She wondered if her mother and father were still living in Hyderabad. She had stowed away on a train when she was ten and had not seen them since. Now, the exact reason why she had left was not clear in her mind. What she did know was that she did it for her mother. She did not want to be a hardship anymore. Even if she went back, she could never find them. They moved frequently because rich people would complain and their hut would be torn down. When the rich sipped their tea on their verandas, they wanted to see butterflies and parrots, not the poor cooking on open fires in front of their palm-leaf shacks. She stood up and shook out her langa. It had already started to dry.

As Maya walked, her stomach rumbled. Up ahead on the open road, a man was spreading out coconut husks he had collected. The lorries and cars would run over the husks and flatten them. The weight of the trucks would help soften the husks. Then the man would weave hospital beds, mats and rope using the coir. Sometimes, people would spread limestone and wait for the trucks to grind it for them. Then they would sell the limestone powder at the market. Servants of the rich decorated the walkway to house entrances with the chalk to ward off evil. There were free "factories" like this all along the road. Maya knew lots of things in India were free if she used her head.

Her hardened soles were massaged by the small pebbles on the roadside. Looking up, she noticed that a woman's sari pallu was hanging out of a rickshaw, Maya ran to tell her. She had heard of women being strangled by their saris when their pallus were eaten by the revolving wheel spokes.

"Your pallu, Ammagaru," Maya yelled as she ran alongside the rickshaw.

The woman pulled on the trail of cloth and smiled her thanks. Maya's mother had taught her to treat others well even though she was poor. She believed that good deeds would be rewarded in some way, if not immediately, then in the next life.

As she passed a powderpuff tree, she heard a baby's gurgling. There was a cotton sari tied between two boughs of the tree, and in this cradle was a baby girl. She looked toward the clutter of huts across the street, but no one was in sight. Hearing a noise, she spotted a woman washing bronze and steel cooking vessels in the distance. Maya wondered if her mother had left her hanging like this when she was a baby. She had always felt she was a burden—an extra mouth to feed. Sometimes she felt they had wanted a boy. Their disappointment, however, had surfaced only occasionally. It was best that she had left. The baby girl cooed and began sucking on her tiny foot. Maya rocked the cradle until she was asleep.

A lorry passed, and flakes of rice husk flew out from under the burlap cover. In the bright sun, they glinted and shone like snow. Her mother had told her about the mountains up north where the white powder stuck to the peaks. In the summer, it would melt, and down would trickle cool water. The aching in her stomach was more noticeable now, and she wondered if it was just hunger for food or because she was homesick.

"Do you know what Maya means?" her mother had asked her once as she washed her at a public pump. "It means illusion."

Now, Maya was living the illusion to the fullest. It was a shame that the people needed to be shocked into pitying the poor. That was what made the pimps kidnap small babies and blind them by squeezing the juice of the milkweed into their eyes or repeatedly break their limbs so they would be crippled. It was what made mothers sacrifice their children into the begging underworld for a small stack of bills. An outstretched hand was not enough. But her mother had taught her how to arouse pity without maiming herself.

Since then, Maya had learned to master the art of illusion. Although, now, she was starting to look her age. The younger beggars did better, because as they reached up, people looked down into their glassy, naive eyes. The older you were, the less innocent you looked, because living on the streets did that to even the kindest souls.

Women were spreading red chili peppers on cloths and laying them out in the sun to dry as she walked into town. She decided to try a spot on the busy street across from the train station. She sat on the ground in the middle of the sidewalk, which was strewn with useless lottery and gambling tickets.

"Amma, please spare a little," she repeated over and over as she held her hand out to passersby.

An old man with a white beard dropped a fifty-paise coin in her hand. She thought this would be her lucky day, but it was not. By the time the sun set, she had given up. She had made a total of one rupee and eighty-five paise. It was obvious to her what the problem was—she looked much too clean today. She got up and walked toward the train station. Out front, she saw an old woman get knocked down by a scooter. The two men began to ride away, until they noticed a small crowd had gathered to see what they would do. Then one of them handed the woman a twenty-rupee note. They hopped back on the scooter and zoomed off. Maya peeled a banana as she watched the woman crawl into the shade of a tree to rest. She wondered if the woman was really hurt or just pretending.

Once inside Kondapalli station, she scanned the tracks for arriving trains.

On track three, there were passengers exiting a train that had just arrived from Hyderabad. She climbed aboard the emptying train and searched the compartments for forgotten luggage or money that had been accidentally dropped on the floor. It was a fun sort of treasure hunt, and she did not resort to train-hopping often. Looking clean was an advantage in this case because it drew less attention when she climbed on the train—the conductors chased beggars away if they spotted them trying to board. As she was searching under the berths, she looked up and saw through the window bars, a pink cake box sitting on a bench. Like the baby in the tree, this cake also did not seem to belong to anyone. Before she could fully weigh the consequences of her actions, she was skipping down the aisle of the train. Her stomach had suddenly come to life, and her mouth was watering. She walked up to the bench, picked up the cake as if it belonged to her and ran into the crowd. It was heavy, and she wondered if it was filled with fruit cream. She did not see the police or the group of people they were interrogating.

"Hey! Come back here with that! Police!" a man screamed as her feet began to move faster. "It has a bomb!"

But she did not hear their yells. Weaving through the people with skill, she held the cake away from her in hopes of not destroying the pretty icing. Her head swam with all of the various cakes she usually drooled over when she pressed her face against bakery windows. She had never tasted a cake like that. Laddoos and jilabee, yes. But a cake like what she hoped was in the box? Never.

"Stop!"

Her mirrored skirt flapped against her legs as she scurried up the stairs, over the walkway and down another set of stairs to the back of the station. She was glad no one had tried to play hero and stop her. Her heart beat with anticipation as she ran behind a mound of loose bricks. She was so hungry for the cake, she could already taste the sugar melting on her tongue. Sitting down, she arranged three bricks side by side and placed the cake box on the makeshift table. The moon was full and cast silver beams down on her like a spotlight. Her hands shook as she tore the string off the box. She lifted the cardboard top and caught her breath. It was pure white with pink flowers dotting the edges. There was something written on it. If she could read, she would have known that it said Happy First Birthday, Ganesh.

She smeared the lettering as she dug a hunk of the cake up with her fingers. The cake was white, and the lemony-pineapple cream inside was cool. She could not open her mouth wide enough, and the fluffy frosting stuck to her cheeks, chin and nose. Some water would be perfect with the cake. It occurred to her then that she would need to wash up or else the ants and mosquitoes would eat her alive that night. As she broke off another piece with her fingers, she saw a shadow looming before her. A policeman. She froze. He froze, too. They stared at one another in awe. She wondered why he had not pulled her to her feet and started beating her. In the next moment, the strange silence filled with his laughter. She must have looked funny with all that white on her face. Another policeman, waving a nightstick, joined him and he started laughing, too.

"The cake is a cake," said the first policeman to the other. "We had better call Vijayawada and tell them to stop rounding up and stripping the hijras."

"We do not have to rush to tell them—let them have their fun."

As they walked off laughing, Maya sat with her fingers fat with frosting and wondered what else a cake could be but a cake.

Giving Birth

D r. Sita Murali didn't understand the justice of it at all. Was there such a thing? Usha had been such an intelligent girl.

"Do you know how smart she was when she was a child?" she told the nurses. "When she was two, she asked my father to tell her stories."

"I don't know any stories," he had said.

"Oh, Grandpa, yes, you do—they are all in your head."

"Well, if they are in my head, how can I make them come out?" he had asked.

"You think about them, and they fall onto your tongue from your head, and then they are born into the world. That is how you will tell me stories, Grandpa."

She was all choked up saying it. The nurses looked at her blankly, and she knew they did not believe her. This drooling woman lying in room nine, how could she ever have been intelligent? How could she have shown such promise and withered away before she turned thirty?

"I know—I am her mother," she said defiantly.

"Room nine," one of them muttered again.

The tall one with all the makeup shook her head as if she knew exactly what she was talking about. Then they all walked away. Maybe they felt the anger swelling up inside her. Maybe they saw her eyes get teary. Maybe they did not know how to comfort a woman in a sari.

When she walked into the room, she began to shake. She did not want to see her daughter lying in a hospital bed.

"You can't even say 'hello'?" Usha said with an edge of hate to her voice.

The bottom of her jaw was cut, and the gauze pad was seeped with blood.

"Nanna, what are they doing to you?"

"Nothing."

"I am sorry."

"For what?" snapped Usha.

"I wish it were me lying here instead of you."

Her daughter turned away and stared at the sun through the blinds.

"I love you, Usha."

Her daughter whipped her head around and looked at her as if she had just confessed to murder. Her eyes were flashing, and she knew what Usha was thinking: She did not believe her. If ever she wanted Usha to know how much she loved her it was now, but she would not believe her. How could she have caused this? How could all the love she poured into this child have turned on itself and bubbled into hate?

"I have something for you," she said as she opened her purse and took out a small package.

Usha was curious, but wary. She watched her pour water into the glass on the bedside table and then drop in five tulsi leaves she had taken out of a wet napkin. The leaves were remarkably fresh considering that they had traveled across the world.

"Your cousin Divya brought tulsi from India," she began. "I think it will help you get better. Tomorrow morning, take out the leaves and drink the water. Will you drink it?"

Her daughter stared at her as if she were speaking another language. But what else could she do? It was the last hope. She recalled various tales of the powerful plant curing the most incurable diseases. There was no medical explanation or proof—just faith.

"Please, Nanna, you must drink it. It will help you."

Usha looked at the green leaves floating in the clear glass.

Sita looked down on her daughter, hoping her mind would click back into place, but she was deteriorating. Usha blamed her for it. All of it. Her eyes told her that. You were a bad mother. Dad died because we moved here. You never loved me enough. You were never home. But where was she? She was working to help support her three children. She wanted to give them the best in life.

There were days when she, too, wished that they had never stepped foot on American soil. Her practice had been burgeoning in Tunuku, and she was making a name for herself. She remembered when the tax bureau had written her a letter informing her that she was to be audited. The bureau said that, according to her patient list, she owed them a great deal more in taxes. She suggested they send someone to Tunuku to watch her work for a week. So, they did—a fellow by the name of Rama Rao. He saw all the patients that filed in sick and filed out better. He saw how many of them were poor and how she did not demand money from them. He noticed the rickshaw drivers who gathered outside the office and greeted her warmly. He heard that a woman had brought her a chicken and she had returned it graciously. That is how she served the sick as a physician. Mr. Rao was awestruck and so impressed that he kindly requested that she and her husband join him for dinner at his house. It was unheard of that an auditor would extend such an invitation in those days, and naturally they had accepted. She was never audited again.

So, why did they come to this miserable country? Her husband's brother and her own sister were doing so well for themselves in the States. Their children would have access to better colleges. No one had said, however, how hard it would be to get a job—that male hospital chiefs did not like women doctors, much less Indian ones. But she was used to fighting—in India, the male doctors had talked right through her as if she were transparent. They did not make it easy for her in the States, but she persisted and was hired as a staff psychiatrist. She stopped wearing saris and started squeezing into itchy polyester pantsuits because that was all they could afford. When relatives had boasted about America, no one had mentioned how hard it would be for her children to make friends or that some teachers wouldn't take into consideration that English was not their first language. No one told her that her husband would sink into a deep depression and eventually die of a heart attack at the age of fifty-two. No one told her his death would trigger a mental breakdown in her eldest daughter. All they said was, come on, it's wonderful here. Come on, we'll help you start your new lives. We have two cars, and we built a mansion. We went to Disney World. Come on.

Pushing the bitterness aside, she reached out and stroked her daughter's hair. It felt strangely artificial, like the strands that sprouted from heads of cheap plastic dolls. She remembered how when Usha had first arrived in the United States, she began campaigning for them to buy her a giant white doll-head that girls painted with eye shadow and lipstick.

"But all the other girls have Pretty Penny," she had whined.

They hadn't been able to afford winter coats, much less such an irrelevant toy. In certain spots, her daughter's hair was brittle as if it had been burned. Usha insisted on perming it, as she insisted on listening to music around the clock and eating junk food. She did everything Sita did not want her to do. And she could not help but think that Usha did it simply to spite her.

"What happened to your hair, Usha?" she asked.

"You're the doctor—you figure it out," her daughter cracked.

"How are they treating you, Nanna?" she asked holding back her tears.

Usha flinched away from her hand.

"Fine," she replied flatly.

"Are they feeding you enough?"

"I'm not hungry."

Usha's eyes were wide and scared. She was paranoid. She did not trust her.

"It is Amma, Nanna," Sita said to soothe her.

She sat down at Usha's bedside. Her daughter had not slept in days. She could see that by the dark circles under her eyes. What were they doing to her? She recalled some of the cold and cruel nurses in the mental institutions where she had worked. When she had reprimanded them for eating the patients' food, at first they had been embarrassed. Then, they said that she was an egotistical doctor.

The joy of delivering a baby when she was a surgeon in India was hard to place now. Sita closed her eyes, and nodded off. She saw a baby's head tearing through a splayed vagina. The head was huge, covered in bloody mucus and embedded with dozens of throbbing veins beneath the translucent skull. She reached out, and it fell with the weight of a melon into her hands. How many children had she birthed? She had lost count.

Then like an oncoming train, this vision took a turn. The tuft of black hair lying wet and sticky and the raw, wrinkled face shining up at her were repulsive. For the first time in years, she was sickened by the sight of the blood. Look beyond that, she told herself. There is life—great creation. But still the horror seized her, and she could not stop it. She had never reacted to birth this way before, yet it was all so vivid. Without warning, her hands pulled away from the baby's head. Its head slid down, tearing the hole wider. Then the baby hit the floor—all the while, crying murder at those few seconds of life. Sita awoke with a start, disturbed by her dream. Smiling, Usha was staring into her eyes. Were they peering out of the same window of fear?

After Sita's husband died, she had lost faith in the medical profession. They could not save him. Worse, she could not save him. Since her resignation, even her identity as a doctor had been stripped from her. Now, she was only a widow who wore saris and had a crazy daughter. Her husband had gambled away their life savings, so she could not afford to admit Usha into a private hospital. She had a mentally ill daughter in a state facility, and she was a doctor.

"How did your chin get hurt?" she asked.

Usha looked at her and blinked. Did she even know she had been hurt?

"Your chin, Nanna. It's cut. What happened?"

"What do you care?"

"I do care. I love you, and it upsets me to see this."

Sita looked at Usha and saw her as a five-year-old.

"They took my radio, Amma."

Amma. The word tolled hollowly in her ears. It was what her three children called her. That was, until they moved to the United States from India. Then they started calling her Mom. That was when the trouble started. How could they have expected any of their children to step out of a culture as if it were a garment and don another? Cultural values mixed, but some didn't, like oil and water. That is what happened inside her daughter. She did not know what was right. She did not understand why she could not move away with a white man. She did not understand that her parents were confused, just like her. How could she? They were supposed to have all the answers. They were the ones who brought her to this strange land. They had showed her all the opportunities, but made the choices for her.

"Those fucking white bitches," her daughter hissed. "They tricked me."

"How?"

But Usha did not answer. Instead, turning away, she shut her out.

"Let me go ask them about it, okay? I'll be right back, Nanna."

Now, she was bloodthirsty. She scanned the halls for the nurses—any nurse. She found two of them in the reception area.

"What happened to my daughter's chin?" she demanded.

"The patient had asked for a lemon to eat, and we gave it to her," the blonde one started. "We were being kind."

"In fact, one of the nurses had bought her a whole bag of lemons because Usha is a favorite patient of hers," interjected the tall one.

"Then, the patient snapped and assaulted two of the nurses by throwing lemons at them," stated the blonde one. "When mental patients are angry, they can be very strong."

"The lemons were very painful—they hit like baseballs," another one passing by piped in.

"When the aides tried to restrain her, she hurt herself," said the tall one, guiding a lumpy mascaraed lash out of her eye.

"Where is the doctor—I need to see him."

"Oh, he's very busy in the geriatric ward," the blonde one said, leading her back to room nine. "He'll call you at home when he gets a free moment."

As Sita walked back to her daughter, temporarily defeated, she heard a phone ring in the hall. Her back stiffened. Lately, she would stare at the phone with hatred. When it rang, her heart leapt. What had happened now? What new tragedy, what new hope? She knew it was a mistake to expect the same treatment from these doctors as she had given her patients as a surgeon. They didn't care as she had cared. The most painful part was that, as a doctor, she knew what a doctor was and was not capable of doing.

"Amma, did I get any mail?" asked Usha sweetly.

"No, Nanna. Not so far. I will bring it to you if you do."

Her daughter was looking at her, and for a moment, she looked like her daughter.

"Do you want anything, Nanna?"

Usha bit her lip as if in deep thought.

"Lemon pickle," she said. "I would like some lemon pickle."

The words stabbed her heart with a pained joy. Finally, her daughter had given her an opening to show how much she loved her.

"I will bring it tomorrow. Okay?"

Usha was staring out the window again, the lucidity in her eyes had completely vanished.

As Sita walked out of room nine, she heard chewing. She turned around and saw Usha with the empty glass in her hand and a tulsi leaf hanging out of her mouth. Her daughter, too, was impatient.

The entrance doors to the hospital swung open, and Sita walked out numbly. Her tanned skin drank in the afternoon sun as she stood on the concrete walk to catch her breath. The jingling of car keys in her hand seemed so far away. As she settled into her car and buckled up, she remembered she had to stop at the store to pick up some milk.

Her daughter's face was searing her mind like an alien sun. No matter where she looked Usha's face was all she could see. She imagined her daughter walking on telephone wires, hovering in trees, sitting on clouds and running alongside her car.

On the freeway, a Trans Am merged abruptly into her lane, and she swerved a little, honking the horn twice. The driver gave her the finger. A part of her wanted to floor the gas pedal and smash the other car to bits. But she did not speed up.

As she drove, a sudden queasiness overcame her. She remembered when her children complained of car sickness or felt as if they were going to vomit, she used to give them wedges of lemon pickle. At that moment, the realization struck her: Usha must have asked the nurses for lemon pickle, and they had given her lemons. Her eyes filled. Why didn't they think to call her? She rummaged through the glove compartment for a tissue and dabbed at the wetness. She knew why. They hated Usha because she was young, beautiful and ill. When they got too close, her schizophrenic eyes evoked those of their own daughters', and they needed to step back. That was why they couldn't understand.

How could they forget one of the side effects of the medicine they were injecting her daughter with was nausea? How could a lemon be synonymous with lemon pickle? Anger seized her as her mind groped to piece it all together—to drive out any uncertainties. When the nurses gave her daughter a lemon, with great difficulty, she had sucked on it. In fact, she ate the whole goddamn thing. What did they say to that? They probably laughed at her—right in front of her they laughed. It was so amusing to watch the crazy Indian girl suck on lemons, wasn't it? Then, the tall one came in with a whole grocery bag filled with them. She was being *kind*. The next day, her daughter was devastated. When a nurse entered her room, she hurled the lemons at her.

"Fucking white bitches," Usha screamed. "Didn't you hear what I said? Don't you understand English? Why doesn't anyone want to listen to me? Am I invisible? Fuck you!"

The nurses summoned the aides, and they banged her about trying to hold her down. In the struggle, her chin was cut. They took away her radio to punish her. What had she done wrong? Nothing at all. She was speaking a different language, although she was speaking English. And so, her Usha lay crumpled, her spirit smashed to bits like a mirror, each jagged piece reflecting her many indignities.

Sita had missed her exit. Her tears were falling freely now, and she could barely see the dotted lines separating the highway lanes. She did not feel that she was driving the car. Someone else was doing it for her. Getting off at the next exit, she took the back streets home. She remembered she had, in the fridge, a big plastic container filled to the brim with peppery lemon pickle. When she had morning sickness while she was pregnant, she had gobbled up lemon pickle. Her mother had said she could not make it fast enough. Now, every day, she felt as she had when she was lying in the hospital bed in Delhi, panting with anticipation, waiting for the doctor to tell her that her first-born child was healthy.

The streets were barren—not even a child playing on a front lawn or a barking dog. She missed the bustling streets in Tunuku, but she could not go back. This was her home now. She had seen too much, she had changed too much. Pieces of her were floating here. She thought how the only satisfying thing in her life was her small garden. The buds that blossomed year-round—the births she saw there—brought mild satisfaction.

She pulled up into the driveway and put the car in park. Engine still running, she watched the twilight horizon extinguish the flame-tip of the setting sun. The yellow and pink were engulfed by the dark house, which suddenly seemed grotesque. Remembering that she was out of milk, she shifted into reverse.

The Party

"D eepti, what are you doing?" called Mrs. Hema Supanni. "Come and hang these clothes upstairs."

"I am wiping the floor in the bedroom, Ammagaru," Deepti replied.

Dipping the rag in the bucket of soapy disinfectant, she crouched on all fours and cleaned the marble floor. This was the part of her job she hated the most. The disinfectant—it was the kind they used in hospitals and railway latrines—ate away at her hands, making them raw and itchy and the fumes made her dizzy. It would not have been so terrible if she had had to clean the floors only three or even four times a week, but Mrs. Supanni liked her to do it every day. After voicing a complaint, Deepti had been told that the upstairs rooms could be wiped up every other day. Deepti was happy to hear it, but she was on her guard, because similar to mixing the cleaning solution, their master-servant relationship could easily turn into a volatile concoction. There was always something about to bubble over in the Supanni household.

Thunder, a panting Doberman who had a penchant for pumping himself on people's legs, strolled into the room. His long toenails clacked on the marble. She smiled as she thought of Mr. Supanni attempting to clip the dog's nails. He covered up his fear of getting bit by jumping back and whooping how he did not want to harm the poor thing. Deepti pulled back as Thunder sniffed and snorted, blowing his foul breath on her cheek. She wished the Supannis had never bought him. These days, many rich people were buying ferocious canines and letting them loose in their front yards to ward off thieves and also to alert the village that they had something worth protecting. Dogs were their guns. Also, owning an expensive and rare breed could be added to the growing heap of status symbols people liked to flaunt, such as serving imported brandy to guests and displaying hard-to-get government phone diaries. No matter that one did not know a single person listed in the diary. The important thing was that the book desired by so many was sitting, not near the phone, but in a showcase collecting dust.

When she walked into the yard, Mrs. Supanni was sitting on a peta, cutting a snake gourd into bite-size chunks. She pushed the lengthwise slice of the vegetable away from herself against the vertical blade and tossed the pieces into a steel vessel.

Deepti walked over to the washing stone. The wet twisted logs of petticoats and saris sat in the two pails at her feet. She picked up the pails by the handles. The clothes were still heavy with water because the washer woman was not feeling well lately. Good thing she had showed up today. Another day and Mrs. Supanni would have insisted Deepti do the laundry. She would have refused, and that would have sown the seeds for an argument.

"Who does that old hag think I am? Am I the boss or what? I cannot believe she is abandoning me a week before the party."

"At least she did not get ill during the week of the party," Deepti reminded brightly.

"Ill? How nicely you defend her, Deepti. Let me tell you, I know all the tricks in the book. I am fifty-five years old, remember. This sickness crap is just a ploy. It is a political punch."

"Ammagaru, I really think she is not well," Deepti replied.

"Oh, do not tell me—everything in India has to do with politics."

She was silent because she knew that Mrs. Supanni was tongue-lashing the laundry woman in front of her for another reason. She wanted to remind her that she had eyes in the back of her head and that she was watching her, too. Deepti just wanted to stay out of her path today. Mrs. Supanni got especially unbearable when a party or other big function was approaching. Deepti walked into the house with the buckets.

"She wants to threaten me by reminding me that I need her. H*ah*. You see these?"

Deepti turned around and saw that Mrs. Supanni was pointing to the onion skins and cucumber peels on the ground.

"I need her like I need these."

Deepti nodded and made her way upstairs wondering who needed whom. Walking onto the second floor veranda, she wrung out the excess water from the clothing. She could get another job if she was told to leave, but she did not want to. Mrs. Supanni paid her well and as long as Deepti stuck to the routine, she did not bother her. True, Mrs. Supanni was in the habit of conveniently forgetting the history of one's dependability and concentrated on the here and now. That meant if the washer woman was late today, then she was always late.

It was the stability that made both of them behave. Although she threatened all the time, the truth was that Mrs. Supanni dreaded the thought of having to search for a new servant. It was a dangerous undertaking, and Deepti was trustworthy. Yes, Mrs. Supanni needed her. She shook out the petticoats and hung them up on the line. Stretching the cotton saris, she laid them flat on the floor of the veranda. The sun was hot, and they would dry quickly. As she turned to leave, Thunder ran onto the veranda and began chasing his tail, entangling himself in one of the saris.

"Thunder!" Deepti screamed, but it was too late.

He was entranced, throwing his head from side to side, the sari clenched in his bared yellow teeth.

"What is that racket?" asked Mrs. Supanni as she walked up the stairs and out onto the veranda. "Thunder! No!" she yelled, clapping her hands twice.

The dog dropped the sari and fled past both of them, his nails skidding down the stairs.

"Damn dog," Mrs. Supanni muttered as she picked up the abandoned sari.

There were several holes in it from his sharp teeth

"It is useless now," she said as she held it out. "You take it, if you like, Deepti."

As Mrs. Supanni plucked jasmine flowers from the bush on the veranda, Deepti laid the sari out again. It was not a favorite of hers, but she would take it home anyway.

At eleven o'clock precisely, the Muslim butcher would park his cycle inside the gate and drop off chopped beef for the dog. Mr. Supanni had arranged for the man to put the meat in Thunder's dish as well. Mrs. Supanni would not touch beef, and Deepti had refused to get that close to the voracious beast. Thunder was familiar with the butcher and always waited patiently as he emptied the meat into his dish. The butcher would sort of throw the bowl down on the ground, snatching his hand away so it would not be mistaken for a tasty morsel.

"We could be starving, and that dog would still be fed like clockwork," Mrs. Supanni joked. "Good thing, too, because if he was not fed, then he would munch on us!"

Mr. Supanni was always out checking on the fields and the lorry business, and Deepti and Mrs. Supanni often ate alone. Deepti sat outside near the dirty dishes, while Mrs. Supanni sat at the dining table. Sometimes, if Mrs. Supanni's mind was whirring with how a relative had insulted her or with another family tragedy, she would eat standing up. Today, she loomed in the doorway slurping up sambar with her wrinkled hand. Deepti took the opportunity to remind her that she would be taking Saturday off next week.

"You do remember that I will not be coming on Saturday, Ammagaru?"

"What? That is impossible, Deepti. That is the day after the party, and I need you to help clean up the house. Although the function will be at the hall we rented, some of the relatives will be passing through here. It will be a mess. You must come in on Saturday."

"Sasi is turning six on Saturday, and Rudra and I would like to take her to the temple. I am planning to cook a special meal, Ammagaru."

"Well, you can just take some of the food from the party and not miss the day of work. Surely I have ordered so much food from the caterers that there will be plenty for you to take home."

"I would prefer to spend the day at home with my family. Ammagaru, I told you about this at least a month ago.

"You did? Funny, I do not remember," she said looking up vacantly at a neighbor's palm tree.

A boy had climbed to the very top and was picking the ripe coconuts and tossing them to the ground. Frightened by the falling coconuts, a crow perched on the wall watching Deepti eat, flew away.

"Ammagaru, I told you before you were even planning to have a party," said Deepti firmly.

"Well, we'll just see."

With that said, Mrs. Supanni put her dirty plate on the ground in front of Deepti and walked into the house. What did that mean? What was there to see? She hoped the old woman was not going to offer her money to come in on Saturday. It would make the whole situation unnecessarily difficult.

On the way back from the corner market, Deepti passed the washer woman's husband ironing a sari on the roadside outside their hut. He earned money by pressing the clothes that his wife laundered.

"How is she?" asked Deepti.

"She is resting inside," he said. "The good doctor on the corner examined her and said it is malaria. He gave her the medication for free."

There were black burn scars on his hands from the iron. She remembered that the washer woman had grumbled to her once that he occasionally drank too much.

"That is good news," said Deepti and walked on.

That was her problem: Mrs. Supanni thought everyone had the luxury of sleeping in rooms with doors and windows they could pull tightly closed at night. She forgot that everyone did not plug in the GoodKnight or All Out! mosquito repellent before closing their eyes. She had to remind her in a respectful way that most poor people did not have electricity. Mrs. Supanni was too engulfed in her own problems—dealing with the uncooperative tailor and her Jayadev's mother-in-law, who was insisting on making the chicken for the party even after Mrs. Supanni had explained to her that she was ordering from a wonderful hotel. There was competition between them, and Deepti wondered which of the two was more manipulative. She knew that Mrs. Supanni was certainly capable of being vicious and evil. But as long as Mrs. Supanni treated her properly, Deepti didn't care about her personal affairs.

When she walked into the backyard, she saw through the open windows that Mr. Supanni was taking his tea in the front room. She put the biscuits and bread in the cabinet and closed the latch on the screened door so Thunder would not get into it. Once, the Supannis found him whimpering in the middle of the night after he had broken a pot of pickled lemon and lapped up some of the spicy relish. The veterinarian had told them to feed him yogurt for a few days and he would be back to normal. If he was such a smart dog, Deepti wondered why he was always doing the silliest things. The phone was ringing, and Mr. Supanni did not make a move to answer it. Mrs. Supanni muttered something under her breath and picked up the receiver.

"Oh, hello, Indu," she said sweetly.

Her husband never took phone calls from his sister in the States.

"Tell her I am in Madras, Hema," he whispered, waving his hand frantically.

Then she, rolling her eyes and horribly contorting her sagging face, spoke to her sister-in-law. She tried to make small talk.

"Wuma's wedding was divine, and the reception was just spectacular. We are having a big party for Jayadevbabu's son, Ganesh. He will be one on Friday."

They hurled their children's achievements at each other like daggers. Often, the sister-in-law would listen for a while and then say something inflammatory such as, "So, where is that brother of mine—out carousing as usual?" Then Mrs. Supanni's tongue would dart in and out of her painted lips like a lizard's, innocuous but ugly. When it came to property and money, they were cutthroats. People like them never had enough. Part of Deepti could not wait for the day when Indu would knock daintily on the Supannis' door. Then they would lunge at each other. She wanted to see the old women tear at each other's colored hair and shred their golden pallus. As Mrs. Supanni chatted, Thunder jumped up on her leg and started thrusting into her thigh. She walked backwards as far as the phone cord would allow, trying to get away from the dog, but he followed, his tail stump trembling. Mr. Supanni began to laugh, and Mrs. Supanni glared at him.

As Deepti walked home that evening, she thought about what she was going to do if Mrs. Supanni did not give her time off on Saturday. She hoped Mrs. Supanni would not forget again. Maybe she would remind her tomorrow. When she walked up to their hut, her mother was lying on a cot outside. Deepti pushed aside the curtain and put the canisters of curries and rice inside.

"Where is Sasi?" she asked, standing in the portal.

Before she could answer, she heard the bells of Rudra's rickshaw.

"Amma!" called Sasi, jumping out of the rickshaw and running to her mother.

Sometimes, Rudra would take Sasi for a sunset ride in the

rickshaw. Deepti picked up her daughter, whose small hands wrapped around her neck.

"Did Nanna give you a fun ride?"

The child nodded her head vigorously.

"Well, you must be hungry then. Go see what I got for dinner."

She put her down, and Sasi sprinted into the hut, her oversized frock swinging on her thin frame. Rudra pulled the rickshaw close to a tree and tied it up with a chain—if thieves tried to steal it, he would hear the chain jangling. The rickshaw was a wedding gift from his parents. Deepti's dowry had been ten thousand rupees, three thousand of which Rudra spent on silver anklets for her. Unfortunately, when Sasi was born, Deepti had to have a cesarean section, and the operation had cost six thousand rupees. So, the anklets were at the pawn shop. Later, she had heard that hospitals were doing cesareans just to make money and that most of the operations were unnecessary, but Deepti refused to believe the rumor. Rudra handed her some money with a half-smile.

"It was a good day," he said and walked past her into the hut, unwrapping the cloth he wore around his head to block the sun, absorb sweat and protect him from head injuries in the event of an accident.

As Rudra, Sasi and Deepti's mother ate around the fire, Deepti stood and served the food. She ate breakfast and a big lunch at the Supannis'. The rice and curries Mrs. Supanni gave her to take home were usually enough for two people. So, Deepti did not eat at night. Sometimes, she would eat whatever Sasi left on her plate.

It was eight in the morning on Friday, the day of the party, and Deepti was not sure if Mrs. Supanni was clear on the fact that she would not be coming in tomorrow. After sweeping the fallen decaying honeysuckle and night jasmine blossoms, she scooped up the dust pile in her hand and threw it in the small garbage pail. Then she washed the walkway and decorated the cement outside of the gate with limestone powder. She pinched some of the white powder between her fingers and "drew" a circle of four lotuses. The party was starting at seven-thirty, and Deepti probably would not get home until eleven o'clock that night. She sighed as she walked past the car and into the backyard. Husband and wife were sitting in the front room when she entered with a rag to wipe the showcase. There was not a spot of dust to be seen, but Mrs. Supanni always said wiping everything every day was the only way to keep it off. Deepti picked up a photo of Mr. and Mrs. Supanni with Jayadev, daughter-in-law Geya and Ganesh—the baby whose birthday party Mrs. Supanni was pulling her hair out over. Deepti's fingers ran over the gold-plated frame. It was beautiful. Every time she dusted it, she was reminded that she did not even have a photo of Sasi. Ganesh could still barely hold his head up, and there were thousands of pictures of him.

"Is it not fit for a god?" asked Mrs. Supanni.

Deepti turned to see what she was referring to. She was holding out a thick gold chain to her husband. He nodded his approval, and then shot Deepti a stern look. He did not like it when Mrs. Supanni showed off their wealth in front of her. Mrs. Supanni clucked and waved off his paranoia. She trusted her.

"Deepti," Mrs. Supanni said.

Deepti turned and faced her.

"I will be needing you after all tomorrow. Before you object, here is a hundred rupees to compensate for the inconvenience."

She held out the money, and Deepti stood motionless.

"But Ammagaru, what will I tell Sasi?"

"I am sure she will understand when you come home with a nice new frock on Sunday," said Mrs. Supanni

Mr. Supanni hid behind the newspaper. Deepti took the money and returned to dusting.

Even as she sat eating lunch at noon, Deepti could not figure out a decent way to break the news to Rudra. Their lives were paved with disappointments, and this would be another dip in the road.

"What can you do?" he would say in a hoarse whisper. Then he would add, a bit more cheerily, "We can use the extra money."

The fried okra she was shoveling into her open mouth tasted like bitter smoke.

"Ammagaru?" a voice bade from over the wall.

"Deepti, see who that is."

She looked up and knew it was the children Mrs. Supanni had shooed off yesterday.

"It's the same children who wanted the kamalas, Ammagaru," called Deepti.

"Oh, I told them to come after lunchtime. Did they not hear me? Go on and give them some fruit."

Deepti opened the side gate, but the three children would not come in.

"The dog," one of them said fearfully.

"Do not worry. He is tied up."

The two girls had on white blouses and blue convent skirts. The boy was in knickers and a short-sleeve shirt. On his head hung the strap of his book bag, which knocked against his back. Mrs. Supanni stood in the walkway, scowling because Deepti had let the children into the yard instead of handing them the fruit over the wall. They stared up at the greenish-orange kamalas hanging in the tree.

"Go on," encouraged Deepti.

The girls were tall enough to reach a ripe fruit, but the boy was not. Deepti picked him up.

"Which one do you want?" she asked, and he pointed to the far right.

He pulled, and the branches bounced back as the fruit was set free. His small brown hands quivered as he gripped the juicy orange.

"Thank you!" they cheered as they skipped through the gate.

Deepti knew what it was like to pass a fragrant tree ripe with fruit while walking to school. She would look up each day, and her mouth would fill with water as she imagined biting into a pink guava or a sweet kamala. She would dream about it until she had worked up enough courage to ring the bell or call into the yard. It was not advisable to refuse pleas for food when someone knocked on your door, be it a beggar or a child flushed with excitement.

"Deepti, I was thinking. Perhaps it would be nice for your husband and child to come to the party," said Mrs. Supanni as Deepti locked the gate.

"That would be kind of you, Ammagaru."

"Good. I am going to the hall to check on the flowers and to make sure the soda was delivered."

Deepti was thrilled to be able to spend some time with her child and husband. Frankly, it would probably be the only time that Sasi would be at a party like this for her birthday. She didn't have to know the party was just for Ganesh.

Deepti didn't know exactly what to do with herself as the hundred and fifty or so guests started filling the hall off Bandar Road. Her duties were to flip the cassettes in the tape player, help guests with the gifts and assist with the cake-cutting ceremony. Mrs. Supanni had bribed her because she was addicted to the power of having a servant at her beck and call. Deepti smoothed the maroon cotton against her legs. The least worn of all her saris, it was crisply starched and pressed. Ladies paraded in, wearing saris heavily laden with jheri and thick braids adorned with jasmine and sampungi. They flaunted thick gold chains, the stock diamond earrings and glittering bangles up to their forearms. Deepti was glad she didn't have to tuck her sari into her waistband so that it wouldn't get filthy. She was not cleaning now. Tonight, Deepti was a guest, not a servant.

"I am so glad you could come," said Mrs. Supanni to her friend Radha. "And Divya! How lovely you look!"

"It is our pleasure," said Radha as Divya handed Mrs. Supanni a large wrapped gift.

Mrs. Supanni, in turn, handed it to Deepti. As Mrs. Supanni and Radha walked into the crowd, the young woman tugged on her richly embroidered dhupatta and lagged behind, already bored to death. Deepti placed their gift on the table beside the stage and directed other guests to do the same as they entered. Looking for Sasi, she saw that she was sitting up on Rudra's shoulders. She was wearing a simple polka-dot dress Mrs. Supanni had given her last Dasara. Without a drop of gold, Sasi still sparkled the brightest. No matter where she walked, Deepti could see her daughter's looped and yellow-ribboned plaits floating above the crowd.

Guests greeted the hostess, her husband and the proud parents of the birthday boy and then gravitated toward the food. The banquet table was covered with seven vegetable curries, biryani, lamb, fish, chicken, yogurt and sweets. Jayadev's mother-in-law's chicken dish was in a small pot in the back. People started stuffing themselves about a half hour after they had arrived. In his hurry, an old man stained the tassels of his white silk shawl with turmeric from dragging it in the fish curry. His wife tried cleaning it with water as he rubbed his belly, stretched smooth like a watermelon under his dhovti. Children chased each other through the maze of saris while using chicken legs for weapons. The sound of all those gnashing teeth was deafening, and Deepti wondered if they tasted what they were eating at all.

She changed the cassette in the tape machine even though the latest cinema music was being drowned out by the loud voices and children's shouts. The video cameraman was on stage, panning the crowd. Then he focused on the birthday cake, which was framed with a backdrop of vertical garlands of pink and white roses. Everything was perfect—except for one small detail. The baker had forgotten to write "Happy First Birthday, Ganesh" on the cake, and Mrs. Supanni was livid. She swore at herself for not opening the box at the bakery and then vowed to set them straight tomorrow.

"I hope they got the pineapple cream right at least," she had muttered all afternoon. "I specifically told them I wanted pineapple cream and not elachi. Modern bakers, *ppfff.*"

After everyone had eaten at least one plateful of food, a children's group performed a dance piece. It was then that Deepti, Sasi and Rudra ate dinner.

"Can I have more chicken, Amma?" asked Sasi.

"You can have as much as you like, baby," she said and filled her daughter's plate with Jayadev's mother-in-law's chicken.

It was so much better than the catered dish. Once they had their fill, the three walked over to the shadow puppet show in the back of the hall. The puppeteer was telling the story of how Ganesh came to be a deity. Some of the children watched, mesmerized, but most were running about and jumping like monkeys on the oblivious adults. Against the wall, in the latest styles of tiger and leopard-print saris, leaned two yawning college-aged women, looking more disengaged than ferocious.

"Amma, look at the elephant," said Sasi, giggling.

She smoothed her daughter's hair lovingly. She was glad Sasi was enjoying herself. Looking over at Ganesh, she saw that he was being cuddled, pinched and passed from outstretched hands to out-stretched hands. She could not help but wonder what would happen if someone dropped him and he was trampled. They cooed in his ear, fingered the gold about his neck and passed him unceremoniously like a ball. She looked down at Sasi, who was now dancing with a little boy in a suit and tie.

"Stay close to Nanna, Sasi," she said.

"I will," she reassured her, blinking her doll-like eyes.

Deepti kissed her on the cheek.

"It is time for the cake," she said to Rudra and walked toward the stage. Thunder was busily sniffing women's saris. Deepti found Mrs. Supanni, and they walked up onto the stage. The cake was still in the box because of flies. Deepti eased it out and placed it gently on the tilted stand.

"Damn modern bakers," Mrs. Supanni cursed. "Tell me, do I have anything in my teeth, Deepti?"

She grinned, and Deepti shook her head.

"Good. Wait behind the curtains."

As Deepti walked away, Mrs. Supanni beamed brilliantly and turned toward her guests. They did not notice, so she cleared her throat in the microphone.

"Good evening," she said. "I would like to thank all of you for coming and helping us celebrate the birth of my beautiful grandson, Ganesh. Today he begins his second year."

The guests applauded, and the photographers flashed their cameras.

"Thank you. Now, for the event we have all been waiting for—the cake-cutting ceremony. Babu."

She looked at Jayadev, and he looked to Geya, who was also empty-handed. Mr. Supanni, white-faced and chewing on killi, shrugged when all eyes turned to him. The crowd shifted as it became clear that the baby was missing. Mrs. Supanni was clearly embarrassed. Deepti peeped out from behind the curtains.

"We cannot seem to locate the guest of honor. So, whoever is holding Ganesh, please bring him up to the stage." Everyone looked to their neighbor to make sure he or she was not holding the baby. They waited, but no baby. Mrs. Supanni wailed into the microphone, and the buzz grew louder as panic crackled through the hall. She ran from the stage and conversed with her husband and son about what to do.

"Maybe someone kidnapped him," Deepti heard a woman whisper.

"They do that these days and ask for a ransom," said another.

"Maybe they just took the chain from his neck and left him alone," offered someone else more optimistically.

"Was anyone suspicious seen with the baby?" shouted Jayadev, who had taken charge.

People talked among themselves.

"I last saw Ganesh with a woman in a red sari," answered a teenage girl.

Within moments, the guests dispersed, piling into the streets on a baby-hunt. Deepti walked down the steps at the side of the stage to rejoin Rudra and Sasi. Just then, Thunder barked and leapt onto the stage, tearing into the birthday cake.

"Thunder, no!" yelled Deepti.

She could see his paws were already white with frosting. Picking up a tray of chicken, she placed it on the stage. Abandoning the cake, Thunder started lapping up the curry. As Deepti ran back to the cake, she knew it was too late. She could smell the cream. Elachi. When she looked down on the cake, she saw it was nearly split in half. It was when she went to have a taste of the icing that she saw the electrical wires jutting out from the center of the cake. She looked up at Rudra and Sasi, who were walking toward her.

"Amma," said Sasi sleepily.

"A bomb," Deepti announced flatly, afraid her voice would set it off.

Without uttering another word, she walked down from the stage and fled with her family into the night. When they found Jayadev in the street and told him about the bomb, he did not believe them at first. Then he started yelling.

"A bomb! Take cover!"

The police had to push their way through the mob of people, some milling about with curiosity and others frantically running in search of their loved ones. As Deepti and her family walked home, she knew she had to return the hundred rupees to Mrs. Supanni and that tomorrow, early in the morning, she, Sasi and Rudra would go to the temple and spend the weekend together as they had originally planned.

The Dancers

Ana trained her eyes to land on people's faces like flies. She only looked at them so she could navigate through the throngs of bodies. They always stared at her no matter what she wore—sari, salwar-kameez, skirts and roomy blouses. If she wore her hair loose, in a bun or plait, she was still singled out. Walking down the street toward the train station, she wondered if it was because she had a pretty face or because they smelled danger.

Once inside, she searched for the ticket booth for Madras. There should have been a separate line for ladies, but the ticket clerks never paid any mind. Women had to be aggressive and stand solidly planted as the mannerless men tried to push them out of the way. As she slid her ticket form under the window, a potbellied man with killi-stained lips tried shoving his paperwork ahead of her.

"Wait your turn," she said firmly, and he withdrew his form immediately.

"One-way ticket Pune to Madras?" confirmed the clerk.

She could hear the fat man laugh sheepishly behind her back.

"Yes, that is what it says there," she said.

She stared at the crisp five-hundred-rupee note in her hand. It was the first time she had really looked at one. It had a nice portrait of Gandhi on it.

"Two hundred and fifty-five," said the clerk.

She pushed the bill through the opening. To further irritate the impatient man behind her, she took her time reading the ticket to check if all the information was correct before she stepped away from the counter. The man glared at her as she walked past him, and she looked him right in the eye and smiled.

"Crazy," he muttered under his breath, his fear crackling under his sheath of superiority.

The compartment was still empty because she had boarded the train early. After sliding her small suitcase under the berth, she leaned her head against the window and closed her eyes. Tomorrow she would turn twenty-eight.

She thought back to her seventeenth birthday. For the first time, she remembered it clearly, and like a movie, it played in her mind. She had helped her mother stir the cake batter of eggs, butter, flour and sugar. Then she had watched her pour it into four small cake tins and cook them in hot sand. Each of them, including her two little brothers, had a cake for themselves that special day, and Ana got to blow out four candles. She remembered the center of the cake was still wet and sticky, but she had not cared at the time. Now, it irritated her to think she had been so gullible and silly. How could she not have questioned such bizarre behavior? If she had at least had an inkling, the horror of the next day would have been cushioned.

Her mother had woken her especially early and told her she had warmed up some water for her bath. She even poured the water over her with a small mug as Ana washed her hair with soap.

"For your birthday, Ana," her mother had said as she handed her a butter-colored sari.

The sari was brand new and had a forest green floral design on the border and pallu. She took it excitedly from her mother and skipped into the hut to put it on. It would set off her golden-ivory skin dramatically, and as she wrapped herself in it, she wished that they had a mirror.

"You look noble," her mother said as she stared at her with teary eyes.

Then she sat in the sun as her mother dried her hair by whisking it gently to knock the water out.

"Your hair is so thick and black," she said proudly. "You must take care of it when I am no longer here."

"But Amma, where will you go?" she asked naively.

Her mother did not answer her right away. Instead, she combed the knots out and braided Ana's hair loosely. Picking up a yellow hibiscus flower, she pinned it at the top of her plait.

"I will not be here forever, Ana. But I will be with you. We are like shadow and light."

Just then, a car pulled up, and her mother stood, heavy tears rolling down her face.

"Who is that?" asked Ana.

"Goodbye, Ana. You take care of yourself and your new family."

She dabbed at her tears with her pallu.

"I do not understand, Amma," called Ana as her mother walked away from her.

Her father got out of the car with a man. He was draped in white silk and had flashing gemstone rings on every finger except his thumbs. Her mother walked out with a plastic bag of clothes and handed it to her.

"Remember, shadow and light."

"Amma, I do not want to leave."

But it was as if her mother did not recognize her anymore. Her mother's usually bright eyes were now cold and small. Her father stood with his hands on his hips.

"Amma!" Ana cried.

When her mother put her hand on her father's shoulder, he

shook it off. That was when her mother vanished into their hut. In his fist, her father tried to hide the folded bills. Her mother was sitting on the cot inside, and only her sari from the knees down and her bare feet were visible. The sun reflected off the two cheap silver rings on her toes. Waist up, she was bathed in darkness.

"Amma!" she shrieked, but her voice was drowned in the noise of traffic.

Her mother did not rise or look out. She sat still, playing with her fingers in her lap.

Ana looked at the compartment door when she heard loud voices. A man paused, stared at her and then down at his ticket, and then kept on going. Her eyes fell on a poor woman begging with an infant girl on her knee on the platform. Beggars were not allowed in train stations anymore. It would only be a short while before a policeman would chase her off. Perhaps, if he felt like it, he would beat or kick her. But that did not matter because this mother was desperate as her own parents. They had sold her because they needed the money for her brothers' education. In desperation, it was hard to think clearly. There was a fly moving across the baby's cheek. Just before it reached her lips, someone walking by dropped a coin in the mother's lap and scared it off.

Ana took out a pack of Goldflake cigarettes and lit one up. She blew the smoke out the window. On the platform, a man in a silk lalchee and matching dhovti stared at her as if she had offended him in the greatest way. She blew a smoke ring into the air, and it floated above his head like a dunce cap as he walked by with a disgusted look on his pocked face.

Eight thousand rupees. That was what they had sold her for. A small smile formed on her lips now because in her beaded purse she had over thirty thousand rupees. She flicked the smoldering butt through the bars on the window and sat back down.

Khalifa, the man her parents had sold her to, was not a bad-looking man. He had a young face, and the age difference between them, eight years, was not immediately evident. They had never married.

"I paid three thousand more than the usual rate," Khalifa had said in an attempt to compliment her as they rode farther and farther from her family.

She stared out of the car window at the blur of the crowd. They passed Muhammad, the old man who sat on the pavement under the shade of an enormous powderpuff tree with his wares spread on a dirty piece of burlap.

"Muhammad!" she cried into the window, which was open a crack.

But he was happily snoring with his turbaned head against the tree trunk.

"Who is Muhammad?" Khalifa asked, arching his back against the seat.

Was he already stricken with jealousy? No. He was afraid of being duped, of buying spoiled goods.

"Tell me, who is Muhammad?" he demanded.

She remembered the busyness of the area. It was near the Gateway to India and a big tourist spot. She had first seen Muhammad there when she was about eight, walking home with some milk for her brothers. His face was the color of wet earth—river mud with tributaries of wrinkles running through it. He let her touch his face and hands, which she stared at on long afternoons as he made bicycles and monkeys out of silver and copper wire. The tourists gobbled up the five-rupee gifts. Muhammad had given her a bicycle and monkey to give to her brothers, who ended up breaking them in two days flat. For her, he had made something special—a copper chariot drawn by a peacock. He told her it would take her away whenever she wanted. When she looked into the hollow loops of wire, she saw the iridescent blue and green feathers. Eventually, after numerous visits, she learned how to make the bicycle and monkeys herself. They made a pact that she would keep his wonderful art alive after he had died. Muhammad would smile a gummy grin because he knew having such a pretty jabbering girl by his side helped his business. When it was a slow day for sales, they would wile away time by telling jokes about passersby. When people said he was rude, she would say that he was simply being honest. Sometimes they would laugh so hard that their heads would throb. She had wanted to be like Muhammad when she was little. He had fun and made an easy living.

"Why did I pay that extra money, Ana?" Khalifa asked, trying to penetrate her psyche.

"Because you are stupid," she said, smiling into the window.

He flipped a thick hand under her chin and turned her to face him.

"Because you are beautiful and untouched. If I find out otherwise, I will have your family killed."

His words dropped with the heat and lightness of red embers and began to sear her skin. She thought of last Independence Day when one of her brothers had accidentally dropped a sparkler on her thigh. Her hand gripped her leg, once again feeling the pain of the burn.

"Muhammad is an old man who sells crafts by the Gateway," she replied numbly.

Khalifa had bought her because of her pale skin. She scanned the crowds they were zooming by and could not find another South Indian who was her color. There were many shades of brown, but her skin color was a rare diamond in a pile of coal. At that moment, she wanted to tear the skin off her bones and hand it to Khalifa and tell him that was what he had bought.

They stopped at an intersection as an elephant decorated with garlands of flowers, red and gold silk throws and kumkum was paraded through the streets.

"Ridiculous Hindus," Khalifa muttered.

The driver drove closer to the elephant, hoping to prompt it to move along more quickly, but instead the regal animal picked up its trunk and decided to halt the procession right there.

Ana let out a snorty laugh. The driver met her defiant eyes in the rear-view mirror. The elephant began to defecate.

"They are so filthy," said Khalifa, his right eye twitching as he stroked his pointy beard.

The thick, wet dung landed in a heap in front of the car. Ana began to laugh. When the elephant walked on, the driver had no choice but to drive over the pile. The strong smell of elephant shit wafted up from the tires, and Khalifa began to cough. Ana's laughs turned into cackles. He looked at her in terror as the possibilities stung him like angry bees. He tried to convince himself that she was laughing so maniacally because she was so young and childish. But her laughter increased in intensity. Did he not know the story of the mogali? It was a shoot from which a fragrant blossom with serrated petals sprouted. Its guardians were thin green vipers that shot up and bit the hand that tried to tear away their paradise—everyone's paradise. Did this fool think he could pluck a flower without studying the nature of its thorns?

Two old men who looked like stiff college professors entered the compartment and sat down. They had two small briefcases that slid easily under the berth. She was glad they didn't move close to the window and sit right across from her, because she didn't feel like looking at their faces. They were staring at her, and it was less intrusive when they did it from a distance. She had grown accustomed to all of them, their mouths hanging slightly open, like lions during the hunt. They had cornered their prey, and now they were drooling to rip into her flesh, bite into her jugular and snap her neck. It was the rush of the kill and the promise of power. But whose limp corpse was hanging from their mouths? Why did the blood taste sweet at first and then turn suddenly to bitter poison? She looked at them and they stared back unabashedly as if she were a billboard for an X-rated movie such as *Stripped to Kill*, movies that featured red-lipped white women with knives at their throats or guns at their heads. Turning, she looked directly at the man staring at her.

"Yes?" she asked with annoyance.

"Madras?" the one with spectacles asked with a small smile.

"Yes, this is the train to Madras," she said and looked out the window.

She knew he was asking where she was going to and not the ultimate destination of the train. She felt they were looking through her sari and trying to picture her naked. Surely they knew most Indian women did not wear underwear. Smoothing her sari over her legs, she tried nipping her self-consciousness in the bud by closing her eyes. Still, she could feel the heat of their gazes slithering over her skin and resting on the beauty mark on her chin. It was rather large, and people always tended to focus on it. When she danced at the Beach Club in Pune, some of the patrons had dubbed her "Beauty" because of the mole on her chin. She didn't mind stripping at the club as long as the men didn't touch her. That was the deal she had made with the management. They liked her because she was the lightest-skinned dancer they had. She missed Kalpana with whom she had been developing a friendship. A part of Ana wished she didn't have to leave Pune, but she feared Khalifa's men had found her, and it was not worth the risk. Ever since that strange man, Ravi, had followed her home, her fear had grown and grown until she had no choice but to leave. Some of the girls gave her some names of clubs in Madras, but she was apprehensive about what she would find there because, although the dancers were nice, they were also terribly competitive. None of that mattered anyway. She had decided to put her past behind her and try to find a decent job. Maybe she could work at a beauty salon doing nails or giving facials. She could do that very well, she imagined. She just needed a good teacher. When she opened her eyes, she saw one of the men was asleep, but the other was still riveted. She ran a hand through her loose hair. Was it her skin or because her hair was free? Did she look brazen and wild? Could he tell she was a cabaret dancer? Did he think she was a whore?

✦

Khalifa was not a typical Muslim. He had two or three wives, was lax in his praying and had a penchant for drinking beer. He supposedly had a palatial home in the United Arab Emirates, but spent little time there. Traveling was a passion of his, and she supposed it was because of his rowdy behavior that he kept moving about. Surely the devout Muslims did not tolerate his carousing. After they had arrived at his house in Hyderabad, he told her to take a bath. A servant girl who could not have been more than eight years old helped her into a huge tub of steaming, soapy water. She scrubbed her back gently with a brush and then drained the tub. When it was refilled, the girl dumped in a mixture of rose and sandalwood oils. Ana sank back into the hot water and closed her eyes. She must have dozed off because when she opened her eyes, Khalifa was on top of her. The mixture of sensations was overwhelming as he pawed her nakedness. His beard dripped with wetness as water sloshed over the sides of the tub onto the marble floor. She screamed, gagging on the perfumed bath water. She tried to push him away, but everything was so slippery from the oil. He was marking his territory like an animal. She bit hard into his fleshy shoulder. Ana could not recall much of the event because she felt as if she had floated out of her body. She did remember, in the struggle, some of her glass bangles had smashed against the porcelain, the slivers digging into her left wrist. It stung at first, and then the pain subsided. As the blood from her wrists, between her legs and Khalifa's shoulder streamed into the water, she was thankful that he had done it in the tub. It made it less real.

Now, she pushed her silver bangles back and looked for the scars. They were barely visible. Sometimes it felt as if there were still a few shards there. Occasionally, she would feel a vein pinch and could almost see her pulsing blood stumble as if over a river pebble. Those times, she decided, were when Khalifa was cursing the day she had walked into his life.

That first night was the last time he had ever laid a hand on her. After he had fallen asleep, she grabbed her bag and ran away. She stole his money purse that he had left on the table and got on the first available bus. Once across town, she spent the remainder of the night in a cheap hotel. In the showers in the hall, she met a woman named Pinkie, who was a prostitute. Pinkie told her about a dance club called the Blue Lotus, and Ana started working there the very next day. The proprietor was a wiry buzzard named Panjit, who froze when she entered. Was he frozen with fright or awe? She did not know then at the age of seventeen, but now she knew it was awe. He did not care if she was Hindu or Muslim. He said he liked the size of her hips and treated her as if she were a white dove he was afraid of scaring off or soiling with his greasy fingers. When she made enough money, she bought a one-way ticket to Pune, where she had been working up until the day before.

A woman slid the door fully open with her bag and settled across from Ana. She had too much luggage, and Ana noticed that she had British Airways flight tags. Dressed in a salwar-kameez, the woman sported short cropped hair and long earrings with red stones. Her right ear was pierced three times and in the other two holes were a moon and star. Around her neck was a wide necklace that had six rows of multicolored beads. She thought about the thieves who snatched necklaces from passengers who slept with their heads close to open windows as the train pulled into a station. But this was not a gold necklace, and gold was what thieves were mostly interested in. On the woman's feet were beige sandals instead of chappals. Her nose was sharp, and her skin the color of a coconut. She looked as if she would have perfect teeth behind her closed lips. As she sat down, Ana pretended to look out the window.

Ana thought about what she had on—a transparent lavender sari with a border dotted with gold stars, and flashy silver hoop earrings. Her chappals sparkled with gold foiled leather, and silver bangles nearly covered her arms up to the elbow. The woman was looking at the tattoo on Ana's right hand. Ana remembered when her mother had finally given into Ana's pleas to get a tattoo.

"Green dot piercing," the woman had called, making her rounds in the neighborhood.

"Do not have her do anything crazy!" her mother had yelled as Ana chased after the woman.

For three rupees, the woman had made a simple lotus on the back of her hand using a needle and leaf juice. The tattoo was a dark olive color on her pale skin. Her mother thought it was nice. Ana had run around the village showing it off for months. It made her feel like an individual.

Now, this Indian woman who lived in Britain was staring at it. The green tattoo was an obvious sign of being lower class. When she saw that Ana was staring back at her, she smiled.

"You have beautiful hands," she said in a slight British accent. "The lotus is striking."

"Thank you," said Ana.

The woman pulled up the sleeve of her tunic and showed Ana her forearm. There, a peacock gloriously spread its green and blue feathers over the woman's hairless skin.

"It's lovely," said Ana, amazed at the intensity of the colors.

The train jerked and started to move forward. The woman covered up the tattoo and took out a book, but within a few minutes, she had nodded off. As they passed a clearing, the sun shone through the dirty windows and bathed her from the waist down in warm orange and gold hues.

The woman opened her eyes as they pulled into the Wadi junction. Some of the boys and men hawking snacks and drinks ran alongside the train to get a headstart against their competitors. She rubbed her eyes and looked at Ana.

"Wadi station," said Ana.

"I guess I was really tired," said the woman.

Ana nodded. The woman stood up and stretched.

"Do you want anything?" she asked, and Ana shook her head.

The woman paused for a second, and Ana knew what she was thinking.

"Don't worry, I'll keep an eye on your bags," Ana reassured her.

She watched her walk out of the compartment and resurface on the platform. The old men had gone out somewhere as well. The woman bought a bag of spiced chickpeas and sipped a Thums Up.

"Here," she said as she handed Ana a Limca through the window bars. "I thought you might need it."

"Thank you."

She drank from the straw like a baby sucking on a breast. The lemon soda deeply quenched her thirst. After the woman returned, Ana took out some money to reimburse her, but she would not take it.

"It's my pleasure," she said.

"You are kind," replied Ana.

Ana felt as if she had known this woman since childhood. She felt as if she were an old friend who had stepped back into her life. It occurred to her then that she did not even know her name.

"My name is Gayatri," the woman said, holding out her hand.

Ana stared at her for a second before she reached out and shook it. No one had ever extended their hand to her before.

"Were you born here or in Britain?" asked Ana.

"In Hyderabad, actually. I moved to Britain only about seven years ago to study homeopathic medicine."

"My mother used homeopathic remedies."

Their conversation sank into a lull, and Ana took the moment to fish out her pack of cigarettes from her purse. She saw a flicker in Gayatri's eyes, and she offered her one.

"Thank you," Gayatri said, casting a side-glance at their compartment mates, who had returned.

Ana held the match for her, and she took a deep drag on the cigarette.

"What are you doing in India?" asked Ana.

"I came for my father's funeral. That was in Vijayawada. After that, I spent a few weeks on holiday visiting family in Pune with my mother. Now, I'm on my way to visit some friends in Madras. It's the first time I'm really relaxing."

"It must have been trying dealing with all of the relatives at the funeral."

"Yes," replied Gayatri.

"Do you miss your father?"

"Yes, but I feel at peace with what happened. This may sound strange, but I think his death is the best thing that could have happened for my mother. She has shed an old skin and begun a whole new life."

One of the men nervously glanced at them, and the women laughed.

"I'm glad she realized it," said Gayatri.

"We die a thousand times," said Ana, and Gayatri was reminded of her own mother's words.

Then, as if in a dream, a small boy with a parrot in a cage stood staring at them from the platform. He was wearing a torn undershirt and dirty knickers. His feet were bare, and his knees scraped. Ana smiled and motioned him to come over.

"Babu, the train is delayed, come inside," she said, and the boy nodded.

As he entered with the parrot, the younger of the two men stood up indignantly.

"They have diseases," he said, and it was not clear if he was referring to the bird or the boy.

"We are all susceptible to diseases," said Gayatri, and the man had no choice but to leave from the heat of the remark.

"I will see what the delay is," he muttered to his friend and stomped out.

"What a beautiful parrot you are," praised Gayatri.

"Hello-hello-hello," cooed the bird.

"Ask a question, and see what answer is picked for you," said Ana as she took out a handful of change from her purse.

There were chunks of guava and idli at the bottom of the cage.

"Will I be happy in love?" asked Gayatri, slightly embarrassed after the question escaped her lips.

Then she fed the parrot a two-rupee coin and waited for an

255

answer. The bird cocked its head and dropped the coin on the floor of the cage.

"One more," said the parrot. "One more."

Gayatri burst out laughing as the parrot hopped about in its cage.

"This is so typically Indian—it's fantastic!" she said, beaming.

The boy grinned as his partner won over their customers' hearts. Ana caught the old man smiling as he sneaked peeks at the fun.

"Thank you—okay—hello-hello," squawked the parrot.

After being fed a total of three more rupees, the bird picked up a card from the floor of the cage and handed it to Gayatri. She looked at it and smiled.

"It says, most definitely—be patient. Oh, you do it, too, Ana."

"Will Gayatri and I remain friends?" asked Ana.

Gayatri smiled. Ana proceeded to feed the bird coins, and after only four rupees, it hopped down from its perch and picked up a card that was buried under several others.

"Let the soul guide you," read Ana.

"Thank you—okay—thank you," sang the bird.

The train began to move, and as the boy turned to quickly make his way off the train, he bumped into the other man, who was returning from his investigation. The women chuckled.

"Hurry," Ana called to the boy.

There was plenty of time for him to get safely off the train. Within a minute, they passed him on the platform and waved. Upon his shoulder, he held the cage, in which the bird was madly hopping about.

The women settled back in their seats, and after a moment of listening to the train pick up speed, Gayatri looked at Ana.

"What are you thinking?" Gayatri asked.

"About tomorrow. It is my birthday."

"How old will you be?"

"I will be starting my twenty-ninth year."

"Does it bother you?"

"Not too much. I just feel like I am still seventeen."

"Well, when we arrive in Madras, we must celebrate. What are your plans there?"

"I must look for work."

"What kind of work? I have some friends who might be able to help you."

"I am a dancer," Ana replied softly.

"Really? I love dancing. I go with my friends all the time in London. It's a grand time. We make up all these strange steps."

"Like what?"

Gayatri stood up and shook her body as if she were being electrocuted. Then she knocked her head from side to side while rolling her shoulders and rotating her hips.

"How wonderful!" cried Ana as she clapped her hands.

This pure jubilation was reminiscent of how she used to tirelessly joke with Muhammad. The old men looked at them with horror, and the two women looked at each other, laughing uncontrollably like inseparable schoolgirls. As Ana clutched her stomach, she truly felt as if she were seventeen again, the joy cutting clean through the layers of sadness that had been strangling her heart.

The Circus

Leeladhar had followed the path that wound up through the dense forest. The wild monkeys frolicked in the middle of the road and were slow to scatter even when a van full of tourists crept up. Parting the bushes, he walked into the dark green leaves, which seemed to form another world. The Karthik temple was behind him, and he could faintly hear the shouts and laughs of children feeding the monkeys popcorn. When would he be able to laugh at the cleverness of a monkey again? He had asked for blessings inside the temple, but he still felt as if a wall were pressing his chest. He walked farther from the voices.

Diagonally cutting through the trees, he found himself on the flat-topped mountain, his bare feet meeting the crumbling edge as he looked down. The jagged rocks looked like fingers, and the valley, a giant hand. He felt himself being pulled into the cavernous earth—into the Devi.

"I forgive you," the Devi whispered. "I will catch you."

He did not believe Her. She had every right to lie. He misused Her trust in him. When the Goddess got him in Her clutches, she would transform into Parvati. Then, with lightning speed, Parvati's sharp claws would wrap around his throat and strangle him with a gentle smile. He would pay for throwing acid on Navina—for destroying her life, for murdering her. Goddess fingers would betray him and dig into his chest, jabbing at his heart as a bird of prey pecks at a carcass over and over again. He knew he was not worthy to live, but he could not pitch himself into darkness. Maybe it was his fate to live the rest of his life in misery. Maybe he would live to be eighty-five. That would be justice! A rock fell and sailed into the depths below. He did not hear it land. But he did hear a branch snap behind him. He glimpsed the flick of an orange tail.

"Wait!" he shouted.

It was a tiger. He ran into the trees, but could not find it. He looked for footprints, but found none. He wanted the tiger to sink its teeth into his flesh and eat him alive. Once in its clenches, he would have no choice but to relinquish his desire to live. He would gratefully perish in the glorious paws of such a beast. But there was not a tiger in sight. Instead he stood staring into the spots of a beautiful doe. How could a doe kill him? She was still, although churning with assessment. The more he looked into her eyes, the more his aching to die grew. The force of his mournful sigh sent her sprinting past a sandalwood tree. She was afraid of him.

His thirst to draw blood was answered when he felt a stinging in his leg. Looking down, he saw that his ankle was bleeding. He wondered how he had cut it. The sight of his feet gripped him. The dirt was caked between the ill-shaped toes, the nails of which were long and yellow. There were curly black hairs growing on three of the bigger toes on each foot. The feet seemed uncharacteristically huge. Had he somehow acquired someone else's feet? What a strange thought! And perhaps that is precisely what had happened. So, someone else was the murderer after all. He was not responsible.

"These are not my feet," he said softly.

The thought broke over his head like a coconut, and childish laughter washed over him.

"These are not my feet!" he proclaimed, bursting into laughter. "These are not Leeladhar's feet!"

But the shrieks of joy that pierced the canopy and tilted parrots' eyes his way subsided. Why couldn't he have just accepted it and snatched the peace by the collar? Why couldn't he have mustered all his strength and beat off those terrible doubts? He wished it would have lasted just a little longer, but it had not. It got away from him like water through the unseen cracks of cupped hands. He looked at his palms. They, too, were filthy. The mud sticking to his fingers made them look fat and unfamiliar. Spitting on his left hand, he tried rubbing away the dirt to check for the scar between his first and second knuckle. Still, he could not see it. His mouth was parched, and the saliva on his tongue was thick and foamy. A bird's whooping call filled his ears. His feet began to run toward its source, planting themselves firmly on the soft forest floor, and he had no choice but to follow.

By the time he spotted the stream, he was wet with perspiration and his pants were torn by thorny branches. He ran right into the middle of the stream and stood there until the rushing water had cleansed his feet. Falling to his knees, he scrubbed himself. It was not until after he had gulped some of the water with his cupped hands that he checked for the scar. He held it up to the sunlight. Yes, these were his hands. Slowly, he began to feel as if he were standing on blocks of ice. As he walked back to Karthik, his guilt dripping a trail, yellow cassia petals drizzled down on him from the heavens.

"See what you cannot have," they were cooing through the clouds.

He looked up and saw that the bird had followed him and was now perched out of reach on a solitary branch, ferociously mocking him.

Only in colors and smells could he describe what made him do it. His mind was dipped in pearly gold and silver, and he smelled jasmine as if he were burying his face in the hair of a goddess. The warm breeze patted his tears dry. He felt safe up there, sitting high on the roof of a temple. He felt right. But they said that he was insane.

"Police!" they yelled.

"He is a madman!"

"There is someone on top of Meenakshi temple!"

They gathered below and stared up at him like a constellation. The yellow moon he was staring into had betrayed him, spotlighting his presence. He was begging for his guilt to be washed by the gentle hands of the goddess with fishlike eyes. But they spotted him and began to point. The hushed voices grew louder and within minutes, a mob surrounded the temple. Their anger was mounting and he wondered if he should just jump and be done with it. But again, he was frozen. How did he get up here? Someone had started to climb up using the rope. Of course, the rope. In the next second, his body was making its way down the temple. If he could not kill himself, they would. He would make his spine limp and let them punish him. The four-sided shrine tapered and was topped with elaborate bone-colored sculptures of devis and worshiping scenes. Every inch of what looked like a hundred-foot stone hat was carved. They watched him, and when he hesitated in the middle, they yelled.

"Come on down, or we'll come get you!"

Their voices startled him, and he lost his balance. His foot caught on a goddess thigh, and his hand grazed a goddess breast. There was a unified gasp of horror at his boldness. But when he looked at the shapely form, he did not see breast or thigh. He saw the Devi. Silence fell as they watched him inch down the rope. He smelled smoldering peanuts and knew he was getting closer to his circus audience. As his feet touched the dirt of the road, they converged on him with not claps, but fists. Someone took a swing at him, and another kicked him in the stomach. He fell, hugging himself when a policeman yanked him to his feet. They looked at him from head to toe, surveying his scraped and dusty body. Then they bombarded him with questions, which he could not find his voice to answer.

"Are you Muslim?"

"He is!"

"Ask him who Meenakshi is."

"Why did you do it?"

"Crazy Muslim."

"Throw him in jail."

"How can anyone doubt that he is a Muslim!"

"Kill the bastard!"

The crowd followed the police as they paraded down the street, displaying the madman who desecrated Meenakshi. He felt the warm blood streaking down his face. He was limping. This was his punishment. Then, someone threw a bottle, and it hit one of the policemen in the head. Their grips loosened, and he began to run. A sacred elephant that was blessing worshipers with his trunk for a few coins knocked another policeman down. Leaving the oil-lamp-lit storefronts and the burgeoning vengeance behind, he stole away into darkness. He ran down a road decked by fields and passed a child hitting a buffalo with a bamboo stick and another transporting chickens leashed together in the basket of his bicycle. It was not until he could hear the uninterrupted song of crickets and frogs that he stopped running.

The next day, he reached the bustling center of Madurai, where the tourist buses were lined up to travel all over southern India. He wandered into a public bathroom to wash up. In the reflection of the water trough, he saw the yellowish moon beside him and his bloodied nose and lips. There was a thin, oily film on the water's surface on which a few bougainvillea blossoms were floating. The bright pink petals made the water more inviting and fresh. He splashed his face and then, in an unfettered second, found himself climbing into the basin to soak his aching body.

The sand was exceptionally hot, but not as hot as the stone road leading from the beach to Ramanathaswamy temple. He felt as if he were walking on coals. The pants that he had stitched himself, and which were once khaki, now hung on his waist, torn and dirty. When he ran a hand over his shirtless torso, he could feel his bones sticking out like twigs. Lately, he found his appetite was sated with dates, almonds and bananas. People sometimes tossed him a few coins when he was resting under a tree, but he immediately gave it away to a hungry child. He was not a beggar.

When he wandered into the cavelike temple, the coolness of the stone floor inside felt like ice on his overheated feet. He stood in a puddle of water under a column for a moment. Taking a deep breath, he noticed the air was cool and salty. He heard the gleeful shouts of worshipers echoing from the theerthums as buckets of sacred well-water were dumped over their heads. The sound of the splashing promised solace from the guilt that still gripped his heart. He had to wash off the blood tainting his mind, just as servant girls methodically swept verandas with stiff straw brushes and water every morning and afternoon.

At the first well, there were three men and an old woman ahead of him. While waiting, he watched as the ocean streams hit the stones on the ground and shattered into drops. When it was his turn and the bucket was raised high above his head, he closed his eyes. The chill made his lungs catch and tighten as an anxious hand around a butterfly. He had stopped breathing. Was it finally over? No. In the next second, like a newborn baby, he began to cough and gasp for air. And when he heard the strange choking noises, it took him a few seconds to realize that it was he who was choking. In the horrible retching sounds, he heard the cries of his victim. As the empty bucket was lowered into the well and refilled for the woman behind him, he began to shiver. He rushed to the next well.

After the initial dousing, the fervor of the bathing increased exponentially. It had become a game of sorts as he walked quickly from sacred well to sacred well. He could not run because the mossy, wet floor was very slick or surely he would have. After the tenth theerthum, he stopped counting. The joyous shouts of others infected him, and he found himself smiling. How quickly he had forgotten that he was here being cleansed for taking another's life! It would have been fine if his conscience had been once and for all clear and pure, but it was not. And as the water shattered over heads, his peace also shattered. So, as the others' bodies shook with laughter from the chill of the water, he saw only the convulsing body of Navina when the acid hit her face. He licked the drops clinging to his lips. When a temple priest ladled water into his cupped hand from the final spring, he slurped it up numbly. He could not say if it tasted salty or sweet. As he found his way out of the temple, he passed the well he had just visited, and what he saw cascading from the buckets onto brown bodies was not water. He ran to the well and knocked the bucket out of a man's hand.

"What is wrong with you?" the man screamed with more astonishment than anger.

"It is blood!" he cried.

The man and the soaked worshipers stared at him blankly.

"Yes, son," said an old man with a white beard dripping with red. "It is the blood of God."

When he ran out of the darkness of the temple and into the bright sun, he did not feel clean although he had had more than twenty baths.

Strangely, he did not remember having walked over a bridge to get to Ramanathaswamy temple. But here it was as solid as a mountain before him. It was the Pamban Bridge and the only way to the temple unless one took a boat or train. He supposed he could have swum, but he did not know how to. He looked down at the single railway track that cut a modern path through the water. A tourist bus pulled over in the distance, and bodies spilled out to gaze upon the Bay of Bengal. In the *Ramayana*, Rama also stared into this rippling green, blue and indigo—the vastness that impeded his search for his love, Sita, who had been kidnapped by Ravana and taken to the island of Lanka. That was when hundreds of monkeys, led by the exceptionally long-tailed and nimble Hanuman, took the stage and began heaving stones into the water. And it was upon these floating stones that Rama walked the eighteen kilometers to the island. As Leeladhar pictured monkeys leaping through the clouds, a vulture coasted above the rows of sand lingams that were decorated with seashells. Below, two shiny brown backsides surfaced near a fishing boat. The vulture was eyeing the bucket teeming with silvery fish. His skin was hot, and he felt dizzy. He only glimpsed the vulture flying toward the boat because he was upside-down, somersaulting off the bridge.

He found himself wandering through an unguarded mango grove that was surrounded by rows of eucalyptus trees. Farmers had to take care when they grew the eucalyptus because once its oil was spilt on the soil, it was said that nothing would grow there. He remembered that eucalyptus oil was medicinal and stopped to crush a few leaves in his fingers, which smelled like fish. Why did his hands smell like fish? He paused for a moment and stared at them as if he would be able to see the past day replayed there, but he saw nothing. Biting into a red mango, he snaked through the trees.

When he reached the village, a tea stall sign told him that he was in Kanniyakumari. As his senses came back to him briefly, he remembered and the desperation seized him once again. It was in this panic that his eyes landed on a man as does a butterfly on a succulent blossom. Sitting against a white wall was a swami shrouded in orange and pink fabric that seemed endless. He sat with his back straight and his legs crossed perfectly. His long hair was slick and black, and around his neck were rudraksha beads, which many swamis wore for meditation purposes. He looked majestic like a peacock, and his presence—although his eyes were closed—was magnetic. That was what made this man stand out from the other "enlightened" types lining the path to Cape Comorin, as the British dubbed the tip of India. That was what set this man apart from a beggar posing to be a mystic. It was his magnetism and the tree. He chose to sit under a palm as the others did for shade, but his tree was at a peculiar slant as if it were a finger pointing south. The most spectacular difference was that from the base of the trunk to about two-thirds of the way up, the tree was straight, but from that point on, it went berserk. It curved every which way, up to the tuft of feathery palm fronds, which were all green except for one that was burnt brown. Leeladhar was reminded of his own youth, a childhood without many worries or decisions. Now, he was caught somewhere in this wild spiral of life of wrong turns and unable to find his way out. The swami must have sensed his need because he opened his eyes.

"Oh, swami, the claws of guilt are shredding my heart," he professed. "I feel like I am dying."

"What have you done?" asked the swami.

"I have changed the course of another's life forever—I have killed."

"So have I. I have killed the urge to smoke and to look in a mirror. I have killed the lust that drew me to brothels, where I shamelessly gazed upon unfortunate women, and to dance-pubs, where I drank myself into a stupor."

"But I have ruined a beautiful woman's life in a fit of lust," Leeladhar choked out in between tears. "I threw acid on her to make her ugly."

"Which was your true desire: to extinguish her beauty or to extinguish the breath of lust itself?"

"I don't know. I feel like an old man, yet I have never held a woman close. My family has disowned me, and I have been wandering for what feels like years."

"Is the earth under your feet not warm?"

The swami turned his open palms toward his knees and looked straight ahead. There was a certain finality to the gesture, and Leeladhar's heart leapt.

"Please, I don't know what to do. I feel like my senses are taking their leave, but they are not. I would much prefer if they did. I haven't slept for at least a week."

"Nor I."

In the sand beside the swami sat half of a seashell holding a few rupees and some paise.

"What can you tell me? I have no money to give you. Please. Where can I go?"

"Here. Sit."

The nervous young man sat down in front of the swami.

"I have been to so many temples, but I have found no solace. I want to kill myself, but I am a coward. What can you tell a murderer, great swami?"

"Nothing, but to sit. Desire of life or death is ultimately still desire."

"I find it hard to be still. You have traveled far distances, and is it not then that you have found yourself and peace?"

"I have not found it by running or sitting. I have lived and died in the same breath. I have been blinded and given sight. I was seared by nakedness, and beyond it, I saw where the continents are one. I saw from where the oceans spring, a place as small as the corner of my eye and as vast as the land that a bird can cover. There are eyes on my hardened soles, and the dust does not offend. I have had to walk far, but have never wiggled a toe because the world is as open as the green of a rice field and as small as a mole above a lip."

As Leeladhar tried to make sense of the swami's mysterious words, he looked at his face for what seemed to be the first time His face, neck and shoulders were horribly burn-scarred. Was this how Navina looked now? He had been imagining the damage he had caused for so long that he was glad to see it face-to-face. As Leeladhar stared in silence at the swami's scars, they did not turn his stomach, but rather filled him with excitement.

"What happened to your skin, swami? I ask you this because I can see you, too, have suffered in this life."

The swami looked away, and Leeladhar could not help but think that he had in some way disappointed him. But he meant no harm by his questions, and he saw no reason for him to take offense.

"Was it a raging fire from which you could not escape?" the young man persisted.

The wise man looked into his eyes, and the intensity Leeladhar saw there hung by a finger from a precipice overlooking a lush gorge of insanity. Time was suspended as if they were falling. The swami's eyes streaked slowly down to the sand like a comet's tail, and he replied matter-of-factly.

"I was burned by an ant."

267

Where the Oceans Meet

It had stopped raining, and the winds had subsided. Now, all
Padma heard as she walked down the moonlit road was a slight
stir as gentle as a baby's breath against the fronds. Somehow, the
monsoon rains had been tamed, and in the vast territories they had
swooped over, they left not horrifying destruction, but rather delib-
erate abundance. There was an abundance of water for the harvest
of rice, vegetables, sorghum, cotton and finger millet. No one was
lamenting over a drought, not in Kanniyakumari, or anywhere else
in India. There was a lush hush that spread over the land that would
be cultivated with perfection this year. Suddenly, the moon was
blocked by a cloud's massive hand and there was darkness. At that
moment, she heard a grunting sound, and her heart jumped.

"Who is there?" she called, her eyes peeling the purplish night.

But no one answered. She had stopped walking, her feet resting
in the cool dirt. Ever since that windy night in Nilambur when she
had been grabbed and lifted high like a basket of vegetables above

their heads, she was more frightened of the dark. In the brief still-ness that followed, she flashed back to the whirlwind—her sari be-ing ripped off her body, her brothers' contorted faces, the humiliation as she was paraded naked to the river, and the artist who had befriended her. His name was Jan, and his skin was the color of an ebony tree. Her brothers said she was a whore for pos-ing for him because they had seen a nude painting of her. She told them that she had not posed for him without her clothes on, but they did not believe her. The cruel hands of betrayal dug at her heart and left it hollow. She hated Jan for breaking her trust, and then she was filled with disappointment. She wished he had asked her per-mission. But what was it that he would ask her permission for? To use his imagination? He could have created that same painting when they had first passed each other on the road. Then what? In all that innocence, they would have still branded her a whore. They would have still stripped her and thrown her into the river they said would cleanse her filthy, desecrated body. Did they think she was a goddess?

She remembered her father telling her about the tribal Koiyas who lived deep in the forests worshiping the Goddess or Devi. She did not have a particular face or name. She was merely Devi. The Koiyas' only contact with civilization was when they had to go into the city to sell honey or dried fruit or to read palms. They bought rice and other necessities with the money they made and once again vanished through the leaves. That night in Nilambur, she believed the Goddess had answered her prayers by sending the monsoon—She told the wind to break the clouds and unleash the rain. The fren-zied crowd's eyes went heavenward, and they left her alone. They began to dance on the bank as she choked on river and rain, de-prived of the cathartic release of feeling her own tears rush down her face.

Naked, she made her way back to town and wrapped herself in a familiar sari. She could hear their muffled cries of ecstasy over the rain they hoped would uncover nuggets of gold she had doggedly panned for over the past six years of her life. Did they believe that they deserved gifts from the Hindu goddess Lakshmi after what they had just done to her? Yes, they truly did. Then she ran as fast as she could into the silvery night. She ran because she knew that they were planning on drowning her—if not that night, then the next.

Again, she heard the peculiar sound. Standing as still as the air, she listened keenly. By now, her eyes had adjusted to the darkness, and she saw a spotted sow running toward her. She laughed heartily as the pig sniffed her feet and then wandered down the road. Resuming her walk, she thought about how she had lured herself into the pre-dawn darkness by remembering what beauty awaited her. She had an urge to hide. So she forced herself to remember nature—the jungly places of shadows and uncertainty that brought her joy once upon a time. With their wretched hands, they had stripped her courage along with her sari, and that was what she hated the most about that day. So, now she routinely drove herself into the brambles of darkness. Mentally, she would recite a mantra and when she had done so about a hundred times, she was at the spectacular peninsular tip of Kanniyakumari. This courage fed on itself and grew fatter with each passing day of living on her own.

Since she lived in a room nearby, she did not need to travel far to her job at the hotel. She cleaned and tidied rooms in a western-style hotel frequented mostly by tourists. Generally, they were the only ones who could afford the lavish prices for rooms, which cost anywhere from three hundred to four hundred rupees. The management treated her kindly, and she knew she was very lucky to have such a steady and painless job. However, she did miss the soothing sound of grit and water in gold pans. When memories of her life in Nilambur surfaced, there were times when her heart plucked as a solitary sitar string, and she pined for what had been. But now her imagination soared in ocean waves rather than in treetops.

When others started joining her on the path and the sky was paling as if veiled in a sheer ivory chunni, she knew she was getting closer to her destination. They started their days early as she liked to do. A boy in a yellow shirt and knickers turned onto the road from a field up ahead. The bundle of red sugar cane he was carrying was bent, bobbing in a flexible arc around his turbaned head. As he made his way into town, the green tufts of leaves scraped the ground behind him, leaving a feathery trail in the dirt.

When she arrived, there were only a few meditating bodies sprinkled on the beach. Sometimes, when she came a little late, the best spots were taken and she would have to strain her neck to see. As she walked a little farther to her favorite spot, she came upon two boys poking at a sea turtle lying on its back in the sand.

"Stop that," she called in Malayalam.

There was a sharpness in her voice, and the boys immediately dropped their sticks and ran off laughing.

"Poor thing," she whispered as she kneeled in the sand beside it. In the white of its plump belly, she could not help but see a vision of herself lying on the shores of the Chaliyar, also broken and naked. As she stared into the whiteness of it, she realized that the turtle was not breathing. But, then again, she did not know how turtles breathed. With both hands, she carefully turned the creature over. Its eyes were closed, and its lipless mouth was sweetly curved. Its shell was spotted as were its four paddled feet and head. What secrets of the sea did this turtle know? Did the turtle know if the water sizzled when the sun slipped into it? In which seacove did the turtle slumber? How many years had passed since its birth? Did it ever run into its mother and father in the blue-green depths? Was there an ocean goddess? Was the powerful ocean as uncontainable as the invisible force of creation itself?

"Tell me, turtle, where do the oceans meet?"

As she stared at her tears sitting in perfect ovals on its shell, she knew that she, too, was voiceless. Picking up the turtle, she walked into the water and returned it to its home—a safe place where it was welcomed by the many hands of the ocean. As she watched the turtle bobbing away from her, she felt something on her foot and saw a translucent crab was strolling over her. Even when she wiggled her toes, it was not frightened. It continued on its path, straight alongside the tremulous waves. She cupped some sand in her hand. The grains were copper-red, black and golden-white.

In minutes, the beach was crowded with spectators who were waiting for dawn to breathe its rosiness into the lightening sky. A donkey laden with salt bags snorted at his owner, and he petted its head, his own eyes straight ahead. Sand still in her hand, Padma focused on where the ocean met the sky. The halo around the rising sun was pearly pink. As the crescent tip rose silently above the horizon where the Indian Ocean, the Arabian Sea and the Bay of Bengal poured into oneness, there was a concomitant exhalation from the crowd. It came from the back of their throat, for at this moment, all these people had one throat, one voice and one thought. In this moment, time stopped, as it often does in the midst of a miracle, and the sky was dusted with golden light. She watched with held breath, as if seeing for the first time, and knew that with each daybreak, she would see so much more.

As men in multicolored lunghees splashed in the sacred waters, Padma's eyes fell on a young girl in a black langa. She was topless, and her bare back was to Padma. The girl's hair was brown and knotty, yet she stood dignified, with her hands at her sides. When the girl turned around, Padma saw her own face. Padma looked down at the copper, black and gold sand at her feet and saw, among these grains, the inseparability of life and death and illusion and truth. She knew then and there, she had to share her thoughts with others.

When she spoke, her voice was clear and strong.

"One day before the rain, I was benighted—a crow whose black and gloss blocked the sun's blaze," she said. "Why not a peacock, you ask?"

They sat in a circle in the sand at her feet, and she began to sing with the freedom of a bird that has just been set free:

> When I sat under the banyan tree
> who was there, who saw me free?
> Braid loosened and eyes wild, swinging

under this tree of trees of
naked trunks and nectardew,
a drop from which my aching grew.
Parting leaves like a pair of lips
and wings fluttered against fingertips;
swallows, sparrows and parrots swooped
away from this cave of emeraldery.

Who was there, who saw me free?
Fleeing darkness, splashing light,
running river, running night;
a pink shell tossed up tenderly
by the dark hands of kama's sea,
the rush of waves, the crush of wind,
the sound of a hundred wings
beating me, beating him,
fear's spring offering.

Who was there, who saw me free?
Head, shoulders, thigh or foot,
what goddess does not like to run
to a pond to witness the sprout
of lotus-seed toward the sun:
root-feet dangling, bangles jangling
and when petal-fingers begin to bleed,
is it not what haunts, this birth,
in the way of pinioned roots,
blind ascension of angel shoots?

Who was there, who saw me free?
And if an answer there may be,
what it is that makes me me,
is that which makes red banyan spring
forth only from the banyan tree?

Glossary

AMARASWARA A Siva temple located in Amaravati, Andhra Pradesh, on the banks of the Krishna River. The temple has one of the few white Siva lingams in existence. See also *lingam*.

AMLA Indian gooseberry or emblic tree; the fruit of this tree.

AMMA 1. Mother 2. A term of endearment similar to "dear" or "baby."

AMRUTHA BALE (literally "nectar") A sweet banana.

ANDHRA A person from the state of Andhra Pradesh.

ANDHRA PRADESH A southeastern state in India bordered by the states of Tamil Nadu on the south, Karnataka on the west and Maharashtra and Madhya Pradesh on the north; principal language is Telugu.

ANDI A term of respect used when addressing a woman or a man, regardless of age.

BABIRUSA A forest-dwelling wild pig of the East Indies, the male of which has long, upward-curving tusks.

BABU 1. A term of endearment, often used for a young male, which loosely translates to son. For an older male, *babugaru* is often used to show respect. 2. In Hindi, babu means "father" and is used as a courtesy when addressing a man, similar to "Mr."

BANGALORE A city of south-central India, west of Madras, and the capital of the state of Karnataka.

BANYAN TREE A tropical Indian fig tree with aerial roots that descend from the branches and develop into additional trunks.

BEEDA See *killi*.

BETEL NUT The seed of the betel palm, which is chewed by itself or with other ingredients, particularly after meals to aid digestion. Also known as areca nut. See also *killi*.

BHAJI Snacks consisting of vegetables dipped in chickpea-flour batter and deep-fried.

BIRYANI (or biriani) Basmati rice made with vegetables, fish or meat and seasoned with saffron.

BODHISATTVA An enlightened being who compassionately forgoes the ideal state of nirvana so that he or she may teach and help others.

BOTTU An ornamental powder, paint or appliqué applied by Hindu women between the eyebrows, or where the "third eye" is said to be, often as a red or black circle, but also now in fashionable shapes for women. A Hindu worshiper, male or female, may receive a bottu of powder or ash during religious ceremonies.

BRAHMINS The first of four classes comprising the Hindu caste system; members of this class, priests and scholars, study and teach the sacred Hindu texts and preside over religious rites in temples.

BRINJAL Eggplant.

CASSIA TREE 1. A variety of Indian shrubs and trees, which bloom with yellow flowers. 2. cassia fistula is used when referring to the dried pods of the drumstick tree.

CHAI Originally, a north Indian term for tea, which is often made from tea dust, sugar, spices and boiled milk. Tea dust is cheaper than the tea leaves, which are exported. The ingredients vary from region to region. There are chai stalls and vendors on practically every street corner in India.

CHAKRAKELI A very sweet banana native to Andhra Pradesh.

CHANDRA BALE A banana that is red in color and cooling to eat.

CHAPPALS Open footwear, similar to sandals, chiefly worn outdoors. It is customary to leave chappals out on the veranda prior to entering a guest's home and they are never worn inside Hindu temples.

CHUNNI A long scarf, often sheer, worn by women with salwar-kameez (pants and tunic) outfits by draping it around the shoulders in a variety of styles; originally used to cover the bust, but now has come to be used as more of a decorative accessory.

DAHL (also spelled dhal or dal) 1. The edible seed of a tropical shrub of the pea family; dahls, such as chick peas and pigeon peas, are consumed daily in some form in most Indian homes. In South India, dahls, lentils, grams and other legumes are the main sources of protein in vegetarian diets. 2. A thick stew made with lentils, onions and spices. See also *legume*, *lentil* and *gram*.

DARSHAN (literally "act of seeing or visiting someone") Special darshan tickets purchased in temples allow the devotee to "visit" with the god or goddess longer than those without a ticket.

DASARA (literally "one taking away ten" sins) A ten-day festival at the end of October or in early November when Hindus worship ten incarnations of Parvati, the goddess of courage and war. For example, adults may worship weapons or tools, a writer worships books, and a businessman worships his financial balance. Young girls often worship dolls.

DEVI 1. (uppercase) Mother Goddess having numerous manifestations, primarily that of Parvati, Siva's wife. 2. (lowercase) a goddess.

DHOVTI (or dhoti) Long cotton fabric, worn by men, wrapped around the waist and then between the legs to resemble loose pants.

DHUPATTA A shawl worn over the shoulders; often richly embroidered.

DOSAI A crispy pan-fried crepe made of rice flour and black or green gram flour; also the name of this dish.

DRAVIDIAN 1. A family of languages—mostly spoken in southern India—including Telugu, Tamil, Malayalam and Kannada. 2. A person who speaks any Dravidian language and who belongs to the pre-Indo-European peoples of southern India.

ELACHI Cardamom, an Indian herb with capsular fruits and aromatic seeds.

ELLORA CAVES Temple caves tunneled and carved into a mountainside near Aurangabad, Maharashtra, and representing Hindu, Buddhist and Jainist faiths.

ELURU A town east of Vijayawada in Andhra Pradesh.

EYE-TEX A commercial brand of black eyeliner used to accentuate the eyes of young girls as well as women. See also *katika*.

FENI A liquor distilled from cashew nuts.

GANESH God of education and the remover of obstacles.

-GARU A suffix added to the name of a person, noun or pronoun to show respect, for example, Ammagaru (Madam madam) or Ashokgaru (Ashok sir).

GITA GOVINDA A poem by Bengali poet Jayadeva, telling of the courtship of the god Krishna and his consort, Radha, and beautifully depicting their spiritual unification.

GOA A union territory of southwest India on the Arabian Sea. This former Portuguese colony attracts many hippies as well as other tourists who sadly envision its white beaches as drug havens.

GRAM Any of the large variety of legumes available in India, which are often soaked and then ground into flour and used as key ingredients in many dishes such as idli and dosai. See also *legume*.

GREEN BALE A long, thin banana that stays green even when ripe.

GUNTUR A town south of Vijayawada in the state of Andhra Pradesh.

HALVA A soft sweet made with wheat milk, sugar, nuts and raisins.

HANUMAN The monkey-faced devotee of the epic hero Rama. Hanuman helped Rama defeat the demon king Ravana and rescue Rama's wife, Sita. See also *Ramayana*.

HIJRA (or kojja in Telugu) An Indian man who identifies as a woman and wears saris and other feminine attire.

HINDUISM A complex body of social, cultural, philosopical and religious beliefs and practices native to and predominant in India, originally marked by the caste system. It is characterized by a belief in reincarnation and one supreme being, by the view that opposing theories are aspects of one eternal truth, and by desire for liberation from earthly evils. The principal Hindu gods are Siva, the destroyer and restorer of worlds; Vishnu, the preserver; and Brahma, the creator. The principal goddesses are Siva's wife, Parvati, the goddess of war and courage; Vishnu's wife, Lakshmi, the goddess of prosperity; and Brahma's wife, Saraswati, the goddess of knowledge. Gods and goddesses appear in other numerous complementary forms and incarnations.

HYDERABAD A south-central city in India, capital of the state of Andhra Pradesh.

IDLI A fluffy, steamed "pillow" made of a fermented ground mixture of rice and black gram and often eaten with sambar, a spicy vegetable and lentil stew, or coconut chutney or relish; also, the name of this dish.

JACARANDA A tropical tree or shrub having pale purple flowers.

JACKET, OR BLOUSE A custom-tailored cotton or silk garment worn with a sari. Cropped below the breasts, the jacket, in a matching or complementary color to the sari, fastens in the front or the back with hooks and can have half, short or no sleeves or be backless depending on the woman's tastes.

JAINISM An ascetic religion of India teaching immortality and reincarnation of the soul, and denying the existence of a perfect or supreme being.

JHERI The glittering thread woven into some saris. Technically, jheri is made by spinning pure gold and pure silver around cotton thread. One can still purchase a sari with gold and silver jheri, although they can be very expensive and also quite heavy. More commonly, cheaper metals, which tend to blacken with time, are subsituted for gold and silver.

JILABEE (or jelabi) A sweet made with a black gram and rice flour batter that is pressed in pretzel shapes, fried in hot oil and then soaked into a hot sugar and rose-water syrup.

KADU BALE A wild variety of banana often eaten to cure constipation.

KAMA (in Sanskrit, literally "love, wish or desire") 1. Enjoyment of the world of the senses constituting one of the ends of woman/man in Hinduism. 2. Blind passion; according to Hinduism, one of the six vices, the other five being anger, jealousy, miserliness, arrogance and possessiveness. Kama is often incorrectly used to mean spiritual love.

KAMALA ORANGES An extremely sweet variety of oranges. The city of Nagpur, in central India, is known for its kamala oranges.

KAMMAS The agricultural subclass of the Sudras. See also *Sudras*.

KAPOK The silky fiber obtained from the fruit of the silk-cotton tree and used for padding in pillows, cushions and mattresses.

KARTHIK A temple for Kumaraswami, son of Parvati and Siva, in South India.

KATIKA A sterile, solid eyeliner applied with the finger. Traditionally, katika is homemade by burning a castor oil wick on a copper plate, collecting the soot and mixing it with sterile butter. Refined camphor is often added for a cooling effect on the eyes. The mixture is collected in a container and then placed in cool water for several days.

KAZA A type of sweet made in various shapes, often coated in honey and topped with shredded coconut.

KERALA A southwestern state on the Malabar Coast of India.

KHADI Traditionally handspun cotton cloth.

KHUS-KHUS (or vetiver) A grass of tropical India that is cultivated for its aromatic roots from which oil is extracted and used in perfumery, as well as for mats, which when wetted down, give off an earthy fragrance.

KILLI A betel nut leaf stuffed with areca or betel nut powder, scented liquid calcium and other flavorings and eaten to enhance digestion after meals; after eating killi, the mouth is temporarily stained red. Beeda is similar to killi and is considered more fashionable because it is artistically wrapped in a funnel-shape. Paan refers to all the ingredients used to make killi. Guests may be presented with a paan tray, from which they can make their own killi, as they sit leisurely and chat.

KOIYA A general term for the tribal peoples who inhabit the jungles in Andhra Pradesh.

KOJJA See *hijra*.

KRISHNA (in Sanskrit, literally "black") God of spiritual love, the eighth incarnation of Vishnu, often depicted as a handsome young man playing the flute.

KUMKUM Colorful powder, often red or turmeric, applied between the eyebrows of a Hindu worshiper. See also *bottu*.

LADDOO 1. A sweet, round treat of which the key ingredients are gram flour, sugar and butter. 2. A nickname for a "sweet, round" child.

LAKH Currency unit equivalent to one hundred thousand rupees.

LAKSHMI Goddess of prosperity; wife of Vishnu, the preserver of worlds.

LALCHEE A loose, collarless tuniclike garment worn by men with a dhovti or matching pants.

LANGA 1. A long skirt worn by young girls with a matching blouse or jacket. 2. A light cotton ankle-length slip that ties at the waist and is worn under a sari; also called a petticoat.

LANGUR Any of various slender, long-tailed monkeys inhabiting Asia.

LANKA The island ruled by Ravana, laying east of the Indian peninsular tip, in the Hindu epic, the *Ramayana*. See also *Ramayana*.

LEGUME The edible seed of certain pod-bearing plants, such as peas and beans.

LENTIL The round, flattened, edible seed of a leguminous plant native to southwest Asia. See also *legume*.

LINGAM A stylized phallus often depicted in conjunction with the yoni, connotating maleness, vitality, fertility and creative power and being an emblem of the god Siva. Yoni (in Sanskrit, literally "vulva") is a figure representing the female genitals serving as the formal symbol under which Shakti is worshiped. Shakti is the creative energy of nature; also life force and dynamic energy of a Hindu god (as in Siva) personified as his female consort.

LORD VENKATESWARA A blending of the principal Hindu gods Siva, Brahma and Vishnu; idols of Lord Venkateswara are represented in black.

LUNGHEE An outer casual garment, resembling a long skirt, for men; this ankle-length, often brightly colored cotton cloth, is worn wrapped about the waist.

MADRAS A southeastern city of India, capital of the state of Tamil Nadu;

principal language in the Tamil Nadu state is the Dravidian language Tamil.

MALABAR COAST The region of southwest India between the Arabian Sea and the Western Ghats mountain range.

MALAYALAM A Dravidian language spoken chiefly in the state of Kerala.

MARUTI A manufacturer of Indian automobiles.

MEENAKSHI A temple for an incarnation of the goddess Parvati.

MEHNDI The art of staining decorative designs on the palms and soles of the feet with henna during celebratory rites of passage, holidays and festivals.

MOGALI A palmlike tree that grows in sandy soil and has thorns and fragrant, pale yellow blossoms.

NANDI A sacred bull and chief vehicle of transportation of the god Siva.

NANNA 1. Father 2. A term of endearment similar to "dear" or "baby."

NARAKASURA (literally "hell demon") The demon that god Krishna fights and kills in a well-known battle, celebrated as Diwali, the festival of lights.

NATIVE BONTHA A green banana for cooking.

NEERA Sap freshly extracted from the palmyra palm tree prior to sunrise and drunk as a health beverage. See also *toddy*.

PAAN See *killi*.

PAANWALLAH A street vendor who sells cigarettes, candy, killi, beeda and other items.

PAISA A subunit of the rupee; one hundred paise are equivalent to one rupee.

PAKODI A deep-fried snack consisting of chickpea flour, onion, chili pepper and sometimes vegetables.

PAKUM, MYSORE PAKUM (literally "hard cake") A sweet made by heating a mixture of chickpea flour, sugar syrup and clarified butter, which is then cooled in a shallow pan and cut into diamond-shaped pieces. Mysore pakum is a popular sweet originating in the city of Mysore.

PALLU (or palloo) The upper part of a sari, which is draped over the woman's shoulder. A pallu often displays the colorfully decorated and/or embroidered border of the sari.

PARVATI Goddess of courage and war; Siva's wife.

PETA A small, wooden seat with short legs that sits a few inches off the ground; often used by Indian women while they cook.

PRASADAM Food that has been offered to, and hence blessed by, a god or goddess and given to worshipers after a puja. See also *puja*.

PUJA A ritual of individual atonement or mass worship during which Hindus pray and make offerings of water, fruit, flowers and incense to gods and goddesses; a puja is performed by priests in temples and by family members in private homes.

PULKA a bread crudely made with wheat flour and water.

PURI A deep-fried, puffed bread made of wheat and often eaten with potato curry.

PUSHKARANI A tank of holy water used for bathing or washing the feet prior to entering a temple.

RAJASTHANI Used to describe the inhabitants or culture of the people of Rajasthan, a state in northeastern India.

RAMA hero of the Hindi epic, the *Ramayana*; considered an incarnation of the god Vishnu. See also *Ramayana*.

RAMANATHASWAMY A temple for the epic hero Rama in Rameswaram on the southeastern coast of India, bordering the Bay of Bengal.

RAMAYANA A Hindu epic telling about the virtues of man through the tale of Sri Rama Chandra's slaying of the demon king Ravana and rescue of his wife, Sita.

RAVANA The demon king of Lanka who kidnaps Sita in the *Ramayana*. See also *Ramayana*.

RIG VEDA One of the four Vedic collections, which is part of the *Samhitas*, a compilation of prayers and hymns.

RUDRAKSHA (literally "Siva's eye") Dried berries that are strung as beads into necklaces and used for meditation and worship.

RUPEE Basic unit of Indian currency, in both paper and coin. One U.S. dollar is equivalent to about 35 rupees.

SAI BABA OF SHIRDI A non-denominational saint with great healing powers, who lived in the village of Shirdi, near Nasik, in western central India, from the mid-1850s until his death on October 15, 1918.

SALWAR-KAMEEZ Pants (salwar) and matching tunic top (kameez) for women popularized in places with cool climates, such as Punjab and Delhi, and eventually made fashionable all over India; often available ready-made or already tailored "in one size fits all."

SAMBAR A thick, spicy stew of vegetable and lentils often eaten with rice or idli.

SAMOSA A deep-fried snack consisting of a triangular pastry wrapping stuffed with vegetables.

SAMPUNGI A highly scented green flower that is often worn in the hair.

SARI An outer garment worn by Indian women, consisting of about six to seven yards of cotton, silk or other lightweight fabric, one end of which is wrapped around the waist to form a skirt and the other which is draped over the shoulder to cover the torso.

SIVA (or Shiva) God of destruction, restoration and fertility.

SRI KALAHASTI A Siva temple near Madras built on the site of an ancient lingam; the belief is that three Siva devotees, the spider (sri), the snake (kala) and the elephant (hasti), all worshiped this very lingam until they became angry with each other, fought and died.

SUDRAS the fourth class of the Hindu caste system comprising artisans, laborers and servants; the Untouchables should be included in a subclass of the Sudras, but are often put in a fifth class all their own since they lived predominantly outside of the villages, away from the other Sudras.

SWAMI A Hindu religious teacher or spiritual guru; a respectful address for such a person.

TAMIL NADU A state in the southeast tip of India where Tamil is widely spoken.

TELUGU The language chiefly spoken by the Dravidian peoples of the Indian state of Andhra Pradesh. In addition to Telugu, English and Hindi are also spoken in Andhra Pradesh.

THEERTHUM 1. Natural wells of holy water in Ramanathaswamy. 2. A general term for sacred water given to worshipers by priests from wells, buckets, waterfalls, and the like.

TIFFIN (of British origin) A light meal, chiefly a snack or midday meal.

TODDY Sap extracted from the palmyra palm tree after sunrise—when the sap has fermented—and drunk for inebriation purposes. See also *neera*.

TULSI Also known as sacred basil; a plant believed in India to have miraculous curative properties.

VADA Gram and rice flour mixed with onion and spices and then deep-fried in various shapes; often eaten with yogurt.

VAISYAS The third of the four Hindu classes, comprising businesspeople.

VEDAS (literally "sacred lore or knowledge") The oldest Hindu texts, composed in Sanskrit and considered sacred.

WOOD APPLE A fruit with a hard, woodlike shell and sweet and sour pulp that is often used in chutneys and drinks.

YONI See *lingam*.

About the Author

Bhargavi C. Mandava was born in Hyderabad, India. She is a contributor to *Listen Up: Voices from the Next Feminist Generation* (Seal, 1995) and *Another Way to Dance: Contemporary Asian Poetry from Canada and the United States* (TSAR, 1996). Her fiction and poetry have been published in the *Asian Pacific American Journal, Bangtale International, California Quarterly, India Currents, Poison Ivy Magazine* and the *Rockford Review*, and her music criticism has appeared in *Alternative Press, Creem, Request, Spin* and the *Village Voice*. She lives in Los Angeles. *Where the Oceans Meet* is her first book.